"They do say that Paris is a place for lovers."

Anna said it softly, hesitantly, watching an entwined couple walk past, whispering to each other. Anna looked at them with envy. "How true that is."

Alex was looking at her intently, and suddenly, taking her courage in both hands, she raised herself on tiptoe and placed her mouth on his.

She felt his initial surprise, his shock, his withdrawal, but she kept her lips on his, feeling him respond and gently take her arms and draw her toward him. His lips began to move. It was the most wonderful, warm feeling. She pressed toward him, longing for him to kiss her deeper—but, urgently almost, he pushed her back.

"No, Anna. This has to stop…"

* * *

Belhaven Bride

Harlequin® Historical #190—June 2006

Helen Dickson was born and still lives in South Yorkshire, England, with her husband, on a busy arable farm where she combines writing with keeping a chaotic farmhouse. An incurable romantic, she writes for pleasure, owing much of her inspiration to the beauty of the surrounding countryside. She enjoys reading and music. History has always captivated her, and she likes travel and visiting ancient buildings.

Belhaven Bride

Helen Dickson

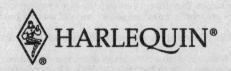

HARLEQUIN®

TORONTO • NEW YORK • LONDON
AMSTERDAM • PARIS • SYDNEY • HAMBURG
STOCKHOLM • ATHENS • TOKYO • MILAN • MADRID
PRAGUE • WARSAW • BUDAPEST • AUCKLAND

ISBN 0-373-30499-4

BELHAVEN BRIDE

Copyright © 2004 by Helen Dickson

First North American publication 2006

Chapter One

1932

It was a wet winter's day in London. Rain lashed at the windows of Mr Rothwell's office, obscuring the forms of bustling pedestrians on the streets. The office was spartan and cold, Mr Rothwell large, solid and humourless. In brusque tones he introduced Anna to a man by the name of Mr Alex Kent.

Stepping forward, Mr Kent expressed sympathy for her bereavement. His voice was deep, resonant and slightly accented—East European, Anna thought. He had a patrician, almost arrogant air about him that suggested education, breeding and money. However, Anna was so nervous and awed by the occasion she paid no attention to him. She was only interested in what Mr Rothwell had to say.

When the letter had come, asking her to make an appointment to attend the solicitors Rothwell and Rankin's office in London for the reading of her mother's will, she hadn't known what to expect—though, of course, she didn't know enough about lawyers and wills to make comparisons. Since then she had worked herself into a knot of anticipation and foreboding.

Mr Rothwell gestured to a leather-covered chair across the desk. 'Please sit down, Miss Preston.'

Dressed in maroon school tunic, blazer, maroon-and-gold striped tie and sturdy black lace-ups, Anna removed her felt hat and placed it on the desk in front of her. Sitting stiff-backed on the edge of her chair, her lips compressed into a thin line, she faced the elderly lawyer across the desk. A shiver of apprehension ran through her. Glancing down at the folder in front of him, as briefly as possible Mr Rothwell explained the terms of the will. Apart from a few of her mother's personal items there was nothing of value—no money, no property.

This came as no surprise to Anna, but what did surprise her was that her mother had placed her in the care of Lord Selwyn Manson. Lord Manson was Anna's maternal grandfather, a man she knew practically nothing about—and the little she did know did not endear him to her. Because her mother had always spoken of him in the past tense, she had believed him to be deceased.

Anna listened in utter silence and in an agony of tightly corked emotion, her fingers tightening on each other in her lap. Her nerves were stretched, teetering on a scream.

'This has come as something of a shock to me, Mr Rothwell. My mother sheltered me all my life, kept things from me. She often spoke of my father, who was an artist and was killed in the war before I was born, but she told me very little of her own background, only the unpleasant circumstances that forced her to leave home. I was not aware that I had any family alive at all, let alone a grandfather—or that he was a peer of the realm.'

'Lord Manson has always been aware of your existence. I am in contact with your grandfather's solicitors—and I am grateful that Mr Kent, who is your grandfather's adviser and associate on several business matters, could take time off from his busy schedule to be present today.'

Anna kept focused on Mr Rothwell, feeling the eyes of the formidable Mr Kent, seated on the sofa behind her, burning holes in her back. 'Why did my grandfather not try to contact me?'

'Your mother forbade him to. However she stipulates in her will that on her demise, until you reach twenty-one, your guardianship must pass over to your grandfather.'

A coldness closed on Anna's face. She shifted uneasily and wondered why pain always had to be concealed in hard reality. 'I don't understand. Why would my mother do that? Why should he care about me?'

'You are his sole heir, Miss Preston, and when he dies—even after death duties—you will be an extremely wealthy woman.'

At that moment the amount of her grandfather's money didn't interest Anna—the disruption the terms of her mother's will would bring to her life did. 'Does he want to see me?' She felt depressed and there was a hollow feeling in the pit of her stomach.

'Eventually.'

'May I ask when?' she asked evenly. Her tone betrayed nothing, neither shock, outrage or pain, which was deeply felt.

'When you have completed your education.'

'I take my Higher Certificate examinations very soon. My teachers have been preparing me for university and I was hoping to sit the Oxford entrance exam. You see, I had set my sights on a career for which a university degree is essential. However, I do not have the means to go to university now, so I am considering doing a secretarial course instead. I must work to support myself, you understand.'

'My dear Miss Preston, you can forget about work.'

'Why? I have to work some time.'

'There is absolutely no question of that. You must reconsider your future. When you have taken your exams, your grandfather has expressed a wish that you continue your education in Europe.'

'And afterwards?'

'That you make Belhaven, which is in Buckinghamshire, your home.'

Mr Rothwell went on to talk further about Belhaven and Lord Manson's plans for her future—coming-out, a Season. Anna gave only monosyllabic replies. She asked a brief question now and then, showing no sense of curiosity about Belhaven or the man who was to be her guardian, and feeling nothing but abhorrence at his talk of a Season. They were interrupted when his secretary knocked and opened the door, beckoning to him that she would like a word. Murmuring an apology, Mr Rothwell excused himself and left the office.

Alex Kent, who had listened quietly and intently, now got up and came towards her. He stood looking down at her slim, informal figure. At seventeen years old there was still a trace of childishness about her; in fact, Anna Preston looked as aloof and virginal as a nun in a convent. She was calm, controlled, which, he thought, was her normal way of doing things, but beneath it all a kind of fierce energy seemed to burn.

When they had been introduced, she had looked at him uncertainly and taken his outstretched hand. Her grip had been surprisingly firm for her age, and when she spoke her voice was soft and cultured. His first reaction had been, 'what a prim miss', and then, more soberly, 'what a pretty—no—beautiful girl'. Her skin was pale, her features small and delicate, but it was the large violet eyes and upward slanting eyebrows that drew and arrested his gaze so that the rest was forgotten. Her hair was long, silken and black, drawn in a maroon ribbon at the back of her neck. Her expression was still and frozen, an expression he understood. It was the look of a girl who had never been happy—who was frightened to allow herself so frivolous an emotion in case it was taken away. He knew her mother had helped keep it there.

'Your grandfather and I have been close friends for many years,' Alex said. 'He realised the problems you would have to face today and asked me to come here to look after you. I have accepted that responsibility.'

'May I ask why he didn't come himself?'

'He suffers from a severe form of arthritis that prevents him moving about. He lives quietly, rarely leaving the house. Aren't you interested to know more about Belhaven—about your grandfather or your future?'

'No, sir, not very,' Anna replied, speaking politely and frankly and looking up at him from her fringe of dark lashes. As she did so she remembered the night when she had been six years old and she had walked in on her mother crying wretchedly for her long dead husband. In her anguished ravings and with half a bottle of gin inside her, her mother had told of the harsh, cruel treatment meted out to her by the very man Alex Kent spoke of.

Her mother, always careful never to show emotion or feeling, had never spoken of it again, but what Anna had seen and been told had affected her deeply. With all the anger and confusion of a child she had craved revenge for what her grandfather had done to her mother. And now that same man was arrogantly demanding control of her life.

'Any interest my grandfather shows in me now is seventeen years too late, Mr Kent. I have worked hard for my examinations in the hope that I can go on and further my education. Do you expect me to turn cartwheels over a house and a man I thought was dead—a man who was so unfeeling he turned his back on my mother for marrying the man of her choice?'

Alex Kent sat on one corner of the desk, gently swinging one elegantly shod foot, forcing her to look at him properly for the first time. Probably twenty-seven or eight, his skin was burned mahogany brown—suggesting an extended holiday in the south of France or somewhere similar where the rich and famous went—contrasting vividly with his silver-grey eyes. The planes of his face were angular, his gaze penetrating. His black hair, as black as her own, was brushed back, with the gleam and vitality of a panther's pelt. Anna noted the crisp way it curled in the nape of his neck, and the hard muscled width of his shoulders beneath his expensively tailored jacket. The firm set of his jaw confirmed her impression that he would stand no nonsense from anyone. He towered above her, making her at once guarded, vulnerable, and acutely uncomfortable as he considered her in lengthy silence.

'Not entirely,' Alex replied at length in answer to her question. 'When your father died your grandfather asked her to return home. She refused, allowing sentiment and not good sense to rule her emotions. If she was unhappy, she had no one to blame but herself. But what of you? Your mother was a secretary to an accountant in the city, living in a rented house in Highgate. You must have known she wasn't earning the kind of money to send you to Gilchrist. Did it ever occur to you to wonder where she found the money to finance your education at such an exclusive school, a school with high academic standards, admitting only the daughters of the very rich?'

Anna grew thoughtful. He was right, Gilchrist was expensive and exclusive, as befitted the daughters of people of class. She had puzzled on this, but, after a while, accepted it. It was easier that way. 'No. But I suspect I am about to find out.'

Alex nodded, his gaze hardening at her tone, which was offhand and with a hint of animosity. 'Your grandfather. Despite their estrangement, your mother was not averse to accepting his money to finance your education—but she would accept nothing for herself. She sheltered you, kept things from you. You never questioned her, which tells me you are either stupid or afraid of reality.' His eyes narrowed when her smooth façade broke. An objection sprang to her lips, which she checked, and her face became flushed, the blood running beneath her smooth skin in the painful way it does when one is young. 'The latter, I think.'

'If I am as stupid and naïve as you obviously think, then I would do better to harden myself in my own way, with my own kind of people,' Anna snapped.

Alex raised an eyebrow. Her remark stirred his anger, and when he spoke his tone was harsh and to the point. 'Your own kind of people have always resided at Belhaven. Harden yourself, by all means, but do it in the right place and with the right people. Perhaps a year at finishing school will help you acquire charm and confidence and, since you are to move in exalted circles, will help you develop a feeling of being the equal of any man or woman—which, being the granddaughter and heir of one of England's wealthiest men, is important.'

Anna blanched and for the space of half a minute she could not speak. 'Forgive me. I really had no idea my grandfather was that rich. So, it is his intention to turn me into a facsimile of a well-bred, well-connected young woman.'

'Which is precisely what you are,' Alex stated, with a distinctly unpleasant edge to his voice. He smiled his rather austere smile, one corner of his mouth curling.

With a sinking heart, Anna wished he didn't make her feel like the gauche schoolgirl she was. It was irritating to be judged on appearances and found lacking.

'You are impertinent, Miss Preston,' he went on reproachfully. 'Gilchrist may apply great emphasis to the values of academic ability, but where manners are concerned it appears to be somewhat lacking.'

Anger kindled in the depths of Anna's dark eyes. Tutored in rules of discipline and restraint, normally she would never dream of arguing with anyone, especially not with an elder. She was far too polite, far too dutiful, but this stranger had a way of getting under her skin and releasing something unpleasant in her. He also knew far too much about her and about her mother for her liking.

'I suppose I must seem impertinent to you,' she admitted, meeting his gaze unflinchingly, her sense of depression growing worse. 'With no family to speak of, with a mother who ignored me thoroughly throughout my life, with no brothers and sisters to keep me in my place and never having known my father, I say all kinds of impertinent things, Mr Kent. Am

I supposed to feel grateful to my grandfather? Because, try as I might, I can find no hint of gratitude within me.'

Alex's anger with her vanished and his expression softened. 'I apologise if I sounded harsh just now,' he said gently. 'I should have known better.' For the first time she had let her guard slip a little and truth over loyalty to her mother prevailed. He was strangely moved by her words. Anna Preston had lived her life in a tight discipline. The extent and intensity of her mother's unhappiness and bitterness at the death of her husband after just one year of marriage—the man she had loved above all else, including her daughter—had been with her through life. Sadly, its tragic effects were visible on the young face before him, and as a result Anna Preston was seventeen going on seventy.

For an instant Anna thought she saw a shadow of sympathy flit over Mr Kent's face. Before she could be certain it was gone, replaced by a faintly ironic interest. She was normally not the sort of person to go around revealing information about herself, let alone to total strangers. In fact, she would normally cut her own tongue out before revealing how things had been between herself and her mother, but there was something about Alex Kent that drew you into his rather intense personality. Realising she had given too much of herself away and that he'd picked up on it, regretting her outspokenness she lowered her eyes. 'I'm sorry. I shouldn't have said that. It's no concern of yours.'

'You're right, it isn't, but I'm a good listener—if you'd like to talk about it?' Alex prompted.

Anna shook her head, thankful that he didn't pursue it.

'Miss Bartlet, your headmistress, has always sent Lord Manson's solicitors annual reports of your progress. She says you've worked hard and done extremely well in class, that you are a credit to your school. Your grandfather is immensely proud of you. He was glad to see the money he provided was well invested.'

'So I'm an investment,' Anna remarked coolly, indignantly

tilting her chin a notch. 'I'm pleased he considers my good marks in class as value for money. I suppose taking his money all these years means that I have to give something back—that he expects it, that it is a debt to be repaid. But what if I choose not to go to school abroad, to turn my back on everything he offers,' she enquired, 'for I need no one's aid or protection?

'I do not in the least mean to sound ungrateful, but I find nothing at all pleasurable in the prospect of having my established order of things turned upside down. It has always been my intention to be self-sufficient, to make my own way in the world.'

'Which is a trait I personally admire in anyone—be it man or woman—unlike your grandfather. It is one of the few things we disagree on. It is his considered opinion that marriage and motherhood is the true career for a woman, that ladies do not take up paid employment.'

This unexpected revelation about Lord Manson was uttered quietly and accompanied by a smile. It was a smile that took all the harshness and offence out of Alex Kent's previous words, a smile that was instantly rueful, conspiratorial and incredibly charming, a smile that said he perfectly understood how hard the situation was for her. Anna was absorbed in the smile, a smile that drew her into a private alliance. He was sitting perfectly still, watching her. Something in his expression made her hastily drop her gaze, but the warmly intimate look had been vibrantly, alarmingly alive, and its effect would remain with her.

Raising her head, she looked at him hard. 'Such prejudice is stupid in this day and age. Women are no longer the weaker sex.'

'I couldn't agree more, but do I detect a hint of feminism in that remark?'

'I just happen to believe women should have the same opportunities as men. If that happens to be feminist then so be it. My mother was of that opinion, too. One thing I am thankful for is that she believed passionately in the education of women, which was why she went to great pains to have me properly educated.'

'And you want to go to university?'

'Yes. I've set my heart on it. Domestic subjects are given low priority at Gilchrist, as you will know, Mr Kent. Academic success is the main goal, with university entrance the pinnacle of ambition—which my grandfather must have known when my mother sent me there. However, I realised when she died that I lack the means to go to university, and if necessary I will take the Civil Service entrance examination instead.'

'And do clerical work?'

'If I have to.'

'I can't see you drumming your brains out on a typewriter.'

'Needs must, Mr Kent,' she said, and her small jaw was set in a way that Alex found so reminiscent of Selwyn he almost laughed.

'Not in your case.'

Alex looked down on Anna's quiet composure, her certainty, and her absolute confidence in herself. 'The Belhaven inheritance by tradition is rightfully yours,' he continued on a more serious note. 'There is no other direct heir, no son or daughter, no other grandchildren to carry on the ancient line. You, Miss Preston, are the last of the line. Should you refuse to have anything to do with your grandfather, on his death the estate will be broken up, its treasures dispersed.'

'I see. So, in spite of his power and wealth, my grandfather has no stake in immortality,' Anna remarked drily.

'No one has that.'

Anna fell silent and averted her gaze. She felt lost and so very alone. She had no one to turn to. No one. Every avenue of appeal was closed to her. Even this man concurred with her grandfather. 'It appears I am left with no choice but to adhere to my mother's wishes and do as my grandfather says,' she said softly, without joy.

'You are his rightful heir, so my advice to you is to accept it with the grace and dignity of your noble lineage. Furthermore, the fact that it was your mother's wish that you make your future at Belhaven with your grandfather makes me fervently believe she would have forgiven him if she'd had the chance that you now have.'

Her ire coming to the fore once more, Anna tossed her head. 'I am not my mother.'

Alex recognised in her remark the same hostility he found whenever he negotiated with any business rival who was being forced by circumstances to sell something he wanted to hold on to. It was her pride that was forcing her to retaliate by making the whole situation as difficult as possible for Alex.

Fearing that she was vacillating, he said pointedly, 'I realise what the loss of your mother must mean to you in a personal sense and I respect your bereavement. But you must consider the effect her death has had on Lord Manson. His feelings for her were passionate and deep. She caused him unimaginable suffering when she defied him and married your father. The fact that she has died so suddenly without making amends, which your grandfather has tried to do since the day she walked out, has affected him deeply. He loved her more than you imagine. Whatever you may think, he is heartbroken.'

Refusing to be mollified and reluctant to change her opinion of a man she had spent her life hating because of the suffering he had caused her mother, suppressing the urge to remark that she doubted her grandfather had a heart to break, Anna said somewhat ungraciously, 'He'll survive.'

Stifling a sigh of impatience, Alex said with unintentional curtness, 'I am sure he will. You are an intelligent young woman, Miss Preston. You'll learn your grandfather's ways quickly. You'll soon come to terms with his system, his peculiarities.'

'My mother told me he insisted upon controlling her. He cast her out. After all he has done, am I to pretend it didn't happen?'

'You are not his judge, but even if you were, don't you think it would be best to be certain of your facts before you pass sentence? Are you to commit your grandfather without hearing his defence?'

Anna looked at him solemnly for a moment, then she said, 'I don't mean to. I will let him put his case. But are you saying my mother was lying, Mr Kent?'

'I hate to be the one to disabuse you of your illusions, but your mother walked out of Belhaven. It was her choice. There is more to the matter than appears on the surface.'

'Then I would be obliged if you would enlighten me.'

'It's for your grandfather to do that. Not me.' Standing up, he picked up her maroon mackintosh and helped her into it. 'There are details to be worked out, but they needn't concern you at this point. Your grandfather's solicitors will contact your headmistress when a suitable school has been found— perhaps in France or Switzerland. Do you have a preference?'

'No,' she answered, unable to keep the disappointment she felt about being denied the chance to realise her dream at university from her voice. But she had to be sensible and practical. 'Since you appear to know a great deal about me already—which, because you are a stranger to me, I must say I find quite unsettling and objectionable—you will know I have never been further than my school in Essex, so either will do.'

Alex was shocked into momentary silence. In his own world and wide circle of friends and acquaintances, everyone went everywhere, and often. It was difficult to accept this bright young girl had never been anywhere beyond Essex. 'All the more reason why you should continue your education abroad for a year or thereabouts. They do say that travel broadens the mind, especially at your age. Afterwards you will go to live at Belhaven. Your grandfather wants you to have the opportunity to enjoy a Season—to look over the eligible young men,' he added almost as an afterthought, a humorous twinkle glinting in his eyes.

Anna stiffened, finding nothing funny about that. 'Does he indeed? He is going to be disappointed. A Season is quite out of the question. I want no presentation at Court, no coming-out. The sole purpose of all that ghastly nonsense is for a girl to procure a husband. The manner in which she is put on parade for gentlemen to look her over like a filly in the ring at a race meeting is quite absurd and so outdated, don't you think?' She paused when she saw Mr Kent's eyes widen and a smile tug at his lips as he nodded his agreement. 'I have no inclination to marry in the foreseeable future—not for years and years, in fact, so it would be pointless.'

Suppressing the smile, Alex smoothed his expression into an admirable imitation of earnest gravity. 'I quite agree, but we will see what happens to you when you are of an age to decide—in a year's time.'

'Age has nothing to do with it,' Anna went on somewhat irately. 'I will not change my mind, but I hope my grandfather will change his. His ideas are stuffy and antiquated. I cannot see the point, or the purpose, of sending me abroad to an expensive school. It will be money totally wasted. If he must spend his money on me, I'd much rather he sent me to university instead.'

'The purpose of spending a year at school abroad is to enrich the mind, not to train it for some exacting occupation. But whatever you do in the future, your education will prove invaluable to you. Plenty of time when you return for university and to develop a career if you want to.'

'Even though my grandfather will oppose it?'

'I'm sure you'll be able to win him round,' Alex said, desperately trying to prove to her she wasn't as powerless as she thought she was. 'Your grandfather is a fine man, Anna—you don't mind me calling you by your Christian name?' She shook her head. 'It isn't natural for two people who are close to be strangers to each other.'

'But after all these years—'

'He wants to meet you. You could make him happy. He is

the finest man I have ever known. I admire him enormously.'
There were few people Alex admired. 'One day I hope you
will understand what I mean. There's no limit to what he can
do for you—if you let him.'

'The role of grandfather cannot be assumed by a total
stranger, Mr Kent, and I cannot be expected to love him to
order.'

'That is the last thing Lord Manson would expect of you.'

Anna found herself quite intrigued by Alex Kent; she
looked at him enquiringly, tilting her head to one side. 'I
suppose you went to university.' For a moment he looked
quite taken aback. Immediately she regretted her impulsive-
ness. 'I'm sorry,' she said sincerely. 'I didn't mean to pry.'

'Don't be sorry. You may ask anything you like—within
reason,' he added an almost imperceptible second later. Anna
perceived that second and she recognised what he was saying—not to pry too deep. 'I will be as honest and direct as I
can,' he went on. 'I did go to university—Balliol College at
Oxford.'

'And got a double first, I expect.' The smile that moved
across his lean brown face confirmed her remark. 'You must
have had to work unimaginably hard.'

'No academic achievement is automatic.'

'Mr Kent, I really don't want to go to school abroad and
the prospect of being thrust into an unaccustomed social life
in the company of hundreds of strangers appalls me,' she told
him earnestly. 'It's a worthless, frivolous life and I would hate
every minute of it. I don't think I will be able to stand it. I've
always known what I want to do with my life. I know it…
perhaps like you did.'

He nodded slowly. 'Ambition comes before everything.
That's a fundamental lesson I learned a long time ago. I can
see you're serious, that you have your heart set on it.'

'Yes. I've always been determined and single-minded about
what I want, and the fact that I might fall at the first hurdle—
that of lack of money and opposition from a man I've never

met—undoubtedly means I am losing both those qualities. Please will you try to make my grandfather understand how important going to university is to me? Don't forget that I don't have to do what he wants. I can still walk away.' Her gaze was steady and meaningful as it became fixed on his.

Alex was silent, studying her seriously, then he began very slowly to smile. 'That sounds to me like blackmail, Miss Preston.'

Anna's expression became sublimely innocent. 'Does it? It was not intended. I'm merely trying to strike a bargain.'

Alex cocked a sleek black brow. 'With Lord Manson? Several have tried—and failed. I must tell you that your grandfather hasn't considered university and will probably say it's an absurd notion, but I promise I will try.'

'Oh, my goodness,' said Anna, her eyes alight with hope, 'do you think you could? I would be most grateful.'

Alex saw her poignant look of gratitude before she masked her feelings with a smile. 'Leave it with me. I'll see what I can do. Now, come along, I'll get you something to eat and then drive you to the station.'

'Thank you, but there's no need.' Her smile broadened—a sudden, dazzling smile that hit Alex somewhere in the region of his stomach. He seemed to be looking at a different person. 'Miss Bartlet very kindly allowed Mr Cherry—that's the school chauffeur, to bring me to town in the car. Goodbye, Mr Kent. No doubt we'll meet again some time—at Belhaven, perhaps.' Placing her maroon hat securely on her head, she turned her back on him and marched briskly towards the door.

'Anna?' Alex called after her.

She stopped and turned. 'Now what?'

'You're doing the right thing—about going to Belhaven,' he said softly.

'I hope you're right, but whatever happens I'll cope—just as I always have.'

Alex watched her go. Never had he been so dismissed. He suppressed a smile. Anna Preston was a tough little madam and his admiration for her was acknowledged. Something warmed him as he watched her go. And the way her face had been transformed by her smile—hope renewed that he might be able to arrange it for her with her grandfather for her to go to university after all. He suspected that she didn't smile often, and when she did it was as if she were bestowing some kind of favour.

He began to wonder what she would be like after three years at university—if he could persuade Selwyn into letting her go—and if Selwyn had not made a grave mistake in what he intended for her. Reserved, proud and young as she was, it would be interesting to observe the maturing of Anna Preston—to assist in it, even. At that moment he didn't know whether she would be a curse or a godsend at Belhaven, but he was looking forward to finding out.

Seated in the back of the car as Mr Cherry negotiated his way through the traffic, Anna gazed out on a dismal London town without really seeing anything at all. The meeting had left her feeling angry and disturbed. It was hard to be told that she had a grandfather by a complete stranger, instead of by her mother, Lavinia, a beautiful, unapproachable, untouchable stranger. As mother and daughter they had respected each other, but they had been neither companions nor friends. Anna had never understood her, and now she was dead she never would.

They had spent so little time together. The small rented house in Highgate was just a place Anna went to for Christmas and organised holidays—none of them happy. Her mother's death from pneumonia had been sudden. She had been buried in Highgate cemetery as she had wished—without fuss and with just a few friends to mourn her passing.

And now Anna's grandfather was to take charge of her life and send her to a school abroad where she would learn the dreary things the girls who were to be next year's vacuous débutantes were taught.

Closing her eyes, she rested her head wearily on the leather upholstery. She felt horribly depressed at the prospect of Mr Kent failing to persuade her grandfather to allow her to go to university, forcing her to put her career on hold, of being indebted, of enforced gratitude to an old man who had made her mother's life a misery. It wasn't fair. It simply wasn't fair.

Chapter Two

The Convent of the Sisters of Magdalene was hushed, the smell clean, sanitised. Flanked by her nuns, Sister Geraldine, the mother superior, paused on her way to vespers when she saw a man who had just arrived. Recognising him, she detached herself from her nuns and moved towards him, her hands clasped into her sleeves, her face sculpted by time and prayer. After greeting him, she led the way down a long stone corridor with niches of plaster saints. So many young women had passed through the convent—only Sonya had stayed. Eventually Sister Geraldine halted before a door and turned to the visitor, smiling reassuringly at his worried countenance.

'I was sorry to trouble you, but I'm glad you've come. It was just a setback, nothing like the last time, but I knew you would want to know. Despite her frail appearance, Sonya is a sturdy young woman. She'll be fine. Go in and see her. She's still sedated so she may not respond or even know you are there, but hearing your voice may help her rest easier.'

'What caused the setback, Sister? Do you know?'

Sister Geraldine shook her head. 'She was at the village fête with Sister Mary. She'd been looking forward to it for days. They hadn't been there long when she suddenly became agitated, crying and quite beside herself, incoherent. She said there was someone at the fête she didn't want to see, someone who meant to harm her, and she wanted to return to the convent, saying it was about to happen all over again.' She averted her eyes, troubled. 'I believe it was the young man who let her down so badly that she saw. She—she still dreams—such terrible dreams.'

A muscle worked spasmodically in the visitor's throat as, with a look of wordless, impotent rage directed not at the innocent mother superior but at the man she referred to, he said, 'Not dreams, Sister Geraldine. Memories.'

She nodded, understanding. 'Yes—yes, I know. Those terrible things she saw as a child, her memories, are still real as they were then. They will not let go. Go and sit with her. I'll come and see you after vespers.'

Sister Geraldine turned and silently went back down the corridor, knowing he wouldn't leave until he was certain Sonya was all right. Over the years Sister Geraldine had become extremely fond of Alex Kent. She had met him in 1919 in London's East End, at a hostel for the homeless where she had been involved in charity work at the time. Alex and his sister were refugees from war-torn Russia. At fifteen years old he was fiercely protective of his nine-year-old sister.

She had watched with interest as he had struggled to put his past behind him and, being academically brilliant, had distinguished himself, and yet he was so absolutely without affectation. He was a fine man, the finest man she knew, and she had good reason to be grateful to him—his donations to the Convent were such that it could not survive without them.

However, that said, the sisters had taken Sonya to their hearts. She had come to them a broken, terrified child. She couldn't speak; such horrors her young eyes had seen in her native Russia, things no child should have to see. Sonya had gathered her little body into a block of impenetrable steel and hadn't uttered a word for a long time. But gradually, with all the love and tender care the sisters and Alex had bestowed on her, they had watched her bloom like a newly watered flower—only to see her cut down by that terrible business four years ago from which they had been afraid she would never recover.

Alex opened the door to Sonya's room and went inside. The furnishings were spartan, the only adornment on the white walls a crucifix and a picture of the Madonna above the bed on which the young woman lay—these Christian images at variance with her Jewish ancestry. Moving closer, he gazed down at her, the slender contours of her body a mere ripple beneath the smooth surface of the covers. His heart wrenched. He looked at her face for a long time, so long he failed to notice the passing of time. At last, as if sensing his presence, or that he had willed her to do so, her long lashes quivered and she opened her eyes, seeing him through a thick haze.

'Alex,' she murmured. She looked up at him with loving eyes, dull and drugged, her tender mouth pinched with pain, though not the physical kind. She was watching him now, remembering—but what did she remember? She had been ill, and worse still her mind had been confused, like it had been twice before—when she had been a child and when she had discovered she was to bear a child of her own.

Bending over her, Alex took her hand and raised it to his lips. 'I don't wish to disturb you,' he said gently, sitting on the bed facing her. 'You've been ill, Sonya. Try and rest. Forget what happened.'

She frowned, the sedative the doctor had administered to her earlier having caused some disorientation. Letting her hand lay trustingly in his, as she had done so often in the past, she sighed sleepily. 'Forget? What do you mean? What must I forget? I don't understand, Alex.'

'No, of course you don't. Try to go back to sleep.'

'I will—and—thank you for not talking about it. I'll be all right if you don't talk about it.'

Like a child she obeyed him and closed her eyes, and for that Alex was relieved. For now she didn't remember what had happened to her—she didn't remember that terrible night when she had tried to take her own life—and why. He hoped and prayed the memory of it was gone forever, for the scale of the misery it would bring would be more than she was equipped to deal with, but sadly he knew she would remember. That night and one other—which belonged to another time and another place—had scorched their memories on her soul.

Gently his fingers brushed the dark hair from her brow and, leaning forward, he placed his lips against it. 'Sleep, Sonya. I love you. When you wake I'll be here.' He sat beside the bed and bowed his head. His silent vigil would last all night, and when she awoke and saw him there, she would be reassured that he loved her, that he would do anything, give all that he had, to make her happy.

Now her exams were over, Anna was in the middle of packing up various books and personal possessions she had acquired over the six years she had been at Gilchrist, when Miss Bartlet's secretary knocked and poked her head round the door.

'Telephone call for you, Anna, in my office.'

Anna stopped what she was doing and stared at her. She was unlike the other girls—no one ever telephoned her. 'Are you sure it's me they want? Who is it?'

'A Mr Kent.'

Anna gaped. 'Oh, I'd better speak to him. Thank you.' Having hurried down the stairs so as not to keep him waiting, she said, somewhat breathless, 'Hello, Mr Kent.'

'Hello again, Anna. How are you? Well, I hope?'

The deep, faintly accented voice from the other end of the line caused Anna's heart to do a somersault. 'Yes—yes, quite well, thank you.'

'I thought you'd like to know your grandfather has agreed to your request to go to university.'

Anna gasped, absolutely thrilled. 'But—but that's wonderful. You cannot imagine what that means to me.'

'Oh, I think I can,' he replied, laughing.

'Thank you so much. Was it very difficult to persuade him?'

'No. In fact, he couldn't be more delighted, or proud. So—go ahead, Anna.'

'I have to get my results first.'

'I won't argue with the inevitable.'

Anna laughed. 'I'm touched. Such faith.'

'Absolutely. I do have another reason for calling you.'

'Oh?'

'I thought you might enjoy some well-earned leisure when you get your results and have secured a place at university. Lord and Lady Ormsby, close friends of your grandfather, suggested you might like to join them. They're taking a villa on the Riviera for the summer. They have a daughter, Tamsin, slightly younger than you. Her education is complete and she's to go to finishing school in Switzerland in the autumn. I think you will like her.' After a slight pause he said, 'So—what do you say? Does a holiday in the sun appeal to you?'

'Why, I—I don't know. I've never been on holiday before.'

'Then it's high time you did.' When she didn't reply, he asked, 'Is something bothering you?'

'It—it's the expense.' This quiet admission caused Anna more shamed anguish than she cared to show. Alex sensed it and was quick to reassure her.

'Don't worry,' he said shortly. 'Your grandfather is to arrange for you to have an allowance, so you'll be able to shop for clothes and whatever else you might need before you go. Lady Ormsby will be in touch with you to arrange things. You must try to enjoy yourself throughout the coming weeks, to think of nothing but what you see and do and pleasing yourself. Will that be so very difficult?'

'It might be. I'm not given to the idle, pleasure-seeking life.'

'I think you should try it just for the fun of it. Have you ever done anything for fun, Anna?'

'No. Not ever.'

'You do want to go?'

'Yes—yes, of course I do.'

'Then that's settled.'

'Just for a few weeks, though. I must get back to prepare for term starting—books to buy, and things.'

'Of course. That can be arranged later.'

'May I ask you something?'

'Anything.'

'Why are you doing this—being nice to me?'

'Because I happen to like you, and I'm going to save you from yourself if it's the last thing I ever do.'

'I don't know what to say.'

'Just say yes.'

'Yes, thank you.'

'You're welcome. Good luck, Anna.'

When she'd replaced the receiver, Anna stood and stared at it for a full minute. She was strangely excited. A holiday! It was without doubt the best thing that could possibly have happened. It solved her problem of what she was to do for the summer at one fell stroke—putting off the day when she would have to go to Belhaven and meet her grandfather. However, she felt the first stirrings of gratitude towards him for agreeing to her request. She would write to him, thanking him, when her results came through.

Anna passed her exams with flying colours and secured a place at Somerville College Oxford to read English literature. The letter she wrote to her grandfather was the most difficult she'd ever had to write. She received a reply from Alex Kent on his behalf. It was short: *Congratulations and well done. You deserve it.*

Having just got back from spending two days at Belhaven going over business matters with Selwyn, Alex answered a knock on his door. The man who filled the open doorway was unexpected and unwelcome. Rainwater dripped from his hat

and shabby coat, making puddles on the floor. Alex stared at
him in shock and disbelief. After a span of sixteen years it
could not be. Something inside him broke and ceased to
move. It was Victor Melinkov, his stepfather, and he was
looking at him from beneath hooded lids over shrewd, calculating dark eyes. They contained a lifeless, haunting emptiness that had not been there before.

He was a large man with a pale complexion, thinner than
he had been before the Revolution. Although no longer in
possession of the handsome looks that had once attracted
Alex's mother, he still commanded attention.

Immediately memories Alex had buried deep tumbled out
of their grave to torment him—his flight from Russia as a
boy, when he had left behind not only the ashes of his mother
and the country of his birth, but this man who had abandoned
his wife and daughter at a time when they had needed him
most, to distinguish himself in the Red Army. Alex was still
haunted by the screams, by the smell of scorched flesh.

'Victor Melinkov. What in the living hell do you want?'
Alex demanded coldly, speaking in his native Russian. His
granite features gave no sign that he was enraged at being
caught offguard by this man he had hoped never to set eyes
on again. 'You have no right to come here.'

'Right? I have every right. It has been a long time, Alexei
Ivanovitch Petrovna.' Victor's voice sounded the same—
forceful and arrogant.

'Not long enough. Say what you have to say and then get
the hell out of my life and stay out.'

'Our paths seem destined to cross. Did you think I would
fade from your life when you have my daughter? When I went
back and found out what had happened—when I saw the
burnt-out village, I thought you were all dead, but then I was
told you and Sonya had not perished. I swore I would find
you. What have you done with her?' He pushed his way past
the younger man and strode into the apartment, as if he expected to find her there.

Alex closed the door and followed him. 'You forfeited the right to call her your daughter when you left her to die with our mother.'

Victor glanced at him, clearly irritated that he should remind him of that. 'How quick you are to anger, to flare up,' he said, reverting to heavily accented English—Alex was quietly impressed by his diligent progress in the language which Victor had been reluctant to learn when he'd married Alex's mother. 'You take after your mother. She used to lose her temper—not like your father, who was a gentle dreamer. I did not leave your mother and Sonya to die. If I had not joined the army voluntarily, I would have been recruited anyway. Had I refused, I would have been shot. You know that.'

In Victor's eyes there was a greedy inner glow as his gaze swept the sumptuous apartment, its contents attesting to his stepson's money and power. He trailed his fingers down a particularly fine, expensive figurine. 'You've come a long way—done well for yourself, I see.'

'Do you think what I have was just given to me? I have succeeded with nothing more than my brain and my wits.'

'You never went back to Russia.'

'The Russia of my youth does not exist any more. I am grateful for what Britain offered me. The Soviet Union under Lenin means nothing to me but depression, enslavement…and murder. Let us get to the point. What is it you want?'

'My daughter. I have come to see Sonyasha.'

'Sonya does not concern you. She is happy to be here in England, with me. To her you are dead.'

Victor took a step forward. A brutal man, his face became set in lines of menacing rage, the cords of his neck standing out, quivering and tense. 'But as you see, I am not dead, in fact very much alive, and I intend to remain that way. Tell me where she is or by God I shall beat it out of you.'

Alex regarded Victor dispassionately. 'You loathsome bastard. Do you think that by coming here and making threats you can terrorise me into submission? Times have changed. I will not cower to you as others have done. Sonya is well and in a place where she is safe.'

'And you are sure of that, are you?'

'As sure as I can be. Where have you been all these years? Why did you not seek Sonya out before now?' Alex demanded, in charge of himself and the situation. He saw a strange hauntingly brooding look darken Victor's eyes.

'I got into some trouble. I was arrested and taken to a labour camp in Siberia, where I spent thirteen years,' he said with more disgust than embarrassment. 'It was a hellhole, a place where men are forgotten, where men give up hope. I was one of the lucky ones. I came out alive.'

'I'm sorry.' Alex was sincere. The horrors of the labour camps were well known to him. 'That must have been difficult.'

'Only those who have spent time in those God-forsaken places will know how hard it was. What I went through, what I saw…such horrors I will never see again as long as I live. When I was released I was in a bad condition and spent some weeks in a reception camp. I had nothing—no money, no family, nothing. I wanted to see my daughter again. I can never be a proper father to Sonyasha, but it is important to me that I have someone.'

This new aspect of Victor worried Alex. There was something there that did not go with his real nature. Alex saw his face settle back into the expression of lifeless formality he had first seen when he had opened the door.

'Somehow I knew you would have tried to get to England,' Victor went on, 'to your mother's people. When I was restored to health I made enquiries and was proved right—and that you had made your fortune. That was when I began to see a future for myself again, that you might be generous with your kin since you have money.'

Alex felt his hackles rise, but forced himself to remain calm. 'And you could not overlook the opportunity to capitalise on it,' he said with bitterness and contempt. 'I could not imagine your actions being motivated by anything but greed. How dare you use Sonya as your excuse to get to me? Do not expect me to feel sorry for you, Victor Melinkov.'

'Why not? I am sure you can manage an allowance for my comfort. I was a generous man to your mother and you while I could afford it.'

Alex could have argued against his claim, but he held his silence. Victor had been known as a man of self-indulgence. On his death Alex's father had left his mother relatively well off. Victor had soon got rid of her money with a succession of mistresses and gambling with his ill-famed friends.

'Have you nothing to say concerning my mother and the manner in which she died? She was your wife.'

Unmoved, Victor shrugged and said gruffly, 'Wife? She never loved me. She never recovered from your father's death. But enough. This is no time for sentimentality. How much will you give me to get rid of me?'

There was excitement, ill concealed behind the words, and Alex eyed him with scorn. The soul that animated Victor Melinkov was a chilling quagmire of avarice, selfishness, wickedness and deceit.

'And what if I decline to give you anything?'

'Then I shall make a nuisance of myself. But I do not think we shall come to that, shall we? Suppose we say five thousand pounds. A reasonable figure, I think.'

Alex's face hardened. 'You have the most damnable effrontery. I am not the Bank of England.'

'I've done my research. Five thousand pounds is nothing to you—a mere drop in the ocean.'

Alex capitulated. It would be worth five thousand pounds to get rid of him. There was no emotion in his businesslike stare. With the quick reflex of a man who will protect what he cherishes most, even with his life, he said, 'I will give you the money, but there are conditions. You must give me your word that you will leave England and do not try to contact either Sonya or me again. She is not your concern.'

Victor's laugh was short and bitter. 'Not my concern? Sonyasha is my daughter. That makes her very much my concern. To hell with your conditions. I will see her. Is it not natural for a father to want to see the child he loves?' He appeared calm, yet the vein in his right temple beat hard against his skin.

Alex was watching him closely. Could it be possible that Victor Melinkov had loved his daughter—even though he had never shown that love—and that he was sincere in his desire to see her? His vein told Alex he was. 'Forgive me if I find that hard to believe.'

'It is the truth. Tell me how she is, about her life, what she is doing. Is she married—has she made a grandfather of me?'

Alex would have thought that Victor wouldn't have cared a damn what happened to Sonya when he'd left, that he was totally devoid of feeling, but it seemed that it did matter. For Sonya's sake he wanted to believe it. He felt a reluctant stirring of compassion.

'No, Victor, I cannot tell you all the good things you want to hear. She is not married—in fact, her life since that day when she was a child and saw the kind of horrors no child should ever see has not been happy. If you wish to know what has happened to your daughter since she came to England, sit down and I will acquaint you with the facts. And you are right. As her father you have a right to know all there is to know.'

Alex moved towards the window and stood looking out over a dispirited London as, quietly and in a voice devoid of emotion, he told Sonya's story.

Victor remained standing, listening to every word. As Alex's voice filled the room at first he appeared to relax a little. For a moment only. As realisation began to sink in, the shock of what he was hearing turned his face cold, his expression becoming frozen in bitter fury. When Alex had finished speaking, Victor reacted to his revelations like all violent men. He rounded on him, his face tight with suppressed rage, his hands balled into fists at his sides.

'And you let this bastard live—after all he was guilty of doing to my child? Alexei Ivanovitch Petrovna, I am shocked. I demand to know the name of this person whom you say hurt my daughter so much she tried to take her own life.'

Alex looked at him through narrowed eyes, matching his direct gaze. 'No. It is over. What is done cannot be undone, and I have no intention of seeing myself hanged for the sake of—' He stopped himself in time, before he uttered the name of the man he despised above all others. 'That would do Sonya no good at all.' Striding into his study, he hurriedly wrote out a cheque for five thousand pounds. 'Here,' he said briskly, coming back and handing it to him. 'Take it and go. I withdraw the conditions I made, but I ask you not to come begging for more.'

Victor stiffened. 'I will not beg.'

'I will give you nothing else. As for Sonya—I will see what I can do. She is in a convent where she is well taken care of. Where are you staying?'

'In the East End—Whitechapel.'

Alex cocked a mocking brow. 'Considering the efforts you went to to escape your Jewish ancestry, Victor, when you escaped the Pale, with a third of the Jewish population of Great Britain living in the East End you must forgive me if I seem surprised.'

'I arrived in London with nothing. There was nowhere else I could go. Now I have the means I fully intend to move out.'

'Let me know where to.'

When Victor looked at the cheque he shook his head. 'I should have preferred cash.'

'I expect you might, but I do not keep such a sum in the apartment. Take it to my branch and open an account. If you have any difficulty, tell the manager to contact me.' Handing it to the Russian, he said, 'Go now. You have what you came for.'

When Victor had taken it and placed it in his pocket, he walked towards the door and left without another word.

Born of peasant stock in the Pale—an area in the west of Russia—Victor Melinkov was a Jew and had always felt disadvantaged by it. Jews in Russia were not treated as citizens and possessed few, if any, rights. To escape the stigma he had fled confinement and moved to a village east of Moscow, where he worked hard at being a gentile, unafraid of pogroms and persecution. His name did not connote any religious adherence, nor did he look like a traditional Jew. It had made no difference to Alex's mother that Victor Melinkov was Jewish, but the marriage had been ill conceived, a costly mistake, and his mother had lived to regret it.

When revolution came, it fed Victor's anarchistic ideals and he realised this was the fulfilment of his dream—to be a true Russian and to shake off the yoke of Tsarist Russia and work towards a super state.

Alex had an uneasy feeling that it would not be the last he would see of Victor Melinkov. The fact that he had taken his money was insufficient for him to consider the matter closed. He'd be back for more when he'd got rid of it.

The Ormsbys were a close-knit family and the familiarity they showed to each other was something new to Anna. From the moment she had arrived in their midst she had encountered friendliness and was overwhelmed by their kindness. The good-humoured affection they seemed to feel for each other and the manner in which they included her astonished her.

Lord Quentin Ormsby was a sweet man, content to live life in his wife's shadow, while Lady Irene Ormsby, an attractive woman who had cultivated a svelte, sophisticated appearance over the years, was both clever and innovative and was used to running things to her satisfaction. She spoke in a well-cultured voice with generations of upper-class breeding. They had produced four children. The eldest, Michael, worked in a

good job in the City, and twins Edward and Charles, boisterous fourteen year olds, had been sent away at an early age to
prep school and were now at Eton. Later they would go to
Oxford, because that was the way in which all Ormsby boys
were educated.

Tamsin was a year younger than Anna. The two girls had
become fast friends almost from the first moment they were
introduced, which was rather odd because they had little in
common.

The two-storey whitewashed villa with green shuttered windows set discreetly in the hills overlooking Monte Carlo—the
exclusive preserve of the extremely wealthy—was superb.
Unaccustomed to such luxury, Anna enjoyed the quiet peace
it provided. There was a calm order and remoteness from the
world.

The days were long and relaxed and, when the heat was
not too intense, they would play tennis or drive down to
Monte Carlo. Mostly they swam in the bright turquoise waters
of the pool and lounged in the shade. They often visited
friends of the Ormsbys who rented villas up and down the
coast, when they would sit around on sunny terraces beneath
trailing bracts of tropical bougainvillaea, drinking Pimms,
pink gins or Martinis.

Anna discovered she was something of a sun worshipper.
Ignoring Lady Ormsby's advice not to spoil her complexion,
she was delighted when her face and body turned a lovely
golden brown. Her time spent at the villa was happy and so
very different from what she had known at Gilchrist.

Throughout her childhood she had been aware of a growing
sense of isolation within herself, an emptiness that not even
the girls at school could fill. With it came the knowledge that
she was deliberately pulling away from people, creating bar-
riers. The habit of reserve she had built up over the years
when she had hidden so much of herself from others could
not be dismantled overnight. She had no family to talk about,
no background of any interest, and she had not known how

to deal with the sophisticated, boy-mad girls she encountered. She was more comfortable in her own company and one or two others who, like her, were quiet and academically inclined.

Tamsin, who had light brown hair cut into a bob and brown eyes, had done much for her self-esteem. She made her laugh, bolstered her morale and boosted her spirits. She was also warm hearted and full of fun; it would be a long time, if ever, before Anna became as buoyant, confident and gregarious.

At that time the whole of Europe was obsessed with everything American, from the music, the dancing and the cars to Hollywood, home of the movies, and the beautiful people—the glamorous stars that made the wonderful films. Tamsin was no exception. Fashion and society magazines satisfied all her literary requirements. Unlike Anna, she was looking forward to her coming-out with a great deal of excitement, and happily contemplating her new wardrobe, which Lady Ormsby insisted on purchasing in Paris.

Lady Ormsby was an extremely likeable, socially ambitious woman who thought it unwise to burden Tamsin with too much education. She had stayed at home to be educated by a governess until it was time for her to be 'finished' in Switzerland. The school Tamsin was to attend was enormously expensive, a school that appealed to well-to-do parents who wanted their daughters to turn out well and enjoyed the kudos that association with such an exclusive school brought them. Anna hated such petty snobbery, but things like that were very important to people like Lady Ormsby.

When Anna had been at the villa for four weeks, Lady Ormsby informed her that Alex Kent, who was driving home through France after spending some time in Cannes, would collect her from the villa and she was to accompany him back to England. 'Your grandfather is anxious to meet you,' she informed her. 'There should be plenty of time for the two of you to become acquainted before the Oxford term starts.'

This latest development sent Anna scurrying to find Tamsin in alarm. She found her sitting on the edge of the pool in her swimming costume and an enormous straw sun hat, trailing her feet in the water and sucking a sugared almond. Since Lady Ormsby and Lord Manson were old friends, Tamsin was sure to have met Alex Kent at some time or other. Fortunately she had, frequently. When Anna asked her what she thought of him, Tamsin settled herself on a lounger and, chomping what remained of the sugared almond, was more than willing to talk at length about him.

'As you must have seen for yourself, he is devastatingly attractive in a mysterious, wicked way. Socially he's very desirable—but hardly a dilettante. He's too serious for that; business always comes first with him and making money is what he's best at. But that doesn't stop the female population chasing after him,' she provided with typical practicality. 'There isn't a woman alive who wouldn't leave her bed—and, in some cases, her husband—in the dead of night for a rendezvous with him.' She sighed, meeting Anna's gaze dreamily. 'He's the type that makes virgins wish they weren't and married women forget their vows.

'He's a proud, infuriatingly arrogant, private individual and for some reason he shows no inclination to marry and scorns any woman who gets too close—which makes him infinitely more attractive and fascinating, I suppose. But there's something cold about him. Up to now no woman's come close enough to thaw the ice inside him.'

'Nevertheless, I have reason to be eternally gratefully to him,' said Anna. 'When my mother died I didn't know what my life would be like, but I decided that it must be a life I chose for myself and not something ordered by somebody else that was inescapable. Alex Kent recognised that, which is why he fought my corner with my grandfather and succeeded in persuading him to let me go to university. Is he very rich?'

'Seriously. He's also ambitious—a man of many interests, with business connections at the highest levels in several of

the world's capital cities. The financial crash that ruined so
many people didn't seem to touch him. Father says he has a
quicksilver brilliance in business matters, which he attacks
with a driving force.'

'I noticed he spoke with a slight foreign accent. Where is
he from?'

'Russia—at least, I think that's where he was brought up.
I believe he's half-Russian and half-English.' She frowned,
suddenly thoughtful. 'He's a bit of a mystery, really. With the
exception of Lord Manson, no one really knows anything
about him or his past, and he never talks about it. All I know
is that he came to England during the war and appeared in
Stainton one day—that's where Belhaven is. His relationship
with Lord Manson is of a peculiar kind—in fact, he's developed an unshakeable attachment to your grandfather.'

'Does he live at Belhaven?'

'Goodness, no. He has an apartment in town—in Kensington.'

'Have you ever been to Belhaven, Tamsin?'

'Yes, several times.'

'What's it like?'

'Lovely—an English paradise—much nicer than our own
Applemead. Despite the war and your grandfather living there
all alone since…' She hesitated, having been about to mention
Anna's mother, and suddenly remembering that her own
mother had told her not to mention her unless Anna spoke of
her herself. In fact, there were a lot of things her mother had
forbidden her to talk about, things about Alex that were better
left alone.

Anna sensed what Tamsin had been about to say and
smiled. 'It's all right, Tamsin, you can mention my mother. I
don't mind when people talk about her.'

'I'm glad. It must be hard for you, but you needn't worry
about going to live at Belhaven with your grandfather. It isn't
rundown or anything—in fact, quite the opposite. Lord Manson is passionate about the house and employs a regiment of

servants to see to his needs and to make sure it's kept spotless. You really are lucky, Anna, going to live at Belhaven. I wouldn't mind living there.'

'And my grandfather? What's he like?'

'Strict…demanding of those he employs. In fact, he has the ability to terrorise those beneath him to jelly with merely a look or a lift of an eyebrow—rather like Alex Kent in that respect. Although he can't be all that ferocious since his employees look after him with a cast-iron devotion. He's terribly frustrated at being confined to a wheelchair, which you can understand. Mummy has known him all her life and is extremely fond of him, and he's always very nice to me. I'm sure you'll get on, Anna. Mummy says he's looking forward to meeting you.'

Anna's newfound knowledge about Alex Kent did not make her feel any better. She was grateful to him, to be sure, but the mere thought of being alone in his company for long filled her with trepidation. As the hour of his arrival approached her stomach was churning frantically at the expected meeting, and by the time his shiny blue convertible swept up the curved drive and stopped in front of the villa, she had worked herself up into a nervous wreck.

Unfortunately, he arrived an hour early. Tennis with the twins in the heat of the day had sapped her energy so Anna was taking a quick dip in the pool before she had to get ready. She had just finished her final lap and surfaced to see a pair of gleaming brown shoes on the white tile surround.

Chapter Three

Treading water Anna followed the feet upwards, her eyes meeting those of Alex Kent looking down at her. Quickly she hauled herself from out of the water like a graceful mermaid, her tanned flesh shining with rivulets of water. She had no idea of the lovely picture she presented in her bright blue swimsuit. As if she were suddenly conscious that she was staring at Mr Kent in a way that was scarcely polite, her face turned scarlet. The effect of this girlish weakness on Alex brought an expression to his face that was at once vibrantly and alarmingly alive.

In one quick glance he saw the change a month in the sun had made. Her skin was burned a flattering golden brown and a few freckles sprinkled her nose. She had a beautiful, fine bone structure—he saw classic beauty rather than sex appeal—and there was a slight dimple in her chin below the curve of her rose-tinted lips.

An inexplicable, lazy smile swept over his face as he looked at her and held out his hand—Anna had the staggering and impossible impression that he actually liked what he saw. *'Enchanté, mademoiselle,'* he said quietly. Automatically she gave him her hand for what she presumed would be a normal handshake, but he covered it with both of his and kept it. His eyes were warm with admiration as they looked straight into hers. 'You look well, Anna—so grown up and *élégante*. France obviously agrees with you.'

'I'm glad you think so. I love everything about it. It fits in perfectly with the picture I had of it in my mind: the heat, the colour, the lack of restraint—yes, I like it very well,' she managed awkwardly, hastily withdrawing her hand from his, annoyed with her attack of nervousness.

With his sunglasses pushed up over his thick black hair, Alex Kent presented a dazzling figure. He was dressed in cream trousers, his white shirt partially unbuttoned, the sleeves folded back over his forearms. His accent was noticeable, adding to his attraction. And yet there were harsh lines on his face and a tension in his manner that suggested some kind of inner struggle unrelieved by success. Anna combed back her dripping wet, heavy black hair and, terribly self-conscious, confused and strangely vulnerable, reached for a towel she had left nearby and draped it round her.

'And are you enjoying yourself?' he asked, quietly touched by her sudden show of modesty.

'Yes.'

'And the heat? Do you find it difficult?'

'No, not really. In fact, I spend so long lying in the sun that Lady Ormsby says I'll shrivel up like a prune. You… you're early, Mr Kent. We weren't expecting you for another hour or so,' she said in a shaky voice.

His voice was gentle as he said, 'Mr Kent is far too formal, Anna. My friends call me Alex. Finding myself with nothing much to do, I decided not to hang about. You don't mind, do you?'

His smooth, accented deep voice wrapped itself winningly around his words, and his powerful charm of manner radiated a rapier-sharp intelligence. Anna was mesmerized. 'No,' she lied, wishing she'd had time to change.

He nodded with satisfaction. 'Good, then you will not object to traveling back to England with me tomorrow.'

'It's very good of you to trouble yourself with me.'

'You are no trouble, Anna, and how extraordinary that you should think you are.'

Clutching the towel firmly in front of her, Anna could tell that he knew she was acutely uneasy with him, and that she was reluctant to go anywhere with him alone, but every instinct she possessed warned her that he could become extremely persistent if he chose.

'Are we to drive all the way to Calais?' she asked, alarmed at the prospect. She wasn't used to keeping company with men at all, let alone one like Alex Kent—and Calais was a very long way away. 'The overnight train from Nice to Paris would have been much quicker.'

A smile quirked at Alex's mouth. 'I know, but not nearly as enjoyable.'

'But isn't that how most pleasure seekers travel to and from the Riviera?'

'Yes, but in my experience trains are overcrowded and lacking in privacy, which is why I nearly always drive myself. Besides, I recall you telling me that your experience of travel is limited, so I thought you might like to become more intimately acquainted with France. Don't worry,' he said when he saw apprehension cloud her eyes, 'I'll make sure you are back in England with plenty of time to prepare for the beginning of term.'

'So, here you are, Alex,' Lady Ormsby remarked, walking across the lawn towards them, looking cool and attractive in a clinging floral-print sheath dress and a large brimmed sun hat. 'I wondered where you'd disappeared to. You must be travel weary after your drive from Cannes. There are refreshments on the terrace. I'm so glad you're not leaving until morning. I'm throwing a small dinner party later—very informal, nothing smart. I'm sure you will know most of those invited. Have you been holidaying in Cannes?'

'A few days, no more,' he replied, kissing her proffered cheek. 'I was in Geneva on business and thought I'd drive down to see a few friends and coincide with escorting Anna back to England. I've spoken to her grandfather and he has no objections.'

Lady Ormsby flashed him one of her brilliant smiles. 'How terribly kind of you to think of Anna. I'm glad chivalry is not quite dead. Some may consider it inappropriate for a young girl to travel unchaperoned in the company of a young man, but, like Selwyn, I have no fears at her being alone in your company, Alex. I confess that I was worried, thinking of her traveling so far alone on the train. She will be glad of your company, won't you, Anna?'

'Yes...very,' Anna answered hesitantly.

'It's rather unfortunate that her first venture abroad is being curtailed so soon,' Lady Ormsby went on, 'but there we are. It can't be helped. I have failed to persuade her to share Tamsin's Season. Nothing would give me greater pleasure than to have a free hand to present her at Court with Tamsin and guide her through her Season with all the honour due to the granddaughter of Lord Manson of Belhaven.'

'I'm sorry, but I could never see myself as a débutante. Please excuse me while I go and change.'

'Very well, dear—oh, and, Alex,' Lady Ormsby said as Anna was about to move away, 'you mentioned something about calling England. Feel free to use the telephone whenever you like.'

'Thank you. I'll do it now.'

Anna watched him go. Lithe, tall, deeply tanned and extremely handsome, there was a vigorous purposefulness in his long, quick strides that bespoke impatience and an active life. When she went inside, the villa was a flurry of activity, with servants preparing for the party later. There were flowers everywhere—orchids and lilies, mainly, being Lady Orsmby's favourites—and bowls of pot-pourri scented the rooms. What Lady Ormsby said was to be a small, informal affair was in reality cocktails followed by a formal dinner for thirty people. Because there would be no one under the age of twenty-five, Tamsin jokingly called it the Martini Set.

When she had changed into a cool dress and tied her hair back, Anna went to join the others. Hearing Alex talking on the telephone as she was about to cross the hall, she paused. He was standing with his back to her, speaking in Russian intently, looking out of the window. Unaware of her presence he began speaking in English, slowly and quietly.

'I'm sorry but I have to go. Goodbye, my darling, and remember that I love you so very much—more than anyone. Take care of yourself, Sonya. I'll see you just as soon as I return to England.' He replaced the receiver and stood staring down at it for several moments, his expression thoughtful and deeply troubled.

Not wishing to intrude on what was clearly a very private moment, Anna backed away out of sight, her heart beating a tattoo of panic, as much from the humiliation of being caught eavesdropping as what she had heard. She went out of the house by another exit, unaware as she left the hall that as Alex turned around, as though sensing an alien presence, a flash of her yellow skirt caught his eye as she disappeared.

Anna was curious as to the identity of Sonya. Who was she and why had he been speaking to her in Russian? Of course, the obvious answer was that she was Russian. Well, whoever she was, despite what Tamsin had told her about no woman being able to get close enough to thaw the ice inside him, Alex Kent was very much in love with her, that much was plain.

When she reached the terrace, Lord Ormsby, wreathed in pipe smoke and reading a newspaper, was seated in his usual wicker chair beneath an awning. When the sun was too strong for him it was his favorite spot. The twins were frolicking about in the pool and Tamsin was reclining on a lounger in her swimming costume, flicking through the latest edition of *Vogue*. Anna went to join her, perching on the edge. When Alex appeared she saw he was frowning, as if he was concentrating on some problem. He looked her way, casting his eyes over her yellow skirt before going to sit next to Lord

Ormsby, whose wife was clinking ice into glasses and pouring fresh lemon juice.

'You're right on time, Alex,' Lord Ormsby greeted him. 'Punctuality always was one of your virtues.'

'Probably my only one,' Alex replied with a smile. He took a moment to look appreciatively at the magnificent view. Beyond the oval pool the ground fell away down the green sloping hills, and in the distance the sea, dotted with pleasure seekers' yachts and small fishing boats, was a glittering blue sheet.

'The view is quite magnificent,' Alex said, 'the villa perfectly situated. Little wonder you choose to come here year after year.'

'Yes, we like it,' Lord Ormsby responded. 'A bit of Mediterranean sun does one the power of good. A lot of our friends come to the Riviera so the social life is pretty lively. Did you manage to get through to England all right?'

From where she sat Anna sensed, rather than saw, Alex tense. 'Yes—thank you.'

Lady Ormsby paused in her task and gave him a long considering look. 'And how are things, Alex? Nothing wrong, is there?'

'No, everything's fine.' He looked directly at Anna, his eyes probing, secretive, as he wondered how much, if anything, she had overheard of his call. There was nothing in her expression that told him she had. 'Selwyn is well. I telephoned him before I left Cannes. He's looking forward to meeting Anna.'

'I can understand that,' Irene said, handing him a long, ice-cold glass of lemon juice. 'I just know she'll be good for him. Poor Selwyn. How angry he was when Lavinia left, and when the anger left him he had nothing. It's been so long...' Irene's expression suddenly became wistful as she looked across at Anna and for a moment she became perfectly still, lost in thought, then, shaking her head, she gave a long sigh. 'Oh, well—like I said, it was a long time ago.'

Whatever it was Lady Ormsby had been about to say Anna would never know. Something in the interchange of words was confusing. When Lord Ormsby had asked Alex about his telephone call the looks Lady Ormsby and Alex had exchanged had been all knowing and secretive, from which everyone else was excluded. Nothing made sense. Who was Sonya? Why had Lady Ormsby purposely avoided mentioning her name? Why the mystery? Alex's expression was shuttered. He was a man who hid his secrets well. Still, it was none of her business and probably not worth bothering about.

Later, Anna and Tamsin made their way out onto the terrace where cocktails and hors d'oeuvres were being served. The terraced gardens were open to the sun, but here and there exotic trees had been planted, making their own canopies of shade. The ornamental urns brimming with bright red geraniums looked especially lovely. Anna observed the glamorous Riviera set milling around, eating and drinking and shifting from one group to another. Tamsin immediately disappeared to get herself a drink.

From his vantage point on the terrace, Alex idly watched the guests arrive without consciously admitting to himself that he was watching specifically for Anna to appear...and then he saw her. Draped in a strappy dress of white satin that clung to her small breasts and minuscule waist and complemented her tan, her stance was one of quiet, regal poise. She had an intriguing, indefinable presence that made her stand out, even in the moving kaleidoscope of movement and colour and animated voices. It was as if everyone and everything was in motion except Anna. Alex headed slowly but purposefully towards her.

'You look lovely,' a deep voice said behind Anna. She turned to find Alex looking at her with a smile of pure masculine appreciation.

Her face broke into a smile. 'Thank you,' she replied, feeling like the dazzled teenager she was. His reaction to her appearance was so flattering that she was instantly glad she'd taken Tamsin's advice to wear the white satin.

'They're a noisy lot, aren't they?' he remarked. 'You meet the same people at these parties, people who know all about each other since they're together every year down here. Must get rather dull, I always think—however, tonight's an exception.'

Anna looked up. 'You mean me?'

He grinned. 'Who else?'

Her eyebrows rose. 'Are you telling me that I'm peculiar in some way—that I don't mix?' she asked defensively.

'On the contrary. I admire your courage. You've fitted in remarkably well. Are you always armed for battle, even when someone makes an innocent remark about you?'

'It wasn't innocent. You implied that I'm different.'

'You are different—and before you raise your defences, that was meant to be a compliment.'

A smile touched the corners of her mouth. 'I'm sorry. I'm just not used to getting compliments.'

'You'll soon get used to it—when everyone gets to know who you are. Being Lord Manson's heir will count—you'll see.' His eyes moved leisurely over the fragile features, pausing at length on her soft pink lips. 'I suppose you're used to these parties by now.'

'I found them strange at first—I was afraid I wouldn't fit in, wouldn't have anyone to talk to. But these people—they're so confident...so worldly...so unafraid to speak their minds. It's as if nothing bad ever happens to them.'

'You have the strangest notion that the world is full of people who have no problems. They do. None of them are perfect.'

'I suppose you're right. I'll just have to find something else to envy.'

'There is nothing and no one in this world you should envy, Anna. You outshine everyone. You just have to learn to trust yourself.'

Alex smiled—a smile that was part of his charm—and at that moment the dormant part of Anna's heart began to stir. The soft glow of the setting sun rested on his face and with a new greed Anna fastened her gaze on him. 'Yes, I suppose I must,' she responded, warmed not only by his smile but by his solicitude also.

'I've been hearing all about you from Irene and Quentin,' he said conversationally, perching his hip on the stone balustrade, watching her almost lazily. 'I should have paid you a visit before now. I'm sorry I didn't. Quentin tells me you've become a real member of the family. I assume that means you like them.'

'I love them,' Anna said. 'They've all been wonderful to me. I'm going to miss them when I return to England.'

At that moment Lady Ormsby came to lay claim to Alex. She wasn't smiling—in fact, she looked extremely vexed about something. With an apologetic smile Alex moved away.

'I'm so sorry, Alex,' Anna heard Lady Ormsby say to him quickly. 'He was certainly not invited. If he hadn't chanced to arrive simultaneously with the Reynoldses, who, as you know, are good friends of ours, he would never have been admitted to the house.'

They continued to talk as they moved out of earshot and Anna frowned, wondering who would have the nerve to come to a private party when they had not been invited. And why should Lady Ormsby feel the need to apologise to Alex about it? She watched him as he began to mingle, thinking how incredible he looked in evening dress. Several ladies were openly admiring. One such lady was Nancy Kirkbride, a red-haired beauty who possessed a ripe sexuality and had an irritating habit of calling everyone 'sweetie'.

Anna watched with some amusement as the incorrigible woman, having first favoured Alex with a smile so devastating that it could not fail to contain a strong element of flirtatiousness, then laid her hand compellingly on his arm and guided him inexorably towards the glittering crowd of people. Unfortunately, Alex did not interact so well with the lady's male partner, Lord Freddy Campbell, the son of an earl, a smooth sort with slicked back fair hair, good looks in a sleepy, boyish kind of way, who was clearly unimpressed.

When Alex first encountered Freddy, his eyes were arrested by the sight of him. Anna observed how both men changed colour—Freddy's countenance flushed, Alex's whitened beneath his tan and froze into a mask of pure undiluted hatred. He cast Freddy a look that would have pulverized rock before he abruptly turned away. Anna realised that Freddy Campbell was the uninvited guest.

Freddy and Nancy were typical party animals; in fact, the pair of them looked slightly worse for drink already.

Alex knew several of the guests—prosperous businessmen and their wives basking in the warmth and wealth of the Riviera. With a smooth urbanity and social polish he was absolutely at ease. Careful to avoid Freddy Campbell, he moved around, perfectly charming, giving the evening new order and fresh life.

'Why is it that whenever men gather together they tend to discuss such boring matters as politics and business?' Tamsin complained with an aggrieved note in her voice. 'Wouldn't you think when they come on holiday they'd leave it behind? I'm going to miss you something terrible when you leave tomorrow, Anna. Are you sure you can't stay and go back with us?'

'You know I can't, Tamsin. I have so much to do. Besides, your mother wants to spend some time in Paris buying clothes to launch her beautiful daughter on to the social scene. Your mother tells me that your brother Michael is to be your partner.'

'Yes. Mummy says it's time he thought about getting married and it will give him the opportunity to find something suitable—an heiress, she hopes, who would be able to contribute in maintaining Applemead in the style to which it's accustomed.'

Anna laughed. 'How very wise, since you will more than likely bankrupt your parents with exorbitant bills for your new ballgowns and fripperies, but I'm certain everyone will envy you your elegance.'

'I do hope so. I'm so looking forward to Paris. I do find these kind of evenings a drag. If only Mummy would invite a younger set, we could have some fun.'

Anna shot her a wry look. 'I don't think your mother would appreciate the kind of fun you mean, Tamsin. They seem a pretty mixed bunch to me.' She observed Nancy moving in to monopolise Alex's attention once more, seeming totally unaware of her scowling partner. Tamsin saw it too and smiled with bland amusement.

'You can see what I mean about Alex being popular, though I bet he's getting pretty tired of Nancy by now. Her father's in trade—new money—and Nancy works hard at try-ing to be la-di-dah while calling everyone sweetie. I read plenty of magazines and Alex has a different glamorous woman with him in every picture I've seen of him, but he never stays with them.'

Anna frowned. Tamsin's comment brought the mysterious Sonya to mind and, for some reason she could not explain, she was reluctant to ask Tamsin if she'd heard of her.

'Nancy always makes a beeline for Alex…' Tamsin sighed '…and who can blame her. He looks like a Greek Adonis.'

'Adonis didn't have black hair, Tamsin. He was blond.'

'Well…you know what I mean. Few men can deny Nancy anything—although she's not as young as she looks. Look at her face—it's an armour plating of make-up—and look at Freddy. They've been together for two years—although, in view of his reputation and the provocation she's given him, I doubt he's been faithful.'

'What a strange relationship.'

'Freddy doesn't seem to mind a bit when Nancy shows interest in other men, either—although Alex is an exception. Freddy's something of a loser, you see. His family lost a lot of money in the crash and never recovered, which was a terrible blow to Freddy.'

'Why do you say that?'

'He has a passion for fast cars. He has a Bugatti and an Alfa Romeo that he's always racing at Brooklands, but it's a hobby that doesn't come cheap. He doesn't like Alex—resents his success and all that—and, looking at him now, I'd say he'd like to give him a one-way ticket to Siberia. Alex can't stand him either and avoids him whenever he can.'

'There must be more to it than that. Plenty of people are successful. Why should Freddy single Alex out?'

'You're right. Before Freddy's family fell on hard times in 1929, Alex already excelled at being successful. He was seeing Freddy's sister at the time—his twin sister, Edwina. Thinking everything was nice and cosy and that in time Alex might marry Edwina, Freddy approached him, wanted to buy into his company. Alex told him to forget it and dropped Edwina like a stone.'

'If he didn't think he could make her happy, then he must have thought it was for the best.'

Tamsin gave her a tight, meaningful smile. 'You've obviously never met Edwina. She's a walking mantrap. To Alex their relationship meant nothing more than an exotic, sensual bit of spice.'

Anna looked at her in astonishment. 'You seem remarkably well informed, Tamsin.'

She giggled. 'It's amazing how much you learn by pretending to read while keeping an open ear to what the grown-ups are saying. I've no idea how Edwina felt, but I suppose she couldn't help being dazzled by Alex. She's awesome, the perfect hedonist.'

'What's a hedonist?'

'A pleasure seeker. Edwina is an acclaimed beauty who lives to enjoy life to the full. All her life she's had things her own way and never sees anything but herself. Anyone who's been hers stays hers, if she wants him, and she wanted Alex.

But he dropped her—and you know that old cliché, ''Hell hath no fury…'' and all that.'

'Why, what did she do?'

'Unable to forgive his public rejection and humiliation of her—no one ever did that to Edwina; there's nothing weak or sentimental about her, you see—she turned her sword against him. Edwina's clever, a survivor. She can survive at depths that can crush the life out of any man. She believed in attacking from strength, and that lay in the hold she has always had on her brother's emotions. She recruited Freddy's cooperation to help get back at him. Together they swore they would see Alex ruined. They spread it around that he could not be trusted and they were certain he would be washed up before the year was out. It was unfortunate for them that the crash happened when it did and the tables turned.'

'No wonder Alex is so angry to see Freddy here tonight. But there does seem something rather endearing about him.'

'There is. He can be an absolute charmer when he's away from that sister of his and so likeable. One can't help but notice how close they are when they're together, but Edwina is definitely the dominant twin. Mummy didn't invite Freddy and she's rather cross about it, but when he presented himself with the Reynoldses, she could hardly ask him to leave. Still, I suppose being the son of an earl enables him to do as he pleases with relative impunity.'

The problem of the uninvited guest solved and the two men's intense dislike of each other evident in their body language, Anna said, 'Perhaps Nancy will leave Alex alone when we go in to dinner.'

Unfortunately, that wasn't the case. Nancy forcefully placed herself next to Alex, directly across from Freddy.

Candles had been lit around the room and on the table, with the setting sun casting a golden glow on the terrace. Anna had Tamsin on one side and Edward—the most boisterous and mischievous of the twins—on the other. As the meal progressed she observed that Freddy Campbell drank a lot. He also smiled a lot and languidly listened to what Nancy—who was being her most dazzlingly social self—had to say to Alex as she simpered and pouted and fluttered her eyelashes at him over the frosted rim of her martini glass.

But it struck Anna that the spontaneity was gone. Freddy Campbell's behaviour seemed studied, every look pointing to the couple directly within his sights. Though Alex's manner remained stoic, Anna could sense his growing agitation with the woman, for his eyes rested on her with a total lack of clarity.

The conversation around the table covered everything from the coalition government in Britain to the carryings on between the twice-married Baltimore-born Mrs Ernest Simpson and the Prince of Wales. The growth of the Fascist movement in Germany and whether or not the newly elected German Chancellor, Adolf Hitler, was a visionary or a psychopath was discussed at length, as was the trade unions and whether or not they were being influenced by the Communists. The rise in Jewish protests in Britain against Nazi anti-semitism raised particular interest, and everyone agreed that the massive unemployment was a problem and that the immigrants infiltrating society only exacerbated the situation.

One or two sympathized with the immigrants, commenting on the fact that conditions in their own countries must be pretty grim to force them out. Freddy was not so sensitive and, on seeing Nancy touch Alex's hand with her finger was, blinded by prejudice and unable to overcome an irresistible urge to pick a quarrel with the infuriating foreigner. To Freddy, Alex was too attractive for his own good and his dislike and jealousy grew more acute the more he found himself in his company. Freddy immediately seized on the opportunity and asked Alex to air his opinion.

'Why don't we ask Alex what he thinks about the Communists and our trade unions—and about the immigrant situation? You, more than any of us, must empathise with them, being an immigrant, a refugee from Russia.' Freddy uttered the words immigrant and refugee with something bordering on contempt. He expected his verbal condemnation to get a reaction, but except for a muscle that began to twitch in Alex's jaw and a hard stare, there was none. 'You are far removed from your beginnings,' Freddy went on, 'but are you content?'

Freddy was leaning back in his chair, watching Alex calmly, his voice flat and the words carefully spaced. The wounding remark made the two men the focal point of everyone's attention. The clink of silver cutlery on bone china stopped, along with conversation down the length of the table, eyes directed at Alex, brows raised in interest.

Anna was inexplicably holding her breath as she looked at him, and she didn't like what she saw. This was a new Alex Kent, his eyes flint hard with pure, cold hatred in their depths as they fastened on Freddy. Perhaps she misinterpreted the look that lingered, but, whatever the reason, the temperature dropped several degrees. Tension hung like a pall over the table.

'I think what Freddy is trying to say,' Lord Ormsby tactfully intervened, 'is do those who have been forced from their homeland because of persecution feel the need to return when the situation improves?'

With a magnificent gesture of unconcern that completely belied his mounting fury, Alex shrugged lightly and said, 'Thank you, Quentin, but I think I know exactly what he meant. It's a general opinion that Communists influence the trade unions, and there are some hotheads in government who are spoiling for a fight. Whatever the truth of it, it makes good headlines, I suppose, but the idea of Bolsheviks hiding under every bed is a joke.

'And you are right, Freddy. I am far removed from my beginnings, from Russia. I am neither the first nor the last to flee persecution—such is the natural progression of things. And, no, I do not feel the need and nor do I have the desire to return to the country of my birth. I know, as you do, that

I am not really one of you, even though my mother was English. When I came here I was treated fairly—after all, we do live in a democratic society. I have much to be grateful for. I have succeeded where others failed,' he said, his eyes fixed firmly on Freddy's coldly reminding him of his own failure, 'which has attracted resentment from some, but not from those who matter to me.'

'Those who matter being men in high places—men like Lord Manson, perhaps?' Freddy said. His voice was cool, touched with slight derision, and he was seemingly unmoved by the blast of Alex's gaze. 'Pity you weren't born into the nobility, Alex,' he laughed, 'for then you would have it all.'

Alex's face hardened into an expressionless mask, but his eyes were like daggers.

Anna was beginning to feel terribly uncomfortable. This wasn't the usual dinnertime conversation. Hostility bordering on pure hatred simmered between the two men, and yet Alex was treating Freddy's impertinent remarks with a cool nonchalance that didn't seem at all appropriate.

Freddy Campbell was a man whom Alex quietly detested to a degree that went far beyond his smiling affability, which he knew masked insolence, and for his blatant lack of moral decency. Freddy didn't seem to realise that his all-consuming desire for hedonistic pleasure had brought about his downfall.

'What an absurdity!' Alex exclaimed, hiding his mounting temper behind a coolly polite façade. 'Of course there is the nobility—the elite, a lot of inherited privilege and wealth—and into that—as was the case in Russia until the Tsar and his family were murdered—one has to be born, such as yourself, but men and women of mean birth are capable of advancement…do advance.'

'You and your like often do, and use any means and anyone to achieve their ambition,' Freddy retorted, his comment slighting. He was completely unable to deal with Alex's ruthless lack of emotion.

'Me and my like?' Alex said with amazing calm, giving no

indication that he was affected by the intended insult. In complete contrast to Freddy, whose expression was beginning to show his feelings, Alex lounged back in his chair indifferently, his expression bland, his long legs stretched out beneath the table. 'Now, I wonder, I really do wonder, what you can mean by that? Do you see me as a rough edge catching the silk? I was not born a peasant, and, if I had been, it would have made no difference to me as a person. I am what I am— a man known for my honesty and integrity—and I have more than I require. Man is, after all, only a creature of habit—and his habit is often his passion.'

'And women? Are they a habit…a passion?' Freddy drawled, a faint contemptuous smile touching his lips as his gaze slipped to Nancy and back to Alex.

Alex said, in a voice ice cold, 'You should know the answer to that—being an expert in the field.'

Anna detected meaning in Alex's remark, meaning hidden from the rest of them, but known and festering between the two antagonists. Was it to do with Edwina, or did it go deeper than that?

Ignoring Alex's sarcasm, Freddy stumbled on. 'From what I see of your zealous attentions, I trust you are enjoying Nancy's company,' he said, unable to find innocent cause why the two of them should have their heads together—although to be fair to Alex, it was pretty obvious to everyone that Nancy was trying it on, and that Alex was doing nothing to encourage her.

'I suspected something else was on your mind but, whatever you have to say, save it until later,' Alex said lightly, trying to divert Freddy's attempt to provoke further argument, but the steel in his voice was in vivid contrast to the expression of bland courtesy he was wearing for the sake of their fascinated audience. 'Let's not spoil the meal any longer than absolutely necessary.'

'Damn it all, Alex,' Freddy flared, finally letting go of his temper, 'Nancy's with me.'

Alex's expression was critical and contemptuous. 'In that case, why don't you pay her some attention—unless you're losing your touch?'

Anna, who had never seen men act this way before, had a sudden urge to run for cover, but Nancy had an equally strong impulse, induced by drink, to giggle at the male hostility she had provoked and reached for her glass. She was not so woolly headed as not to know that it was not her antics that actually made Freddy angry, or even her flirtations, it was the simple fact that she had chosen to do it with Alex.

With spurs of anger and jealousy pricking him to a painful depth, Freddy shot her a withering glance. Balling his napkin up, he dropped it on the table, accidentally knocking his glass of wine over in the process. The dark red stain spread in every direction.

'I think the drink has clouded your mind,' Alex drawled, getting in one more verbal thrust. 'You're high as a kite, Freddy. Why don't you go outside and clear your head?'

Freddy stood up and pushed his chair back. 'I think I will. Please excuse me, Irene, Quentin, and thank you for a delightful meal. I'm sorry. It was not my intention to make a scene or to give offence.'

Casting about for something to say to diffuse the tension, Lady Ormsby seized on tomorrow's cruise on Lord Tyrone-Scott's yacht moored in the harbour at Monte Carlo. Meanwhile, Anna watched Freddy go out on to the terrace, where he stood for a moment to light a cigarette, before disappearing. She felt sorry for him—as she would for anyone who got on the wrong side of Alex Kent.

'Oh, dear! Poor Freddy,' she said to Tamsin in a tense, quiet voice. Alex had not so much as glanced at her since they'd sat down for dinner, but, hearing her words, he turned his head and looked straight at her. She would have been dumbfounded to know that, as she returned his stare, he was seething inside.

Chapter Four

The strains of 'It's Only a Paper Moon' could be heard coming from the gramophone in the next room. Some of the guests were already dancing.

'Come on, we might as well dance,' said Tamsin.

'You go. I'd like a minute to cool off.'

Guests were standing in small groups, laughing and talking beside the bar, which had been set up beside the pool. Lights, set up in the trees, created circles of yellowish light attracting night insects. Anna went down some steps and paused, leaning on a stone balustrade. The night was hot and still, the aroma of tobacco and the murmur of conversation drifting down to where she stood.

Listening to the cicadas beat out their rhythm, she gazed at the panorama of twinkling lights fanning out along the coastline. It wasn't until she turned her head that she saw Alex standing a short distance away. He looked a solitary figure, cloaked in silence. She moved closer.

'I suppose the quiet out here is infinitely preferable to the mood inside the villa,' she murmured. He turned, his harsh face defined by an iron jaw and dark brows. When he saw her, the stern line of his mouth relaxed into a lazy smile. He wore an expression of polite concern, but Anna saw his hand clenched tight as it rested on the balustrade, and the line of tension that ran through his body. He was strung up like a harp.

'You're right—and the company is better by far.' Alex saw the pleasure that lit up her face, and it warmed him with its astonishing intensity, softening the hard streak of cynical indifference that was his norm.

'Still, you shouldn't be down here all alone.'

'I felt the need to be by myself. Don't you ever feel like that?'

'Yes,' she admitted, 'but this is a party.'

'I don't have to be in the middle of it,' he pointed out meaningfully.

'No, of course you don't.' After a moment's pause she said, 'Was I mistaken or did Freddy have an axe to grind?'

The effect was immediate. Alex's features tightened and he fixed his gaze on the sea. At length he spoke, and in a constrained manner said, 'Was it that obvious?'

'I'm afraid so. It's clear the two of you don't get on.'

Anna sensed, almost felt, the rage that was being kept under ruthless control—it came towards her in waves of heat. Yet the voice was cold when he said, 'Freddy Campbell is a useless and thoroughly unpleasant character, irrepressible and fatally addicted to gambling and other vices, which I shall not go in to. They are not for the ears of a respectable young lady. Seduced by blue skies and loose morals, he appears on the Riviera every summer. He may be the son of an earl, but the man's a charlatan and a scoundrel of the worst kind.'

'Oh, dear—as bad as that,' Anna said, beginning to wish she hadn't mentioned Freddy Campbell. She noted that when Alex was angry a stronger than usual accent seeped into his voice.

'Every bit. The man's a radical, a fascist, one of Mosley's set.'

Anna knew about Oswald Mosley. He had been a socialist and a member of the Labour party before being expelled and forced to the right. His turn to fascism was a response to the failure of the government to adopt radical reform to prevent the continued economic and political decline in Britain, and to cure unemployment. Drawing inspiration from Mussolini's Italy, in October of 1932 Mosley had formed the British Union of Fascists.

'But surely you can't hold a man's politics against him?'

'Some may find their ideas interesting,' Alex ground out, 'but personally I think they are deeply dangerous.'

'Oswald Mosley is the leader of a legitimate party with legitimate views, even if you don't agree with them.'

'That doesn't alter the fact that the movement's style is aggressive and attracts political violence. It believes in force, restriction of free speech and its members are brutally racist and anti-semitic. Often thousands of police are unable to quell the violent rioting that breaks out between the fascists and their opponents.'

'I was under the impression that the authorities' view of the BUF is far more objective than the attitude it takes towards left-wing movements and the Communist party, and that the police sympathise with the discipline and control of the Blackshirts at their public meetings unless provoked. Many people think Mosley is brilliant and that his ideas are exciting. They believe his economic theories are sound, that what is needed is a realistic program of action to deal with the economic and wretched social crisis affecting Britain just now. They want a shake up of the established authorities, to take control to apply a complete reformation of the system.'

'They would do all that—with force, if necessary,' Alex retorted drily.

'No, by persuasion. The party is doing awfully well.'

'So well that it's failed to convince the nation that the authoritarian methods necessary to solve Britain's economic and social problems will work, and, for a party whose purpose is to solve these problems, it is conspicuously unsuccessful in recruiting a mass following.' Alex stared at Anna suspiciously. 'You speak with the voice of a radical, Anna, and appear to be remarkably well informed on the affairs of the BUF.'

'Not really. I only know what I read in the newspapers.'

He considered her without a hint of expression, then with slow deliberation he said, 'I sincerely hope you are not attracted to the fascist cause. That would be most unwise.' His tone promised terrible reprisals if she chose to ignore him.

Anna bristled. 'Of course I'm not. But if I were,' she said, unable to thrust down her feeling of pique at being told what to do, 'it would be entirely my own affair. Everyone is entitled to their views—even me. How long have you known Freddy?' she asked, quickly changing the subject and looking away.

'To my everlasting regret, ten years, and he's never been any different.'

'Why, he must have been what—nineteen—twenty when you first knew him? At that age he can hardly have had time to sink into such depravity.'

'Believe me, Anna, he was every bit as bad then as he is now, wicked, devious—and controlling,' Alex added softly, almost to himself. 'I met him at university. Half the undergraduates went to Oxford simply to grow up; Freddy Campbell went up solely to have a good time—fast living and academic indifference—with absolutely no intention of learning anything.'

'And then he met Nancy,' Anna remarked, wishing she hadn't a moment later. Alex's expression became darker and more ominous. The hard line of his jaw tightened until a drumming pulse stood out in his cheek. He was furious, Anna thought with a jolt of fear. Quickly, apologetically, she said, 'Alex, I'm sorry. Forget I mentioned her.'

Making a visible effort to control his fury he asked tautly, 'Why not? Why shouldn't you mention her?'

'She—she seems nice.'

'Being nice won't hold Freddy Campbell, but money will.'

Anna ignored his remark. 'Does she usually impose herself

on you like that? She has a way of looking at you that must
alarm Freddy.'

'You are very perceptive, Anna; however, I have no interest
in Nancy—and the only kind of attraction she has for Campbell is that she has money enough for him to live off. Nancy
is an attractive woman, but not a sensible one, otherwise she
would get rid of him.'

'I can see why she doesn't. Freddy is very good looking
and always charming. I've seen them at several parties—although we've never been properly introduced. Don't you
think Freddy might have cause to be hurt by Nancy's easy
defection—that his pride was at stake?'

Alex's face hardened and there was a feral glitter in his
eyes as they searched her features. 'Is that a criticism?'

Anna's small chin lifted and her spine stiffened at his chilling tone. How could he treat her with the same brutal contempt he'd treated Freddy? 'Of course not. It's not for me to
criticise anyone. But, sitting beside her at dinner—'

'Which was a situation I could not avoid without causing
a scene,' he was quick to point out.

'No, I don't suppose you could, but I—I merely thought
your attentions might have provoked him, that's all.'

'It seems to have escaped your notice that I was not the
only male Nancy Kirkbride latched herself on to tonight,'
Alex pointed out tightly.

'No, it didn't, but you're the only one that mattered to
Freddy.'

'How quick you are to defend him, Anna. Perhaps you are
attracted to him yourself. Do you admit it?'

Anna was indignant. 'I admit nothing of the sort. You are
mistaken if you think that. It's a ridiculous thing to say. But
in spite of everything I find him pleasant—'

His voice cut across hers with the slashing force of a knife
blade. 'Don't make the mistake of falling for him. That would
be a foolish thing to do. Whatever sentiment Freddy Campbell
has created, you have been deceived—although with his looks

and that smooth charm of his, his success is not to be wondered at,' he mocked sarcastically. When Anna opened her mouth to argue, he said, 'Drop it, Anna. You will oblige me by refraining to speak of something about which you know nothing.'

Anna sighed with capitulation. The lines of his face were angular and hard with determination, but behind the cold glitter of his eyes lay a fathomless stillness. 'I'm sorry if I've offended you, Alex. I didn't mean to. Would you like to dance?' she asked impulsively in an attempt to relieve the tension vibrating in the air between them.

Alex tilted his head towards the strains of the music. He looked neither shocked nor flattered by her bold request. His answer when he gave it was firmly spoken. 'No, not now.'

Anna turned her head in the direction of the tune that started playing, slow and romantic—George and Ira Gershwin's 'Someone To Watch Over Me'. In some strange way it reminded her of herself and Alex, for wasn't that what he was doing; watching over her?

The piercing sweetness wrapped itself round her. She was aware of the man beside her and wished he would smile and take her in his arms and dance with her, that he would place his lips against her cheek and— She checked herself. She wished…she wished so many hazy, impossible things. Humiliated and hurt by his firm rejection, she stepped back.

'You're right. Better not. I should have known better than to ask. Please excuse me. I must find Tamsin.' She left him then, trying to retreat from a predicament into which she should never have put herself in in the first place.

Instead of joining her friend, Anna wandered past the pool and into the shadows, sitting down at a table to nurse her wounded pride. Alex Kent was no longer her knight on a white charger, but a monster. When a cloud of cigarette smoke curled round her she realised she was not alone. Freddy

Campbell sat across from her, looking languid and extremely bored. He was smoking a cigarette and calmly watching her.

He smiled slowly. It was a nice, winsome smile, which made his eyes crinkle at the corners. Extinguishing his cigarette in an ashtray, he said, 'Hello. I've seen you before tonight, but we haven't been properly introduced. I'm Freddy Campbell.'

'I know,' Anna replied, closing her mind to everything Alex had said about him and flattered that he should have remembered her. Looking at him properly, she saw his good-looking face was marred by a hint of sulkiness about the mouth.

'Pretty young thing, aren't you?' he remarked. 'Does this pretty young thing have a name?'

Anna warmed to the admiration in his glance. His aura was so magnetic that no one could resist his advances. 'My name is Anna—Anna Preston.'

'Naturally dark, too, and the eyes to go with it. Where did Alex find you?'

'He didn't—find me, I mean.'

'You are travelling with him to England, aren't you? I've heard it mentioned.'

'Yes, but I don't know him very well.'

Freddy nodded. His eyes gleamed across at her. 'No—no one seems to know very much about our Mr Kent,' he drawled in silky tones. 'Man of mystery and all that. You don't mind talking to an outcast, do you?'

Anna laughed lightly. 'Of course not. I often feel like one myself.'

Throwing her a look of amused empathy, he pushed a glass across to her. 'Oh, dear! Like that, is it? Have a drink?'

She sipped at it—cognac—wrinkling her nose. She didn't like the taste.

Freddy clinked her glass. 'Cheers, Anna.'

'Do you often come to the Riviera, Mr Campbell?'

'I give you leave to call me Freddy, dear girl.' His eyes

were hooded, his smile mocking. 'It suits me here. England's not so good these days—national government—too many socialists for my liking. Unemployment, high income tax—that's bad.' With an expression of disgust he downed his drink in one.

Anna watched him reach inside his jacket and remove a small leather pouch, which he opened and extracted a white powdery substance. Tapping some on to a cigarette paper with some tobacco, he rolled it up and licked the seam.

'Life's better here,' he went on, 'relaxed, cheaper, fun. You can do exactly as you want, when you want and with whom you want—no one expects anything of you.' He lit the cigarette and inhaled deeply, appreciatively. The strangely scented smoke wreathing out from between his lips curled about them, mingling with a heavy perfume which rose from the thick candle on the table. 'How old are you, Anna?'

'Eighteen.'

'Eighteen. That's young—still a child.' His eyes swept over her, gleaming in the dim light. He found her innocence and naïvety delightful. It drew him on, the way the tip of her tongue touched her bottom lip. Freddy had only ever seen her briefly in the company of the Ormsbys, but he felt he knew her intimately. He had only ever seen such perfection once before—in someone best forgotten. He caught the scent of Anna and smiled lazily. 'And still a virgin.'

Anna felt a tell-tale flush sweep over her face, but all she could do was sit and stare at him. Freddy Campbell was like a sinful genius that needed to be surveyed at close quarters.

He laughed softly. She was not clever enough to mask her inexperience. 'Ah—I see I shock you.' His voice was husky. 'Virginity is a word not to be uttered out loud in the presence of respectable young ladies. It might suggest that she knows what it means. But of course you are virginal, and delicious—a treasure beyond price—but for how long will you remain *virgo intacta*, I wonder? You're like a passion fruit ready for plucking—but make sure when the time comes you only give it to the man of your choosing.'

This was Anna's first experience of men like Freddy Campbell. It was all so strange—but dangerous, and there is no drug on earth more addictive than danger. She was appalled and stimulated by the conversation and, to her wide-eyed innocence, excited and intrigued. Embarrassing though this was, with everything Alex had said about him still fresh in her mind, there seemed to be nothing malevolent about Freddy just now—and she found his relaxed detachment an antidote for Alex's coldness.

'Here,' Freddy said, holding out the cigarette. 'Be my guest—won't bite. Have a good time.'

Knocking the little demons that rose up to do battle away, Anna reached over. 'Thank you.' At precisely the same moment a figure appeared beside her and pushed aside her hand.

'What the hell do you think you're doing, you son of a bitch?' Alex exploded, looking at Freddy, his voice vibrating with fury and contempt. 'She's eighteen years old.'

Pushing her chair back, Anna stood up, annoyed by Alex's interference. 'If you don't mind—'

His face hardened into a mask of freezing rage, Alex turned on her. 'I do mind.' Anna was surprised how much she minded his look of contempt. 'That was a stupid thing to do. Have you any idea how dangerous this stuff is?' Snatching the cigarette from Freddy's fingers, he dropped it on the ground and ground it beneath his heel, wishing he could do the same with Freddy.

Anna was furious. 'It's none of your business.'

'You little fool! Don't you know what it is? It's heroin.'

Anna looked at Freddy, who remained unmoved by Alex's anger—as did his smile. He sat inert, as loose limbed as a lurcher, and even in the dim light she could see his expression was blank and that his pupils had grown large and black. 'I—I didn't know,' she confessed tightly, her voice having lost none of its angry indignation, but her anger directed at herself and her gullibility.

'Of course you didn't. How could you?' With one exasperating look at Freddy, who had unconcernedly begun rolling another cigarette, and taking Anna's elbow in a none-too-gentle grasp, he said, 'Come with me. It's useless trying to get through to him in that state.'

Standing on the terrace where she had parted from him just a short while before, Anna looked at him darkly, shook his hand off and moved away. He stood still, taut, fierce tension marking his mouth. 'You really shouldn't have done that. I have a right to do as I please.'

Alex closed the distance between them and placed his hands firmly on her shoulders, forcing her to look at him. For a second she appeared mutinous, then she sighed and lowered her gaze. 'Anna, listen to me. I know what I'm talking about. Heroin is dangerous. It's addictive and I've seen what it can do to people—the misery it brings. It ruins them and their families. It gets to them, takes over their lives so that they live for the drug and nothing else. Promise me that you will steer clear of it.'

Anna nodded. Everyone knew drug taking was the darker side of High Society life. She had heard of dope parties where drugs were passed around. In fact, morphine, which was a popular party drug, could be bought over the counter at the chemists. She should have known what the white powder was that Freddy had rolled into his cigarette. 'Of course I will. I'm not such an idiot—only—only I thought...'

'What exactly did you think?'

'That it was just a cigarette. I—I acted without thinking. I'll know better next time.'

Alex's harsh expression relaxed and his tone was gentle. 'Of course you will. But let's hope there won't be a next time.' Suddenly his gaze narrowed on her face. 'There are tears in your eyes. Why?'

Anna felt her control collapsing. 'Because I am stupid, embarrassingly naïve and gullible.'

Alex thought he heard her voice break, and his conscience tore at him. Any fury remaining within him died abruptly. As he looked down into her tear-bright eyes, his stomach clenched at the thought that if he hadn't followed her to apologise for his harsh words, she would have taken Freddy's doped cigarette.

'Anna.' His low voice was filled with concern, his hands gentle on her shoulders. 'I apologise for my behaviour earlier. It was unforgiveable. The last thing I want is to upset you. Freddy Campbell and I go way back and things have happened that are impossible to forgive or to forget. What you said about his pride having taken a battering was right. A man is most sensitive about his pride when he knows he has little of which to be proud.'

He dropped his arms to his sides. Anna stood looking up at him. A satin shoulder strap slipped down her arm. She didn't seem to notice. His eyes were very intent, very serious. They held hers as if she was in some way worthy of close study. She could not look away. They drove into her, like a physical touch. She could feel her whole body responding, a strange stirring deep within her. He smiled faintly, and she just went on staring at him in fascination, savouring the strange moment, exploring what she felt.

'You have lovely eyes,' he murmured. 'It was the first thing I noticed about you.' Moonlight played on her face and shoulders, bestowing on her an unearthly kind of beauty. The sweet smell of lilies permeated the air.

Nothing anyone had ever said to her had stirred Anna so much. She went on staring at him, afraid to speak. Very slowly he adjusted the fallen strap. She shivered uncontrollably at his touch. And then suddenly he dropped his hand.

'You should go to bed,' he said quickly covering his feelings. 'We have an early start.'

Without a word Anna turned and left him, and in spite of

what he'd said about her eyes, she felt unhappy and foolish, rejected in some way, and for some reason totally hopeless.

The hour after dawn was Anna's favourite time of day to swim in the pool. The house was cool and seemed deserted as she padded through to the terrace. After a hot and sticky night she felt her spirits lift as she breathed in the salty sea air and felt its familiar presence. Her flesh welcomed the cold water. Floating on the surface, she closed her eyes, feeling the sun's heat on her face. She felt detached, languid, but at the same time very alive, in that state of semi-consciousness where thought is slowed but physical sensations magnified.

After several laps she hauled herself out and sat in a wicker chair in a corner of the terrace, rubbing her hair dry and gazing at the sea. The Riviera had been hot, hot enough to melt the flesh from her bones, but it had been fun, and she was sorry to be leaving, but she was also eager to get on with the next stage of her life.

Someone came through the French windows. It was Alex. He made straight for the pool, not having noticed her. Tossing his towel and robe on to a chair, he dived in like the blade of a knife, parting the water with brisk strokes. Anna stood up, intending to leave, but something compelled her to stay. After several laps he got out, scraped back his hair and began towelling himself dry.

Anna's breath caught in her throat on being confronted by this superbly fit and muscled body not twelve feet away. Alex Kent was six foot three inches of splendid masculinity; he had wide shoulders and chest, covered with a light dusting of black hair. His hips were narrow, his stomach flat, his thighs hard.

Alex didn't look up, but his mouth quirked in a slight smile. 'I hope what you are looking at meets with your approval.'

Disconcerted and embarrassed by the way the sight of his bronzed body was affecting her, and mortified that he knew she'd been looking at him, Anna's gaze flew past him to the garden. She fixed her eyes on a rather splendid geranium with the fascination of a naturist watching a praying mantis eat its prey. 'Yes, I always think the garden looks its best at this time of day.'

'You weren't looking at the garden, Anna,' he said softly.

'I—I wasn't?' She dragged her eyes to his.

'No,' he replied.

There was a long silence then she said, 'I don't know what you mean.'

'Oh, my dear girl,' he remarked, half-laughing, half deadly serious, as he looped the towel around his neck and moved towards her, 'if you don't know that, then you really are a child.'

'Oh,' Anna said quietly. Alex was looking down at her scantily clad body in such way that made her turn liquid inside.

It was her costume that made Alex pause. The cut was demure, but the wet fabric clung to her slender body faithfully, hinting at the dimple of navel. It outlined the curves of breasts and buttocks and the V-shaped mound above her thighs. His lips curved in a lazy smile. 'But don't worry. I think you look extremely nice, too.'

She returned his smile uncertainly. 'You do?'

'Absolutely. Now, come along. It's going to be hot, so we'll leave immediately after breakfast.'

'Are you ready?' Alex asked.

'All packed and ready to go,' Anna replied, thinking how young Alex looked, in his shorts and cotton shirt.

'Is this your luggage?' he asked, pointing to a large suitcase and hand baggage by the door.

'Yes.'

Picking them up, he blithely stalked outside, giving Anna time to say her farewells as he stacked her luggage in the boot of his two-passenger roadster. There were quick hugs and an instruction to Tamsin to get in touch as soon as she arrived home, after which Alex propelled her around the front of the car and into the passenger seat, before sliding behind the steering wheel.

Leaving the villa and the waving Ormsbys behind, Alex turned and looked at his companion, thinking how young and fresh she looked in her cotton dress and trimmed straw hat. She stared straight ahead, her expression set and slightly sad. Her self-possession was such that he had forgotten how very young she was. 'Do I detect a touch of remorse, that you are already regretting leaving the villa?'

Anna shook her head, managing a slight smile. 'I enjoyed my time there enormously and Lord and Lady Ormsby have been very kind, but I'm glad to be returning to England and keen to begin university.'

'Certain? Think carefully while there's still time to turn back.'

She stared at him. 'Would you really take me back?'

'If you wanted me to,' he answered.

'It would take some explaining to my grandfather if you did—but I'm sorry to disappoint you. I realise how irritating it must be for you having to escort me all the way back to England, but since it's your idea to travel by car instead of the train, I'm afraid you will have to learn to live with me.'

'That should be interesting,' he commented softly, and watched in amusement as a pink flush of embarrassment tinged her cheeks.

'I see nothing funny,' she blurted.

'You don't? Perhaps you lack a sense of humour.' As Anna opened her mouth to rebut the charge, he turned and gave her an arch look before fixing his gaze on the road.

Alex didn't speak again until the car began to climb. With the sun shining on the mountainous backcountry of Provence, the scenery was quite spectacular. 'The mountains are particularly beautiful at this time of year. Don't you agree? We'll stop shortly and have some champagne. I think the occasion merits it.'

'But it's only eleven o'clock.'

He grinned. 'I know. But one of the compensations of being on holiday is being able to do exactly as one likes, when one likes, and there's no rule that says champagne can't be drunk before dark.'

'You must enjoy driving, to drive the full length of France,' Anna commented after a minute's silence, feeling that she must say something.

'I'm particularly fond of France—especially the mountains. Spending so much time in the city as I do, I usually come for the skiing—to enjoy the sport and relax, to recharge my batteries.'

Anna sneaked a glance at him. Turning slightly, he caught her gaze, and she was amazed by the expression she saw in his eyes. It had a yearning quality, nostalgic almost, allowing an open vulnerability to slip through the sardonic arrogance he usually sported. It was as if he was tormented by some insupportable distress and he came to the mountains to gain relief from it.

'Did my grandfather ask you to collect me?'

He nodded, changing down a gear to negotiate a rather sharp bend.

'Do you always do everything he tells you to?'

'No. He suggested it. I was happy I was able to help.'

'Does he intimidate people?'

'You might say that.'

'Even you?'

'No. Your grandfather and I understand one another. When you know me better, you will realise I am not in the least intimidated by anyone—especially not by Selwyn, who always intimidates those who are not as successful as he is.'

'Are you saying he judges himself on his accomplishments and wealth and others don't?'

She was so direct and perceptive that Alex, amused by her

genuine unguarded questions, was finding it difficult equating her with his idea of a schoolgirl. He grinned. 'I think you'd better ask me something else.'

'Will you tell me about Belhaven?'

'All in good time.' Alex knew Belhaven was a place she was going to not for sentimental reasons, but because she was swallowing her pride and acting out of duty. 'I will answer any questions about your new home, and your grandfather, that you put to me before we reach England, but for now I am anxious that you relax and enjoy the journey.'

'You must be very close to my grandfather,' she persisted, 'to know so much about me.'

'We are friends, good friends—and he's told me a good deal about you. I know that your father died before you were born, leaving your mother with nothing to support either of you.'

'Sadly that's true. My father was a painter, did you know?'

'I have heard it mentioned.'

His reply was terse, causing Anna to look at him. He was looking straight ahead, his expression showing faint pity.

When Alex felt her gaze on him the expression vanished, his face instantly resuming its look of good humour and inscrutability. 'Do you paint?'

'Very badly, I'm afraid. If my father hadn't been killed during the war, my mother said he would have been a great artist.'

Anna noted how Alex's face closed up in a particular way, which caused her to suspect that he disagreed with what she said and did not like what he had heard about her father. Reluctantly she let her mind go back over the years, recalling how she had heard one of her mother's friends say that if her father hadn't joined up he would have gone to prison. Anna had felt unease descend on her then as she thought that perhaps her father had not been the saint her mother would have her believe. That same unease descended on her now, bringing with it an unfamiliar rush of resentment towards Alex Kent.

'What else has my grandfather told you about me?' she asked tightly, changing direction.

Alex was relieved that she did since he held a very low opinion of her father and had no wish to be the one to shatter any illusions she might have. However, the stubborn lift of her chin indicated that she'd sensed his dislike of the man.

He made a visible effort to soften his tone. 'Oh, that you have worked hard, aiming high for academic achievement, and succeeding—which I know—and that you are to read English literature at Oxford. You excelled in sciences and classics—the same cannot be said for your gym classes. You hated hockey, I believe, and you have just told me you dislike art.'

'No, I didn't,' she countered obstinately. 'I told you I couldn't paint, which is not the same thing. As a matter of fact, I do like looking at paintings, even though I don't always understand what I'm looking at.'

'Since art is a passion of mine, I shall enjoy showing you. Your grandfather also told me that at school you were quiet and reserved, enough to provoke ridicule from some of the other girls.' Turning to look at her, he grinned. 'Don't worry. We all have our faults.'

'I'm glad to see you include yourself among the imperfect,' Anna retorted, turning away from his condescending smile.

'I'm just as flawed and human as any man, Anna.'

'I suppose I should be flattered that you have taken the time to take an interest in me—although I sense you find me rather pathetic.'

'Not at all. I was extolling your virtues.'

'It didn't sound like I was being complimented. Despite what you've been told about me, after just a short acquaintance, is your vanity so colossal as to lead you to think you can understand me?'

If Alex felt the barb of her riposte he didn't show it. 'I know that you are caring and thoughtful, honest and sincere and self-sacrificing. I don't think it's amiss to pay a compliment and say you are a very pretty young woman—also a very determined one,' he added. 'I have a notion you will succeed at anything you choose to do.'

Anna's cheeks pinked. She wasn't completely lacking in human feeling. 'Thank you,' she replied tersely. 'I intend to try.'

Alex turned and looked at her. 'Don't be so aggressive,' he told her quietly. He was going to have the devil of a job breaking her out of that straitjacket she had placed on herself. 'I want to talk, not argue. I have no desire to quarrel with you.'

'Then do not try to provoke me. It's extremely ill mannered of you to badger me. Why do you do it?' she asked sternly, no longer daunted by him.

Her words were accompanied by such a well-bred, reproving look that Alex laughed in spite of himself. Still smiling, his mouth wide over his excellent teeth, he looked at the outrageous young woman who dared to lecture him on his shortcomings. 'It's as well to test the mettle of one's allies, as well as one's enemies.'

Anna found herself quite intrigued by this confounding man. She saw there were tiny lines around his eyes from squinting against the sun, which gave strength and depth to his handsome face. Her mouth quivered in the start of a smile to match his own. 'And in which category do you place me?' she asked, her antipathy of a moment earlier melting away in the most curious way.

'I will just say you stand in the middle just now. Where you end up depends on how we get on on the journey.'

Chapter Five

Alex booked them into a small, delightful hotel. With ivy clinging to its walls it stood in a small courtyard filled with tubs brimming with flowers and a wonderful view of the mountains, which glowed blue, rose pink and white in the setting sun.

Later, having freshened up and changed into a dress she had bought in Monte Carlo for formal occasions—a sleeveless, narrow lilac crepe, the hem flaring gently around her slim calves and modestly high at the front—Anna made her way down to the hotel bar.

Alex was sitting on a high stool at the bar, sipping a whisky as brown as he was. His face was sombre, almost severe, and Anna wondered what occupied his thoughts. He hadn't seen her enter, so she took a moment to quietly admire the way he looked. His suit and shirt were impeccable, his features distinguished, and vitality and intelligence radiated from him. She sighed, wishing he might find her as pleasing to look at as she found him—then she decided that wasn't a good idea at all.

He turned and saw her and smiled, watching her approach, thinking what an enchanting girl she was. Her dress clung to her slender figure and showed off her silky black hair. It was unfashionably long and parted down the middle, drawn back from her face with two small diamante clips. His look appraised her when she reached him, a lazy smile sweeping over his face, totally unaware how the glamour of that smile did treacherous things to Anna's heart.

'Very nice,' he murmured. 'I've taken the liberty of ordering you a glass of wine—or perhaps you would prefer a martini?' He frowned as a thought suddenly occurred to him. 'You do drink alcohol?'

Anna smiled at him directly. 'Of course I do, and, yes, please, a glass of wine would be lovely.'

'Hungry?' he asked, handing her the wine.

'Yes, I am ráther,' she replied, taking a sip.

'Then let's go in.'

Several people were already dining in the restaurant. They were shown to a table by the window, where they settled into their seats across from each other. The atmosphere was one of intimacy. Anna felt suddenly awkward. Glancing around she saw how the other women were looking at Alex. Suddenly she felt extremely self-conscious, conspicuous and very immature. He was so incredibly confident and good looking that everyone must be wondering what he was doing with someone as plain and uninteresting as she was. Sitting straight-backed in her chair, nervously she avoided her companion's penetrating gaze, concentrating her attention on the view of the mountains.

Her withdrawal from him stirred Alex's annoyance. 'Anna, tell me something,' he demanded curtly. 'Why are you uncomfortable when you are with me?'

Anna felt as stupid as she sounded. 'I don't know. I can't explain it.'

'But you are?'

She nodded. 'Sometimes.'

'Do you have a problem with me?'

'Not exactly.'

Looking across into those long lashed eyes raised to his, Alex forgot how impatient he'd been with her a moment before. 'Then I can see I shall have to work harder to make you relax.'

'You mean you already were—working hard, I mean?'

Amused, he said, 'Not hard enough, apparently.'

Anna saw the sudden gleam in his eyes, the slight curve of his lips, and saw something distinctly sensual in that. His look was much too personal. It made her feel vulnerable, defenceless. She stiffened. 'Alex! Are you flirting with me?' she asked bluntly.

'No,' he replied, equally as blunt.

'Good, because I've quite enough to contend with just now without that. Besides, you're far too old for me. However,' she said, tilting her head sideways and thinking of voluptuous, man-mad eighteen-year-old Alexandra Manning, one of the most popular girls on the Riviera, 'I have a friend who I am sure you would like. Her name's Alexandra. She's terribly attractive and mature for her age. I'm certain she would like to meet you—and, yes, she would be perfect for you.'

Alex's brows rose when he realised she was trying to fix him up with one of her friends, which he found unprecedented and insulting. The smile disappeared immediately. 'I don't think you should say any more. I think we should revert to how we were before—silent—before my ego takes a battering,' he said coldly, all good will having gone from his voice. Scowling, he looked down at the smoked salmon the waiter had just set before him and attacked it with his fork.

Anna knew he didn't intend to speak for some time. Her lips curved in a mischievous smile. 'Oh, dear,' she murmured, picking up her cutlery and stabbing a piece of the pink fleshed fish. 'Who am I to dent the ego of Mr Alex Kent?'

Alex could hardly believe his ears. His eyes darted to hers and he saw her puckish smile. His scowl relaxed into a reluctant grin, and he tried to negate it by chiding as sternly as he could, 'Impertinent minx. I'll thank you not to poke fun at me in future.'

Unchastened and unrepentant, Anna met his gaze head on.

'Why? Because it is you that lacks a sense of humour?' she remarked, reminding him of the very thing he had accused her of earlier.

He nodded slowly in acknowledgement of her scoring a hit. '*Touché*. You weren't serious about pairing me up with Alexandra—what's her name?'

'Of course not—and she's not really my friend, more an acquaintance, but you rose to the bait like a trout for a fly,' Anna confessed. 'To be fair, I don't think you'd care for her at all—and be assured there's no guarantee Alexandra would be attracted to you. You will be relieved to know she prefers men with blond hair and blue eyes, and preferably younger.'

Astonishment registered in Alex's expression as he realised that at twenty-eight she evidently regarded him as long past the age of eligibility for marriage. 'Now you make me sound like Methuselah.' There was something about the girlish joke, something about her engaging smile and the laughter that caused an unexpected, uncontrollable and, under the circumstances, bizarre reaction from Alex. He started to laugh, a good, rich sound, causing several heads to turn their way. He was laughing at her audacity, at her impertinence. After a moment he smoothed the laughter from his face and took a much-needed drink of wine.

'I think you'd better eat your salmon. Oh, and just for the record,' he said on a more serious note, 'I never flirt. Behaving like a lovesick, besotted idiot is not my style.'

'No. I don't suppose it is.'

'And one more thing,' he said quietly. A dark shadow dimmed the brilliance of his eyes, then it vanished behind a deliberately offhand smile. 'You have to remember that I'm your escort and escorts are not allowed to make passes at their charges, so I'm afraid you're out of bounds where ravishing is concerned.'

Anna returned his smile. 'I'm relieved to hear it.'

The mood of conviviality continued. The meal was a feast of gastronomic delight. They sat through it in the soft glow

of the lamps surrounded by the murmur of voices and the soft
clatter of cutlery on plates. Anna lapsed into silence and con-
centrated on the delicious salmon, noting that her second glass
of wine was definitely affecting her, making her feel so relaxed.

When he was finished eating, Alex settled back and tried
to concentrate on the next stage of their journey, but in a state
of sated relaxation he was more inclined to dwell on his
charming companion who was spooning up the last of her
dessert.

Dabbing her lips with her napkin, replete and flushed, Anna
sighed. 'That was delicious. I can't remember eating a crêpe
Suzette that tasted so good.' In thoughtful silence she sipped
her wine, while contemplating the man reclining opposite.
Meeting his gaze, she smiled. 'Tell me what you have planned
for us tomorrow.'

'Ah, I see I have aroused your interest at last, now the meal
is out of the way and you are replete. Dare I hope that smile
denotes a softening in your opinion of me?'

'I have no opinion of you,' Anna said calmly.

'I disagree. You have a very strong opinion of me. In reply
to your question, I will tell you that I want to make an early
start. Mainly following the route Napoleon Bonaparte took
when he escaped from exile on the island of Elba and landed
at Cannes, we'll head for Geneva and on to Burgundy and
Dijon by way of the Côte-d'Or. Burgundy is very beautiful,
with impressive medieval villages, abbeys and castles to see—
a tourist's paradise. It's also renowned for good food and fine
wine, so you have much to look forward to.'

'As long as you don't expect me to eat the snails,' Anna
commented, pulling a face. 'I definitely draw the line at
snails.' Another of her smiles appeared, gorgeous, wholesome
and luminous, lighting up her whole face. Alex melted beneath its radiant heat. 'Does my grandfather know you're tak-

ing me on holiday, by the way, and, more to the point, would
he approve?'

'He knows, approves and trusts me implicitly. He wants
you to enjoy yourself now your schooling is complete.'

'Do you work for my grandfather?'

'No,' Alex answered firmly.

'You obviously occupy a position of some influence.'

'We are friends, your grandfather and I,' he said, regarding
her coolly, 'as well as partners in several business ventures—
which you already know.'

'He's very rich, isn't he?'

Alex nodded. 'Considerably so.'

'Didn't he lose a lot of his money in the crash of 1929 like
everyone else?' she asked, referring to the Wall Street crash,
when an economic blizzard had swept across the Atlantic
from the United States.

'He survived. He did lose a considerable amount, and it
would have been a good deal worse if he hadn't had the fore-
sight to move funds out of the country before it happened.'

'Did you advise him to do that?'

'I suggested it.'

'Tell me about the Mansons. I have so much to learn.'

Alex nodded. 'I will tell you as much as I know. Not only
are they rich, through the ages they have possessed something
very desirable—breeding. Their ancestry can be traced right
back to William the Conqueror. Since Stuart times they have
been in attendance at the royal courts and fought with dis-
tinction for the King's forces in the civil wars and later under
Wellington against Napoleon. Several have married in pursuit
less of love than sizeable dowries, building up in the process
the Belhaven estate.

'Your great-great-grandfather made a profitable marriage
alliance that brought with it 2000 acres in Scotland—with its
own castle, I might add. But it was one of your ancestors in
the nineteenth century who made the Manson fortune in India,
trading in spices and all manner of exotic goods.'

'Goodness, how impressive. I can see I'm going to have my work cut out learning all about them. But what about you? How come you live in England? You're Russian, aren't you?'

'How do you know that?'

'Well, it's perfectly obvious you're not English. You speak with an accent—and Tamsin told me. I—I asked her,' Anna confessed hesitantly. 'What were you called when you lived in Russia—Kent sounds extremely English?'

'Alexei Ivanovitch Petrovna was my name then. It seemed less complicated to change it when I came to Britain. Kent was my mother's maiden name. What else did Tamsin tell you about me? All complimentary, I hope.'

'Some of it. Some of the girls I met at the parties we attended seemed to know all about you—there's often things written in the newspapers and magazines about you, you see. They were quick to voice their opinion when they discovered you were coming to collect me,' she said, careful not to give him the impression that Tamsin was a tittle-tattle, or that four of the party girls had unanimously given him ten out of ten in the attractiveness ratings.

Alex raised his brows slightly, in a gesture that silently, and very effectively, managed to convey his annoyance. 'I must count myself fortunate that young ladies take such scintillating interest in my personal life and that they are so eager to share what they know of it with each other,' he said drily and with a hint of sarcasm. 'What did they tell you—that I am a cold, arrogant, insufferable Russian immigrant, whose affairs are notorious and too numerous to count?'

'You're rather harsh on yourself. No, they said nothing like that,' Anna answered, startled by his sudden brusqueness, and uneasy under his relentless gaze.

'Nevertheless, do you believe it?'

Hurt by his change of mood, puzzled by it and uncertain how to proceed, Anna glanced away as if to gather courage, then she looked at him calmly. 'I don't know what to believe. You seem to be such a complex character, so full of contrasts, that when I am with you I feel as though I am running down several roads all at once. Should I believe all those things you say you are?'

'You should,' he replied quietly, restrained and guarded, unable to hide the displeasure he always felt at any unprecedented and unwelcome preoccupation with his private life.

Anna didn't fail to notice the implacable warning in his deceptively mild voice. Sensing Alex Kent would not endure curiosity about his personal life from her, she had no intention of asking him about it. So many things that would be possible with an ordinary man were not so with him. Looking across at him, she tipped the balance of power into her favour by saying, 'I'm sorry. Have I said something to offend you?'

The anger within Alex died as quickly as it had risen. Seeing Anna's anxious expression, his stomach clenched at the thought that he might have hurt her. Wisely suppressing the urge to put his hand against her cheek and try to reassure her that she had said nothing wrong, which would undoubtedly panic her, he said quietly, 'No, it's not you. It's me. I like to keep my personal life private. It's my own affair, and I hate it when people pry and try to come too close. I especially mean the newspapers and the sanctimonious society gossips with nothing better to do,' he told her, his voice suddenly iced with loathing.

Anna sympathised with him. Studying him surreptitiously, she saw the indomitable pride, intelligence and determination chiselled into his features. She'd listened to the girls she'd met gushing on about him, about his love affairs and his rise in the financial firmament, defining him in terms of big Hollywood stars like Gary Cooper and Clark Gable who stared out of the silver screen.

Anna decided that nothing that she'd heard described him. In real life there was a powerful charisma that had nothing to do with his handsome looks and that mocking smile of his. He had already done and seen all there was to do and see, things, she suspected, that had affected him deeply and perhaps hardened him beyond recall. He kept those experiences locked away beyond reach, behind an unbreachable wall of polite charm and sophistication.

And that was his appeal, Anna realised, the challenge that confronted any woman who met him, that made them want to break down that invisible wall, to discover the real man behind it, to find something deep and profound, something more lasting than the mindless pleasure of an affair.

'I do understand—truly. In fact, I feel a bit like that myself when people ask me about my past—about my mother. I don't like talking about that, either.' The look he gave her told her that he understood, and the slow smile that swept over his face did treacherous things to her heart rate. 'When do you expect to reach Calais?' she asked, thinking it wise to change the subject at that point.

'That depends on how long it takes us.' Resting his arms on the table, he leaned forward slightly. 'Anna, look at me,' he said in a low, velvety voice, the kind that usually sent tingles of excitement darting up a woman's spine. He spoke in earnest. 'You are on holiday—the first holiday of your life—and have plenty of time before you begin at Oxford. Tell me what you did in Monte Carlo?'

'Tamsin and I swam a lot and played tennis—when it wasn't too hot, that is—and the evenings were sociable— Lady Ormsby saw to that. Villas along the Riviera were filled with partying English. Almost every night we were at a party or dining at one of the restaurants in Monte Carlo, so we were never bored—although Lady Ormsby watched us like a hawk to make sure we didn't misbehave.'

Alex grinned knowingly. 'Irene was running true to form. As you will have observed she is fiercely proud, combative, and tough minded. She is also brilliant and amusing and puts great importance on doing the right thing, on upbringing, society gossip, titles and society events and associating with the right people. The seriousness with which she addresses the social calendar always amuses me.'

'I know. I—heard her saying how kind it was of you to go to the bother of taking me back to England. Won't you find it tiresome trailing a schoolgirl around France, like a pet poodle?'

He grinned. 'A skittish Irish setter more like. You are no longer a schoolgirl, but an extremely charming, lovely young woman, and it will give me enormous pleasure showing you the places I have come to know and love. Besides, I will appreciate some feminine company. Promise me you will try and enjoy it.'

'Yes—but—'

'Good, because there's no way out of it. You have a lot of catching up to do. I'm sure you've been taught much about France at school and from the history books, but sometimes living life teaches us far more than books. There are so many wonderful things waiting to be discovered. And if our relationship worries you, then you can look on me as an older brother.'

Anna gave him a wry look. 'I see you as many things, Alex, and an older brother is not one of them. How old are you? Twenty-seven? Twenty-eight?'

'The latter is spot on.'

'Well, I suppose ten years is a conceivable age difference—if you were my brother, that is.'

'What I am offering is my friendship, my company and attention. Is that too difficult for you to accept?'

Anna looked at him thoughtfully. His offer of friendship was genuine—she could see it in the warmth of his eyes, hear it in the gentleness of his voice. She could not turn his offer aside, even though a voice inside her head was warning her that she was plunging into dangerous, uncharted territory. 'No, it isn't.'

The following morning Anna awoke with the determination to enjoy the rest of her holiday, and it was hard to believe the handsome, complicated, sophisticated Alex Kent was to be her companion until she reached Belhaven.

They set off straight after breakfast, stopping when they felt like it to see anything of interest and to take coffee and lunch breaks, and spent the nights in quiet, out-of-town hotels. They drove north to Geneva, where they spent two days. Anna was sorry to leave the alpine scenery—thoroughly rustic in character, with simple, hardy villages and vineyards, cool, peaceful pastures and dairy cows with clanking bells. They travelled on to Burgundy, stopping to take in the sights at Dijon before driving across the Morvan to the ancient town of Avallon. They strolled within the calm and peaceful old part within the ramparts, where nothing dates from later than the eighteenth century. And then it was on to the Loire Valley. Anna absorbed everything she saw, gazing in wide-eyed wonder at ornate Renaissance châteaux and noble estates.

As the days passed and their friendship flourished, Anna was discovering herself and Alex was her guide. He had the power to make her do anything, even love herself. Looking back in later years, she would remember the sensation of coming out of dark, empty loneliness into an environment of affectionate, humorous delight. She drank the delicate Burgundy wine and ate so many wonderful meals she told Alex she was in serious danger of bursting. He laughed at her, telling her with mock severity that she was too thin anyway and that she should eat more.

From Orleans they headed north to Fontainebleau. The beautiful palace left Anna breathless. When she stood in the Cour des Adieux (Courtyard of Farewell) in front of the principal façade, so named, Alex explained to her, since it was here that Napoleon Bonaparte took farewell of his weeping soldiers, before leaving for exile on the island of Elba in 1814, she was almost able to feel the sadness of that time. It was as if it still haunted this beautiful place. Her gentle heart rejecting Napoleon's proclaimed guilt, Anna was unable to hold back the tears.

Alex was deeply moved by her sensitivity. 'What a truly tender, sensitive soul you are, Anna Preston, to feel so much sympathy for a beleaguered emperor.'

Immediately Anna dashed away her tears. 'Perhaps the legend plays him false—I'd like to think so. And I am sensitive, I suppose—but tender?' She shrugged. 'I've never thought about that.'

'Your reaction just now leads me to think you are.' He smiled. 'Heaven help us when I take you to see Versailles and you hear the heartrending tale of Marie-Antoinette, when the Paris mob went to the palace to assassinate her. No doubt you'll weep buckets and we'll be in serious danger of drowning.'

'You are beginning to know me too well, Alex,' she said, laughing lightly. 'As a child I was told never to cry. I was taught obedience, self-control, the recognition of authority and respect for my elders.'

'And I have no doubt that you followed those instructions most conscientiously.'

'I tried, but it wasn't always easy. I learned from an early age to keep my emotions in check and it was always difficult for me to show them, so tears do not come easy. You must think me stupid crying at old, worn-out tales, but suddenly I cannot help it and I don't care any more. For the first time in my life I know what freedom feels like and I'm enjoying it enormously—thanks to you. I keep having to pinch myself to prove I'm not dreaming. I admit I'm looking forward to seeing Paris.'

The sombre way her companion was looking at her made Anna burst out laughing, and Alex found himself captivated by the beauty, the infectious joy of it. She was trembling with life, like a butterfly waiting to emerge from its chrysalis. He'd heard the melodic sound of her laughter many times during the time they had been together—it tinkled like bells on the fringes of his mind—had seen it glowing in her eyes. And now, as she gazed up at him with those appealing, tear-drenched orbs, by the heady sweetness of just being with her he realised that if he didn't make it back to England soon, there was every chance he was going to find this utterly refreshing and delightful female irresistible as well, which he must avoid at all cost.

There were many visitors in Paris in July. Alex booked them into a small, luxury hotel on the Right Bank off the main boulevards, close to the Palais-Royal. The street had a discreet charm. It was quiet at night and convenient to many sights.

To Anna, Paris was heaven. Throbbing to its own frenetic rhythms, it was the most wonderful, invigorating place on earth and she was as excited as a child discovering Christmas. They lunched at Maxim's, strolled along the banks of the Seine and the Champs-Elysées and drank coffee at the delightful pavement cafes. She lost her breath at the magnificent view from the top of the Eiffel Tower, admired the Tuileries, kept close to Alex when he took her to Pigalle with its seedy bars and the Moulin Rouge. The Moulin Rouge was a nightclub where people were drawn out of nostalgia, fantasising about the days of Renoir, Toulouse-Lautrec and the fabulous cancan girls.

Montmartre was where tourism was at its ripest. It was a Bohemian, different, colourful world, home to artists and writers. Anna was able to see beauty in the sinister as they explored the pealing and shabby alleyways of the Paris underworld: secret—violent—drug-filled exotic dreams—often fatal. They strolled along picturesque streets, browsed in the little shops for trinkets, and climbed the hill to the white domed Basilica of Sacré Coeur.

The days were full and they walked a great deal. Alex was keen to show Anna as much of Paris as was possible, so that at night she was so exhausted she would tumble into bed and be asleep the moment her head touched the pillow. When she opened her eyes it would all begin again.

She felt fiercely happy—Alex had much to do with that. She had never felt so close to another person. The newly found intimacy she found exciting and exhilarating, and she clung to each moment, savouring it to the full. Not only had she been his first consideration the whole time, but he seemed to have an immense knowledge about so many subjects. He knew all about France and its history and art, of which he had a great understanding and therefore appreciation. He had a special love of music and promised her that before they left Paris he would take her to the ballet and the opera. He indulged her and surprised her all the time. Each day she learned more and more about him, but he was guarded, giving nothing of his past away, always careful not to come too close, not to overstep the bounds of friendship.

Everything was going splendidly until Alex casually suggested a visit to one or two of the fashion houses. They were having breakfast and Anna was just about to pop what was left of a warm croissant into her mouth.

'But I have enough clothes, Alex. Are you saying there is something wrong with the way I look?'

'No, not to me—you are perfect. But it's how you look that makes people want to find out more about you.'

Anna gritted her teeth. 'I'm not bothered about that. I don't place any great importance on looks.' This wasn't quite true. She did care, but in the past she'd had little in the way of an allowance to do anything about it. And in Paris everyone dressed so beautifully she felt dowdy by comparison.

'There is nothing wrong in making yourself look nice. Women have been doing it since time immemorial. Isn't it natural to want to look attractive? Let's face it. In the battle of the sexes you are more capable, with the weapons on hand, of wreaking the most damage. Your mother should have been your guide, shown you what being a woman means.'

Anna had put down her croissant and was looking at him warily. He paused. From the first day of their journey they had both avoided mentioning her mother—it was like an unspoken agreement between them that they wouldn't—but now, if Alex was going to succeed in getting her through the doors of one of the Paris fashion houses, he would use any means at his disposal.

'Your teachers taught you what they could, but there are things they couldn't teach you. Only experience can do that. You've known nothing of the world outside school. You have never lived it and it's time you did. You may have achieved academic status, but in every other respect you are ignorant. You, my dear, Anna, are world illiterate.'

Anna gasped, and Alex saw her reel from the blow of his words. He grinned. 'Sorry if I sound like a stern headmaster, but I am trying to get to the root of your hang-ups.'

'Alex, how dare you? I don't have any hang-ups.'

'No?'

'No.'

'Then why won't you allow me to indulge you? Paris is the centre of fashion—and who knows, you might even enjoy trying on some of the latest creations. Besides, before we leave Paris I want to take you to the opera and the ballet, and I would like you to wear something appropriate. So I think a couple of new dresses, at least, are in order.'

Anna's eyes narrowed suspiciously. 'Has my grandfather put you up to this—told you to buy me some new clothes?'

'He—suggested it.'

She was indignant. 'So between you, you want to take me in hand and create an entirely new me—new clothes today, new face tomorrow. You may want to foist a new image on me, Alex, but I have no intention of letting you make it a false one.'

Alex shook his head. 'I have no intention of doing so. You are well worth looking at the way you are—and as for cosmetics, you don't need all that. Why tamper with perfection?'

They argued some more and in the end Alex won—as he knew he would.

Alex took her to one of the fashion houses that had a high-class clientele. The salon was busy with well-to-do ladies, but Madame Roche—a woman of impeccable good manners, infinite tact and an arbiter of elegance and good taste—gave them her special attention.

When Anna looked as if she favoured something in black, Alex waved it away, fingering through others on the rails of a more colourful hue with knowledgeable expertise. Finally he conferred with Madame Roche, who ushered them into a small room where Alex sat down and Anna was taken behind a concealing screen. Here she undressed down to her chemise and allowed Madame Roche to transform her.

Anna presented herself to Alex time and again in outfit after outfit, so utterly astounded by her reflection in the cheval mirrors that she was rendered speechless. Confrontation with her image was something she had always taken little interest in; now she gazed long and incredulously, turning this way and that, slowly examining every inch of her undiscovered self and liking what she saw. It was when Madame Roche slipped a black evening dress over her head—a sliver of silk and tiny black beads—that she stepped from behind the screen for the last time to present herself somewhat shyly to Alex.

Throughout the trying on Alex had looked quietly at this lovely, compelling young woman as her slender form was set off to perfection by the new clothes. The colours were subtle, youthful, perfect for her dark hair and golden skin, and now as he gazed on her attired in this latest creation, the whole effect classical, mature and restrained and devastatingly elegant, the result was a metamorphosis.

Anna turned from the mirror and looked to where he sat with one long leg crossed over the other, his elbows resting on the arms of the chair and his fingers steepled under his chin.

'Well, Alex?' she ventured, shy and self-conscious, her voice quavering with uncertainty, for he had at first scorned the black, stating it was a colour for old ladies and funerals. 'What do you think?'

'I take back what I said. The dress becomes you perfectly. From now on we will dine in style, so you can wear your finery. But, however am I going to regard you as "Miss Anna Preston, fresh out of school" in the same light again?'

For a moment his gaze held hers with penetrating intensity. The clear silver depths were as enigmatic as they were silently challenging, and, unexpectedly, Anna felt an answering frisson of excitement. The narrowing of Alex's eyes warned her he was aware of that brief response.

Anna passed it off with a light laugh and turned and went behind the screen to remove the dress.

Before they left the premises—Anna shoving a newly purchased bottle of Chanel No.5 into her bag—Alex paid the amount due, leaving the address of the hotel where the clothes and accessories were to be delivered.

'There's just one more thing we need to do to complete the image,' Alex said, taking her arm and briskly guiding her along the pavement.

Anna shot him a warning look. 'Which is?'

'A visit to the hairdresser.'

'Just a minute,' she protested, coming to a halt. 'I love my new clothes, but one thing at a time.'

He grinned down at her. 'You need pampering.'

'You've pampered me enough already.'

'Indulge me. I want to pamper you some more.'

Alex refused to back down, and after further persuasion her small pocket of resistance was overcome and he marched her into the hairdresser. He was content to sit and read the daily papers and drink coffee while Anna was whisked away and her hair was washed, trimmed and styled in a sleek pageboy to her shoulders and gleamed like well-polished jet.

'That's more like it,' he approved when she presented herself to him once more. 'Now let's get some lunch. How does a return to Maxim's sound?'

Anna laughed. 'Perfect.'

Chapter Six

Anna never tired of lunching at Maxim's. She loved the atmosphere, the Lautrec paintings, the Tiffany lamps and the stylish Parisiennes who filled the restaurant, pushing dainty morsels of food around china plates.

They had just finished their meal when she looked up and saw a woman detach herself from her male partner as the waiter was showing them to a table and move in their direction. Looking as though at least two personal maids had helped her to achieve her flawless tidiness, she was glossy in her perfection. Her hair was blonde, short and well dressed, her bones covered with just the right amount of flesh. Wearing an ivory silk sheath dress faintly blushed with pink, a diamond brooch pinned to her right shoulder and a mink stole dripping from the left, she possessed a sensuality that killed at a distance. Drenched in a very exclusive scent, she swept towards them with the magnetism of a woman who is confident of her beauty. Her eyes were fixed on Alex.

Alex's head snapped up. His shoulders stiffened and he rose awkwardly—Alex, who was never awkward. An expression Anna could not recognise flicked on his face, and his eyes seemed dangerously bright in the subdued light.

'Edwina! Radiant as ever, I see.'

His voice was dry and heavily laced with sarcasm that was

not lost on Anna. She stood up, clutching her napkin. Confronted by so much sophisticated elegance, she felt plain and insignificant by comparison. Her instinct told her that this was Edwina Campbell, Freddy's sister—and Tamsin was right, the woman was awesome. Anna didn't like her. Her personality was forceful, her assurance verging on arrogance that bordered on contempt, and the way she pouted her bright red lips at Alex, her eyes giving him the come-hither look, reminded her of a Hollywood vamp.

Anna was shocked by her own reaction to Alex's one-time lover. It was a feeling so strange she was unable to put a name to it. It took her a moment to come up with its source. Jealousy.

'Alex, what a pleasant surprise,' Edwina purred.

'Spare me your lies. You are no more pleased to see me than I you.'

'My, my, what a beast you are—such a beast as any woman should delight in keeping for the pleasure of taming…if, indeed, you could be tamed,' Edwina said, her voice low and exact. Her eyes narrowed, her smile was unpleasant. 'I recall from my own experience that it was much more fun when I failed to tame you, although I also recall that there were times when you were as soft as butter in the proper hands. It's been a long time, Alex.'

'Not long enough,' he said flatly.

Edwina ignored his cutting remark. 'I understand you've been holidaying on the Riviera.'

'You've been talking to your brother.'

'He told me the two of you met.'

'Your information is indisputable,' Alex replied with crushing formality. 'We would not have met had I been able to avoid it.'

'Dear me, how hard and unforgiving you are, Alex.'

'I am forgiving of those worthy of forgiveness. Neither you nor your brother fall into that category.'

Edwina gave him her most freezing stare. 'Still simmering over that little disaster that befell—'

'Your brother played a major role in that "little disaster",' as you so callously put it,' Alex was quick to point out, 'but do not try and pretend you didn't lead a full supporting cast.'

It came to Alex that, next to her brother, he hated this woman. How vindictive she had been when he'd ended their brief affair. He wondered what lies she had fed Freddy about her uncaring lover—he didn't know, but he could well imagine. The truth was that he had tired of her, but now the threads of tangled lies Edwina had wrought could never be undone.

'Oh, for heaven's sake, Alex! Why so stony faced and bitter? You and I go back too far, and as you can see I have survived our relationship without scars.'

Alex's jaw clenched so tightly that a muscle began to throb in his cheek. He gave Edwina a look of unwavering distaste and said in a voice of tightly controlled fury, 'The same cannot be said of someone who is known to both of us, who is less worldly than you, Edwina, someone who was manipulated by a conniving witch and a despicable scoundrel. I compliment you on your complicity and treachery.'

Bemused, Anna looked from one to the other. She had no idea what they were talking about or whom, but it was clearly of a very serious nature.

Edwina tossed back her head and laughed. It was full of contempt and mocking cruelty. 'Any compliment from you is always welcome.' Tapping her clutch bag tucked beneath her arm with one long, vividly red fingernail, she looked at Anna with little interest, but Anna felt there was a seething curiosity behind the well-bred façade. 'It isn't like you to forget your manners, Alex. Aren't you going to introduce me to your friend?' she asked, blithely ignoring the simmering rage emanating from her former lover.

'Miss Anna Preston,' Alex said tightly. 'Anna, this is Edwina Campbell. You are already acquainted with her brother.'

Anna met Edwina's frosty, assessing gaze with quiet composure. On closer inspection there was something porcelain-hard about her that was unattractive. 'Freddy—yes. We met in Monte Carlo.'

Edwina arched her brows at Alex, her red lips curved in a derisive smile. 'A trifle young for you, isn't she, Alex?'

Anna's face burned with indignation. How dare the woman be so rude? 'Alex is very kindly escorting me back to England,' she was quick to point out.

'Alone? You have no family?'

Anna met the penetrating inspection with unflinching hauteur. 'I was an only child. My parents are both dead.'

'Edwina belongs to the aristocracy,' Alex explained sardonically. 'Is that not so, Edwina?'

'Of course, but if you're acquainted with Freddy then you'll know all about that.'

'And you can trace your ancestry all the way back to the seventeenth century,' Alex quipped, his tone sarcastic, his whole expression one of cynicism.

With a look that told Edwina she was not daunted by pretensions of grandeur, Anna said, 'How impressive, but one has to be able to trace one's ancestry back to William the Conqueror to belong to the old nobility—like my own. My grandfather is Lord Selwyn Manson of Belhaven. You will have heard of him.' She met Edwina's eyes, saw them flicker, and knew she had scored a hit.

Alex struggled to suppress his admiration, despite his anger.

'I see. I was unaware that Lord Manson had a granddaughter.'

'Now you know.' Alex took Anna's arm. 'Excuse us.'

Edwina stepped back to let them pass. 'Far be it from me to detain you. I shall be in Paris for several weeks. We may bump into each other again.'

Alex paused and regarded her with undiluted loathing. Anna could feel the tension in his hand holding her arm. 'If you are wise,' he said in a blood-chilling voice, 'you will avoid me very carefully, Edwina.'

In stunned silence and walking with quick steps to match his own, Anna was escorted out of Maxim's. She would never have guessed, never imagined, that Alex was capable of the kind of virulent hatred she had seen in his face when he had looked at Edwina Campbell. He was silent for a long time afterwards. Anna stared at his profile, but of course, as always in moments of complex emotion, it was inscrutable.

For a brief awful moment she felt wholly cut off from him, as if a door had been closed between them, and in that instant some sixth sense told her that if she were to ask him what he and Edwina had been talking about, she would be entering very deep and dangerous waters indeed. He never mentioned Edwina again.

Their last night in Paris would always stand out in Anna's memory. From the moment she put on her new black dress it became an enchanted evening. She was buoyantly happy and out on the town in the most romantic city in the world with the most attractive man in the world. They drank champagne at the Ritz before going on to the opera, and when they were leaving Alex presented her with a single orchid. However, as the evening drew to a close, despite their discussion of the music and pleasant exchanges, Anna was aware that Alex's mood had been disintegrating since the interval.

Although he'd specifically told her to enjoy herself, to treat the evening as a festive occasion, there was an indefinable tension about his features, becoming more pronounced as the evening wore on. She told herself it was because their time in Paris was at an end, and that he was as reluctant to leave as she was—or was it something else? Was it his meeting with Edwina Campbell that played on his mind, or the phone call he had made to England before they'd left the hotel? Who had he been telephoning? Was it Sonya the woman he had spoken to with so much tenderness at the villa, the woman he had told he loved more than anyone?

Determined to enjoy the evening, she had carefully extinguished the ridiculous flare of jealousy she had felt at the time, but the more she thought about it, the more it continued to wrench at the softest part of her heart.

In the orange glow of the gaslights they strolled along the banks of the Seine, watching the boats go by. The night was gently warm, the air filled with the scents of summer, a blanket of stars overhead, the moon bright and casting a silver sheen on the surface of the river. Seduction was everywhere. A gentle breeze lifted Anna's hair and caressed her face.

Alex paused and, still clutching the orchid, she turned to him. He was staring down at the swirling water, his hands shoved deep into his pockets. Uncertain of his mood, Anna remained silent. In the moonlight his profile was harsh. He looked like a man in the throes of some deep, internal battle. Suddenly it seemed colder and she shivered.

'I suppose we ought to be making our way back to the hotel,' she suggested when some time had passed and his silence had become unsettling. 'But before we do, I would like to take the opportunity of saying to you that these have been the happiest two weeks of my life.' She felt a wave of gratitude, and something else, too—a desire to show her appreciation, and not to allow the evening to disintegrate. 'Thank you for showing me France, for my holiday. I shall always treasure this time.'

Alex turned and looked at her. 'It was my pleasure.' He meant what he said. Beneath the heavy fringe of dark lashes, her eyes were amazing, mesmerising in their lack of guile, and her smooth cheeks were flushed a becoming pink. Strands of shining black hair brushed her face. She was, he decided, refreshingly open and honest, with a gentle pride he admired.

His reply had a deep, hypnotic quality. Anna gave a wistful, almost shy smile. His handsome face was sombre. She was acutely aware of his powerful male body looming over her, tall and strong—of a man who had gallantly taken care of her and shouldered all her burdens for the past two weeks. The combination of all that was becoming dangerously, sweetly appealing.

'How I do so love Paris,' she murmured. 'Wouldn't it be lovely if we could stay here for ever—just the two of us.'

Anna didn't know how explicit her expression was—like an open book, exposing what was in her heart. Alex saw it and was immediately wary, and in that moment he realised that eliminating her from his life when they reached Belhaven was going to be harder than he'd imagined.

'One day you will come back, perhaps when you meet the man of your dreams—a man who will have your head spinning and your legs turning to jelly,' he teased, trying to sound light-hearted and casual while knowing he was being deliberately cruel, but it was necessary.

His words penetrated the fog of Anna's senses, bringing her back from the languorous narcosis into which the magical evening, the moon and the stars and their stroll by the river had sent her. She felt as if something were shattering inside her—a raw illogical panic slithered into her. She hadn't wanted him to say that. It spoiled the moment.

'They…do say that Paris is a place for lovers,' she said softly, hesitantly, watching an entwined couple walk past, whispering to each other. Anna looked at them with envy. 'How true that is.' Alex was looking at her intently and suddenly, taking her courage in both hands, she raised herself on tiptoe and placed her mouth on his.

She felt his initial surprise, his shock, his withdrawal, but she kept her lips on his, feeling him respond and gently take her arms and draw her towards him. His lips began to move on hers, his tongue to explore. It was the most wonderful, warm feeling. She pressed towards him, longing for him to kiss her deeper, but urgently, almost, he pushed her back.

'No, Anna. This has to stop. I'm sorry. I deserve to be horsewhipped.'

'No, you don't,' she said. 'It wasn't you. I made you do it. And please don't say you're sorry—because that means you regret it. I don't.' She saw Alex's shoulders stiffen and he took a step back. She could see by his expression that she had gone too far. 'I'm sorry, Alex. I've put my foot in it, haven't I? I shouldn't have done that. It isn't what you want.' Her lips trembled into an apologetic smile. 'Too much champagne, I expect. I'm still not used to it. But you are the nicest man I know.'

Their gazes linked and held, hers open, frank, with gratitude in its depths, his a blend of seriousness and sadness and frustration.

She sighed. 'Why must we go home? I don't want to.'

'We must. I have work to do. I've been gone too long as it is.' Even though his voice was soft, it was steady and resolute, and there was a hardness in him now.

'Thank you for looking after me.' Her words were sincere and heartfelt. Reaching out, she placed her hand on his arm. The gesture was spontaneous, but one she immediately regretted, for Alex drew back, resisting her. It was a moment before she realised that he must be startled, because reaching out to him was something she had never done before—not to anyone. She dropped her arm and he stepped back, his smile a curious blend of withdrawal and self-derision.

'The holiday is over the moment we board the boat at Calais, Anna. When you reach Belhaven you will begin a new life, meet new people your own age.'

Anna understood the rules of their return to England, because his manner and his expression made it clear: no tears, no regrets—just memories. 'I know I will, but I'll never forget this, any of it. The only foolish thing I've done is caring too much for you.'

Alex jerked away, his voice condescendingly amused as he tried not to look too deeply into Anna's wounded eyes, eloquent in their hurt, which remained fixed on his face. 'I never intended for you to do that. I think you are very lovely and very special, Anna. I can't believe how lucky I have been to have had you with me, but in many ways you are still a child—naïve and inexperienced—'

'And still wet behind the ears,' Anna interrupted sharply, deeply hurt by what he said. His callousness was not to be borne. 'Please don't insult me by ridiculing my feelings, Alex, or treat me like a child. It's cruel.'

'I know. I apologise—but I was about to say that friendship is no basis for a love affair. When you get to Belhaven I want you to remember this time in France—but forget about me, there's a good girl. That's what I want you to do.'

Anna felt as if he'd slapped her and that he was treating her like all the other women who tried to get too close. She stepped back, wrapping her arms around her waist as if to fend off the hurt he was deliberately inflicting on her raw emotions. Alex read her every reaction and was satisfied his words had had the desired effect.

Anna knew Alex was trying to get rid of her, she could feel it—and why shouldn't he? she asked herself. He saw her as a child, a stupid, pathetic schoolgirl who had been a pleasant diversion for a while, who had a lot of growing up to do. She couldn't even begin to compare with some of the beautiful women he associated with and he had only been nice to her to please her grandfather. How could she ever have assumed a man like Alex Kent would be interested in her? Never in all her life had she felt so humiliated.

Her wounded pride forced her chin up. 'You're right,' she said with dignity, trying especially hard to appear composed. 'There is nothing left to do or say—at least, nothing that you want to hear.'

'No,' he said. His expression was stiff and aloof.

Anna heard the absolute finality of that word and knew it would be futile to argue. Fighting desperately to hold on to her shattered pride, she said, 'I think it's time we were getting back to the hotel before I make an even bigger fool of myself. It's late and you said we have an early start in the morning.'

As she was about to walk on, she paused and looked at him, struggling to keep her voice steady. 'And you were wrong about the holiday ending when we reach Calais. It's over now, Alex, and the sooner we get to Belhaven the better.' Dragging her gaze from his, she bent her head. She could no longer look at him, or run from him without giving her feelings away, so she carefully turned and began to walk on ahead.

Alex thought he had heard a catch in her voice and his conscience tore at him. Something floating at the water's edge caught his eye. It was the orchid he had given Anna earlier. She must have dropped it—whether by accident or deliberately he had no way of knowing, but he sincerely hoped it was the former. Cursing softly in Russian, angry with himself but none the less inclined to change nothing, he strode after her.

Hanging back for a much needed whisky in the hotel bar, he watched Anna climb the stairs to her room. He'd hurt her because he had to, he reminded himself—the one person whose feelings he'd been most careful not to hurt. He couldn't let her waste one moment of her precious new life believing she was in love with him. He had done well, not letting her know how much he had come to care for her, how much she belonged in his heart. But it was hard, no matter how he tried, to still his emotional rebellion against the rational reason of his mind.

Alone in her room Anna climbed into bed. The memory of what had passed between them was intolerable. In all her eighteen years she had never cared for anyone very much, and certainly not enough to kiss them and say to them such a tremendously important thing like she had said to Alex. Somehow she had lost control of the situation. In doing so she had overstepped the bounds of friendship and found herself in unfamiliar territory. She'd made no demands on him. She'd made a gift of telling him something she'd never uttered to another human being—that she cared for him. And he'd trampled on it, making a fool of her.

No, she'd made a fool of herself, indulged a daydream. For the first time in her life she had fallen for a man—a man who looked on her as a child—with a speed and thoroughness she would not have believed possible. Her unhappiness folded around her like a cloak and she wished with all her heart that she had never come to France, had never laid eyes on Alex Kent. Then she would have gone straight to Belhaven and her grandfather and conformed to his mores with the same detachment that had carried her through life.

Utterly overcome with shame, she drew her knees up tight to her chest and began to cry. When her tears were spent she went into the bathroom and washed her face. The cold water had a calming effect on her and, going back to bed, she closed her eyes and uttered a prayer. Only it wasn't really a prayer. It was a strengthening of her own will.

Alex stopped the car. They were on the edge of a hill, which dropped down into a gently sweeping basin below. The Buckinghamshire countryside was lush and green, with the sleepiness of summer.

Anna glanced at Alex. 'Why have we stopped?'

'I thought you might like to see Belhaven.'

His eyes went past her and Anna followed his gaze.

In the bottom of the valley was the most gracious private dwelling Anna's eyes had ever beheld. Lawns adorned with flowerbeds and statues gave way to a park-like vista. Belhaven was beautiful, and the longer she looked at it the more beautiful it became. It was a huge redbrick mansion with long, leaded windows. Part of the building was timber framed, with bricks arranged in diagonal patterns between the old beams. The walls were covered with ivy and a profusion of flowering creepers—a pastoral paradise, she thought, a scene of prosperity.

'That's Belhaven?'

'Yes. Your home. If you like Belhaven, it is in your power to remain there for as long as you wish—for ever, if you will.' His eyes were filled with meaning, his expression softer than it had been since that last night in Paris.

Anna ignored the subtle hint and murmured, 'Home. How empty the word sounds. How can it be home when I am a stranger there? There was a time not so very long ago when I believed I could make my own destiny. Suddenly I feel that I am at the mercy of fate.'

'Maybe it's a bit of both. We are born with things that define us—personality, humour, resilience—but we can make our own future, too.'

'I want so much to believe that. What is he really like, my grandfather? All I know is that he and my mother were estranged, that he is extremely wealthy, old and ill. You have told me he knows practically all there is to know about me, so I would like to know more about him before we meet—so that I am not entirely at a disadvantage. Is he as awesome as I imagine him to be?'

Alex saw that sudden, questioning vulnerability. It required an answer. 'No—although you may think so when you first meet him. Your grandfather is a tough man, Anna—eccentric perhaps, unorthodox, and he considers old age an affront. It's hard for him, being confined to a wheelchair. He'd been used to an active life until arthritis got a grip on him. Now he sits in his room, dictating letters to his secretary, reading the newspapers and writing letters. There is nothing wrong with his mind—his brain is still as active as it ever was.'

'Isn't he lonely, living in that great house all by himself?'

'He has his moments—although he would die rather than admit it—and there are those who would say he is not the kind of man to feel lonely. He missed your mother when she left—that I do know.'

'Then he shouldn't have been so set against her marrying my father. If he had given them his blessing, she would never have left.'

'He couldn't do that. He had his reasons—good reasons. In time he might explain, and perhaps then you will understand.'

Anna could not control the impatience in her voice as she said, 'But what did he have against my father? Was he some kind of monster—or a criminal, perhaps?' As so often in the past, she was assailed by misgivings about the man whose name she bore.

'I told you when we first met that it is for Selwyn to answer any questions you may have on that particular subject. I never knew your mother, and when she left I had not met Selwyn, so what I know is only hearsay.'

'But my grandfather told you, didn't he?'

'He has told me many things in confidence, over the years. Your mother disappointed him when she went against his wishes and married your father. He hoped that when your father died she would come to her senses and return home. But her feelings towards him were deeply bitter. He wrote to her, telling her the door to Belhaven was always open, that she could return any time she chose. In reply, she sent him one brief note telling him she never would.'

'How I wish they had mended their quarrel. I never knew anyone who had so much self-discipline, such control over herself as my mother. There was a lot I couldn't understand, when my understanding was that of a child. I learned that what couldn't be cured had to be endured, and to endure was unrelenting and doomed from the start.'

Shifting her gaze to the house she became quiet, so quiet and so still that a small white butterfly drifted close, attracted by the bright colour of her dress, but she continued to stare at the house, deep in her own thoughts. Alex sat watching her, filled with compassion, for she spoke in a tone of unutterable sadness.

After a while she spoke again, her voice sorrowful, almost vague. 'There was some kind of fatalism about my mother. Contrary to popular belief, I have found the passing of time and the dulling of grief have little to do with one another—

at least, that was the case where my mother was concerned. She never rejected me—she just didn't see me, only herself. I was a responsibility grudgingly accepted. One thing I learned about her was that something deeper and more complex was involved, that it was the hardiness of her spirit that drew sustenance from her memories of my father. I didn't understand her. In fact, I was slightly afraid.'

'Afraid of letting her down?'

'I don't know. But I never, ever aroused in her the same kind of feelings she had for my father.'

Alex thought he had never heard such desolation, or felt it. He felt a surge of reverent admiration for what Anna had achieved, for what she had overcome, and his admiration was reinforced by the pain and loneliness she had endured throughout her short life. He silently cursed Lavinia Preston to hell for her despicable treatment of her daughter, and, unable to trust himself to speak, it was a full minute before he said, 'Are you ready to meet your grandfather?'

Anna looked into his face. He was looking at her hard. He smiled and his eyes were suddenly warm—warm with what? Understanding? Pity? She hoped not. She couldn't abide pity from anyone, least of all from Alex. Quickly she looked away. 'Yes. Best get it over with.'

It seemed to Anna that she was entering a new world as they passed through the gold painted wrought-iron gates. As the gatekeeper drew them together, sudden panic seized her. She felt trapped, cunningly, yet unwittingly so. She had allowed herself to be drawn to Belhaven as it lay waiting, patient as all traps.

What was she doing here? Who was the man that was waiting for her behind those redbrick walls? And who was this man who was taking her there? The journey from Paris had not mellowed him, she thought sadly, just the opposite. Now there was a cynical edge to his voice and a coldness in his eyes. He had changed and she did not know why. He had become a dark and ominous figure at her side, transporting her to an unknown world in which her happiness had become plagued with remorse and fear.

The car came to a halt at the foot of a low flight of stone steps on which a smartly dressed man in Harris tweed stood to welcome them.

'There's Giles,' Alex said, climbing out of the car, smiling broadly. The meeting between the two men was cordial and relaxed. 'Giles—good to see you.'

'So, the voyager returns.' Giles laughed, stepping forward to open the door for Anna. 'Good to see you, Alex, and in fine fettle too, I see.'

'Anna, this is Giles Burnet, your grandfather's secretary-cum-general factotum, of many years.'

'Welcome to Belhaven, Miss Preston,' Giles said, bowing his head politely and shaking her hand. 'It's a pleasure to meet you at last.'

'How do you do, sir.' Giles Burnet was fortyish, with dark brown hair and eyes to match. Though he was brusque in manner, there was a quiet air of kindliness about him. Anna liked him immediately and knew they would get on.

'Come along in. Your grandfather has instructed that you be sent in as soon as you arrive. He's impatient to meet you. He insisted on being brought down to the library—pride demands that he makes light of his infirmities,' he confided to Anna. 'I'll have Sefton see to your baggage, Alex.'

'Just Miss Preston's, Giles. Leave mine. I won't be staying.'

Alex's words caught Anna unawares. Her eyes flew to his, the sharpness of her disappointment taking her by surprise. 'You—aren't staying?'

Alex heard the sudden break in Anna's voice. It was so touching and tragic, suggesting something very like distress, that he was moved in spite of himself. He shook his head. 'I'm sorry, Anna, but I'm afraid I have to go. It's important that I leave for London as soon as I've seen Selwyn. I have pressing matters to attend to.'

His tone suggested such finality that Anna turned her head away. It shouldn't hurt so much, being told that he was leaving her totally undefended and among strangers. But it did. Was he going to Sonya, the woman she had heard him tell he loved more than anyone? Was he so impatient to be with her that he couldn't wait to be rid of her, Anna? 'Then of course you must go,' she heard herself say. 'I quite understand. I have taken up far too much of your time as it is.'

Before she could move away and follow Giles, who had disappeared inside the house, Alex had closed the short distance between them and grasped her arm. When he looked at her, Anna could see the light in his eyes and the crinkle of laughter lines at the corners.

But Alex wasn't laughing. He searched her face for a long moment, then reached up to gently touch her chin with his forefinger. 'Anna, believe me, you'll be fine. I've enjoyed our time together. It was perfect. But it's time to return to reality—for both of us.'

She looked into his fathomless eyes, and for the first time she realised he wasn't handling their parting as easily as she thought.

Chapter Seven

Anna found herself in a large panelled hall. She stood and looked with awe at her surroundings. It was opulent, with beautiful artefacts reposing on gleaming tables, and on the walls were paintings of long-dead family members in gilded frames, while shadows from the dark corners whispered money. The house exuded an indefinable quality—a sense of order, centuries of happiness and disappointments, memories of men and women who had lived and breathed within these walls—all folded into the fabric. The house was living, breathing, but empty of life. She shivered.

'How is Selwyn, Giles?' Alex asked, his concern for the old man evident in his expression.

'About the same as when you left. Doctor Collins called yesterday and spent some time with him. The pains in his joints continue to trouble him but his will's as strong as ever—more so now,' he said, his gaze fixed meaningfully on Anna. 'Your coming here means a great deal to him, Miss Preston. Today he actually agreed with me when I said it was a lovely day and he smiled at Mrs Henshaw when she brought him his breakfast—and failed to rail at the parlour maid for being late taking him his morning papers.'

Anna stared in amazement at this astonishing information.

'I think it's time we went in,' Alex said. 'Selwyn has ears like the proverbial bat and will know we've arrived.'

Anna was conscious of a small contingent of curious servants lurking about as Alex led her down the hall. Open to their searching scrutiny she was aware they stole lingering looks at her. She managed to direct a self-conscious smile at one or two, but her mind was braced on the meeting with her grandfather. After knocking lightly on a pair of doors, Alex opened them and drew her inside the library.

The room was sun filled, polished and scented, but Anna was not aware of any of this as her feet passed over the Aubusson carpet. The first thing she could make out was a wheelchair. Its occupant was a man who was watching her intently. Arthritis and the years had worn away the muscles of his youth, leaving behind a hard shell of leather. Moving closer, she could see his face was sunk and lined, but even so it bore a strong resemblance to her mother's. His eyes, pale, sharp and intelligent and showing no film of age, were fixed relentlessly on her. Alex stepped past her.

'Selwyn, it's good to see you, good to be back. How are you?'

Selwyn took Alex's hand and gripped it hard, looking at the younger man with genuine affection. Anna had little experience with which to judge the strong bond that tied Alex to her grandfather, but as sometimes happens when two people are very close, it gave a stranger the uncanny impression he and Alex were more than friends—more like father and son.

'I've never felt better,' Selwyn answered, his tone strong and deep.

'Glad to hear it.'

Selwyn looked past Alex to Anna. Alex turned and offered her his hand. She took it and allowed him to draw her closer to the man in the wheelchair. His legs were covered with a tartan rug. She met his hard, discerning stare, began to look away, then forced herself to return his appraisal with a measuring look of her own. The years had not been kind to him, but the feelings that welled up in Anna and drew her towards him were cruel, for she could not hate him as she believed he deserved. She felt he was a forceful man, secure in his own strength and will—just like her mother had been. She still clung to Alex's hand, unwilling to let go.

'Selwyn, this is Anna.'

The older man's eyes narrowed. 'Come closer.'

Alex let go of her hand and edged back towards the door, quietly letting himself out.

Selwyn took in every inch of the young woman before he spoke again. 'So, you are Lavinia's daughter. I'm glad to meet you at last. Please sit down.' He indicating a chair in front of him. 'No need to stand on ceremony.' He waited until she was seated, perched uncomfortably on the edge of the chair. 'I trust Quentin and Irene looked after you in France?'

'Yes—they were extremely kind. I enjoyed my stay with them.'

'I knew Irene's father. We were good friends. Irene and your mother grew up together—same school, came out together and all that.'

'Yes, I know, although we never discussed it.' Anna had felt Lady Ormsby would have liked to, and that she was waiting for Anna to ask, but she'd preferred not to.

'No, well—I knew Irene would take care of you, see you enjoyed yourself. Did you like France?'

'Yes, very much.'

'And Alex?' he asked, watching her intently. 'Has he made an impression on you?'

Anna glanced behind her, not having realised until that moment that Alex had left the room. 'Alex is a very impressive person. We were together a great deal. He took me to many places and he knows so much about France that it made me realise how little I know. He made me see things differently.'

'So, you got on well together.'

'Yes—I think so. He was very attentive and amusing.' The

way her grandfather nodded his head slightly conveyed to Anna that for reasons of his own he was pleased by this. 'I must thank you for your financial support through my years at Gilchrist. I am grateful—truly. Without it I would never have secured a place at university. I realise you still believe in the old emphasis on the importance of the female role as wife and mother—Alex told me,' she confessed when he raised his eyebrows a notch, 'but I want more than that. Perhaps my relationship with my own mother may have something to do with that.'

'That's not surprising. And now you are to go to Oxford to read English literature. You've done well. No one can achieve that without a special talent and application,' Selwyn said with a note of grudging pride.

'Thank you,' Anna said, a reluctant little smile curving her lips.

'Did your mother tell you about me—about Belhaven?'

'Not very much—and absolutely nothing about Belhaven and that you were a peer of the realm. I was led to believe you were dead, that I had no family on either side—and that you disowned her when she told you she was marrying my father.'

A sadness entered his eyes. 'So, she told you that. How you must have reviled me.'

'Yes,' she said frankly. 'I did. It was Alex who defended you to me.'

'I did not tell Lavinia to go. I refused to give my blessing to her marriage, so she left. And you have suffered for it. How do you feel now? Are you not angry that your mother deceived you?'

'She must have had her reasons.'

'Reasons known only to Lavinia. You don't resemble her. Facially you're more like your grandmother. She had the same dark hair.'

'So did my father. I also have my father's eyes,' Anna was swift to add.

Selwyn's thin face hardened. 'The artist's eyes.'

'His name was Robert Preston. Why did you dislike him so much?'

'Dislike is putting it mildly,' he said, his tone betraying the bitterness he so clearly felt. 'I didn't like him, or their marriage. Lavinia could have done so much better.'

'He loved her,' Anna said gently. 'Does that not seem to you sufficient reason? I never knew my father. I have a photograph of him—him and Mother on their wedding day. He...he was very attractive—I can quite understand what my mother saw in him. She told me he was charming—a talented artist. She was hurt badly when he was killed. I wonder why she never returned to Belhaven, why she steadfastly refused to heal the breach between you.'

'Because she was stubborn and proud. Anna, it hurts me to disillusion you, but your mother kept things from you. There are things about your father that you must be told.'

Anna gazed at him with polite interest, and a complete lack of understanding, although the whispered conversations she had sometimes overheard between her mother and her friends concerning her father and his wild ways, hovered like dark shadows on the perimeter of her mind. 'Told? Told what?'

With a shaking hand, Selwyn reached for a glass of weak whisky and water on the table beside him, swallowing it straight down. It was as if he needed it to give him courage, then he said, 'Robert Preston's main interest in your mother was her fortune. He was an opportunist. He was also the son of a common criminal who was doing time for embezzlement.'

Anna gasped, shocked. 'Surely not.'

'It is true. Your father was like him. He was handsome and charming, I grant you that, and it was easy to understand why women were attracted to him. It was Lavinia he wanted—and what she would inherit when I am gone. He was a penniless, unprincipled rogue who saw a chance of becoming rich. He pursued and manipulated your mother relentlessly, worming his way into her world—into her heart.'

The words scraped against Anna's raw nerves, threatening to break the slender thread of control. 'That's not true. I don't believe you. If you're saying these things about my father because you're trying to justify turning my mother out, you're wasting your breath.'

'Don't be afraid of the truth, Anna. It is obvious to me that you are a young woman of considerable courage and conviction. I respect your loyalty to your father, however misguided, and it is no simple matter for me to discuss things with you that are still intensely painful to me. For your own sake, I suggest you listen to what I have to say, even though the truth may hurt you.'

Anna braced herself. 'I'm strong enough to look unpleasant truths in the face. In that I'm like my mother. Please continue.'

'To support his grandiose ideas of becoming a great artist— and in that I and many more doubted his ability; he was second rate and always would be—Preston elected to marry her. She became besotted—he saw to that. I refused to consent to a marriage between them, even going so far as to threaten to cut her off without a penny if she went ahead, but Lavinia was headstrong and refused to listen. So she ran off and married him.'

'But that doesn't make him a bad person,' she argued. 'He must have had some redeeming features.' Her grandfather's look of disdain conveyed to Anna that he hadn't. Her heart began to beat painfully in hard erratic thumps, for she knew from her grandfather's manner that there was something else he hadn't told her.

'There's more, isn't there?' She saw him hesitate as he shifted his gaze from her face. 'Tell me. I have to know everything. Mother found my father's death hard to handle, you see, and all my life he's been lying around like an unexorcised ghost. When I was a child I accepted everything she told me about him without question, but I always suspected, from the things I overheard, that it wasn't all roses between them. Only when I know the truth will I be able to lay his ghost to rest.'

Selwyn shifted his gaze back to her face. He hesitated to tell her the rest which, in the presence of so much innocence, seemed suddenly monstrous. His voice was oddly gentle when he spoke. 'That depends on the truth and how well you are able to deal with it. I don't want to hurt you more than I probably have and I am wondering how you will take the remainder of what I have to confide.'

'I want to know.'

'Very well. Like his father, Robert Preston was a common criminal with a record when she met him. Your mother didn't find out until after they were married, but I don't think it would have made any difference if she had. She wanted him, and that was that. Preston was a thief—London mansions, which he robbed of irreplaceable collections of jewellery, paintings and *objets d'art*, were his target.

'And then he was involved in a quarrel and a scuffle ensued with a man in a bar. He was not inclined to view the incident as serious until he discovered the man had died as a result of a heart attack. The man's wife swore it had been brought on by the injuries sustained in the attack—as to that and not having access to the doctor's report, we'll never know.'

Anna struggled to find a way to avoid condemning her father. Dragging her voice through the knot of emotions in her chest, she said with as much force as she could muster, 'I do not believe he was a murderer.'

'Neither do I, but you can't deny that he was a thief. Deciding to leave and leave quickly before the police came knocking on his door, Preston joined up and was sent to France, where he was killed soon afterwards.'

Battered by this revelation, Anna stood up, fighting to control the wrenching anguish that was strangling her breath in her chest. 'It can't be true,' she said, as calmly as she could.

'I cannot believe my father was capable of doing such terrible things.'

'How do you know? You never knew him.'

'My mother would have told me.'

'What? And ruined the illusion she had of him? Who can claim to know what moves a woman's heart? I imagine her love for the man blinded her to his faults. At all events, I have not lied to you.'

Every instinct Anna possessed told her that her grandfather was telling her the truth. She knew it. She could feel it.

'But—how could my mother have kept it from me?' she burst out, her voice shaking with bitterness and pain. 'How could she have been so unutterably cruel as to let me believe my father was perfect, that he was some kind of saint? How could she have let me spend my entire life trying to make myself worthy of her, of my father's memory—a man who was a thief and not worthy to be called a gentleman?'

'I told you, Anna. Lavinia loved an illusion, not Robert Preston, an illusion she created because she was innocent and idealistic—'

'And blind and gullible and stupid!' In her anguish Anna turned away from the sympathy her grandfather was trying to offer her.

'Anna, listen to me,' Selwyn said, cursing his crippled body that prevented him from going to her. 'I know this has come as a shock and that you will need time to come to terms with what you now know. I'll ring for Mrs Henshaw and have her show you to your rooms. We can talk again later.'

The shock of what he had told her sent Anna reeling into a black hole of desolation so deep she felt she would never get out of it. But she had to. She braced her shoulders, forcing herself to turn round, trying to close her mind to the tormented images of her mother's folly.

'No, I am quite all right. There is just one thing I have to ask you, and then we will let the matter rest for now, but it is important that I know. Do I have any family on my father's side that I should know about.'

'No close family—as far as I know. Your father had two brothers—both killed in the war. His mother, your grand-mother, was a victim of the influenza outbreak that claimed so many lives at that time, and his father died shortly after being released from prison in 1925.

'Anna, I'm sorry I had to tell you all this, but you had to know. It is your right. I am not without my part in the way things turned out, and that's something I have had to live with—will have to live with until I die. I may not have been the perfect father, but I like to think that people change—that I will make a better grandfather.' He paused and bowed his head. When he again raised his eyes and looked at her, Anna shivered at the unhappiness she saw in their depths. His face was quite transformed with grief, tender, somehow undone.

She dragged her eyes away from his and looked around, and for the first time since entering the room she became aware of her surroundings. The room was large, with three of the walls lined with leather-bound books. On every polished surface there were photographs, mainly of her mother: as a baby on her mother's knee; her first pony; on holiday by the sea; leaning against the railing of a huge ocean-going yacht with a dazzling group of her society friends, laughing; glam-orous in white on her début. She looked at the face that gazed back at her, a face with eyes that were extraordinarily alive.

For Anna there was a great poignancy in this confrontation. Until that moment her mother had been to her an embittered, world-weary woman. The beautiful, vivacious young woman portrayed here touched her in the deepest places of her heart, but it aroused her bitterness, also. She felt cruelly cheated.

However, all these photographs proudly on display testified to the love her grandfather felt for his only child—a love she herself had doubted. With tears misting her eyes, she looked at the old man in the wheelchair, who was patiently waiting for her to speak.

'I wish I'd known her then. I can see you loved my mother very much.'

'She never knew how much,' he said, his voice hollow with emotion. 'For all my harsh words, when she left Belhaven the door was always open. But she was proud, unbending, with the strength and determination—'

'That marked her as your daughter,' Anna finished for him softly. She could see he was valiantly trying to cope with his own grief.

He nodded slowly. 'Perhaps. I bore her no ill will for repeatedly rejecting my peace offerings. And now you are here. When I am gone Belhaven will be rightfully yours—I have no doubt Alex has explained it all to you. It is my dearest wish that you will not walk away from it. There is no one else, and I can't bear to think of the old place being broken up, being sold to strangers.'

Anna gazed at him, at his misshapen hands, and instinctively knew the pain that the breaking up of his estate would cause him. Deep inside this awesome, formidable old man was a profound loneliness, his separation from her mother its wellspring. It was a loneliness she understood. She made up her mind there and then that whatever the case, no matter what had happened to cause the estrangement between her mother and her grandfather, she was determined to make friends with this one remaining member of her family.

'Will you stay?' Selwyn asked. When he saw her hesitate, he thought she was about to refuse and, leaning forward, his hands gripping the sides of his chair, he pulled out all the stops. 'You are a Manson and your place is here. Moreover, it is your duty to honour Lavinia's wishes, and she specifically wished for you to come to Belhaven.'

Anna stood looking at him for a moment in silence. His eyes were fixed on her, pleading with her, which she found strange. She hadn't expected to see this weakness in him. And suddenly she knew she couldn't walk away.

'All right,' she heard herself saying. 'I will stay.'

Selwyn sighed deeply—it was a sound that tore through the very fabric of the room. 'Thank you. You cannot imagine what that means to me. Generations of Mansons have lived at Belhaven since it was built three hundred years ago. There is always a great deal to be done, and, now you have decided to stay, a challenge lies before you. Are you up to it?'

'I don't know. I don't know anything about being a Manson—and it may be eighteen years too late to begin. But I will try to learn.'

Selwyn nodded. He believed she would. 'That's good enough for me. I have instructed Mrs Henshaw to have Lavinia's rooms prepared. Should you have any objections there are plenty of others you can choose from. Change them to your own taste if you wish. They are yours to do with as you like. This is your home. This is where you belong.'

'Thank you.' She turned and moved towards the door.

'Anna? Granddaughter?'

Two words, but there was a world of feeling in them. They conveyed to Anna his need for warmth and friendship. 'Yes?'

'This house—it's too big for me. I need someone. I've waited for more years than you can imagine for this moment. May I say it's very good to have you here. Welcome home.'

There was a silence between them. Their eyes met and held with an intensity that was beyond words. Selwyn watched her go, triumph stirring in his heart. It seemed to him suddenly that the house would begin to live again, that it had got its soul back, now his granddaughter was home.

Anna encountered Giles Burnet in the hall. She looked around and beyond him, her eyes searching for Alex. 'Mr Kent? Where is he?' She hoped desperately that he hadn't left without saying goodbye.

'He's in the office, waiting for you. I'll show you where it is.'

Giles opened the door to a room across from the library, leaving her alone with its occupant. Alex was seated behind a desk, going through some papers. When she entered, he rose and quickly strode towards her. He stood close, studying her face with concern.

'How did it go?'

Anna stared at him, her eyes filled with pain and disillusionment, feeling like a blind person suddenly restored to sight, the shock of seeing things as they really were almost too much. 'Not as I expected.'

'Was it very bad?'

She shook her head. 'No, not really. He told me about my father. You knew, didn't you, Alex, what he was like?'

He nodded, looking at her intently, as if to assess the effect of this latest bombshell. To be told you have a grandfather you thought was dead—a titled and extremely wealthy grandfather—had been a shattering experience for her, but to be told your father was a ruthless, self-seeking crook—a thief—could be soul destroying.

'Oh, Alex, it's just too awful.' She turned and moved away from him, filled with a repugnance so powerful she could hardly trust herself to speak, while he stood very still, watching her. She felt as if she had been physically beaten. Her mind couldn't seem to absorb the shock. When she turned she was shaking, her voice trembling, the words spilling from her mouth in a terrible burst of distress. 'Why didn't my mother tell me? Dear God in heaven, why didn't she tell me?'

'Would it have made any difference if she had?'

'Yes. I know it would.'

'How? It would only have made you more miserable than you already were. Besides, I believe your mother was so besotted by your father it made her completely blind to his faults. He may have been bad and dangerous in his own way, but he was everything your mother wanted. He made her happy—if just for a short time. He may not have been right for her, but love is never convenient. He was clearly the love of her life, however disastrous, and she went on loving him until she died. You, more than anyone, must know that.'

She nodded, swallowing hard, averting her gaze. 'Yes, yes, I did. But he can't have been all bad. I won't believe that. I can't. He was my father, after all. And we must not forget that he was killed in France fighting for his country. But...I feel so let down, so disappointed—cheated.'

Alex placed his hands on her shoulders, forcing her to look at him. 'Life is about being let down. One has to learn to deal with it. Your mother was spoiled, Anna, selfish and wilful. Not even Selwyn could tell her what to do. Perhaps a man like your father was just what she needed—though God knows why—and all the upper-class decent young men your grandfather would have had her marry were not.'

Anna was silent. Then, 'I don't know what to do. What should I do, Alex?'

'Oh, my darling girl, I can't tell you what to do. No one can tell anyone that. You have just had one of your most cherished illusions destroyed, and now you must begin to realise that what you have learned has released you from the bonds of loyalty and devotion that binds you to both your parents. By always trying to be what others wanted you to be, and by trying to be worthy of your parents—to make your mother notice you—you were in danger of turning yourself into a starchy, rigidly prim and proper young miss—which is really rather funny,' he said, a smile lighting his eyes, 'because your true nature is anything but rigid and starchy.'

She managed a wobbly smile, warming to his nearness. 'You mean that was how I was when you first met me—and now I'm not?'

'That's about the size of it.' He grinned. 'I could express it more charmingly, but it might go to your head.'

'Oh, Alex. I wish I was as wise as you.'

Mild cynicism marred the handsomeness of Alex's lean features. 'My dear girl, I do assure you that no life has been lived less wisely than mine. As for you, now you can move on. Your life can be what you want it to be—if you will let it. Keep your ghosts in the past. Take stock of what you've got, lose what makes you miserable, and hold on to what makes you happy.

'You are eighteen years old, heiress to a fortune, with a grandfather who desperately wants to get to know you and you are about to fulfil your ambition. You are on the brink of a brilliant career, new experiences, meeting new people. Don't let the past intrude. Will you stay here at Belhaven for the time being?'

'Yes. What else can I do? I am beholden to my grandfather—and grateful. I cannot walk away.' Anna looked at Alex. 'You are leaving?'

'Yes, I must—after I've spoken to Selwyn.'

'When will you come back?'

'Soon.'

'Before I leave to go to Oxford?'

'No, Anna.'

'Then—when shall I see you again? I will see you again, won't I, Alex?' The thought that she might not tore at her heart. She took an involuntary step towards him and Alex, catching a whiff of her scent, stepped back. 'Until I went to France, I didn't know what it was like to feel so happy.' She gave him a slanting look, a question in her dark eyes. 'I have you to thank for that.' She swallowed. 'I—I wish—'

'I know,' Alex said quickly, gently. 'Believe me, Anna, I do know.' With a sigh he placed his hands on her shoulders once more. 'I think there is something I should say to you before I leave and I want you to listen to me very carefully.'

Anna looked at him, holding her breath for what was to come. His face was as still as his body, expressionless, except for his eyes searching hers. She felt those eyes, felt them as a physical force, as a powerful, physical force, probing deep within her.

'I want you to know how much I both like and admire you. I think you are an extremely attractive young woman, mature and very brave—you've had more to contend with in life than most girls and you have coped magnificently. There have been times when I forgot how old you are, and if I have treated you as if you were a great deal older, led you on and given you reason to think there could ever be anything between us, then that was very wrong of me and I am sorry.' He smiled. 'I forget how grown up girls are in this liberated age—how much they know.'

'We did study biology at school. They know a good deal more than you imagine.'

'Thank goodness. Having said all that, I admit I am attracted to you and its been one of the hardest things I've ever done to resist you. But that's where it must end. I don't want you to feel rejected, spurned and humiliated. You are very special to me. I like and respect you too much. You do understand, don't you?'

'Yes, I think so.'

'And I haven't made things worse?'

'No,' she said, feeling better suddenly, no longer stupid and embarrassed about the way she had thrown herself at him in Paris. But it didn't alter the way she still felt about him and made her wish she was a good deal older.

Dropping his arms, Alex looked at her hard, tracing every line of her face, every warm, beating part of her. He breathed in the essence of what lay between them, as if to imprison her image into his memory. His manner suddenly changed, becoming brusque. Going to the desk, he picked up the invoices he had been looking at when she'd entered and began thumbing through. 'I have to see Selwyn on business matters, you understand, which means I have to make frequent visits to Belhaven. It's more than likely we'll bump into each other if I come when you're here on holiday.'

Anna searched his face for some indication that he was sorry they were parting, but his expression was completely unemotional, his tone suggesting such finality that she turned her head away. Haunted by the memory of their kiss, she wanted him to put his arms around her, to offer her the comfort she yearned for, but he was unlikely to do that. Even his companionship was to be denied her in the days ahead. He had fulfilled his obligation and now he was doing his utmost to distance himself from her. It shouldn't hurt so much, but it did.

She was wise enough to accept that this special friendship they shared was all there was ever going to be. That was the moment when she realised the old Anna had been cast off and, newly awake, she had stepped out of childhood.

It remained only for her to extricate herself from this awkward situation as gracefully as possible. Trying to maintain her control, she stepped away from him. She could tell that in his mind he had already left her. Forcing a smile to her lips, she managed to answer, 'I'm sure we will. Thank you for looking after me. You've been very kind—I'm extremely grateful. Goodbye, Alex.'

Alex steeled himself to let her go. He was torn between an impulse not to go after her and prolong their goodbye, and another to offer her some sort of support and comfort. The latter impulse was the stronger, but it was the first that won out.

He held back, assailed by that last night in Paris, and he wondered if he'd ever go to Paris again without remembering the time he'd spent with Anna. He could still hear her musical laughter, see her glowing dark eyes and jaunty, heartrending smile. They had been together just two weeks and she had made more of an impact on him than any other person.

At fifteen years old, when he'd left his native Russia and come to England, apart from his mother and his sister, he had not believed in the inherent goodness of anyone, until he'd met Selwyn—and now Anna. With her he had relaxed his guard and allowed her to come closer than he'd intended. With the exceptions of Anna and Sonya, there wasn't a woman of his acquaintance who wasn't faultless and was capable of feelings that were sincere.

As a result, his attitude to the female sex was highly critical, his opinion low. He had no desire to form a lasting relationship with any woman—not now or in the future. He was unattached and unattainable and would stay that way for the time being. While he had been working hard to achieve his ambition, he could not afford to yield to the pull of love's destructive influence. Love was a whirlpool that sucked you in, drowning you forever, preventing you from the means of achieving your goals. And so with the skill he'd perfected when he was fifteen years old—already restrained, guarded and world-weary—he picked up the invoices from the desk and went to see Selwyn, calmly dismissing Anna completely from his mind.

Chapter Eight

Anna settled into her new life at Belhaven with remarkable ease. She forced herself to listen and learn, to become at the very least efficient and worthy of the Manson blood in her veins in spite of the emptiness in her heart caused by Alex's absence. Every day there was a constant stream of people calling at the house to see her grandfather. Giles took her on a guided tour of the estate, to the tenant farms and tied cottages, formally presenting her to every man, woman and child connected with Belhaven.

It was all so strange to her at first, but she soon began to get a feel of the place and she encountered friendliness everywhere she went. Stainton was a large picturesque village and a bustling hive of activity. Shops lined the narrow main street and the small school, church and green were its focal point.

The kitchen, larders and laundry rooms at Belhaven were a rabbit warren of domesticity, which Mrs Henshaw ran like clockwork. Anna's own rooms were lovely—a sumptuous haven of oriental rugs and heavy silk curtains in cream and pale blue, her mother's favourite colours. But the instant she stepped inside, even after all this time, she noticed the faint, achingly familiar scent of her mother's perfume. The pain of her loss seeped into Anna's very bones, and yet, she felt strangely comforted by the scent being there. Yes, she decided, looking at the rooms, they were beautiful, but she would change them.

As Anna explored her new home she began to relax beneath the unfolding luxury. Trailing her fingers over smooth surfaces of marble, cool alabaster, polished wood and stone, the smell of the house—of wood and damp and the smokiness of log fires—would always remain with her. Something came alive within her—a longing for things of beauty she had kept locked away because the chance of having them was so remote.

Sunlight spilled through the windows into the long gallery on the first floor, which, Giles informed her, had been used for dancing—for Christmas celebrations and hunt balls—in the past.

'What was it like in those days, Giles, before the war, before my mother went away?' Anna asked, trying hard to imagine how it might have been.

'Bursting with life, I'm told. Some of the older servants remember and often reminisce. They were thrilled when they knew you were coming—and I think I must tell you that most of them live in hope that those days will be revived. When you get to Oxford you'll meet plenty of young people to invite for weekends.'

'Won't Grandfather mind?'

'Take it from me, he'll be delighted.'

'Were there always lots of people staying here?'

'It appears so—which is often the case with large country houses. Your mother always invited her friends to stay. There was tennis and fishing and sailing on the lake—all very relaxed, of course. Then there were the weekend house parties that usually followed the London Season, bridge parties, the winter shoots and hunting. Do you play croquet, by the way? Belhaven boasts a splendid croquet lawn.'

'No, I don't, but I fully intend to learn.'

And she meant it. Silently she vowed that whatever it took

she would figure out how to bring Belhaven back to life. She was unprepared for the effect the house was having on her. It was gradually becoming a part of her. Her universe had moved, turned upside down, and all her certainties, her hopes and wishes for the future had changed, become refocused on this place. Belhaven had become a cure for her loneliness, an easing of sadness. It was home—a promise of happiness.

Giles dug an old bicycle out of an outhouse in the stable yard. It was something of a bone-shaker, but by the time Harry—a youth from the village who helped in the gardens— had finished with it, it was perfectly suitable for her to ride. She fully intended taking it with her to Oxford if she could get it into Giles's car or fasten it to the boot, for he had very kindly offered to take her there himself and see her settle in.

One day Anna pushed her grandfather along the paths to the lake, which caused something of a stir among the domestics for he rarely left the house. She sat on the bank beside his chair, tucking her legs beneath her skirts. They sat in companionable silence. How lovely it was. How peaceful. Selwyn gazed over the water, his eyes coming to rest on the little boat fastened to the small jetty.

'I thought I might never see this place again,' he murmured, almost to himself. 'I've looked on the lake as being my own ever since I was a small boy. When I was miserable, if my father had scolded me or something was worrying me, I would come here and take the boat out into the middle of the lake and everything would seem all right. But it's had its dark moments, too—some tragic, best forgotten.'

He paused and Anna waited, puzzled by his remark, hoping he would enlarge on it, but when he folded his hands in his lap and looked down at the lovely young woman who had come to him so late in life and already enhanced it beyond anything he would have believed, a smile replaced his sombre expression.

His gaze moved past the edge of the lake, coming to rest on a heron as it speared a carp, its spindly legs showing above the water's edge. 'How I love this place,' he said with a musing inflection in his voice. 'There was so much laughter here once…it only seems like yesterday. And now there will be again—the pleasures will be yours, although one can hardly imagine they will be the same in today's progressive world. The years when Lavinia was at Belhaven were the happiest of my life, yet I never appreciated them until it was too late. I hope you will be happy here, Anna.'

'I will be,' Anna assured him. She watched as the heron took flight, sending a shower of sparkling water droplets into the air and giving her a moment for thought. Her grandfather was a man given to hiding his emotions—he was embarrassed by them—and not given to sentimental talk. His was the direct way, the way of action, but with her—perhaps because of what had happened between him and her mother—he was trying to be different.

The strange, new, growing relationship between them—to him a gentling in the way he dealt with people—they both welcomed. He watched carefully to see how she was settling into her new home, the tension in his eyes that had been present on her arrival easing, and she often caught him looking at her with what might even be called tenderness.

'I'm glad Giles is showing you around—giving you a proper tour of the place. It's only right that you know how things are done, and what might be expected of you in the future. You might like to honour the tradition of local public service that your position as my granddaughter demands. Not now, but when you finish at Oxford. I suppose you're missing Alex.'

She nodded. 'Yes. I've got used to him being around. When do you suppose he'll come to Belhaven?'

'When he has business to discuss, I expect.'

'He—he left in a hurry.'

'He had pressing matters to take care of.'

'Business matters?'

Selwyn considered her averted profile for a moment, then he nodded. 'And personal.'

'How long have you known Alex, Grandfather?'

'Since he was fifteen years old. After fleeing war-torn Russia, he came to Stainton in search of his mother's family. Her father was the doctor here and he hoped to find relatives.'

'And did he?'

'No, sadly they were all dead.'

'How did Alex's mother come to marry a Russian?'

'She took a position of governess to a Russian family and went to live there, met Alex's father and never came back. When Alex came to see me here at Belhaven, right from the start I was under no illusion as to his ambition. He was only a youth at the time, but he had an energy and spirit of enterprise immediately recognisable to me. He was filled with a burning ambition to learn all he could, to make something of his life. Deprived of my only child, I took him under my wing.

'All my life I never trusted anyone, but I trusted Alex—and he proved himself worthy of it. He worked hard, his ambitions were high, and he was as dedicated as I had been in my youth. Perhaps Alex was more so. To help him realise his ambitions he had a certain charm I had never possessed, and he used it as a means of getting the better of someone in a business transaction.'

'How did he begin?'

'With the stock market—buying quietly, carefully—and buying and selling plots of land all over the place. He was particularly skilful at spotting what he called development potential, waiting until a firm came along wanting to build on a plot, holding out, raising the price and eventually selling. For a man to succeed, he needed strength and the ability to grasp opportunities and to make strategic decisions—Alex had both. His meteoric rise in the world of business was swift, and his reputation is now such that any new deal is assured of success. After the war I saw the world change in many ways—not all for the better—and since the crash in 1929, I realised that perhaps it was time for meteors, for men like Alex. He is my friend, my business partner and advisor—my window to the world, if you like.'

'And like the son you never had,' Anna stated quietly.

'Yes, he is that, too.' He fell silent and Anna thought he wouldn't say any more. But Selwyn had no intention of leaving it at that. 'I was in love with Alex's mother, you know.'

No pronouncement could have stunned Anna more. All she said was, 'Oh. No—I didn't.'

'We fell in love when I was betrothed to Margaret, your grandmother. It was doomed from the start—we both knew it. The differences between us were enormous and there was too much opposition from both families. Alex's mother made the sacrifice and went away—far enough away to make our separation final. When Margaret died three years after Lavinia was born, I tried to reach her—too late. She had married Alex's father and was happy.'

'Did—did my grandmother know?'

'To this day I think she did—knew and must have understood, for she never said a word. Despite my feelings for Alex's mother, I loved Margaret. Ours was a good marriage and I missed her when she died.'

'And Alex? Did he know?'

'Yes. His mother told him. That was his reason for coming to Belhaven—to tell me she was dead.' They were silent for several moments, letting the hawk hovering overhead and the shadows playing across the far side of the lake seal the new covenant between grandfather and granddaughter. Suddenly Selwyn raised his head and sniffed the air like an old warhorse. 'Rain,' he said. 'There will be rain before morning.'

'Yes,' Anna agreed, watching the clouds thickening in the west, 'I think you could be right.'

From the first Anna loved Oxford. Everyone else seemed to take it for granted, but for her it was a dream come true and she felt immensely proud and privileged to be there. It was a place where she laid many of the anxieties of her childhood to rest. She was in a new life with new friends who accepted her without question, and with each month she knew she was becoming less like the Anna she had been.

However, it was like entering a single-sex world where the sight of a woman from Somerville or St Hilda's College in the quad of one of the all-male colleges would frequently cause looks of disapproval. Anna thrived on the intellectual environment. Anna and her new friends belonged to a generation that had its own variety of the rebellious spirit endemic to students the world over, of over-emotional prejudices and violent crusades. Taking part in debates helped her grow in confidence and she discovered a talent for conversation and putting her point forward that surprised her.

Isolated in childhood and pained at being an outsider at Gilchrist, she found a niche for herself at Oxford. For the first time in her life she felt comfortable and accepted and at the end of each term she was content to go home, to spend her vacation at Belhaven.

She ate with her grandfather—they took tea in the drawing room in front of the fire, toasting crumpets and playing backgammon. He taught her to play chess, and when Thomas, his valet, had helped him to bed, she would sit with him and read. She was touched by his genuine pleasure in having her there.

Despite all the frightful things she had accused him of in the past, there was an element that was endearing about his gratitude to her for rescuing him from loneliness. She was surprised by her willingness to talk to him, to ask questions, content to listen as he reminisced about his life and, full of enthusiasm, told her vividly about her ancestors, stories she stored in her memory.

For the first time in her life she had someone she felt close to, someone she could love, someone who loved her for herself.

*   *   *

When Alex arrived at her lodgings in Oxford two days before she was due to leave for the summer vacation to inform her that her grandfather was gravely ill, her concern was deep and genuinely felt.

She was packing some of her books into her case when her landlady, Mrs Hicks, knocked on the door to tell her she had a visitor—a gentleman by the name of Mr Kent. Mrs Hicks was a motherly sort who welcomed Anna's student friends, providing them with sandwiches and cups of tea, but she laid down plenty of house rules, one of them being no gentlemen in the rooms.

Anna was taken completely unawares. She went down immediately and stared at Alex in disbelief. She felt absolutely bewildered, every emotion, every thought, lost to her. All she could think about for the moment was being with him again, and how happy that made her. He was darkly bronzed from the sun, and in contrast his silver-grey eyes seemed to shine like bright jewels. Just when she had thought she might get over him, that he no longer affected her, he appeared, and all her carefully tended illusions were cruelly shattered. The violence of her feelings for him continued to shake and shock her.

'Alex!' she exclaimed, giving him one of her unforgettable smiles. 'What brings you to Oxford?' He took her hand and kissed her cheek. She felt it, not just on her flesh, but treacherously in other places, secret places inside her, stirring into life.

Being with her again made Alex realise just how much he'd missed her, how much he wanted her. 'I'm sorry, Anna, but I've come to take you to Belhaven. Selwyn has taken a turn for the worse.'

She stared at him, ashen faced. 'Is he very ill?'

'Pneumonia.'

'Goodness! I knew he had a chest infection, but I had no idea it was so severe.'

'It worsened. I thought you'd like to be there.'

'Yes, of course—thank you. I was due home anyway the

day after tomorrow—Giles was to fetch me. Poor Grandfather. I fear he's a poor subject for so serious an illness. How is Thomas coping?'

'Giles has engaged a nurse to help him.'

'He's that bad? Sorry, Alex, of course he is, otherwise you wouldn't be here.'

'His prognosis isn't good, but Selwyn is a fighter. He won't give in easily.'

'Just give me a little time to pack my things.'

Her anxiety over her grandfather and the shy self-consciousness that Anna didn't seem to be able to overcome as she sat beside Alex as they left Oxford, her bicycle strapped securely to the boot, Alex eased by asking, 'Well?'

'Well what?'

'Don't keep me in suspense. How are you enjoying Oxford?'

'Very much. It's hard work, but I'm enjoying it tremendously.'

'And your studies? What great literary works are you reading?'

'A whole range—from the classics to James Joyce, Galsworthy and a host of others and, for my own interest, the novels of Virgina Woolf. P. G. Wodehouse is also one my favourite authors.'

'And mine. What matters is his style. He's a master of exquisite prose. I'm also a fan of D. H. Lawrence.'

'Me, too—I particularly enjoyed *Sons and Lovers*. However, I must confess that I'm looking forward to the holidays and giving my eyes a rest.'

'Enjoy a bit of well-earned leisure.'

'Something like that. I promised Tamsin I'd go and stay with her in London for part of the Season, but unfortunately she's contracted glandular fever and has missed her presentation at court. Do you know if the Ormsbys are at Applemead?' Applemead was the Ormsbys' country residence. It was just two miles from Belhaven and of great architectural merit, but not as fine or as old as Belhaven.

'For now. Irene considers the country air will be more beneficial to Tamsin than London.'

'I'll ride over and see her when I can. She's devastated that she's had to put off her presentation until next year.'

It took them over an hour to reach Belhaven. It was dark when they arrived. Giles came out of the house as they got out of the car.

'How is Grandfather, Giles?' Anna was quick to enquire.

'He's not had a good day, but if his strength keeps up he may take a turn for the good.' His smile was reassuring. 'Your being here will help. He's been asking for you.'

'I'll go straight up.'

The room was dark and sombre and smelled like a sickroom. The light in the room suddenly became brighter when the nurse turned on a lamp and left. Her grandfather was propped against the pillows with his eyes closed. He looked dreadfully ill. His frame looked shrunken, his features gaunt, and his breath did no more than flutter in his throat. Sensing her presence, he opened his eyes slightly as she approached the bed. He smiled, but it was a weak smile, expressing pain and weariness. Anna bent over and gently kissed his brow.

'Don't try to speak, Grandfather,' she whispered softly. 'I just wanted you to know that I am here.'

At first she thought he wasn't going to be able to speak, but then in the merest whisper he said, 'Dearest Anna. I'm very tired—so glad you came. Alex…'

'Alex fetched me from Oxford. I had no idea you were so ill. I would have come sooner had I known. Don't try and talk,' she said, knowing that doing so would consume what little strength he had. 'Now I'm here you're going to get better. You'll soon be well, I promise.'

In that moment the past was forgotten, the future would be irrelevant without this last remaining member of her family she had come to care for a great deal. She wanted so much for him to get better. Clasping his hand, she sat with him until he slept. She then quietly left the room and went down stairs, finding Giles alone in the drawing room.

'He's very poorly, isn't he?' she said, sitting down and taking the much-needed cup of tea Giles handed her. 'When is Dr Collins expected again, Giles?'

'Tomorrow morning, unless we have need of him before that. Is there anything I can get you?' She shook her head, drinking her tea. 'Then if you'll excuse me. I have one or two telephone calls to make before I turn in. Lady Ormsby called earlier. I promised I'd let her know when you arrived. Alex is out on the terrace.'

Setting the cup and saucer on the table, Anna went on to the terrace in search of Alex. It was a warm, balmy evening, the moon a huge yellow orb in the sky. In the soft glow of the lights attached to the house she found him standing with his shoulder propped casually against a wooden post, his arms crossed over his chest. He was looking out over the garden. She paused for a moment to observe him. With his dark hair ruffling in the gentle breeze, his sternly handsome face stamped with power and pride, he looked as invulnerable as the steppes in his native Russia.

Sensing her presence, he turned his head and looked at her. A lazy smile curved his lips. With his hair dipping casually over his brow and a cream shirt that was open at the throat and tucked into brown-coloured trousers, he looked incredibly handsome. Trying to ignore the treacherous leap her heart gave at the sight of that enthralling, intimate smile, Anna moved slowly towards him.

'How did you find Selwyn?' he enquired softly.

'Very poorly.'

Alex searched her eyes for what she was feeling. Her face was sombre in thought. 'And how do you feel?'

'Better for having seen him.' She swallowed hard, but her voice was husky. 'I've known him for such a short time. I simply cannot believe he might disappear. He's become the centre of my world. Every day since he came into my life it's seemed such a new and wonderful place to be. I gave him my love, my trust. He was proud to have them—he gave me the same. I can't bear to think he might die.'

'There is a chance he might pull through, Anna. He won't give in without a fight—especially now he has you.'

'I do so hope you're right.' She gazed up at Alex, her eyes warm with gratitude. 'You're really very sweet, Alex.'

He grimaced comically. 'Are you trying to ruin my carefully constructed tough-guy image? Generally I'm described as being hard, calculating and ruthless.'

'That's to the people you deal with in your business world—although in my opinion it's a gross injustice. How could they think that?'

'Because it's absolutely true,' he stated with calm finality.

'Well, I won't believe it. No man could be like that and feel what you feel for my grandfather.' She saw pain slash its way across Alex's tanned features, and in that moment Anna knew he loved her grandfather with the everlasting devotion a son would feel for a beloved father. 'This can't be easy for you either, Alex. I know how special Grandfather is to you.'

'He is.'

'I'm sorry,' she whispered, feeling a lump of constricting sorrow in her chest, and all the sympathy and warmth in her heart was mirrored in her eyes.

Alex hesitated, and for a moment Anna thought he wasn't going to say more. When he did, his voice was strangely hesitant, almost as if he was testing his ability to speak his feelings aloud. He looked up at the stars twinkling in the black velvety sky and said, 'To me Selwyn has always seemed eternal. From the day we met we have moved through the years together, the two of us, like a couple of soldiers supporting, protecting and defending the other. I can't imagine a world without him in it. He gave me my life. Everything I am is because of him. I could never thank him enough for what he has done for me, never make him understand what it means to me.'

'I think he knows. You are just as special to him as he is to you. Will you stay?'

'I won't leave while Selwyn is so ill.'

Alex looked down at her. Her hair blew against her cheek, driven by a puff of warm wind. She lifted her face and smiled at him. For Alex it was as if a shutter had been flung open and the sunlight had rushed in. Her smile was compounded of a luminous gentleness in her dark eyes.

Tenderness washed through him, and he wanted to pull her into his arms, but instead he said, 'You're pale, Anna. You look tired. I think you should go to bed and get some sleep. I'll tell Mrs Henshaw to bring you something to eat and some cocoa—unless you'd like to stay and join me in a brandy.'

'I don't like brandy. Don't you remember?' she said, reminding him of the times she had refused it in France.

'Of course I do. How could I forget?' he said softly.

Beneath his impassive gaze Anna was unable to look away. Her fine-boned face, framed by a halo of black hair stirring in the flower-scented breeze, was a dainty image of fragility as she stood before a man who dwarfed her. Memories of France were prominent in both their minds, memories of shared happy moments, when they had revelled in each other's company, when they had laughed together. Memories that now separated them.

They were both a little older now and wiser, and convinced they were strong enough to withstand and ignore the feelings, the warmth, building between them, pulling them under a strange spell that seemed to enclose them on the terrace.

The silence was inhabited by the living presence of the insects attracted by the light. Alex contemplated her for a moment and Anna stood, riveted by his sparkling gaze filled with a penetrating intensity.

'You really are very lovely, Anna.'

Drawn by the softness of her lips slightly parted to reveal

moist, shining teeth, he moved closer. But Anna, recalling
their parting at Belhaven ten months ago, and the things he
had said to her on that last night in Paris, stepped back.

'I think I'll settle for the cocoa. I'll look in on Grandfather
first. Goodnight, Alex.'

Alex watched her walk away, flaying his thoughts into obedience. He remained on the terrace and stared into the dark
shadows ahead of him. He had known and made love to many
beautiful women, but he had never wanted any of them as he
wanted Anna. What was it about her that he found so appealing? Her innocence? Her sincerity? Her smile that set his
heart pounding like that of an inexperienced youth in the first
throes of love? He frowned. No, not love. Love was for others, not for him. And yet Anna affected him deeply.

He closed his eyes to shut out her image, but he could still
smell her perfume in the air. He told himself that what he felt
was the ache of frustrated desire, but he could not deny that
whenever he thought of her his mind was beginning to dwell
more and more often on love.

The day following Anna's arrival Selwyn began to show
slight improvement, and to everyone's relief over the days
that followed the improvement continued. The strength of will
and the dominating power of life shone in his eyes once more,
filling the room with his presence.

Unable to leave until he was satisfied that Selwyn really
was well on the way to recovery, Alex worked from Belhaven. Anna saw little of him during the day, but after dinner,
which they took in the dining room with Giles, they would
stretch their intellectual curiosity by discussing the politics of
the day and other interesting matters. Anna already knew Alex
had an immense knowledge of many subjects. His love of
music was great, and it was when they listened to it together—either a classical concert on the wireless or something
selected from her grandfather's huge collection of gramo-

phone records—that she came to a greater understanding and therefore appreciation of it.

Often they would settle down in Selwyn's room to play cards or backgammon, when Anna would try to outmanoeuvre him—more often than not without success. It irritated her that Alex clearly had the most superior brain when put to the test, until he suggested chess.

'Do you play?'

'Grandfather taught me.'

'Did he now? But are you good enough?'

'There's only one way to find out. I don't play very well, but I am learning,' she said innocently, taking her seat on the sofa and tucking her feet beneath her.

Alex glanced at the bed. Selwyn gave him a smile and a wink. 'Learning well enough to make Selwyn rue the day he taught you.'

'Nevertheless, you have the advantage. You've been playing longer than I have.'

'True,' Alex admitted, smiling impenitently, 'but I promise not to take advantage of my vast experience.' Fetching the heavy chessboard and placing it on the low table between them, he quickly set up the pieces and cast her a challenging smile. 'Prepare to be trounced, Miss Preston,' he said, one dark brow arrogantly raised. 'Soundly.'

Beneath carefully lowered lids Anna slanted him a long considering look. 'Don't underestimate my ability, Mr Kent. I am a quick learner—I've had a good teacher.' She threw her grandfather a rather smug look of gratitude.

Alex laughed good humouredly, moving his first piece into position. 'Perhaps we should abandon the chess. Would you prefer pistols at twenty paces instead?' he teased as she made her move.

Anna smiled warmly into his silver eyes. 'No, but you might—after the game,' she replied with a jaunty impertinence that made him laugh out loud. 'Your move.'

After much thought each made their moves skilfully, confident they could outsmart the other, careful not to underestimate the other's ability. Initially the game moved at a fast pace, but as it progressed it slowed considerably.

Engrossed in the game, abandoning her chair and sitting on the carpet, leaning forward so that her hair fell forward and shadowed her face, Anna removed two of Alex's pawns and a rook before he finally managed to concentrate on the game. It soon became evident that she was no novice and Selwyn had taught her well, for she was proving to be a skilled opponent. When Alex inadvertently touched his bishop and quickly realising his mistake removed his hand, she reared up at him like an indignant cobra, the colour heightened on her cheeks.

'Alex, you have to move it now. It's the rule, you should know that. Once you've touched a piece you have to move it. You cannot change your mind.'

He flicked her a lazy grin. 'If you say so.' Obediently, he did as bidden and reluctantly moved the offending bishop, only to have it jumped on by her queen.

'Serves you right,' Anna crowed triumphantly. 'You should concentrate harder. It could cost you the game.'

Alex gave her a wicked grin. 'The game is far from over, young lady. I have your knight.'

'And I have one of your bishops and a rook—not counting your pawns,' she countered.

'And you talk too much. Are you trying to put me off my game?'

'Certainly not. I believe in fair play.'

Absorbed in their game, they failed to notice Selwyn's expression of absolute delight as he looked on from his bed. With a well-satisfied smile he watched Alex. He couldn't remember when he'd seen him look so relaxed. Alex's eyes were fastened on his young opponent, and from the way he was looking at her Selwyn strongly suspected his interest was not in the game. It warmed him to see the two people closest to his heart together at last, and if it would keep Alex at

Belhaven a little longer then maybe it was in his own best interests not to improve too quickly.

While she waited for her opponent to make his move, Anna sat with her elbows on the table, her chin cupped in her hands as she seriously contemplated her next move.

It was unfortunate for his game that Alex was unable to do the same, for while Anna thought out her next move, with her dark lashes curving against her cheek and nibbling on her bottom lip—a characteristic gesture that made his blood run warm—she presented to him a captivating picture of bewitching innocence. He became preoccupied with how adorable she looked in that particular pose, and without warning he felt desire pulsating to life within him—unexpected and undeniable. Sitting back and crossing one leg over the other, he was in no hurry for the game to end—in fact, he had no objections to it taking all night if need be—until she plucked his queen from the board.

Summoning every ounce of his self-control, with an effort Alex dragged his eyes away from the captivating figure she presented and shifted his thoughts to his predicament, for somewhere in the back of his mind he knew that if he didn't buck his ideas up this adorable creature would beat him.

And she did. Anna took her king round the back of his pawns and captured them one by one, his black king too far away to prevent it. Finally, covering his king with her white queen she pronounced, 'Check.'

Her game had been executed with such flawless technique that Alex couldn't believe she had trounced him. Eyeing her in frank admiration, he grinned and knocked down his king in surrender. 'Mate.'

Chapter Nine

The days that followed passed in something of a haze for Anna. Like the time they had spent together in France they were golden days, days to treasure and be remembered. Alex didn't work quite so hard and found time for the odd game of tennis and long energetic walks through the countryside— although Anna couldn't understand why he always avoided the lake. When she suggested they might take the boat out and do a spot of fishing his manner became abrupt, and he informed her coldly that he didn't like fishing. Having no wish to spoil the idyll, she didn't mention it again.

One afternoon they drove over to Applemead to visit the Ormsbys. Tamsin was still quite poorly, but she was over the worst.

It was when they were leaving and Anna was saying good-bye to Tamsin that she happened to overhear part of the conversation between Alex and Lady Ormsby.

'I'm so happy to see you and Anna are getting on so well, Alex. It must have been a great comfort to her having you at Belhaven while Selwyn was so ill.' A twinkle entered her eyes. 'I will even go so far as to say you look very handsome together—ideally suited, in my opinion.'

Alex betrayed no sign of emotion, but that was the moment he decided it was time to return to London.

He was quiet on the drive back to Belhaven. When they were passing the village and several pedestrians gave them friendly waves, to restart the conversation Anna said with a lame attempt at humour, 'The people of Stainton really like you, don't they, Alex? But according to Mrs Henshaw they find you something of a puzzle. Mr Kent's a dark horse, they say. In London one minute, flying off to Europe the next, back to Belhaven and up to London again.'

'True, my life does seem to be like that. Speaking of which, it's back to London tomorrow. Selwyn's much improved. There's no reason for me to stay.'

Anna's happiness evaporated before harsh reality. She looked away, suddenly feeling so desperately hurt. Alex said there was no reason for him to stay. Had the days they had been together meant nothing to him? The thought that it might took away the pleasure she had had in seeing him again. With a feeling bordering on despair, she knew he was trying to rid himself of her. Just like before he was afraid she was getting too close.

'Is there something wrong, Alex?'

At her gentle use of his name the muscles of his face tightened. 'Wrong? Not that I know of.'

'When we were leaving, I happened to overhear what Lady Ormsby said to you. Is that why you're going?' It was a humiliating thing to have to ask him, but she had to know. He turned and looked at her. Her eyes saw the changing expression on his face—a look that seemed to warn her and to shut her out. The old dread that he was returning to London to another woman stole up on her. In an instant she felt cold, lost and alone.

'No, you mustn't think that. I have a company to run and I'm scheduled for several meetings—in fact, I have a very important board meeting tomorrow afternoon. I must get back. I've been away too long as it is.'

'It's all right, you don't have to explain. I understand perfectly.'

'I'm only sorry Selwyn's illness was the reason for our meeting again, and not a happier one, but that said, these have been pleasant days, have they not?'

'Yes, I've enjoyed our outings, but I've taken up a lot of your time.'

'The time was well spent, Anna. It was how I wished it to be. You know that, don't you?'

She nodded. 'I'll miss you—and I know Grandfather will.'

'I'll soon be back. I'm in daily contact with either Giles or Selwyn—and as for you, you'll quickly find some other diversion.'

'You were never a diversion, Alex,' Anna was quick to point out. 'But you are right. I have a lot of work to catch up on. I—assume you'll be staying for dinner?'

He nodded. 'I'll leave in the morning.'

The following morning Anna followed him out to his car. Everything seemed to be happening in a dream. Alex was wearing a dark suit. His raven hair was immaculately brushed. His tanned face was drawn, his mouth held in a tight line, and his eyes were expressionless. Neither of them spoke as he opened the boot and placed his bags inside. She wanted to beg him not to go, but she couldn't. Pride and self-respect were all she had left. He came to her and embraced her briefly. She closed her eyes.

When he released her she stood back and looked up at him, forcing a smile to her lips. The sun slanting through the boughs fell on his dark head. 'Have a good journey, Alex.' Her voice was surprisingly calm.

'Goodbye, Anna.'

He climbed into his car and she watched him drive away. It seemed her heart would break. But it didn't. She got through that day—keeping busy, purposely exhausting herself, refusing to give in to her anguish—and she got through the next day and the week and the week after that, and then she went back to Oxford. Determination saw her through.

Anna was in her second year at Oxford when she became reacquainted with Freddy Campbell. She was lying on the grass by the Cherwell, totally engrossed in *Carry on Jeeves* by P. G. Wodehouse. Olivia Pilkington—a young woman who was at the same college and shared her lodgings—lay beside her studying an essay she was writing, when she made Anna aware of a man seated on a bench close by. He had been there for quite some time. At first he had been reading a newspaper, but now it was folded on his lap and he was looking in their direction, watching Anna.

'Don't look now, Anna, but there's a chap over there giving you the eye.'

Unable to resist, Anna lifted her head and looked straight at him. He was good looking in a sleepy kind of way, and vaguely familiar. Meeting her gaze and smiling quizzically, he rose. Tucking his newspaper under his arm, he sauntered towards her. Then she recognised him, even though it was nearly two years since they had last met. Standing up, she had a feeling that the meeting was not accidental.

'I would have known you anywhere,' Freddy said smoothly, his tone light, caressing and lingering. 'I'm delighted to meet you again, Anna. You left Monte Carlo in rather a hurry. There was no time to say goodbye.'

'I'm flattered that you should remember me after all this time—almost two years, in fact.' She smiled. 'You see I remember you, too. I did leave in rather a hurry. I had to get back to England—quite a lot to do before starting at Oxford. I'm surprised to see you here.'

'I have friends in Oxford. My home is near Reading. It's conveniently in reach of Oxford, and London—where I have a flat. It behoves a man to be stationed in two places—one close to my family and the other where I work and play. Might I perhaps take you for tea tomorrow to show there are no hard feelings over our last encounter? I enjoyed our chat, by the way.'

Recalling that encounter and their chat—as well as Alex's savage reaction to it—Anna found herself acutely embarrassed to be reminded of it, but strangely she was not offended. Because of Alex's dislike of Freddy she was reluctant to accept his invitation, but, unable to come up with an excuse, she said that tea would be nice.

They met the following afternoon and after taking tea they strolled along the banks of the river. Freddy told her of his fondness for Oxford and, confirming what Alex had told her about him being an enthusiastic follower of the British Union of Fascists party, without preamble he extolled the policies of Oswald Mosley—who, it appeared, was a close friend of his.

Freddy's tone was polite, in no way arrogant or provocative as it had been on their previous encounter. He had a natural refined elegance, which true-blooded aristocrats displayed in the way they walked and talked—a blend of generations of breeding and environment. He was classically handsome, yet there was an earnest, boyish quality in him that was so appealing, so direct and charming, that Anna could not dislike him—she wanted to because Alex did, but it didn't work that way.

When they parted Anna thought she wouldn't see him again, but a week later he telephoned her. He had arranged to have dinner with half a dozen friends and thought she might like to come along. With nothing better to do and term almost at an end, she accepted.

At first she was apprehensive, but it turned out to be a relaxed evening at a homely restaurant with a Bohemian ambience. The food, accompanied by fine wine, was delicious. The conversation was daring, witty and immensely stimulating, its content—from D. H. Lawrence to International Pacifism—interesting, and far removed from Anna's orbit. They laughed a lot, their banter was sensuous, they recounted provocative, funny jokes, which would have offended Anna before she had come to Oxford. And yet they exemplified another side of society.

Freddy's friends, both men and women, had a liberal attitude to life and were committed fascists. Knowing very little of the BUF party and years younger than those present, Anna was content to listen, perversely fascinated, as they smoked their strange-smelling Turkish cigarettes. She was used to listening to scholars expounding their theories on political matters, but this was different. She was intrigued by the party's political creed and promise of something new and dangerous—and sinister.

When her attention began to wander she caught Freddy's ever-watchful eye. He smiled and she returned it. On the one hand Freddy epitomised everything she disapproved of. He was extremely popular with the opposite sex, terribly lazy, philistine and hedonistic and very right wing. On the other hand he was charming, attentive and fun to be with. She recalled Alex telling her that Freddy was wicked, devious and controlling. At the time she had wondered what he had meant by that—he had not enlarged upon it—but at this present time Freddy seemed none of those things.

When he was driving her back to her lodgings in his rather splendid Alfa Romeo, he said, 'I hope you enjoyed yourself tonight.'

'Yes, I did. What interesting friends you have, Freddy.'

'I'm glad you liked them.'

'Do you still see Nancy?'

'Not any more. We parted last summer.'

'Oh, I'm so sorry. I shouldn't have asked.'

'Why on earth shouldn't you? I'm glad you feel comfortable enough to do so. Nancy and I simply decided we weren't right for each other and decided to go our separate ways. We were deeply infatuated with one another when we met, but we both began to grow restless. And so the adventures began, first me and then Nancy—we were both broadminded and accepting. It's the way of the world. We weren't compatible. You must nave noticed.'

'No, I can't say that I did. You went to Oxford, didn't you, Freddy?'

He nodded. 'I remember my father telling me that those three years would be the best time of my life.'

'And were they?'

'Absolutely,' he said, grinning, 'but I must confess that there wasn't much work done. I—and my clique—wasted both time and money with glorious and reckless abandon. In those days we belonged to the notorious Hypocrites' Club—so named from the Greek "water is best". Drinking was a social activity—and there is nothing like the aesthetic pleasure of being drunk.'

Anna looked out of the window, fixing her gaze on the beautiful fourteenth-century spire of the university church of St Mary the Virgin. She was disappointed with Freddy's reply. When she had first come to Oxford she had been prepared to take in everything, but she felt uncomfortable with this side of things. The Hypocrites' Club had soon come to her attention, notorious for its drunkenness and flamboyance—she found it distasteful. Being the son of an earl, no doubt Freddy's undergraduate life had been that of a rich and glamorous elite with high incomes, the kind she encountered in all the male colleges, the kind she was beginning to despise. They were greatly influenced by wild and extravagant behaviour, hard drinking and were sought after for their cars and the wild parties they gave.

Sensing what she was thinking, Freddy glanced at her and laughed lightly. 'I see you don't approve. I can't say that I blame you, but at least I wasn't sent down and I did come out with a first—which pleased my parents.' A silence fell between them and after a few moments he took her off guard by saying, 'Do you still see Alex Kent?'

Anna's heart missed a beat. His question, coming out of the blue, was an unwelcome intrusion that brought her pain. 'Not since last summer. Alex and my grandfather are good friends and have business connections. He is often at Belhaven, but I haven't seen him in months. How well do you know him?'

'We were at Oxford at the same time—although we didn't have much to do with each other. Not much in common. You're on vacation next week, aren't you?' he said, quickly changing the subject.

'Yes,' Anna replied, glad that he had.

'I've invited some of the people you met tonight to Bishop Storton—that's the family pile, by the way—the weekend after next. Why don't you come along? I know my parents would love to meet you—and so would Edwina.'

Anna thought it odd that he never mentioned Edwina, or that Edwina and Alex had had an affair. He had told her he had a twin sister, but that was all, until now, and Anna was in no hurry to reacquaint herself with that particular woman ever again.

'Thank you, Freddy. It's terribly nice of you to invite me, but I can't. I have to pay a brief visit to Belhaven to see my grandfather. I've promised to spend a few days with him before I go to London. Lady Ormsby has invited me to stay with them—Tamsin's Season and all that.'

'That was last year, wasn't it?'

'I'm afraid not. Poor Tamsin contracted glandular fever so it had to be postponed. No doubt Lady Ormsby will plan it with enormous care and impeccable attention to detail—no extravagance spared. I promised Tamsin I'd be there for some of it. I don't want to let her down.' And, Anna thought, staring dreamily out of the window, she hoped she might see Alex. Would he be in London? Dear God, let it be so.

She thought of him constantly and devoured every newspaper and magazine article about him. She had seen a picture of him in the *Tatler* with his hand on the elbow of a young woman in a fur coat, dark haired like herself and extremely pretty. It didn't say who she was and Anna had wondered if it was Sonya. Did he still see her? Did he still love her?

'I shall make a point of calling on you in London,' Freddy said, breaking into her reverie. 'I'll take you to Ascot and I'd like you to see me race at Brooklands. It makes for an exciting day out. You might also like to come to a BUF rally—see what it's all about. You might find it interesting.'

'I don't know. I'm really not that right wing. I'll have to think about it.'

'I hope you do. We're always on the lookout for new recruits. Tell you what, we'll try and arrange dinner again before you leave Oxford. How does that sound?'

'I'd like that.'

'Good. I'll call you.'

They had reached Anna's lodgings. Freddy stopped the car and got out. Walking round to her side, he opened the door. They said goodnight. He made no move to touch her, and as Anna went inside she couldn't help thinking that it was all very civilised.

As she climbed the stairs to her room she thought of Alex and how hopeless it was for her to continue to think of him. The fact that he went to great pains to avoid her hurt her deeply, but she took solace in knowing he never failed to ask Selwyn about her when he went to Belhaven, and took a keen interest in her progress at Oxford. Perhaps if she were to meet someone else she would forget him. Was this how a woman healed her heart, by forcing out the image, the spirit of the man she loved, and filling the void with another that was less illusion and more real?

Anna had never known sexual pleasure. She knew of it, she had read of it, and she had wanted to experience it herself— with Alex. He had ruffled her feathers, made her aware of her dormant desires.

Freddy didn't make her feel that way. He was glamorous, a spellbinder, an enchanter, with that special charm that rendered his imperfections endearing, but she was in no danger of falling for him. There was something about him that wasn't quite right—something illicit, something not quite proper.

Anna was always learning something new, discovering a flair for doing things. It began with lessons on buying clothes from Lady Ormsby when she went to stay with them at their London house—an immensely grand residence in Curzon Street.

On visits to only the best couturiers Anna was told she had excellent bones, that clothes looked good on her. Vivid colours went with her hair, brought a glow to her skin. Soon, without realising it, she was holding her head higher, standing straighter, and she began to see hints of the kind of confidence and sophistication that seemed so natural in Lady Ormsby. She knew her features were attractive—she knew it from the affirmation in the stares she received wherever she went.

The summer of 1934 was hot, and the days Anna spent in London slipped past—golden, idyllic days. Tamsin had been presented at Court in May. This was followed by a few weeks of hectic social life: balls almost every night all over London, luncheons and parties, with country-house weekends, Ascot and Henley still to come. So far Tamsin had been a great success. Her photograph appeared constantly in all the society papers and magazines.

Tonight was to be the high spot of her Season—her own ball. Lady Ormsby considered the Season to be an essential part of Tamsin's life—an essential requirement whatever the cost—and she was determined that her ball, which would be preceded by a small dinner party, would be a truly splendid affair.

Anna chose to wear a gown made by Molyneux. It was fashioned in oyster pink with a halter neckline, and in her gleaming dark hair she wore a matching rose. As she made her way downstairs with Tamsin, she had to listen as Tamsin told her for the hundredth time about her presentation at Court and what she had worn. Following rigid rules laid down by the Lord Chamberlain's Office, all débutantes to be presented had to wear white Court dress and train and a headdress of three small white feathers—the Prince of Wales Plume.

'I spent hours practising my curtsy, Anna. You would have died laughing. Afraid I might get my feet tangled in my train, Mummy made me practise with a tablecloth for weeks before. And you cannot imagine the jockeying for position to be the first in the queue in the Mall and all the débutantes waiting in the anteroom to be summoned into the presence chamber.'

Anna's smile was one of patient interest, but her thoughts moved along a different, more cynical path. She could imagine perfectly what it had been like. The scene would have been reminiscent of a cattle market.

The house was glittering with lights. All the rooms had been thrown open to give a perspective that dazzled the eyes. In a short time these rooms would be filled with guests from all strata of society, but before that the family and a few chosen friends would enjoy cocktails and a private dinner.

Anna was still smiling when she reached the bottom of the stairs. Drinks were being served in the drawing room, but she had scarcely taken four steps when her eyes were arrested by the figure of a man. Impeccably groomed, faultlessly arrayed in white tie and tails, tall and dark and athletically built, he was standing a short distance away, watching her. She stopped as abruptly as if she had walked into a sheet of glass and stared at him; the silence held for what seemed like an eternity as all the memories she had tried so sensibly to forget overwhelmed her.

Alex had watched Anna literally float down the stairs and his heart soared at the sight of her. All the beauty in the world was embodied in that single female form. Her dark hair fell in a sweeping pageboy to her collarbone and her face was like a jewel above the soft, tubular gown that sheathed her body like a second skin.

Mesmerised, he stood there, watching her incredible smile,

and the shattering tenderness he felt made him ache. She looked stunning, adorable, although a little thinner than he remembered. Her eyes and cheekbones were more prominent now than before, her skin iridescent perfection, the colour of mother-of-pearl. Dear Lord, how he had missed her, and he swallowed over the knot of guilt in his throat when he remembered how hard he had tried to dismiss her from his life.

Débutante balls were not on his social calendar and he'd had no intention of making more than a brief appearance at dinner, but now, intrigued as always by Anna, and with his heart beginning to hammer in deep, aching beats, he was loath to leave.

Deprived of him for so long, all Anna could do was gaze at the sternly handsome face that had haunted her dreams for almost twelve months. Nothing had changed. Her feelings where Alex Kent were concerned were the same—although perhaps that was not quite true. Now they were deeper, more profound. She met his eyes, his warm, smiling eyes, and then her enchanting face was aglow with surprise, and Alex's spirits soared madly, simply because she was pleased to see him.

Moving towards her, he took her hand and, leaning forward brushed her cheek with his lips. 'Hello, Anna,' he said, his accented voice deep and resonant.

The touch of his lips against Anna's flesh stirred her blood.

'You look exquisite,' he said.

She gazed at him with a tentative half-smile, something subtle, full of promise and intimacy. 'I'm so glad you think so.'

'By the end of the night you will have every young man present at your feet.'

She laughed, her laughter a pure cascade of sound. 'I sincerely hope not. It would be most improper—and disappointing, to say the least, for all the débutantes.'

'And which dance shall you save for me?' he asked, indicating the card she carried.

'The first,' she answered without hesitation, wanting to add 'and all the rest'. 'But—this is a surprise. I had no idea you were coming.'

'To be honest, I didn't know if I would make it. I've been in France and didn't get back until this afternoon. Have you been to Belhaven recently?'

'Yes, before coming to London.'

'I haven't seen Selwyn for several weeks. How is he?'

'Quite well. He's getting used to having me around for the holidays and the occasional weekend. I've promised to spend some time with him before term starts.'

Alex nodded slightly, his gaze deep and probing. 'I'm glad you're getting on. He always speaks very highly of you. No regrets about accepting your inheritance?'

'No. In fact, I wonder now why I made such a fuss.'

He grinned. 'So do I.' Taking her arm, he guided her towards the room where cocktails were being served.

As if in a trance Anna sipped her cocktail and allowed Alex to lead her into dinner. Everyone was taking their places at a long table laid out with crystal, silver, monogrammed linen napkins standing to attention on china plates, and a centre-piece of magnificent orchids. Anna was placed across from Alex, and even though they didn't speak he was a palpable presence. When the wine had been poured, he raised his glass to her and mouthed, 'to you'. Anna gazed back at him, her eyes aglow, and then smiled faintly and raised her glass to her lips, feeling in complete harmony with the world.

Afterwards, when guests began to arrive and the orchestra began to play, Alex escorted her into the brightly lit ballroom. The floor was already filling up with awkward, shuffling young couples.

Alex met Anna's gaze, tipped his head towards the musicians and said with teasing formality, 'May I have this dance?'

She nodded, her enchanting smile aglow. 'It would be a

pleasure.' It was a waltz, slow, dangerous, unsafe, but she didn't care. She felt euphoric and radiantly alive.

The eagerness of her reply and the soft look in her eyes were almost Alex's undoing. Mesmerised by the feelings unfolding inside him, his gaze locked to hers, he slid his arm around her narrow waist, drawing her close against him, while the strains of the music wove its spell around them. Alex was physically shaken and unable to believe the desire that pounded through him when he felt her body coming into intimate contact with his own as she matched his step with effortless grace. All the other couples seemed to vanish in a haze as he looked at her. He wanted to crush her in his arms and drown in her sweetness.

Anna found that dancing with Alex was a strangely sensual experience. Beneath the chandeliers they danced the first dance, and then the second—each one lasting about twenty minutes to enable the débutantes to get to know their partners—and by the third it was a scandal. Blissfully unaware that they'd become the object of every eye in the room, Anna danced with no one but Alex. By the fourth waltz everyone was staring at them and pointing them out, society photographers vying excitedly with each other for the best pictures for their magazines.

Anna tilted her head back a little and looked up at her handsome partner. Being in Alex's arms was like stepping back into a mad, fantastic dream. She watched as his gaze dropped to her lips, and in a state of anticipation that had mounted to dizzying heights throughout the evening, she could think of nothing she wanted more than for him to kiss her. Perfectly aware how unseemly it would be for him to do so with mothers and chaperons looking on—and that he might not want to anyway—she covered her disappointment with her brightest smile.

'The impropriety of dancing more than two dances with the same partner has been noted, Alex. Perhaps we should sit the next one out.'

His lips curved in a lazy smile. 'There is no impropriety. You are not a débutante, remember.'

'Yes, I do, and I'm glad—although, despite my misgivings, the débutantes do have a wonderful time.'

'You're happy?'

'At Oxford? Yes, I am.'

'That wasn't what I meant.'

'Oh.' He knew her too well. 'Oxford apart, I am happy, Alex. I'm happier than I've ever been.'

'It shows. You look exquisite—radiant. In fact, I'm the envy of every man in the place.'

Anna smiled, for his compliment was contrived to sound both casual and wholly sincere.

'Why are you smiling?'

'No one has ever said that kind of thing to me before.'

'I can't imagine why not.' Looking down at her upturned face, he felt his stomach clench at the thought of making love to her. 'Tell me something,' he asked softly. 'Do you still think legend plays Napoleon false? And do you still feel sad when you think of Marie-Antoinette?'

'Do I what?' she said, slightly puzzled as she studied his softened features. 'Oh, now I remember—we talked about it at Fontainebleau—and, yes, I do. I haven't changed, Alex—although I have grown up in many ways since I last saw you.'

'So I see,' Alex remarked with a mixture of tenderness and desire. He became distracted when he glanced through the open doors to where a disturbance was taking place. He grimaced. 'I swear the vogue for gatecrashing gets worse by the year.'

Anna followed his gaze, seeing a group of rather boisterous young men in evening suits. Gatecrashing had become the norm. The young found it divinely amusing to tour Mayfair and drop into any house where there was a party. Hostesses were resigned to the fact that their dances would be invaded and so tolerated these uninvited guests.

Alex looked down at his partner. 'Why don't we get out of here—go to a night club or something?'

Reduced to an exalted state of beaming, biddable acquiescence, it never occurred to Anna to say anything other than yes.

Chapter Ten

Lady Ormsby raised an eyebrow but uttered no objection to their leaving, but she did make Alex promise to look after Anna and not to be too late bringing her back. As Anna settled herself against the car's leather upholstery Alex put it into gear and set off.

'I learned to drive last summer—after you left,' Anna informed him brightly. 'Giles taught me.'

'I know. Selwyn told me all about it. I was surprised you drove the old Austin. Heaven forbid! That ancient relic should have been consigned to the scrap heap years ago. Can't you persuade Selwyn to buy you something more reliable?'

'He offered, but I told him I'm quite happy with the Austin. I don't wish to appear too extravagant. Besides, I love the old car—although the gearbox can be a bit temperamental at times. It symbolises my freedom. It's so convenient being able to drive between Belhaven and Oxford. It means I can get home more frequently at weekends.'

After a short drive through London they arrived at the Embassy Club at the lower end of Bond Street. It was exclusive, with a more salubrious clientele than most, one that minor royals and the Prince of Wales frequented. It was exceptionally busy, full of glamorous, glossy people. Everyone was chatting to friends or dancing energetically to 'Forty-Second

Street'. Alex slid the fur stole from her shoulders and handed it to a waiter.

'Would you like to dance?'

She shook her head. 'Can we sit for a while and talk first?'

'For as long as you like.'

Sitting close together Anna watched the people dancing, sipping her wine. Never having been to a nightclub before, she was fascinated. The slender women in clinging dresses with spaghetti straps—mature, sophisticated women dancing with men in evening dress—were so unlike the débutantes she had left behind at Tamsin's ball.

Content to sit and look at Anna, Alex remembered the times they had spent sitting exactly like this and he smiled. 'I forgot how good it was to sit like this—just the two of us.'

Anna turned her head and fixed him with a level gaze. 'You're thinking about France.'

It was a statement, not a question, and he cocked his brow and smiled. 'I also forgot how perceptive you are.'

'Not perceptive. Not really. I was thinking about the same thing.'

Leaning back in his chair, surveying her, Alex said, 'Are you enjoying London?'

'Yes, but I'd much rather be at Belhaven. Sometimes I regard the behaviour of high society as ridiculously superficial and frivolous. I promised Tamsin I'd stay until she retires to the country, so I have Ascot, Wimbledon and Henley to contend with yet—not to mention the numerous lunches, cricket matches and more balls.'

Alex laughed. 'It sounds like exciting stuff. I'm sure you'll enjoy every minute of it.'

'I'll do my best, but I don't think I'm cut out to be a social butterfly.'

'You made quite a good job of it in France. It may be a while ago, but I've never forgotten—certainly not the first time I took you to Maxim's.'

'I remember that, too. It was a tremendous adventure for

me—fun while it lasted.' Falling silent, she let her attention
wander to what was going on around her.

Settling back in his chair, Alex stretched his long legs out
in front of him, crossing his ankles and rolling his glass between his hands as he contemplated his thoughts. He was
caught between torment when he remembered their parting
last summer, and tenderness for what she had become.

Gazing at her now, what he saw was the image he had of
her two years ago at Belhaven. He recalled the wrenching
look on her face when he'd told her there could never be
anything between them and he was to disappear from her life.
He'd hoped to God he hadn't hurt her, but she'd been well
on the way to being infatuated with him, he'd known that,
and he hadn't wanted to be burdened with an infatuated young
girl. Besides, he had invested so much emotional energy in
Sonya that he felt he had no room left for a serious relationship.

At Oxford Anna would soon forget him, make new friends,
get on with her life. That was what he had told her, what he
had wanted her to do. It had been a lie. He'd been unprepared
for his own sense of loss. It had been like a bereavement.
He'd had to stop himself communicating with her, telling
himself he was a fool, when all the time he wanted to look
upon her face, to hold her in his arms—to make love to her.
And then Selwyn's illness had thrown them together last summer. He'd hurt Anna again when he'd left so abruptly. Irene
had made him realise what was happening, when she'd told
him that he and Anna were ideally suited.

Back in London, for the first time since coming to England
he had stopped to reflect on how far he had come, and how
pathetically lonely he was. Throughout their time apart
Anna's image had haunted him. With his eyes closed he'd
traced every curve of her face in his mind's eye, relived in
his imagination every minute he had spent with her, recalling
their every conversation. Time after time he'd imagined what
it must be like to hold her, to make love to her, to drown in

her incredible sweetness and surround himself with her laughter.

But as the weeks became months, his memories of those brief times they had been together were no longer enough. He'd wanted to see her, to discover the person she had become. He realised there would be a change in her, that she would have matured into a woman. Selwyn kept him well informed of her life and progress at Oxford, and he was inordinately relieved that there was no man in her life.

'I would like you to tell me all about Oxford.' Spotting the beginning of a shrug, he held up his hand to arrest it. 'And don't tell me there's nothing to tell because I won't believe you. I've been there, remember. I'm interested.'

His words warmed Anna. 'All right,' she said, her smile bright and amenable. It was the effect he always had on her. That hadn't changed. 'Although it's difficult to know where to begin.'

More wine arrived and Alex replenished their glasses. 'Let's begin with what I already know, that you're at Somerville College and doing extremely well, according to Selwyn, who is forever singing your praises. Tell me about your friends—the societies you belong to and how you amuse yourself.'

The one thing she left out in the telling, the one thing she couldn't tell him because she was afraid of what his reaction would be, was her friendship with Freddy. Being with Alex made her realise how different the two men were. Freddy was all charm, weakness and decadence, whereas Alex was quite the opposite. Apart from being a vital, strong, compelling man, he was terribly intelligent, obdurate and successful. He was also the most private individual she had ever encountered.

When the band began to play 'Someone To Watch Over Me', Alex rose and held out his hand. 'Shall we dance? The last time I heard this tune you asked me—remember?'

Anna did. It had been her last night at the villa when she had heard it and asked him to dance. She remembered how she had thought the song appropriate at the time, that Alex was there to watch over her. Even when her mother had died and she thought she had nothing, he had been there for her, understanding her, ready to help. He knew she'd get through somehow, knew she'd be safe. She recalled how disappointed she had been by his refusal to dance and was touched that he should remember it now. Taking his hand, she rose. 'I'd love to.'

It was late when Alex drove her back to the house. The rooms were empty now and strangely silent. Flowers were beginning to wilt in the heat the dancers had created and crumpled napkins littered the tables. Dawn light shyly invaded the rooms and birds were beginning to sing.

Alex stood, looking down at Anna. 'Thank you, Anna. I've had a supremely memorable evening.'

'So have I. Shall—shall I see you again, Alex?'

His expression became serious. 'There's something I haven't told you. I'm going to America in a couple of days—it's been planned for some time.'

'Oh.' Her reply was half-resentment, half-disappointment. Already she could feel the loneliness creeping over her, as if she stood in a room full of people and she was the only stranger. She tried to keep the hurt from her voice. 'How long will you be away?'

Her face was turned from him so Alex couldn't tell what she was thinking. 'I don't know—six months, maybe longer.'

'I see.' Her voice was tight in her throat. 'Do you have to go?'

'Yes.' Because his feelings for her were deep, and because parting from her was so suddenly and intensely painful, looking for some way to ease it Alex said, 'I will try and see you again before I leave. Perhaps dinner at the Dorchester. How does that sound?'

'Yes. I'd really like that.'

'I'll call you later today or tomorrow to confirm it.'

They were unbearably conscious of one another and that something was happening, as it had before. Alex knew it as well as Anna did. Somehow he couldn't kiss her on the mouth as he wanted to—the quiet voice of conscience wouldn't allow that—and he was afraid of where it might lead. Instead he put his hand against the side of her face and bent his head, gently brushing her cheek with his lips, as he would a sister. They drew apart and Anna stood on the steps and watched him climb into his car. Starting it up, he looked to where she stood.

'Goodnight, Anna.'

Anna watched his car disappear from view. She remained there long after he was gone, until she heard the servants moving about in the house. Slowly she turned and went to bed, her throat and eyes hurting from the tears she adamantly refused to shed, dazed from her futile effort to shut out the painful knowledge that Alex was to leave her once again as soon as he had reappeared in her life. The realisation hit her, leaving her more desolate and bewildered than before, and she wondered what she would do if he simply disappeared from her life altogether.

The following morning when the butler sought Anna out to tell her there was a gentleman on the telephone who wished to speak to her, she hurried to answer it thinking it was Alex. Her heart plummeted when she heard Freddy's voice on the other end of the line.

'Hi,' he said. 'Remember me?'

'Hello, Freddy,' she replied, trying to keep the disappointment from her voice.

'I told you I'd be in touch when I was in town. Anna, there's a rally tomorrow night at Olympia. Love to take you along—show you what it's all about. Tell you what, I'll pick you up—'

'No, Freddy, I can't possibly,' she interrupted quickly. 'I promised Tamsin I'd go with her to the shops in the afternoon, and later we're dining at the Ritz with friends of her parents'. Some other time, perhaps.'

'Shopping can be put off and I'm sure you can be excused dinner,' Freddy said impatiently. 'This rally's a big one, Anna. You have to come.'

'No, I don't. I never said I would. I said I'd think about it and I have. I'm not happy about it. I don't want to be carried away on a tide of emotion—brainwashed into believing something I don't. I cannot support a movement that believes in dictatorship, anti-semitism and the corporate state. The BUF is too right wing in my view and I'm really not all that interested, Freddy. Can't you find someone else to take?'

'No. You haven't been listening to me, Anna,' Freddy said sharply. 'I want *you* to come.'

Anna could hear the anger and frustration in Freddy's voice, but she didn't care. She didn't want to go. 'Don't be angry, Freddy, please.'

'Anna, you're crazy to pass up an opportunity like this. Mosley has a huge following from ordinary, decent people. He's a superb orator. He speaks with passion about his country and the cause and I know you'll enjoy listening to him. Look, come with me as an uncommitted observer. I'll come to the house anyway, wait outside—about four.'

This was the last thing Anna wanted. It would cause a great deal of embarrassment and awkward explanations if Freddy should be seen loitering outside the house. He sounded adamant, not to be deterred. 'Oh, very well,' she relented coolly, 'if it's that important to you I'll come. But don't come to the house. I'll meet you outside Lyons Corner House instead.'

'Right, good girl. I'll see you there then. Don't be late.'

Anna replaced the receiver full of trepidation, with a feeling of doom. She would regret what she was about to do, she just knew it.

'Who was that?'

Anna spun round to find Tamsin behind her, bleary eyed and stifling a yawn.

'Oh, dear,' Tamsin said, 'with a frown like that it's clear it wasn't Alex.'

'No—no, it wasn't,' Anna replied, wary suddenly and not meeting her eyes.

Tamsin regarded her closely. 'Anna, is something wrong? Tell me.'

'Oh, Tamsin, I've done something extremely foolish.'

'Why, what is it?' When Anna sighed and turned away, Tamsin pulled her down on to a window seat and sat facing her. 'Don't stop now. You've got to tell me.'

'Promise you won't say anything—not to anyone?'

'Cross my heart.'

'I've told Freddy Campbell that I'll go to a BUF rally with him and I wish I hadn't.'

Tamsin stiffened, astonishment leaping to her face. 'Freddy? Freddy Campbell? I didn't know you were seeing him.'

'I'm not—at least, not in the way you mean. I had dinner with him a two or three times, that was all.'

'Two or three?'

'Well, three, actually,' Anna confessed sheepishly. 'Oh, dear, don't tell Mummy, will you? She wouldn't understand.'

'But I can't see why my seeing Freddy should matter so much.'

'Of course it matters. Mummy can't stand him—and with good reason.'

'What reason, Tamsin?' Anna asked, eyeing her steadily as she recalled the evening in France when Freddy had arrived uninvited at the party and Lady Ormsby had been extremely put out about it. 'It's not just what you told me about Alex jilting Freddy's sister—or the fact that Freddy tried to buy into his company and Alex turned him down. There's more to it than that. I know there is. Something else happened between Alex and Freddy, didn't it?'

Tamsin looked uncomfortable. 'Yes—but—I don't know all that much—honestly I don't.'

'Is it a secret?'

'No…I don't think so—what I do know is that the subject's taboo and I'd rather not talk about it. I'm sorry, Anna, but I can't. I promised Mummy. Can't you phone Freddy and tell him you've changed your mind.'

'No. He's persistent. He'll come to the house, I just know it. I'll just have to go through with it. I told him I'd meet him outside Lyons Corner House at four o'clock tomorrow afternoon.'

'But I thought we were going shopping. You were going to help me choose something to wear for the Listers' party next week.'

'I know, and I'm sorry to let you down, Tamsin. We'll go the day after—and don't look like that,' she reproached when Tamsin scowled. 'There's nothing to worry about.'

'But there is. Anna, please don't go. It's really not a very good idea. There's often trouble at those rallies. Violent rioting nearly always breaks out between the fascists and their opponents. You might be hurt. And what about Alex?'

'What about him?'

'Well—you adore him,' Tamsin said quietly, having diagnosed the state of Anna's heart with unerring accuracy. 'That was plain to everyone last night. You didn't dance with anyone else and then the two of you disappeared to a nightclub and he didn't bring you back until dawn. I had no idea you felt like that about him, but I suppose the two weeks you spent together in France brought you close. He'll be furious when he finds out you're seeing Freddy Campbell of all people.'

'Yes, I admit it, I do adore Alex, but it's one sided, Tamsin. Besides, he's going away again in a couple of days—to America—probably for months. I don't think he'll care very much what I do, or who with.'

Anna could not have been more wrong. When she had left to meet Freddy, Alex, impatient to see her, arrived at the house to arrange their dinner date for that evening, and to apologise to Irene for stealing her away from their planned evening at the Ritz. Surprised not to find her at home with Tamsin and curious as to her whereabouts, he asked Irene where she might be. Irene was as puzzled as he was regarding Anna's absence. It was only when they questioned a rather nervous and guilty-looking Tamsin that they found out where she had gone and who she had gone with.

Irene was shocked and extremely mortified, whereas Alex was thoroughly enraged. She saw his face blanch and the muscle leaping in his clenched jaw. 'Alex, I had no idea. I had no idea Anna was seeing Freddy Campbell. None at all.'

Something shattered inside Alex, splintering his emotions from all rational control. A million thoughts and feelings spun in a chaotic turbulence and he was scarcely able to contemplate this enormous débâcle. Had she gone with any other man he would have shrugged off what Tamsin had divulged. But this wasn't just any other man. This was Freddy Campbell—a charlatan, a man of no substance, cruel, slothful and hedonistic.

It was difficult to show anything other than loathing towards a man who had almost killed his beloved sister. Knowing how he felt towards Campbell, how dare Anna play him for a fool? What was it about her that demolished his rationality? In France she had made him feel like an emotional yo-yo, and now it was happening again.

'I'll go after her,' he said, his voice harsh with anger.

Olympia Stadium was a massive building. Anna was amazed to see how many people had come to hear Mosley speak, ten thousand or more, from the high and mighty and the most cultured members of society to lowly dustmen. Débutantes were armed with Union Jacks draped round their shoulders. Mosley's Blackshirts—both men and women— were in evidence, some of whom were acting as stewards.

She could see no sign of the police, although Freddy told her they expected trouble and there were some officers in reserve.

There was an unpleasant surprise awaiting Anna. Looking very sleek and modern in trousers and smoking a cigarette in a long holder, her lips perfectly drawn in bright red lipstick, Edwina Campbell was devoting her attention to the men on either side of her. Upon seeing Anna, she became alert and gave her a hard stare, and then she smiled, a forced, false smile that did not reach her eyes.

'Glad you came, darling,' she greeted effusively. 'You'd have been sorry to miss the fun. I was most surprised when I discovered who Freddy has been pursuing with such avidity. He told me you might come along. It's so delightful to meet you again after all this time—Paris, wasn't it? You were with Alex.'

Anna met her gaze steadily. Her greeting was exaggerated and there was something slinky and slithery about this older woman she didn't like. 'Yes, it is a long time since we met— two years, in fact—and it was in Paris.'

'And how is darling Alex?'

Was there something sour in her look? Was she remembering how it once was between Alex and her? 'Very well.'

'Do you see him often?'

'I saw him only yesterday.'

'I know. You were at the Embassy.' She laughed when Anna gave her a questioning look. 'The Embassy is a very public place, Anna. You were seen with Alex and it was remarked upon. Alex doesn't go anywhere without being noticed. He's not the kind of man one can ignore. He's always an interesting subject for the gossips—and I, for one, positively thrive on gossip.'

And creating it, Anna thought cynically.

'I understand you've been seeing Freddy for quite some time now. It's time he settled down. His wild oats stretch throughout the length and breadth of Europe. What a pity we've not yet had the pleasure of entertaining you at Bishop Storton.'

Anna wasn't fool enough to agree that it was a pity. 'I've been busy—exams and all that.'

'Yes, Freddy said.'

Anna's look was direct and unsmiling. 'Freddy and I are not going out. We are friends, nothing more than that.'

'Not yet—but you will be,' Edwina stated flatly. 'Relationships that begin like an overshaken cocktail usually end in disaster.' She waved an impatient hand as the people surged around her. 'You will be well advised, Anna, to stay close to Freddy during the rally. Political violence is a possibility as the Communists—who are, how shall I put it, red agitators from the ghettos—plan to disrupt the meeting.'

There was no time to say more because at that moment Sir Oswald Mosley, the founder of British fascism, and, in Freddy's opinion, the finest public speaker in British politics, made an entrance into the hall surrounded by banners and a blaze of spotlights. When he began to speak he did so in an almost theatrical style and the atmospheric use of lighting and the huge audience were typical. When hecklers interrupted his speech, he stopped speaking. Searchlights pinpointed the hecklers and they were removed by the stewards and dealt with outside.

Anna was uneasy and already wishing she hadn't come.

All the way to the rally Alex struggled to restrain his rage, telling himself that this was a situation which called for care, calculation and a cool head, but by the time he reached Olympia, parked his car, fought his way past the strong opposition of Communists—mainly women—outside the hall, strode over the beaten and bloodstained hecklers who had been dragged out and treated with thuggish violence, and entered the building, his anger had risen to boiling fury.

The main body of the hall was heaving with people and it took him some considerable time to locate Anna and Freddy

Campbell. They were standing towards the back with Edwina, listening to Mosley. Anna looked stunning in a stylish burgundy georgette suit with a matching silk scarf fluttering from her neck. At any other time Alex would have looked his fill, but he was too furious to notice. Campbell's eyes were glued to the fascist leader and he was smiling smugly, a smile Alex wanted to wipe off his face forcibly. Pushing his way through the throng, he made his way towards them.

Anna turned and looked at the large, looming figure bearing down on them. She stared in horror, her heart beginning to pound in genuine terror as recognition flashed into her eyes. His clenched jaw was as hard as granite, and he was emanating wrath so forcefully that her knees began to tremble. 'Alex! It's you!'

Freddy glanced at the newcomer. 'Why, Kent. I didn't expect to see you of all people here today. It would seem we have more in common than I realised,' he retorted, referring to the political content of the rally. He bared his teeth in what might have been politeness, but wasn't.

'Like hell we do,' Alex ground out with withering scorn.

Glancing at Freddy Anna saw that he had paled, though he remained otherwise unruffled, but it occurred to her that he might possibly be as unnerved as she was by Alex's arrival.

Alex ignored Freddy, giving Anna the full force of his fury. 'Damn you!' he bit out savagely, his glittering eyes alive with rage. He took hold of her arm, his features taut. 'What the hell do you think you're doing?'

Anna's face had gone deathly white with shock. She jerked her arm, trying to free herself. 'Let go.'

Alex tightened his grip. 'You'll come with me and you'll do it now.'

Edwina had sidled towards them, her eyes fixed on her former lover. 'Alex,' she purred silkily, 'don't you think you're overreacting?'

Alex spun round with an expression of contempt. 'Shut up, Edwina.' His voice curled round her like a whiplash. 'Keep out of this.' Without more ado he pushed Anna in the direction of the door.

So unnerved and disorientated was she that she made no protest when he dragged her with him, just as a man standing a few yards away smashed his neighbour over the head with a walking stick.

'Kent—let her go,' Freddy demanded, following them out of the hall as more stewards rushed in to quell the riot the walking-stick incident had incited.

'It's all right, Freddy.' Anna spoke, her voice low and trembling, but loud enough to be heard over that of Mosley's. A frisson of alarm shot through her when she saw fighting had broken out close to where they had been standing, and in the foyer she looked on, horrified and dismayed, at the violence being meted out to the hecklers who had been removed by the Blackshirts. The police intervened just in time to prevent further injury. She felt as if the whole world had suddenly gone insane.

Standing apart from the aggression, she turned on Alex. Her features, no longer fearful, were defiant. 'How dare you?' she flared, angry and embarrassed at being so ignominiously hauled out of the meeting. 'What are you doing here, Alex?'

'Looking for you, you little fool. Where the hell should I be with you taking it into your head to attend a rally of this sort? Why didn't you tell me what you meant to do?'

'Because I didn't know about it then and if I had I wouldn't have told you. You'd have tried to stop me, that's why.'

'Damn right I would. Good Lord, I'd have locked you up— tied you up, if necessary, to prevent you. Of all the stupid, flea-brained notions—'

'Shut up,' Anna fumed, giving him a hearty push in the chest and making a move to walk past him.

Alex's hand caught her and pulled her back. 'I'm in no mood for tantrums, Anna. Push me once more and by God you'll regret it.'

Never in her life had Anna seen such controlled, menacing

fury, nor had anyone ever looked at her with such scathing contempt, not even her mother.

'Let her go, Kent. Leave her alone,' Freddy demanded, almost choking on the words. His face had gone an unhealthy shade of red. At this point he seemed to notice that those around them were staring at them, one of the stewards none too friendly. Freddy glared ferociously and took Anna's wrist. 'Come back inside, Anna. He can't force you to go with him.'

'Yes, I can. She's going nowhere with you, Campbell—and definitely not back in there. They're rioting already,' Alex said in a voice iced with loathing. He looked at Anna. 'Wait for me by the door, but don't set a foot outside until I come. There are people out there who will assume you are a fascist and tear you apart.' When Anna moved towards the door, he rounded on Freddy as he was about to follow her. 'Leave her. I want a word with you, Campbell.'

Freddy whirled on his heel and faced him, hands fisted against his sides. He was struggling to control his manic fury. Kent's personality always made him feel at a disadvantage, which was a unique experience for a man accustomed to obedience and servility from all those around him. How he would love to better Alex Kent, to dominate him, but he was incapable of exerting the necessary force of will.

'A word, is it? And what have you to say to me that you haven't said already?' He smirked in the face of Alex's rage. 'Regarding a certain young lady known to both of us.' It was gratuitous malice, and it hit its mark.

The words hung in the air in an oasis of stillness. The wariness in Alex's eyes froze into a pale sliver as cold as glacier ice. From where she stood, Anna could see his right fist clench—the only outward sign of his feelings. What she had witnessed told her that Alex Kent was a dangerously unpredictable foe, and if he'd had a knife in his hand, his hatred for Freddy was such that he looked fully capable of committing cold-blooded murder.

There was no hiding the dangerous, highly charged antagonism between the two men. She watched them speak quietly, too far away to hear what was said, but she saw shock flash over Freddy's face like summer lightning and his shoulders slump. He was about to say something, but his mouth snapped shut abruptly, as though he were afraid to say more. And then, without a glance in her direction, he stalked back into the hall. When Alex walked towards her his face was expressionless, but his lips were white.

'What did you say to Freddy?' Anna demanded under a fresh onslaught of fear and dread.

'Nothing that concerns you.'

Catching her wrist, Alex pulled her outside. She was unprepared for the ugly, surging crowd of flag waving, seething, shrieking women, some wielding hatpins. They had to fight their way through. Someone grasped Anna's hair and almost dragged it from its roots. Alex shoved whoever it was away as she was struck by something sharp in the arm. She felt pain, but she was so afraid they wouldn't make it past the mob alive that she thought nothing of it. Her heart was thudding like a sledgehammer, her mind, sharpened by shock, darting in a dozen directions at once. She felt vulnerable and enraged that she should be judged in this fashion to be a fascist.

At last they reach the car, which Alex had sensibly parked away from the hall. He yanked the door open.

'Get in, before you make an even greater spectacle of yourself than you already have today, and if you do one more thing to annoy me,' he said in a tone of such undiluted fury that Anna cringed, 'I'll make you regret it for as long as you live. Do you *understand* me, Anna?'

'Yes,' she whispered, getting into the car, unable to stop the trembling in her legs. Her exhaustion and sore scalp, and the painful throbbing in her arm had a lot to do with her capitulation. She was not up to arguing with Alex.

Slamming the door shut, with ground-devouring strides Alex went round to the driver's side and got in. His black mood was infectious. He drove through Hammersmith in tight-lipped silence.

As she stared straight ahead, tears gathered in Anna's eyes as she relived what had happened. She drew a shattered breath, trying to hold them back, but the humiliation she felt would not go away. When they ran down her cheeks, she fumbled in her bag.

Hearing a suspicious sniff, Alex glanced at her, at the lovely, frightened face, seeing her tears and wondering if they were feigned in hopes he would relent. He dismissed the thought. Her tears were real, he knew that. Anna hadn't feigned anything in her life. 'Now what's the matter?'

'I have to blow my nose,' she said thickly. 'Do—do you have a hanky?'

He gave her the handkerchief out of his pocket. 'Never in my life would I condone abuse of any kind, but, by God, I understand what makes people do it. I feel very much the same right now.'

Anna wiped her eyes and stared at the unfamiliar surroundings, trying to stem her mounting alarm. The direction in which he was heading did not go to Mayfair. 'Wh-where are you taking me?' she asked hesitantly. He was coldly silent. 'Alex?' she almost begged. 'This is not the way to Curzon Street. Where are we going?'

'I'm taking you to my apartment in Kensington, and don't argue,' he said, when he saw her mouth open in protest. 'There are one or two things I still have to say to you.'

Eventually the car stopped outside a tall building. Anna sat in a state of helpless paralysis. Alex climbed out and came round to her side of the car and opened the door.

'Get out.' When she failed to move, he said, 'Anna, get out. Don't make this harder on yourself than it needs to be. I'll take you to Curzon Street when we've talked and you've tidied yourself up.'

For a second Anna was too humiliated and too miserable

to move, then she blinked back the tears of futility and got out of the car.

As they went inside the building they were unaware of Victor Melinkov watching them from across the street. He had started forward when the car had stopped and Alex had got out. But it was on the young woman that his eyes had fastened. She was slender and dark haired, but he couldn't see her face. A flare of satisfaction reared its head. Could this young woman be his daughter? He knew if he watched and waited long enough she would eventually come to where Alex lived. Had his patience paid off?

Chapter Eleven

Anna reluctantly entered the reception hall in the grand building where Alex had a mansion flat. A porter in a green uniform and gold braid presided over the acres of royal blue carpet. Taking the lift to the second floor, when the metal gate clanged shut behind them Alex took Anna's arm and led her towards one of several doors. He unlocked it and held it open, standing aside and motioning for her to go in.

She didn't dare look at him as she walked past him. The apartment was startlingly spacious, luxurious, essentially masculine and tastefully furnished. At any other time Anna would have been awed by what was the most sumptuous apartment she had ever seen, but she was too upset to give it more than a passing notice. She was conscious of nothing but disaster and felt very much like Mary Queen of Scots must have felt when she'd put her head on the block and was waiting for the axe to fall.

'Sit down,' Alex snapped, striding to the sideboard and pouring two stiff brandies. Handing one to her, when she shook her head, about to refuse, with a voice like ice, he said, 'Drink it.' He watched her gulp it down. She grimaced with distaste as he tossed his own back in one.

Anna sat in an armchair and looked at her executioner. Alex—clever Alex, who was well experienced in the art of wielding power—remained standing. He looked very tall, very authoritative, and very menacing. The brandy coursing through her veins warmed her, but did nothing to stop her trembling limbs. Unconsciously she pressed herself into the soft upholstery, waiting in tense silence for what she was certain was going to be another explosion of verbal blasting. She didn't have long to wait. He twisted round, his gaze narrowing on her face. Nervously she averted her eyes.

'Now,' he said briskly, 'we can talk. Are you listening?'

She nodded mutely.

'Then look at me.'

Anna somehow brought her eyes to the level of his chest.

'That's better. Have you any idea of the seriousness of your actions today? You should know better than to hang around with Campbell and his friends. The man is a perpetual evil that has to be kept at bay. How could you have been so abysmally stupid?'

'Very easily,' Anna replied, her courage rising as always when she was cornered. She considered Alex's treatment of her and the severe reprimand for her behaviour totally undeserved. She met his gaze at last. 'You never did tell me why you despise Freddy so much. It's got nothing to do with me anyway, and I happen to like him. I find him and his friends interesting and amusing.'

'No doubt—and degenerate and decadent and dope addicts.' His scathing sarcasm sliced into Anna's highly sensitised emotions like a razor blade.

'I haven't seen any of that.' Alex came to her and braced his hands on the arms of her chair, putting his face close to hers, his eyes, glittering like shards of ice, impaling hers. She could feel the warmth of his breath on her face, feel the rage in him.

'God knows I have no interest in Campbell or his friends, but I don't like to see you with him. I don't like it and I will not endure it.'

Anna felt a new, violent rage herself. '*You* will not endure it! Who I associate with has nothing to do with you. It is none of your business.'

'I'm making it my business. It's you I'm worried about, Anna, and the effect this will have on Selwyn, the embarrassment it will cause him, when he learns of it. Either it stops now or you will find yourself sucked in and any hope you have of completing your Oxford degree will go out the window.'

'On the contrary,' Anna argued. 'Despite what you say, Freddy strikes me as a sensitive, kind and honourable man, and I can find no trace of the corrupting force you speak of.'

'Can you not? Then he has influenced you more than I realised. Socially his parents are beyond reproach—the same cannot be said of their son. Campbell is a sybaritic layabout, living each moment like a well-fed cat in the sun. Women are drawn to his engaging personality—and I don't suppose anyone can blame him for playing to his strengths. There might well be an heiress who will find him irresistible. To embark on any kind of relationship with that man I can only regard as disastrous. He has only one purpose in seeking you out. It wouldn't have taken him long to discover you are an heiress. He's a fortune hunter, Anna. It's your money he wants.'

Anna shifted uncomfortably and turned her head away from his penetrating gaze. She didn't like what he was implying. 'Stop it, Alex. How dare you talk to me like that—as if I were a mentally deficient schoolgirl.'

'I will tell you exactly why I do dare, Anna. It is because I consider it my absolute moral duty to make you see sense. As your grandfather's friend and your friend—'

'Oh, be quiet!' she cried, her colour gloriously high, her eyes stormy with hurt indignation. 'You are not behaving like my friend, you're behaving like my goalor. If you care about me at all you will treat me as an adult—as an adult woman ought to be treated. I don't want to talk about Freddy anymore.'

'Too bad,' he bit back, unwilling to let her off the hook. 'I haven't finished and you're going to listen. He's under enormous pressure from his father to marry—preferably a wealthy woman whose money can replenish the family coffers. Imagine how elated he must have felt when he sought you out at Oxford and you fell for his charm—you, Lord Selwyn Manson of Belhaven's heir! What could be better? No other woman of his acquaintance is richer than that. No other woman comes close.'

'Thank you, Alex. Thank you so much,' Anna raged, deeply hurt by his insulting remark. 'Has it not occurred to you that Freddy might be attracted to me as a person and not my inheritance?'

'No,' he replied coldly. 'Not for one minute. Campbell and his fascist friends are going down the drain and I don't want them to take you down with them.'

'Stop it, Alex,' she cried, her battered nerves crying out for relief. 'I've done nothing to deserve this. Do you have to be so cruel?'

'It's a cruel world, Anna. One has to be hard to be realistic.' He stood up straight and stepped back.

Anna got up and walked across the room, her arms wrapped around her waist. After a moment she perched on the edge of one of the sofas. Feeling the tears come to her eyes once more, she let them fall, too exhausted, both emotionally and physically, to stop them. She was paralysed with remorse and anguish, and the horrors of the rally, followed by Alex's arrival, his fury and the long drive to his flat, had robbed her of all sense of reality. Added to all this was her mortification about what her grandfather would say. Knowing how terribly hurt he would be made her tears flow faster.

Studying her in frozen silence, all at once Alex's heart filled with empathy. The anger he'd felt earlier melted, greatly alleviated by what he assumed to be her capitulation where Campbell was concerned. She seemed so young, so small and vulnerable. He went to her, towering over her, his broad shoulders blocking out anything but him. Gently placing his hand beneath her chin, he tilted her tear-drenched face to his.

'Forget you ever met Freddy Campbell, Anna. He can do you nothing but harm. I, more than anyone, know that. You could have been in serious trouble today, don't you see?'

She shook her head, thrown off balance by what sounded like gentleness in his voice.

He dropped his hand. 'Do you really believe what Mosley has to say?'

'No—no, I don't—but then I know very little about politics.' Her voice broke, and she pulled Alex's handkerchief from her pocket to wipe her tears. 'I—I told Freddy I didn't want to go to the rally but—he—'

'Wouldn't take no for an answer,' Alex finished for her derisively. 'That's typical of him. How long have you been seeing him?'

'I haven't—at least, not in the way you mean,' she sobbed, dabbing her eyes. 'I—I met him at Oxford a few weeks ago and he invited me to tea and then dinner. And then yesterday he telephoned me at Ormsby House and asked me to the rally.' Crushed by the responsibility for her stupidity, her gullibility, and all the misery those two traits had brought down on her, she lowered her gaze as the tears continued to flow. 'I'm sorry, Alex,' she whispered helplessly. 'I haven't been very clever, have I? What do you want me to do?'

'What I want is to forget all of this happened. Is that understood?'

'Yes,' she said in an agonised whisper. 'What about my grandfather? I—didn't think—the last thing I want to do is make pain for him.'

'What he doesn't know isn't going to hurt him.'

She looked up at him, startled, blinking through her blinding tears. 'You—you mean—you won't tell him.'

He nodded.

'Oh, Alex, thank you,' she gulped, gratitude brimming her heart. 'I don't deserve it.'

'No, you don't.' Her sincere thanks after all he had put her through in the last two hours demolished what was left of his reserve. His throat constricted around an unfamiliar knot of emotion as he looked at the tears streaming down her face, wetting her lips and clinging to her sooty lashes, her eyes looking like two damp purple pansies. At this moment of raw emotion he had never been more moved by her loveliness, her tenderness. Telling himself that he was acting purely out of concern and friendship, in an attempt to comfort her and savour the sweet feelings swelling inside him, he sat beside her and with aching gentleness he wrapped her in his arms.

'I'm sorry, Anna. I'm a brute, I know. I didn't mean to make you cry.' Without a word she turned her face to his chest and cried harder. Silently Alex held her, stroking the soft silk of her hair, cursing Campbell for preying on her innocence and cursing himself with equal savagery for making her cry. He punished himself with the sound of her muffled sobs and lashed himself with the tears that drenched his shirt.

After a while Anna stopped crying and raised her eyes to his. 'Are you still angry with me?'

Looking down at her and having to resist the urge to kiss her wet cheeks and soft, trembling lips, he drew a long fortifying breath and tenderly kissed her brow instead. 'As to that I'm not sure. From the moment Tamsin told me you had gone to that damned fascist rally with Campbell, I haven't been sure of anything.'

Anna drew back in his arms. She felt absolutely exhausted, limp and bedraggled. 'I'm sorry, Alex. I must look a sight. I—feel terrible.'

Something in her pale face brought an instant response. Brushing her hair from her face, Alex smiled. 'Then why don't you have a bath while I telephone Irene to let her know you're safe? I'll prepare us something to eat. You'll feel better.'

'Really? Could I have a bath?'

'Yes. Then I'll take you back.' Standing up, he held out his hand. Like a child Anna took it and stood up. 'The bathroom's this way.'

Aware of the pain in her arm, Anna rubbed it as she followed him through a sumptuous bedroom with an en-suite bathroom. It was all white tiles and sleek Italian fixtures, sparkling mirrors and soft towels on heated rails. Alex put in the plug and turned on the taps, sprinkling some scented salts into the steaming water. Turning back to her, he frowned when he saw her rubbing her arm, seeing blood had seeped through to the fabric of her jacket. Only then did he realise she'd been hurt leaving Olympia.

'You're hurt. Why didn't you tell me? Here, let me take a look.' He helped her remove her jacket, seeing a long blood-congealed scratch down her upper arm. Anna hid her inner disquiet as he took her arm and inspected the injury. 'It's a nasty scratch but nothing serious. This isn't your day, is it?' he said tenderly. 'If you were a little girl I'd have to kiss it better.'

Anna withdrew her arm. 'But I'm not a little girl, Alex. I'm a woman.'

'I do recognise that.' Going to the bathroom cabinet, he took out a bottle of disinfectant and cotton wool. 'When you've had your bath, dab some disinfectant on it just in case. We don't want infection setting in.' With a smile he went out and closed the door.

Stripping off her clothes, Anna stepped into the bath and with a huge sigh rested her head on the rim. The hot water caressed her bare flesh, soothing and relaxing. Lulled by the serene stillness as time ceased to exist, she closed her eyes.

It was the mouth-watering smell of grilled steak that roused her. Her stomach rumbled. She was famished. Climbing out of the bath, she rubbed herself dry and dabbed disinfectant on the scratch, wincing as the acid liquid penetrated the wound. Seeing a white towelling bathrobe hanging on the door, she slipped it on. It was much too large, but it was lovely and soft next to her skin, and it smelled of Alex. Following her nose, she wandered into the kitchen, which was streamlined and clean.

Clad in beige trousers and white shirt, the sleeves rolled up over his forearms, Alex was stirring something in a pan on the cooker. When she entered he looked up, temporarily immobilised by what he saw. Anna was oblivious to the vision she presented to him. She had looked striking in her ball dress, but in his oversized bathrobe she was alluring beyond description. The very sight of her wrenched his vitals in a painful knot, and the urge to go to her and pull her into his arms savaged his restraint. If she knew the full force of that emotion he held in check, she would turn and run for her life.

Putting down the spoon, he crossed his arms over his chest and leaned casually against the cooker, watching her with a lazy smile. With her cheeks still rosy from her bath, her hair damp and forming a torrent of dark silk tresses, with adorable tendrils clinging and curling around her face, and the robe open at the throat—soft flesh showing provocatively to his hungering eye—and tied tight about her minuscule waist, she looked incredible. The heat of his gaze ranged the full length of her in a long, slow, appreciative stare, and then back to her face.

'Very nice,' he murmured. 'Shame about the fit.'

Anna flushed, trying to ignore the treacherous leap of her heart at the sight of that enthralling, intimate smile. 'I hope you don't mind.' The oversized robe slipped off her right shoulder and she quickly pulled it back in place.

'Be my guest. You look adorable. It looks far better on you than it does on me. How do you feel? Better?'

'Yes—much better,' she replied, stunned by his reference to her as being adorable and deciding he meant nothing by it except empty flattery, which she deeply regretted.

'And your arm? Is it painful?'

'No, not really. It's stopped bleeding, thank goodness, and isn't deep. Thankfully I've good healing flesh.' Joining him at the cooker, she dipped her finger into a pan containing something that looked like garnish. 'Mmm,' she murmured appreciatively, perching on the edge of a high stool. 'That's delicious. What else is there?'

'Steak. How do you like yours?' he asked, prodding two sizzling juicy steaks under the grill with a fork.

'Not too rare. Don't you have anyone to look after you?'

'Do I need looking after?' he countered, looking at her, his eyes twinkling with humour.

'I thought all men did. Somehow I never saw you as a cook,' she remarked, adding the fact that he could to the long list of things she loved about him.

'I like cooking—and, yes, I do have someone to look after me. Her name's Mrs Harris. She lives near by and is an absolute gem. She comes in daily and spoils me dreadfully. Today's her day off.'

'I see.'

'And then there's Battersby—butler and valet *par excellence*. He wields authority with great skill over Mrs Harris— or likes to think he does. It's his day off too, so that leaves just you and me and a nice cosy dinner for two.' He turned and looked at her, a lazy smile sweeping over his face, unaware that the glamour of that smile was doing treacherous things to Anna's heart rate.

She felt herself blush beneath his gaze, but managed to ask with admirable calm, 'What is it that you do exactly, and where is your place of work?'

'I have offices in the city. As for what I do,' he said, turning over the steaks, 'among other things—one of them being the burgeoning film industry—I invest in all kinds of industries, such as plastics and petroleum, but my main interest is in land development. I also buy companies that are young and sell them when the market capitalisation hits a high.'

'Gosh! You must be seriously rich.'

He grinned at her, getting the plates out of the warming oven. 'I've done well, I can't deny that; you see, there was no better time than the depression to make money. When people didn't have the nerve to purchase when prices were low, I had the confidence to do just that. I bought anything I could lay my hands on. The depression that ruined so many proved to be my foundation for wealth. I invested in manufacturing industries—motorcars, aviation. I bought some land in the States—in Hollywood, several years ago—after the crash when it was cheap. A film studio wanting to expand has shown an interest in buying it, which is my reason for going over there.'

'And what do you call your company?'

'Kent Enterprises—its subsidiary company is Kent Overseas Construction Company Limited. Hungry?'

'Starving,' Anna replied, terribly impressed by his business acumen and full of admiration for all he had achieved.

'Good. It's nearly ready—though not nearly as grand as the restaurant in the Dorchester, which was where I'd planned to take you tonight, but I don't think you'll be disappointed.' He poured two glasses of red wine, handing one to her.

'Can I do anything?'

'Yes—go and sit down,' he said, tipping some steaming baby carrots into a bowl. 'Try and relax—drink your wine.'

'As long as you let me help with the washing up.'

He chuckled at that. 'It's a deal.'

Anna did as she was told and wandered back into the living room, where a small table was laid for two by the window. Taking a gulp of wine for courage, she sat on the sofa, curled her legs beneath her and waited. The mere fact that she was alone with Alex in his flat was even headier that the wine she was drinking.

Later, when they had eaten and Anna had complimented Alex on his cooking abilities, they sat close together on the sofa, drinking coffee. Despite the harrowing emotional and physical events of the day Anna felt strangely happy and content as she gazed across the room at the dusk gathering over

London, but the thought that she would have to get dressed and return to Ormsby House saddened her.

She'd momentarily forgotten Alex was to leave for America in the morning, but the packed suitcases waiting in the hall reminded her. Her heart wrenched at the thought of him going away. She was going to miss him dreadfully.

'Alex,' she said softly, 'about Freddy.' He turned and looked at her. 'There—there really is nothing going on between us, you know. It's terribly important to me that you of all people believe that.'

'I do. More importantly, do you believe me when I tell you the man is no good?'

'Yes,' she whispered, not entirely convinced that she did since Alex had still given her no explanation as to why he hated Freddy so much, but she didn't want to argue about Freddy any more. She didn't want to talk about him. In the safe silence of her heart she realised just how much she wanted Alex. She wanted to make him happy, she wanted his trust, but more than anything else she wanted his love.

Alex heard the break in her tearful voice. Raising his hand, he placed it against her cheek, his thumb arresting a rogue tear. 'No more tears, Anna. You've cried enough,' he murmured, his voice hoarse. 'I can withstand anything, but not your tears.'

For a moment they didn't move. Alex studied her with heavy-lidded, speculative eyes. Suddenly Anna saw something exciting and welcoming kindle in those eyes and her heart soared.

'I think I'd better take you back,' Alex murmured softly.

'Won't you let me stay with you a little longer? No one's going to miss me.' Her gaze was fixed on his firm lips and her heart was beginning to do strange things.

'You're wrong,' Alex countered, as reluctant for her to go as she was to leave. 'Irene's extremely concerned and upset that you didn't tell her of your intention to go to the rally.

She considers herself responsible for you while you're staying at Ormsby House.'

'Oh, dear, I didn't realise.'

'Clearly. You must also understand how horrified she was to discover Freddy Campbell had taken you there. She's worried about the effect it will have on your grandfather.'

'What? That I attended a fascist meeting or that I went there with Freddy?'

'Both. Selwyn's views are absolutely conservative.'

'I didn't even know my grandfather knew Freddy.'

'His opinions where Campbell is concerned are no different from my own. Do you know what I'm saying, Anna?'

'I think so. My mother all over again, you mean.'

'Something like that. There are similarities.'

'But one big difference. My mother was in love with my father. I'm not in love with Freddy. I never could love him.'

'Can you know yourself as well as that? You are certain?'

'Yes, I am.' Her eyes darkened with a love she wasn't trying to conceal from him any more and she managed to hold his gaze as she quietly and shyly admitted the truth. 'Because I love you, you see—quite desperately, in fact. Oh, it's all right,' she said quickly when she saw his eyes widen with astonishment, 'you don't have to say anything, make any declarations of love and things like that. But please don't say I'll get over it because I won't. I shall love you all the days of my life. I fell in love with you in France. That hasn't changed. It's a fact. There it is.'

She was looking at Alex with eyes as large as her soul and as dark as midnight. Her sincere, heartfelt declaration of love struck a chord of intense feeling deep within him. A huge, constricting knot of tenderness and desire tightened his throat and he wanted to pull her into his arms and openly declare the love she had told him she didn't expect him to utter.

Anna sat there, staring at him while he coiled a strand of her hair round his long finger. The emptiness she felt at his going away began to fill with something disturbing, something strong and dangerous, and, as his fingers tenderly brushed her temple, it became a desire so strong it was like an intense pain—urgent, a need to be fulfilled. She shifted, raising her legs on to the sofa, and knelt, facing him, then took his face between her hands and beyond all rational thought kissed his mouth, just as she had done once before, in Paris. Her lips were as soft and gentle as a butterfly's wings and as sweet as newly extracted honey. She kissed him with a strange combination of naïve expertise and instinctive sensuality that almost drove Alex wild.

Alex's face remained strangely expressionless, but his eyes told her he felt the same. Dozens of feelings raced through her mind, among them doubts and uncertainty that she was doing the right thing, but over it all was a joyous feeling that he wasn't going to reject her.

Drawing back a little from his face, she sighed. 'I can't believe I did that.'

Alex was stunned by the feelings unfolding inside him, at the tenderness and desire throbbing through every nerve ending in his body. They sat without moving, their gazes arrested, magnetised by the silent communication of sexual attraction.

'That's the second time you've kiss me,' he said in a thickened voice. 'I can't let you have it all your own way. I think it's about time I kissed you—to show you how it's done.'

'How?' she whispered, her warm breath caressing his skin. Moistening her lips with the tip of her tongue, she was unaware of the sensual invitation of her action.

'I'll show you.'

Anna watched his gaze drop to her mouth and in a state of anticipation that was reaching dizzying heights she waited. After what seemed to her like an eternity he shoved his fingers into her luxuriant mass of hair and drew her face close to his. His hands were gentle and controlled, yet unyielding, and then he found her generous mouth with his own. It was warm and exciting, his kiss devastating. As his tongue probed for entrance, she opened to him, wanting his possession.

She was hardly aware that his hand was gliding into the opening of the robe until she felt his fingers curl around her breast. The resultant surge of heat that raced through her shocked her. She pressed herself against him, answering his passion with the same wild exquisitely provocative ardour, feeling a burgeoning pleasure and immense joy that was almost beyond bearing.

When Alex released her lips and raised his head, her mouth curved in a smile. 'So you do feel something,' she said softly. His eyes mesmerised her, held him to her.

'Dear God, you're incredible. Have you any idea how lovely you are—and how rare?' he whispered hoarsely, touching the smooth cheek of this unpredictable, artless young woman with unconscious reverence. Desire, potent and primitive, poured through his veins.

His words, combined with the touch of his fingertips against her cheek, and the deep, compelling timbre of his voice, had the seductive impact Anna had always dreamed of. She could not believe the pulsing happiness that glowed inside her, or the exquisite sensations speeding through her veins. For a long moment they gazed at each other, each feeling more exposed to the other than ever before.

'I—I never knew I could feel this—this wonderful wanting,' Anna breathed, gently placing her lips at the corner of his mouth. 'I want you to love me, Alex—properly. This is as far as my knowledge goes. What lies beyond a kiss I cannot imagine. I want you to tell me what to do—to show me.'

His senses drugged with the scent of her, the feel of her lips on his flesh, with the last shred of rationality he possessed, Alex looked at her. He was accustomed to having women desire him and his lovemaking always followed a familiar pattern. But with Anna it would be different. She was not like any of them—she was sensual, a virgin and inexperienced, urgent but unschooled. 'Are you sure, Anna? Are you sure it's what you really want—that it's me you want?'

'Of course it's you I want—no one else. I've never been

more sure of anything in my life.' A detached thread of thought warned her that there might be no lasting future for her with Alex, but she didn't care. Had she not shrugged off a life of convention when she had gone to Oxford? Was it not freedom she had chosen, equality in a relationship, the need to do as she wanted without question?

Without removing his gaze from hers, Alex stood up. 'There's a bed in the other room.'

Taking her hand, he drew her from the sofa and led her into the bedroom. Eager for him, unashamedly Anna slipped out of the robe and stretched her lithe and slender form out on the bed. She heard Alex's quick intake of breath as his eyes fastened on her wraithlike slenderness and the shapely peaks of her breasts that were high and firm. A smouldering glow entered his eyes. He bent over her, his mouth covering hers. Anna was burning. She had never wanted anything the way she wanted Alex—the feel of his mouth on hers, his hands, his body joined to hers.

Standing up he tore off his clothes and came back to her. The feel of his body pressed to her own was just as masculine as Anna expected it to be, iron-hard flesh and sinews. His lips, dominant and tender, lazily coerced, brushing across her own, fitting them to his, breathtakingly insistent, lethal and effective, and all the while his hands touched and caressed with exquisite gentleness, as if he had all the time in the world to explore.

Moonlight flooded the room, lightening Alex's dark skin, turning Anna's as white as alabaster. 'Dear Lord, you are so lovely,' Alex murmured, his mouth against her breast, aroused and absorbed by her in a way that astonished him. His hands, vital and strong, explored the curves of her body, caressing and arousing, as if she were the first woman he had ever known.

Anna was touching him, learning the feel of the hard muscles in his shoulders, the dark hairs on his chest, the narrow waist. The scent of him was intoxication—a lingering trace of sandalwood, but above all essentially male. As the heat of his lips laid siege to her senses and she felt his hardness against her flesh, sanity fled. Her body moved of its own accord in shameless pleasure. She couldn't lie still. 'I'm sorry,' she whispered, ashamed of her eagerness. 'I want you so much.'

'Never say you're sorry, my darling girl,' he said hoarsely, covering her, his hands raising her hips. 'Ever. There's no shame in wanting. We want each other and there is such joy in wanting.'

He was aware that all the months of wanting her, of self-denial and frustration had finally driven him beyond restraint, but, he told himself as his kisses became demanding, almost savage in their need, he was determined—if he could manage it—that she would experience the full depth of pleasure between a man and a woman before she left his bed.

A small cry pierced the quiet room as the thrusting heat of him entered and filled her, and even as she cried out she took his face between her hands and kissed him, hungry with longing. Carefully allowing her body to accept what was happening, his movements were gentle, but Anna was having none of it. Alex soon realised he had roused the sweet young girl into a tantalising creature who breathed passion and sensuality, whose need was as urgent and as savage as his own. He let his control and reservations shatter as he claimed her fully. Gentleness was displaced by a sensual frenzy until release exploded simultaneously between them.

Alex smothered her cries of pleasure with his lips. They lay together, facing each other, his arms about her. After a while, with the night still young, pressing herself close, she felt the leap of his response and gloried in her power to rouse and bring pleasure to this wonderful man.

Anna felt an overwhelming sense of wonder that their bodies could react to each other in an instant, that they could become one. The wonder soared within her as his lips murmured against her mouth, his body claiming hers. They moved together in a timeless rhythm and Anna thought everything was perfect and would last forever.

Waking with the dawn, Alex raised himself on one elbow and looked down at the dark-haired beauty asleep in his bed. Consumed with a feeling of part awe, part reverence, his gaze was one of tenderness. Fragile perfection, she looked like Eve, newly touched by her creator's hand. Anna had bewitched him with her metamorphosis from the quiet, well-bred young woman to passionate siren. Their lovemaking had been quite unique in his experience, satisfying yet leaving him wanting. It had contained everything—sweetness, tenderness, violence and discovery—and afterwards he had been shaken, almost shocked by what they had achieved.

He entertained some vividly erotic thoughts of rousing her warm, tantalising body from her sleep, but he had a train to catch; since he had to take Anna to Curzon Street, he must hurry. He'd taken time off from their lovemaking to phone Irene and tell her Anna wasn't feeling too well and was to stay the night. Irene had sounded disapproving and he hoped she wouldn't give Anna a hard time about it. Getting out of bed, careful not to wake Anna, he crossed to the bathroom.

Anna opened her eyes and look dazedly around the spacious, but wholly unfamiliar bedroom. Beside her the bed was empty. Running water and splashing noises coming from the bathroom revealed Alex's whereabouts. For several moments she lay still, staring fixedly at the ceiling. The euphoria that had gripped her into the early hours had evaporated, leaving her strangely numb and beset with doubts. She reluctantly allowed herself to contemplate the outcome of what had happened.

She had told Alex that she loved him and had coerced him into making love to her.

Her heart began to hammer as the reality of that reckless, irrational act roared inside her brain. *She* was the one who had taken the initiative. *She* was the one who had asked him—no, begged him—to make love to her. How could *she* have issued such an invitation? Alex hadn't told her he loved her, so what did he think of her? Was she just another conquest? She had presented him with what any woman could give him, and he had taken it. Her mind scorched with the memory of the wild abandon with which she had given herself to him. What if, now he had made love to her, he would think of her as just another woman devoid of morality or self-respect?

Already the magic was over, but of one thing she was certain. They weren't the same any more, not after last night. Now they had become lovers her life had changed forever.

Lying naked in his bed, still able to feel the heat of him inside her, she felt the first tingling of shame. Somehow she managed to shake off her unjustified internal tirade and break off the guilt and panic that were causing it. In the bright light of day, without the nearness of Alex to blur her senses, it was obvious that she had let her love and sentimentality drive her to do something that was incredibly impulsive. She had humiliated herself by letting him know how she felt, how she craved his touch, his body. She had been too guileless to hide it.

Shoving back the sheets, she climbed out of bed and draped the towelling robe around her. Padding into the kitchen, she had a drink of water to quench her thirst. On the way back to the bedroom she glanced into Alex's study, seeing neat rows of books lining the walls and a large desk with neat piles of papers and pens and a pad of blotting paper. A photograph was propped on the polished surface. Curious, she went to have a closer look, her heart giving a painful wrench when she saw it was the same woman she had seen him with in the *Tatler*. Across the corner was written *with fondest love, Sonya*.

Suddenly all she wanted was to leave, to get out, to be anywhere but in Alex's domain. Backing out of the study, she returned to the bedroom. Thankfully Alex was still in the bathroom. Without any particular awareness of what she was doing, she began pulling on her clothes. She was filled with shame for her lack of will and a love that she could not control, for if he were to see her now she would let him pull her into his arms. Hastily she scribbled him a note, telling him not to worry, that knowing he would be pressed for time she would take a taxi back to Curzon Street, and that, besides, she hated goodbyes.

Outside she looked around for a taxi, too engrossed in her dilemma to notice the man standing against the wall. On seeing her he stepped forward. Anna was only aware of his presence when a hand clamped down on her shoulder and spun her around. Glancing up in surprise, her body chilled on finding herself looking up into the eyes of a stranger.

From the quality of his clothes he was a gentleman in his middle years. His dark hair was greying at the temples, his features were distinguished yet gaunt and, she thought, sensing an inner aggression, he was used to bullying his way through life. His appearance intimidated her and her throat dried with sudden fear as his eyes searched her features.

'Kindly take your hands off me, and if you do not let me pass I will most definitely scream so loud it will wake the whole of London.' She tried to move past him, but her shoulder was still firmly seized.

The man began speaking to her in a foreign language— Russian, she thought. She shook her head, 'No—I don't understand what you're saying. Please speak in English.'

'Sonyasha? You are Sonyasha?' the man asked in broken English.

'Sonyasha? Who is Sonyasha?'

'Sonya. You are Sonya?'

Anna stared at him in horror and disbelief. 'I am not Sonya. I am Anna—Anna Preston. I don't know anyone called Sonya.' The man looked at her hard for what seemed an age, then appeared to believe her. He dropped his arm.

'No, I can see you are not. You know Alex Kent?'

'Yes. Alex is a friend.'

'I am sorry. I have made a mistake. I mistook you for someone else—someone I have not seen in a long time. Pardon me.' With a slight inclination of his head he turned and walked quickly out of the square.

Anna watched him go, shaken by the encounter. Sonya! Twice within the space of half an hour the mystery woman had made her presence felt. Who was she? What did the stranger want with her and why had he mistaken her for Sonya? And what was he doing loitering outside Alex's flat? If he wanted to see Sonya, why didn't he ask Alex? None of it made sense. Hailing a taxi that rounded a corner of the square, she thought it was all so very confusing and disturbing.

Chapter Twelve

Halfway to Curzon Street, unable to face an afternoon shopping with Tamsin, Anna asked the driver to take her to the Embankment instead. Here she paid him off and walked beside the river in an attempt to sort out her thoughts. What must Alex be thinking, finding her gone like that? Would he come after her? No, there wasn't time. His train left Victoria at ten o'clock.

As she strolled and the sun warmed her, gradually her hurt subsided and she felt dreadfully unhappy instead. She shouldn't have left like that. She might be wrong about Sonya. She should have stayed and given him a chance to explain about the photograph. She looked at her watch—nine thirty. Alex would be at the station now. Could she get there in time to say she was sorry and to say goodbye? Fuelled by a sense of urgency, she hailed another taxi and directed it to Victoria Station, telling the driver to hurry.

Anna ran into the station. Glancing quickly at the clock, she saw his train was due to leave at any minute. She darted ahead, then she saw him walking towards a first-class carriage. Her heart lurched, but as she hurried towards him, crying out his name and raising her hand to wave, she froze and halted. Slowly she lowered her arm.

A dark-haired young woman in a stylish green suit and

matching hat suddenly appeared by his side. It was the same woman who had stared out at her from the photograph earlier. Anna watched in disbelieving horror as, smiling tenderly, Alex held out his arms and she walked into them as though she belonged.

His arms closed around her with stunning force and he held her tight, as if he never wanted to let her go. After a moment the woman tilted her head back and looked at his face. Lovingly she touched his cheek with fingers like the wings of a frail, gentle bird. She said something that made him draw her back into his arms and press his cheek against hers.

When finally they drew apart Alex placed his arm possessively about her waist and, followed closely by a porter carrying the young woman's baggage, escorted her along the platform. She was accompanied by a woman clad from head to toe in the black robes of a nun.

When they reached their compartment Alex turned to give instructions to the porter as the two women said their goodbyes. All Anna could do was watch as Alex and the young woman boarded the train and disappeared from sight as it slowly began to move. The nun stood for a moment and then turned and walked away.

Anna couldn't move. All over the station people were saying their goodbyes and climbing onto trains, but she was insensible to everything but what she was feeling. She was in a nightmare, the most horrific nightmare of her life. What did Sonya mean to Alex and why had he taken her with him? She was beautiful, with a small heart-shaped face and fine, ethereal features—rather like a china figurine.

Feeling terribly alone and unwanted, with her whole world seeming to be crumbling about her, she turned and walked down the platform. Despair flooded her whole being, a dark, terrible despair that pulled her down into an abyss. Alex had someone else. This woman—Sonya—had been there all along. For the first time in her life Anna experienced a real, bitter jealousy. It was a cruel emotion. It was tearing her in two.

It made no difference to him that he had made love to her, Anna, last night. She had to face the fact that she was nothing to him and never would be. His kindness, his dutiful tenderness, she had mistaken for something deeper. At the time she had deluded herself into thinking it was love. The enormity of her pain was like an inner death consuming her with hopelessness. She was hurt beyond all endurance. If loving someone meant being this vulnerable, this wretched, then she never wanted to love anyone again.

Outside the station, with a heavy heart she stopped and leaned against a wall, reflecting sadly on her future. She no longer had any desire to remain in London. So as not to disappoint Tamsin, she would stay for Ascot, and then she would go back to Belhaven to heal, so that grief would be banished from her consciousness.

Alighting from the taxi at Ormsby House she tried to pull herself together, seeing how imperative it was that no one should know how distressed she was. Her immediate difficulty lay in her meeting with Lady Ormsby and behaving as if nothing out of the ordinary had occurred. She found herself unable to think of Alex just then…perhaps later, but that time was apparently beyond her power to imagine at that moment.

Lady Ormsby was alone in her sitting room, seated at a small table sifting through some correspondence. She got up when Anna entered and sat on the sofa, patting the space beside her.

'Come and sit down, Anna. I think you and I should talk. Are you feeling better?' she inquired when Anna was seated.

'Better?' Anna asked blankly.

'Alex told me you were unwell.'

'Oh—yes, I'm feeling much better, thank you. Lady Ormsby, I would like to say how very sorry I am for any concern my absence yesterday may have caused you.'

'My dear Anna, there was certainly no need to ask my permission, but I wish you had told me you were going out,' Irene said, most displeased by yesterday's events. 'And as for Alex—well—he should have brought you straight home. I have strong principles about what is acceptable and what is not. Alex's behaviour was totally out of character and quite reprehensible.

'And as for that dreadful rally you attended… The publicity in this morning's papers is most unfavourable. It would appear that fighting broke out and many sustained injuries, which is hardly surprising considering the nature of the rally and the fierce opposition those fascist meetings always receive from Communists and the like. I'm so relieved you are unhurt.' Suddenly her expression became one of concern. 'They didn't hurt you, did they?'

'I am quite all right, truly. The fighting began as I was leaving—with Alex,' Anna was quick to reassure her, considering it best not to tell her about the slight injury she had sustained to her arm.

'Thank goodness. But to go there with Freddy Campbell, of all people—well, what can I say other than it is absolutely unacceptable. Alex was furious. Indeed, I've never seen him like that.'

'Neither have I,' Anna said quietly. 'He made me feel very young, very naïve and very stupid.'

Irene looked at her, her expression tender, thoughtful. 'I'm sorry, Anna. Was he very angry?'

She nodded. 'About Freddy mostly.'

'Well, that's understandable. I dread to think what your grandfather will make of all this.'

'But why? Please tell me why no one likes Freddy. Alex told me that if I went on seeing him it would be like my father all over again. You knew my mother, so you must know what my father was like,' she pleaded, desperately wanting to focus her mind on something other than Alex. Yesterday she had discovered that another Alex existed, but he could not be allowed a place in her memory just now. The path to remembrance of what had occurred between them was guarded by a terrible feeling of betrayal.

'Yes, I did,' Irene replied.

'Won't you tell me about her? The only person who can tell me anything is my grandfather, but you were her friend.'

Irene smiled, her expression tender as she remembered Lavinia. 'Your mother and I were very close. We went to school together, spent our summers together doing childish things. We came out together and were caught up in a heady haze of parties and dances.' She smiled at the memories. 'Our photographs appeared almost daily in the society papers. We were rich, beautiful and admired and the life we led was very glamorous. Lavinia was happy then. But then she met your father.'

Her expression hardened but her voice continued to remain level throughout her monologue. She was staring across the room, and as Anna watched she clenched her hands on her lap in an attempt at self-control.

'He was most unsuitable. Your grandfather forbade Lavinia to see him, but that only made matters worse. Many distasteful scenes ensued. I tried talking to her and did everything I could to make her see sense. She wouldn't listen. She—she turned against me. I didn't see her after that. Like everyone else I found the notion of her marrying Robert Preston horrifying. I know he was your father, my dear, and I do apologise if what I say hurts you, but he was quite definitely not a gentleman by English standards.

'I am sure your grandfather has told you most of it, so I will not chronicle it in detail. Lavinia made her choice. Her defiance was harsh and cruel. She didn't think of what she was doing to her father. She thought only of herself and her lust for Robert Preston. I wrote to her often, telling her I did not want this to come between us—our friendship meant a great deal to me. She returned my letters unopened. She never forgave any of us, you see, for refusing to accept Robert. Your grandfather could never make his peace with his loneliness.

His hope was that he would become reconciled with Lavinia, but her death thwarted his wish.'

Irene looked at the huge dark eyes looking back at her from an enchanting face, and she felt a constriction in her throat as she reached out and cupped Anna's face in her slender fingers. 'But now he has you. You have made a great difference to his life, Anna. He has come to care for you deeply.'

'I do know that, and I love him dearly. Before I went to live at Belhaven I was convinced I was worthless and unlovable. My self-esteem was so low it was almost non-existent. It was my grandfather who taught me to have faith in myself. My mother was cold, unemotional and unapproachable, whereas my grandfather is warm and human and real. I will never do anything to hurt him—not intentionally.'

'I know.'

'But why is everyone so against Freddy? I know he and Alex have had their differences in the past, that Alex had an affair with Freddy's sister and that Alex refused to let him buy into his company. But there is more to it than that. I know there is. Freddy has the greatest respect and regard for me, and has always shown me politeness and consideration.'

Irene looked at her steadily. Her mouth, which could harden in a second, hardened now. 'I'm sure he has. He has to be on his best behaviour; it is imperative that he marries money, you see, to replenish the family coffers and to finance his costly passion for fast cars—anything so that he doesn't have to work for a living. He can't afford any unwise flirtations.

'Anna, far be it from me to meddle in your affairs. You're a young woman of the world. You don't need me to remind you of the hazards of forming relationships—but I must warn you against forming any kind of relationship with Freddy Campbell. His pedigree cannot be faulted, and men like him are subject to temptation, but he has a past. Distance yourself from him. He—he is evil. There is no other word for it.'

'Evil? That's a strong word to use.'

'It fits.'

'He must have done something very bad.'

'He did.'

Anna was filled with confused frustration. Why wouldn't she tell her what Freddy was guilty of? 'I cannot make any sense of it. What did he do? It's to do with Alex, isn't it?'

'Yes—but I can't tell you. You know how Alex guards his privacy. I'm sorry, my dear, but if you want to know any more you must ask him. I beg of you to avoid Freddy Campbell in the future. If you continue to see him, your grandfather will be deeply hurt.'

Anna knew there was no further point in defending Freddy. 'I will consider what you've said and tell you now that nothing is going to come of my acquaintance with Freddy. I don't care for him in a romantic sense. I've decided to go back to Belhaven next week. I—I don't know what Alex said to Freddy yesterday, but I doubt I'll see him again.'

'Don't be too sure about that, Anna. If he discovers Alex is out of the country, he might very well seek you out. But must you leave London so soon? Tamsin will be so disappointed. She is hoping you'll still be here when Wimbledon starts. You know how much she adores the tennis. She will miss not having you along.'

'There are lots of other people she can go with—and I will be here for Ascot. You'll be returning to Applemead when the Season ends in July, so Tamsin and I will have plenty of time to spend together before I return to Oxford for my final year.'

At first Alex had been surprised to find Anna gone—his surprise quickly turning to anger that she should have left without saying goodbye. Looking down into the square, he had seen her pulling away in a taxi. He'd wanted to go after her, but checking his watch, realised he was running late.

It was imperative that he was at Victoria Station before Sonya arrived. Afraid that Victor Melinkov might get to Sonya at the convent while he was in America, he'd decided for his own peace of mind to take her with him, hoping some time away from the convent would do her good.

Alex maintained the trappings of a peculiar relationship with his stepfather. With the money Alex had given him, Victor had moved out of Whitechapel and found accommodation above a nightclub in the West End. He'd become an active member of the Communist party, a gambler and bought himself a fast car. He was suddenly enjoying life and London enormously.

A frequent visitor to Brooklands motor-racing track, he cut a very dashing figure in his white Maserati. Alex was deeply anxious about the effect his appearance might have on Sonya, whose state of mind had been precarious over the years. In order to avoid any set-back, he continued to keep her whereabouts from him, which infuriated Victor, but Alex stood firm on this.

With so little time he'd have been forced to order Anna a taxi to take her back to Curzon Street anyway, but he cursed her idiotic stubbornness. When he reached Southampton he'd telephone her and demand to know what she was playing at.

When the Ormsbys' butler told Anna Mr Kent was on the telephone, asking to speak to her, she shook her head. 'Please tell Mr Kent I'm out, will you, Smeaton?' She lacked the strength to speak to Alex just then. He called twice more, and each time she told Smeaton to tell him she was not at home.

Loneliness and despair engulfed her. She wished she had someone to talk to, to tell her what lay behind Alex's hatred of Freddy, to tell her about Sonya, to tell her what to do, but no one could help her. She was going to have to bear this alone.

The ocean liner taking Alex to America sailed through the Solent and slipped smoothly into the English Channel. Sonya was blessedly happy that Alex had insisted on taking her, and her high spirits were a joy for him to see. She was taking a lap around the ship while he dressed for dinner.

Alex was livid. He simply could not understand Anna's behaviour. Did she regret what they had done? Had her feelings for him, which she had so unashamedly and sweetly divulged, changed? That was an agonising, infuriating thought. In a state of frenetic restlessness he paced the carpet of his spacious cabin. Being away from her tore at him, along with other worries about her—like whether or not she was pregnant. Feeling like a complete degenerate, that was when he turned his fury on himself and berated himself severely for his irresponsibility, for taking the innocence of that headstrong, beautiful girl.

He was filled with remorse that he might have done anything to hurt her—the only woman he had ever truly loved, as he had once loved his father and mother, unquestioningly, without borders, without limits. She was a single-minded, serious young woman, one hundred percent devoted to him. Fortunately, he was not so utterly lacking in morality as to offer her an arrangement that would rob her of her virtue and all chances of respectability, and he had no intention of messing her around.

So why had she refused to speak to him? Within the confines of the ship and with the entire width of the Atlantic Ocean about to separate them, helpless either to touch her, to comfort or regain her, he told himself, combing his trembling fingers through his hair, he had to put her out of his mind before he went insane. But already he was sitting at the desk and reaching for pen and paper.

The countryside was clad in full greenery, the air heavy with the scent of flowers for Anna's first visit to Ascot with the Ormsbys and some of their friends. Ascot marked the highest point of the London Season, and after that came slowing down. Tamsin was excited. There was an added sparkle to her eyes, for she hoped to see Hubert Standing, whose attentions at her ball she had welcomed and shamelessly encouraged. He was a deb's delight, which meant he was acceptable and eligible.

It was Gold Cup day and despite the heavy congestion on the roads between Windsor and Ascot they were in plenty of time before the first race and to see the royal party drive up the course in open landaus. The noise, the colour, the ladies dressed to kill, raised Anna from the depression that had consumed her since Alex's departure and she entered into the spirit of things.

It was all so enjoyable. There were the usual parades in the paddock after each race, the usual criticisms of other people's clothes, refreshments in one of the tents set up on the vast concourse, the usual queries as to what would win, and the usual laments as to why a certain horse had not been backed, after it had won.

Strolling to the paddock with Tamsin, she glanced at her race card to study the runners in the second race.

'Isn't it exciting?' Tamsin remarked, waving to someone she knew in the crowd. 'Are you glad you came?'

'Yes. It's just what I needed after—'

'After the rally.' Tamsin quietly finished what she had been about to say. 'What a frightful day that must have been. Freddy should have known better than to take you there. I—expect you're missing Alex, too,' she said tentatively. Like everyone else, she wondered what had really happened between Anna and Alex that day, but Anna had been disappointingly unforthcoming.

'Yes,' Anna admitted. 'I do miss Alex—but, more importantly, is he missing me?' she said softly, almost to herself.

Tamsin was so engrossed in animated conversation with Hubert that Anna watched the last race by herself. After seeing her horse lose, she began walking away from the winning post to join the others. Her heart plummeted when she saw Freddy walking up the course towards her. He looked quite splendid in his morning coat and top hat, the *Sporting Life* tucked under his arm.

To avoid any awkwardness she would have liked to pretend she hadn't seen him, but now they had come face to face she couldn't ignore him. Despite what had happened at the rally and not having spoken to him since, he looked perfectly composed, his moody eyes appraising.

'Are you leaving?' he said, his words slightly slurred with the excess of too much champagne.

'Yes, Lord Ormsby wants to beat the congestion on the roads.'

'Did you win?'

'Yes—just the one, Felicitation in the Gold Cup. My stake was a modest one, but it was exciting to see it win.'

'Congratulations, I didn't do so well.' Anna began to walk on and he fell into step beside her. 'I had hoped to bring you to Ascot myself,' he remarked, reminding her of his invitation at Oxford. 'So, is the world of horse racing what you expected—you've enjoyed yourself?'

'Yes—which surprises me. Usually I dislike these kinds of sporty gatherings.' She glanced sideways at him and smiled. 'You must find me awfully dull.'

'Not dull. Just quiet—shy.'

'Shy? Oh—I hadn't thought about that. You can't be accused of being shy, can you, Freddy? You're the opposite—self-confident, and you love being the centre of attention.'

He grinned. 'That's where you're wrong. It's mere camouflage. I'm quite nervous really underneath. That's why I like being with you. I can be myself.'

'Can you, Freddy?' she asked, touched by his simple admission, sincere, she hoped, but she never felt quite sure with him.

'I don't have to put on an act. That's why I was so put out when you went off with Alex Kent at the rally—and I must apologise for taking you there. It was a mistake, I do realise that now.'

'Yes, Freddy, it was.' They carried on walking in silence, then after a moment Anna said, 'I want to ask you something, Freddy, and I want you to be perfectly honest with me. When you came to Oxford that day, when we met, your being there wasn't accidental, was it?'

'Of course not,' he admitted frankly. He turned and looked at her, his look hungering, which made Anna uneasy. 'When I see something I like I go after it. I didn't have to be Sherlock Holmes to find out you were at Oxford. By the way, do you like Alex Kent?'

Confused and embarrassed by his question, which had come out of the blue, she looked away, sure, somehow, that Freddy knew perfectly well how deeply she felt for Alex. The mere mention of his name had made her relax her guard. 'Alex? Why—yes, he's a good friend. I—I am fond of him.'

'Fond in the way you're fond of me?'

'No—it—it's different.' Seeing a light in his eyes she mistook for humour, she said, 'Freddy, stop it. Don't tease.'

'I'm not teasing. I want you to know I'm deadly serious. You might as well know I'm fond of you—more than fond— and I should hate it to be one-sided.' He grinned boyishly but there was a sly gleam in his eye. 'I might go out and shoot myself.'

'You don't have to do that. Think of what the loss would do to your friends.'

'And you, I hope.' He was watching her closely.

Anna didn't reply. She was beginning to feel extremely uncomfortable in his presence.

'Anna, I would like to talk about us.'

'Oh?'

'I'm damned jealous of Alex Kent—I admit it. You say you're fond of him—and really you shouldn't be. He's such a dark horse—Russian immigrant and all that—who knows where he comes from? I get really angry when I think about you and him.'

'There is no me and him. What makes you think I should be interested in Alex?'

'Don't play that line with me, Anna. I know women, and I've watched you together. The way he came after you at the rally, and the way the two of you were glaring at each other was enough. I can see his attraction—his looks and his money, and how noble he must have seemed when he showed his knightly qualities and rescued you at the rally that day. He must seem to be a better proposition than I.'

'Stop it, Freddy,' Anna retorted sharply, quickening her stride. 'You are talking nonsense.'

Suddenly he stopped and caught her arm, pulling her behind a small marquee where they were less likely to attract attention. He turned her to face him. 'I will not be flouted. I want us to be more than friends. You're so beautiful, Anna.' His voice was coercing. 'I am obsessed with you. I can't get you out of my mind. You're angry because I took you to the rally, I know.'

'Now you are being ridiculous. This has got nothing to do with the rally. Please don't say any more. You are wasting your time.'

Her rejection triggered his anger. His face twisted with cruelty and when he spoke there was an underlying violence in his tone. 'Damn you for a tease, Anna. Every time we've been together the invitation in your eyes has enticed me. You led me on—admit it.'

That he should deliberately misinterpret her actions made Anna furious. She tried to wrench her arm free, but his grip tightened viciously. He came so close to her that his face was almost touching hers. For the first time she was seeing something that Alex had told her about. Never had she seen such ugliness in Freddy's face. His eyes were slits. There was a coldness, a meanness about his features she had never seen before. She was seeing a different Freddy, someone angry, let down, hurt, who might retaliate by hurting her.

'It's Alex Kent who's responsible for this,' he hissed. 'I

can well imagine what he's said to you. No doubt he listed all my evil traits—told you how that sour-faced shrew, that dark-haired Jewish whore Sonya deceived me—and warned you to keep well clear.'

Anna felt the colour drain from her face. She couldn't believe what was happening, what she was hearing. As Freddy dissolved into a taut, violent stranger, she felt as if she were witnessing the opening of a door to reveal unspeakable horrors beyond. She glimpsed a dark side to his personality she had never seen before. But then he looked away as if he knew his eyes were betraying him, pulling down the shutters of that dark side. But too late, for Anna had seen how strong he was, disciplining his violent emotions and thoughts, but beyond that she sensed other, harnessed emotions—guilt, pain, misery and despair.

'As a matter of fact he did—at least, something along those lines—but he never speaks to me of anyone called Sonya.' She managed to wrench her arm free and moved away from him. 'I think I have a great deal to learn about you, Freddy, and I feel that when I do I won't like it.'

'And will you heed Kent's warning?'

Anna heard something that sounded like desperation in his voice as she walked away from him. 'I am able to make my own decisions. And since you want more from me than I care to give, I think it would be for the best if you don't try and see me again.'

'You don't mean that. Why are you doing this to me, Anna?' he cried, with the voice of a wilful, petulant child who has been rebuffed. His tone did not stir her compassion.

'We don't want the same things from life, Freddy. I don't love you. I never will.'

'I don't believe you. Don't do this to me. I don't want to lose you.'

Anna stopped and faced him, her expression resolute. 'How can you lose something that was never yours in the first place? I may be younger than you and inexperienced in the ways of the world, but I am no fool. When you sought me out at Oxford it was my money that attracted you to me, not my sweet, delectable self, I do know that. Go and find some other unsuspecting woman to dupe, Freddy—there must be someone out there who will find you irresistible.'

Anna moved away from him, wanting this to end. The day was ruined and she wanted to go home.

'This isn't over, Anna. I swear it. I swear I'll get even.'

'Goodbye, Freddy.'

Walking back to the others, she felt exhausted and shaken. Alex had told her Freddy was no good, that he was a dangerous man. She should have listened to him after all. In his anger Freddy had mentioned Sonya. Was she the reason why there was so much enmity between him and Alex? Had she rejected him in favour of Alex? No, she thought. There was more to it than that.

Several yards away from Anna and Freddy stood Victor Melinkov. He'd had a decent day on the horses and he was about to leave the course when he'd seen Freddy Campbell. They were slightly acquainted through the club at Brooklands. Also he'd often seen him at the Phoenix nightclub in the West End where he came with his friends to smoke and inject their dope.

Victor had no time for people who took drugs—drinking, gambling and women he could understand, but never drugs. He would turn away when they went to indulge their filthy habit in one of the rooms set aside for such activities, and it could be hours before they staggered out. Victor had paused when he'd seen Campbell stop and talk to the young woman, whom he recognised immediately as Anna Preston, the woman he had spoken to as she left Alex's flat.

He observed the altercation between the two with interest. They were arguing, that was obvious. To appease his curiosity he moved closer to listen to what they were saying, and, on hearing Campbell mention a woman's name, Sonya, in their heated exchange, and calling her a Jewish bitch, the rage that smouldered so near the surface of Victor's nature threatened to burst into a raging flame.

He nearly challenged Campbell there and then, but a caution he had acquired in the labour camp, which had saved his life many times, made him step back. Without any confirmation that it was his own Sonyasha to whom Campbell had referred, he restrained that first impulse, but he would enquire into Campbell's background. Should he find it was his daughter Campbell had spoken of with such derision, that he was the man who had driven her to want to take her own life, then Victor swore he would make Lord Freddy Campbell sorry he had ever been born.

Selwyn was in bed when Anna arrived at Belhaven late in the evening. She went straight up, entering when he answered her knock. Crossing the room, she went to him and, bending over, kissed his forehead. Still in a state of anxiety following her altercation with Freddy and missing Alex so dreadfully, the attempt to appear normal was a strain.

'Giles told me you were in bed. You are not ill, are you?'

'Of course not.' He smiled at her, thinking how young and lovely she looked, but studying her closely he could see she looked tense. Something was troubling her. 'I'm never ill, you know that.'

'Now that's not strictly true, but I won't argue.'

'It's good to have you back, although I didn't expect you quite so soon. Was London not to your liking? Didn't you enjoy yourself?'

'It was fun, I suppose,' she said, sitting on the bed and taking his hand in hers, 'and I don't doubt Tamsin's ball was the event of the Season, which will please Lady Ormsby enormously.'

'Irene always did know how to do things properly. You saw Alex, didn't you?'

'Yes.'

He was looking at her intently. 'And how was he?'

'Oh, you know Alex,' she said, her lips curving in a shaky smile. 'I hadn't seen him in months and he's still the same.'

'He's gone to America?'

Pain seared through her when she recalled the scene she had witnessed at Victoria Station. 'Yes.'

'You're unhappy, my dear. Irene telephoned earlier and told me you are not quite yourself. She was right. You don't look it. I wish you'd talk about it.'

'There's nothing to talk about. I'm a bit tired, that's all— quite unaccustomed to Lady Ormsby's society do's—so many balls, tea parties and such. I have to say I found it all terribly exhausting and couldn't wait to get back to the peace and quiet of Belhaven—and to you, of course.' She smiled.

'But you did enjoy seeing Alex again,' Selwyn persisted. His eyes were sharp and uncannily piercing.

Anna looked down at their hands joined together on the quilt. 'Yes—yes, of course I did,' she whispered in acknowledgement.

He nodded. 'So that is it.'

'What do you mean?'

'I mean Alex is responsible for the change I see in you.'

'I don't know that there is a change.'

'Take it from me that there is. But don't worry, my dear. Alex will be back from America before you know it.'

Back at Oxford for her final year Anna absorbed herself in her studies as never before. She trained herself not to think of Alex, to close her mind to him, not to hurt. She succeeded—even going so far as to refuse to answer his telephone calls—until his letter arrived postmarked America.

Taking it to her room, she closed the door and stared at it for some considerable time, paralysed with shock, feeling the world begin to tilt and spin around her. With shaking fingers, she tore it open and looked at the bold handwriting that seemed to leap off the page at her.

My darling Anna, he wrote. Her heartbeat quickened as she read the opening, unbelievable endearment. The letter continued as a condescending lecture. He asked her what the hell she thought she was playing at, leaving his apartment without a by your leave and refusing to answer his calls. When he returned he would demand an explanation, so she'd better have a convincing one prepared.

Then there came a change of tone. He went on to tell her how much he was missing her, that he was thinking of her all the time and how much she meant to him. He couldn't bear to think he might have hurt her in any way and made her unhappy. He told her that because of the night they had made love, how concerned he was that she might be pregnant.

I miss you Anna, he finished. I miss you so much—I will show you just how much when I get back.

Anna read the letter over and over again, unable to focus because of the tears that fell from her eyes. She wept with joy that he'd spared the time to write to her, to say the things she wanted to hear, that he was thinking about her, that he was concerned about her, and she wept because of his betrayal.

How could he do this to her? How could he say these things when he was in America with another woman—a woman who came from the same kind of background as himself? A woman who had so much more in common with him that she would ever have.

Was it nothing more than guilt that had made him put pen to paper and write to her, because he thought she might be pregnant? Thank God she wasn't. A baby was not on the agenda at this crucial part of her life, and certainly not to a man who would stand by her out of nothing more than a sense of duty.

Her joy in the letter was overwhelming. But no sooner had that thought consoled her battered spirits than sharper ones began to pierce her in rapid, relentless succession. Drowning in humiliation she moaned aloud, wrapping her arms about her waist, but the mortifying recollections wouldn't stop. She had given herself to Alex shamelessly. She had let him do all manner of intimate things to her, and then he had gone to Sonya to do those same intimate things to her. No wonder he hadn't uttered any undying declarations of love, she thought bitterly.

He was a monster, a selfish, egotistical monster. How could he be so unutterably cruel? How could he expect her to be waiting for him on his return, to fall loyally at his feet? And how could he speak so harshly of Freddy when he himself had betrayed her with Sonya—had betrayed Sonya with her?

He was unprincipled, unfaithful and morally corrupt, and she made up her mind there and then that she wanted nothing more to do with him. She sent him a brief and to-the-point cable, thanking him for his letter and his concern for her health, and that there was absolutely nothing for him to worry about.

Anna drove to Belhaven to spend a quiet Christmas with her grandfather. After weeks of intensive study she was tired and looking forward to some time away from Oxford. It was dark when she arrived. She parked her car beside one she didn't recognise—a shiny new dark-blue Rover. It couldn't be Giles's because he was spending Christmas with his family. Keen to get inside to the warmth, she dragged her suitcase out of the boot and let herself in. The familiar smells of the house greeted her: bee's wax and wood fires and Mrs Henshaw's cooking.

'I hope you had a pleasant journey,' a smiling Mrs Henshaw said, entering the hall as Anna was struggling out of her coat.

'Yes, thank you, Mrs Henshaw. It's good to be home. How is Grandfather? Is his cold any better?' He'd been quite ill for the past week and she'd been rather worried about him.

'It's about the same as when you telephoned earlier to let him know when to expect you. Doctor Collins called to see him this afternoon and says he's on the mend. Thomas is just helping him into bed, but I'm sure he'll want to see you just as soon as he's comfortable. Can I get you anything—a cup of tea?'

'Thank you, that would be most welcome.'

'There's a visitor waiting to see you. Mr Kent arrived about an hour ago.'

Anna was immobilised. Joy and a wild, glorious happiness exploded in her heart, obliterating all memory of his deceit, but then, remembering, she recollected herself. 'Mr Kent? Oh—I see. Where is he?'

'In the drawing room.'

Like an automaton, screamingly aware of his presence, Anna moved towards the partly open door and went inside. With his hands shoved into his trouser pockets Alex stood in front of the fireplace, where a log fire glowed red in the grate. He'd taken off his suit jacket and tossed it carelessly over the back of a chair. Anna found herself looking full into his arrested grey eyes, eyes that could melt or freeze her. His face was inscrutable. The sight of his handsome, chiselled features almost sent her to her knees.

'Hello, Anna.'

Chapter Thirteen

There was no mistaking that achingly familiar deep voice. It was calm, carefully modulated, sending a sliver of fear sliding through Anna's already overstretched nervous system. His long, muscular frame was well turned out in a charcoal grey suit, the colour's starkness broken by a crisp white shirt. He had the look of a businessman and seemed most worldly.

'Hello, Alex. Forgive me if I seem somewhat surprised to see you.' Her voice was flat and emotionless.

Alex studied her. Her stillness was a positive force. 'I telephoned Selwyn earlier to let him know I was on my way.'

'I see.' It was like coming face to face with a cold, impersonal stranger. It unnerved her, especially when his eyes locked on hers with a piercing, questioning intensity. Alex removed his gaze from her face, his eyes slowly raking her before connecting with hers once more. It was all Anna could do to face his unspoken challenge and not back away.

'I see your cable did not lie.' Even as he looked at her Alex thought it strange that the memory of that one shared night should return and warm his loins.

'Lie?' Anna asked blankly. 'What are you talking about?'

'You are not pregnant.'

She looked away. He was angry and she could feel her own

anger beginning to mount. 'No, I'm not carrying your child,' she said coldly. 'You may rest easy on that score.'

He moved closer. Anna was aware of the clean, fresh scent of his cologne. Taking a deep fortifying breath, she intended to remain distinctly detached, erecting a wall between them to achieve that end. It had been an affront to her pride, her outraged, abused pride, to see him with Sonya, to see him take another woman in his arms. Her pride ached for some assuaging vengeance, but, determined not to let her emotions become entangled again, she relaxed her features. She would not humble herself to ask about Sonya—or plead with him to want her again.

'I wrote to you. Why didn't you answer my letters—and my calls?' Alex asked forcefully, looming over her. 'What in God's name do you think you're playing at? Have you any idea how much time I've spent on transatlantic calls, dealing with endless delays and stupidities of switchboards, waiting for endless minutes while connections were made, only to be told on finally getting through to your lodgings that you were out or could not be located?'

She shrugged, forcing her trembling voice to steadiness. She wouldn't give him the satisfaction of letting him see just how deeply he had penetrated her defences. 'I'm sorry, that could not be helped. I've been working hard. You of all people should know how it is—final year—exams.' She sounded flippant, she knew, but she had to. 'No doubt you have come to see Grandfather on business matters.'

Alex's jaw tensed. 'There are things we have to discuss, but my main reason for being here is to see you.'

Eager to put as much distance as possible between them, Anna turned and walked towards the window, looking out into the darkness beyond. 'Why? You never have before. You've always made a point of coming to Belhaven when you knew I wouldn't be here.' What did he want from her? He loved another. Why didn't he just go and leave her with the tattered remnants of her love?

In four long strides, Alex closed the distance separating them. Gazing down at her dark head, on a gentler note he said, 'Why did you leave, Anna? What happened to make you run off like that?'

'I didn't run. I was quite calm when I left. I had to. I told you in my note. I don't like goodbyes. Besides, you had a train to catch and you were running late. I didn't want to delay you. You would not have had the time to take me to Curzon Street yourself.'

In the glow from the lamps his face was suddenly grim, his dark eyebrows drawn together in a straight line. Looking at his reflection in the black window pane, Anna shuddered. 'Do you know what you put me through—finding you gone like that?' Alex demanded. 'Havè you any idea how concerned I have been about you?'

'No, not really. How long have you been back in England?'

'Two weeks.'

She turned and faced him squarely. 'Two weeks? You have been home two weeks and you haven't telephoned me? I don't care much for your concern, Alex.' Her voice was brittle and stinging with scorn and sarcasm. How she wished things were different between them. It would be so easy to reach out and touch him, to have him take her in his arms. For a moment she was tempted, but then she remembered Sonya and all the emotions that had warred within her since their parting rose to do battle.

'I don't choose to explain to you my other reasons for leaving, Alex, and please don't add insult to injury by asking again. Just get what business you have to do with my Grandfather done and leave.'

'Selwyn has invited me to spend Christmas here at Belhaven.'

'I didn't know.'

'Obviously.'

'And—will you?'

He nodded. 'Unless you have any objections.'

'Would it make any difference if I had? I suppose Grand-father will enjoy having someone else to talk to, especially since Giles is spending Christmas with his family.'

'It is you I have come to see.'

'Do what you want, but leave me in peace.'

Alex was being pulled in a tug of war between anger and despair. What had he done to make her behave so? Nothing made sense. 'Do you regret that night we made love, Anna? Is that what this is all about?'

She looked away. 'It was a mistake.'

'Do you mind telling me why?'

'I cannot pretend it never happened, or that I wasn't your willing partner, but that night changed matters between us. Don't you realise that? It spoiled our friendship—that special relationship we had before.'

'We ceased being just friends when you disclosed the na-ture of your true feelings to me,' Alex reminded her harshly.

'Spare me your sarcasm, Alex. I'm trying to be honest.' She dragged her eyes back to his. 'That was a mistake, too. I regret—I shall always regret my behaviour and the things I said, and if you were a gentleman you would forget all about it.'

'Forget? Something wonderful happened between us that night. I never want to forget that. Anna, something's very wrong. Tell me what it is. You're not still angry with me for dragging you from the rally that day and the way I spoke to you about Freddy Campbell? I thought that was settled be-tween us.'

'It has nothing to do with that. I behaved like a sexual illiterate. How you must have laughed. Unfortunately I didn't find it amusing, but I should have stayed. I should have let you see that what we had done didn't mean anything to me either.

'I should never have told you how I felt. For a woman to disclose such things—even to a man she—she—' the word loves stuck in her throat '—before he has said similar things to her—the man automatically believes she is lacking in self-respect. But you see, Alex, I was as naïve and innocent and gullible as the proverbial newborn babe. I should never have told you. I should have known better than to say such things to a man with an eager body and an empty heart.'

Alex stared at her in stunned amazement. 'What the devil are you talking about? Is that what all this is about—a trifling matter of you telling me you—'

Huge dark eyes, fierce with the most desperate emotion, blazed into his. 'Don't you dare remind me of what I said or call it trifling,' she cut in furiously, flaring up like a brushfire.

'Then do you mind telling me what it is you want?'

'I want what every woman wants, and that's not to be the mistress of a notorious womaniser.' Alex didn't explode; in fact, his manner was infuriatingly calm and superior. He looked at her with a faint, deprecatory smile on his lips, which she longed to remove.

'I am not a womaniser and nor have I lived as a saint, but you would do yourself a favour by not believing everything you read in the newspapers. And you are not my mistress.'

'Do you deny there was seduction on your part?'

'There was no seduction.' That was the truth of it, but it didn't stand a chance.

When he made a move to draw her closer, Anna shook her head, pushing herself from him by pressing a trembling hand to his chest to hold him back. 'No, Alex. Don't touch me. You've done enough damage. When you left for America you left me alone when I might have been carrying your child— while you—you sailed off into the sunset with…' She hesitated, unable to bring herself to utter Sonya's name; in fact, the mere thought of that other woman was more than her taut nerves could withstand. 'Whatever happened between us was a mistake.'

Alex caught her hand and held it fast within his grasp. Never had he wanted a woman as much as he wanted Anna, and never had he felt less sure of his ability to get what he wanted. 'There are some mistakes, Anna, that can easily be put aside.'

'Not this. Not ever.'

As she faced him she felt a terrible pain inside. She couldn't believe this was happening. She longed to respond to the pressure of his hand holding hers, to feel his mouth on hers setting her blood on fire. But the image of Sonya with her angelic features and her loving smile stood between them. She wanted to scream at him and shake him and make him realise how much he had hurt her, but she didn't say anything. Her pride prevented it.

'You are heartless and I should never have let you touch me. I shall never forgive my stupidity for ever trusting you,' and loving you, she thought. Snatching her hand from his grasp as if she had been electrocuted, she turned and walked quickly towards the door. His voice halted her half way across the room.

'I intend to find out what's behind this, Anna. It isn't over between us.'

Anna turned and looked at him, meeting his eyes head on, every bit as stubborn as he was persuasive. She sensed the power that he had, that he would always have, over her. It came to her in waves across the distance that separated them.

'It is, Alex. I can't let it happen again.'

'You can't prevent it. I promise.'

'I must! I will!'

'Just don't bet on it.'

Alex watched her go. The door slammed shut behind her and he heard her hurried footsteps cross the hall and climb the stairs. Although he longed to go after her he didn't. Combing back a wayward lock of black hair from his forehead with impatient fingers, he stood looking into the firelight, wondering what it was all about.

Was she ashamed of what they'd done? He didn't think so. She'd told him she regretted confessing how she felt about him—was that because her feelings had changed, that she

hadn't enjoyed making love? On recalling the passionate, irresistible temptress he had aroused in his bed, of the pure
bliss they had each felt in their union, he knew that wasn't it
either. The one thing that stood out from that night was the
pleasure they had shared.

It had to be something else, something that had happened
in those few minutes when he had been in the bathroom. She
had told him she didn't like goodbyes—he didn't accept that.
She had also said that he was already late for his train and
she didn't want to delay him. He didn't accept that either. In
her distress she had referred to something obliquely but he
had discounted her words. Yet now he began to wonder anew
and try to recall what she had said. She'd accused him of
leaving her alone when she might have been carrying his
child, that he had sailed off into the sunset with...

Then it hit him, and in that one abbreviated moment he
knew.

His memory was like a book being opened wide for the
first time and the answers were staring him in the face.

His mind rebelled in disbelief.

What a blind, stupid idiot he was!

'Sonya!' The name was like a pained sound in the room.

Anna knew about Sonya, that was the answer he'd been
searching for, but it was obvious she didn't know who she
was. Sworn to secrecy over the tragedy that had befallen his
lovely sister, no one had told Anna about her. He recalled the
time at the villa when he had been speaking to Sonya on the
telephone and how he had felt a presence in the hall and seen
the flash of a yellow skirt disappearing when he'd turned.
Anna must have heard his endearments, might have seen the
odd picture of her with him in the newspapers. And, seeing
Sonya's photograph in his study, she had assumed the worst.

Pondering the matter, he placed a knuckle against his lips
and then he laughed suddenly at the sheer absurdity of it all.
Turning on his heel he went to see Selwyn, who confirmed

Alex's belief that, out of loyalty to Alex, no one had spoken of Sonya to Anna. He then went in search of Mrs Henshaw.

Her aged face broke into a smile when he walked with jaunty strides into the kitchen. Mrs Henshaw had known Alex since the day he had come to Belhaven as a gangly youth and had grown extremely fond of him over the years. She found him endearing and always clucked about him like a mother hen when he came to stay.

'Dinner will be half an hour, and I've done your favourite—steak and kidney pie.'

'Excellent. Tell Miss Preston I'll be waiting for her in the dining room, will you, Mrs Henshaw?'

'I'm afraid you're going to be disappointed. Miss Preston says she's extremely tired and asks to be excused—and would I take her dinner up on a tray.'

Alex's grin was tigerish. 'Did she, indeed? Kindly inform Miss Preston I expect her to dine with me, and that I have something to tell her that will make her feel a hundred per cent better.'

Alex's invitation was so incredulous that Anna decided to dine with him to see what it was all about. After checking on her grandfather, she entered the dining room with all the enthusiasm she would have felt for a public execution.

They dined at eight o'clock, with Alex seated across from her at the long dining table. Using the flower arrangement in the centre as a barrier between them, apart from speaking to Mrs Henshaw when she brought in their meal, Anna maintained an uneasy, cool and formal silence. Whatever it was Alex had to tell her, he was deliberately prolonging her suspense. She certainly wasn't going to ask. As soon as she had eaten dessert she rose and excused herself.

Laying his napkin aside, Alex stood up. Striding round to her side of the table, he pulled out her chair. 'I've asked Mrs Henshaw to have coffee brought to us in the sitting room. There are certain matters you and I need to discuss, Anna.'

'But I—'

'Please,' he interrupted. 'I find it most unpleasant being at loggerheads. Besides, Selwyn has the eyes of a hawk. It won't take him long to detect something is wrong between us and will give each of us a severe talking to.'

Despite the rancour she still felt, Anna smiled.

Alex's eyes twinkled. 'Dare I hope that smile denotes a softening in your attitude towards me?' he asked lazily, loosening the knot of his tie and unfastening the top button of his shirt.

'Not at all. I was merely visualising my grandfather giving *you* a dressing down. Somehow I can't for the life of me imagine that anyone would be brave enough.'

'Selwyn's an exception.'

Closing the door of the sitting room, Anna poured the coffee and settled herself on the sofa, where Alex joined her. After taking a sip of his coffee, he set his cup on the low table in front of them and sat staring into the fire with single-minded concentration. After a few moments he turned and looked at Anna.

'We have to talk.'

'Yes, I think we must.' Setting her cup down, she sensed she was about to learn about Sonya at last. After all the months of agonising it came as something of a relief.

'Tell me, Anna, was Sonya the reason why you left that day—when you saw her photograph, when you read her endearment and assumed she and I are lovers?' Seeing the answer staring agonisingly out of her eyes, he smiled. 'You idiot. Sonya is not my lover. She is my sister.'

Anna stared at him in disbelief. The colour drained slowly from her face. 'Your sister? And you didn't think it important enough to tell me?' She stood up abruptly and moved away from him, trying to come to grips with what he had told her. 'How could you?' she said, her voice shaking with bitterness and pain. 'How could you let me go on believing she was your—your…? Oh, Alex, how could you?'

Alex met her fury with equanimity. He heard the violence of her emotions, saw the expressive face go through a range of changes, and he finally understood the inexplicable anguish she had needlessly been through. A look of sympathy softened his grim features.

'Anna, listen to me,' he said, going to her and grasping her by the shoulders. 'I didn't know. Believe me, I had no idea you knew about Sonya. I owe you an apology. It was wrong of me not to have told you, but I had my reasons, and if you will sit down I will tell you. I would never hurt you intentionally. I want you to know that.'

Anna saw that he was looking at her openly and with a passionate warmth. 'You've always had my best interests at heart, haven't you?' she capitulated softly. 'I shall always be grateful to you for that, and what you've done for me, and I do not pretend it could ever be otherwise.'

'Nevertheless, the past must be dealt with before we can go on with the future. There is so much to tell, it's knowing where to begin. Come and sit down.'

Anna did as she was bade, her legs curled beneath her. Beside her, with one arm draped across the back of the sofa, Alex settled back and propped his ankle on the opposite knee, watching the flames dancing in the hearth.

'The last thing I want is for you to rake over some repellent, painful past, but you are right, Alex, to go on we must be open with each other. Why don't you begin by telling me about Sonya. Where does she live?'

'In a convent just north of Oxford. In order for you to understand why she is there, I must start at the beginning, by telling you a little of what it was like for us in Russia when the Revolution came. That Lenin intended to rule by methods more violent than any Tsar soon became clear. He was one among many bewildered millions who completely knew his own mind.

'When an attempt was made on his life, the Soviet Political Police force executed or imprisoned people by their tens of thousands. With the country already in ruins, it was a struggle for Bolshevism fought by the Reds against the Whites, who were united to overthrow the Soviet government. There was no organisation, only chaos everywhere. Red—white—it didn't matter. They were as bad as each other. The bulk of both sides consisted of apathetic peasants impressed at gunpoint.'

'Where did you live?'

'East of Moscow. My stepfather, Victor Melinkov, who is Sonya's father, was eager to distinguish himself in the Red Army and left to fight. He forced me to go with him, leaving my mother and Sonya completely alone at a time when the White Army was closing in.'

Anna saw his eyes harden and heard the note of bitterness in his voice when he spoke of Victor Melinkov. 'You didn't like your stepfather?'

'I loathed him. Unlike my own father, he was a hard and brutal man, and he soon got rid of what money my father had left. I watched my mother become a beaten woman and I hated him for that. When he left her and Sonya, fearing for their safety I escaped and went back, but I was too late. Refusing to turn over their horses and what meagre food supplies they had to the Whites, the villagers had put up a courageous resistance. The reprisals were terrible. I can see the scene still—the fire so hot it melted the snow, and sounds of screaming people running in all directions to escape the guns and the flames as they were being herded into the burning church.

'It was mayhem. I did everything I could to get my mother and Sonya out, but I succeeded in saving only Sonya. She was in a state of numbness for a long time, then total despair—then something else—something much worse—shock, the doctor said to whom I took her to tend her injuries.'

Anna listened to him in horror. 'Alex, how dreadful it must have been—and your poor mother. Was Sonya badly burned?'

'No, thank God. Her injuries were only superficial and soon healed. But it was appalling for her. She took what had happened very badly. I was patient with her—as patient as a fourteen-year-old youth can be—but it was very difficult. She was alternatively angry, hostile and frantically and fearfully dependent on me. She would cling to me, making me promise not to leave her—I wouldn't, of course. I loved her.'

'What made you come to England?'

'There was nothing for us in Russia any more. People were being killed on a massive scale. Blood-crazed mobs slaughtered master and servant alike, indiscriminately, and those who were left were starving. I saw what human beings could do to each other. It was every man for himself. I knew hunger and despair. The tide had turned, the previously established order of things had gone. Everything I had known, everything to do with family, home, order, had crumbled into dust. Lenin and the Bolsheviks were in control. Russia was doomed. I decided to find my mother's people. Fortunately I had a little money. We went south to the Crimea where I managed to get visas and passage on board a ship for England.

'In London we were taken to a refuge for immigrants in the East End, and it was there I met Sister Geraldine—a true angel of mercy. Alarmed by Sonya's condition, she took us to the convent near Oxford where she ran a home for unmarried pregnant girls. Sonya had nightmares about what had happened, what she had seen, so bad I worried for her sanity. Then she became quiet, withdrawn, absolutely so, and I began to worry even more.

'Eventually she settled down. The nightmares became less frequent. She felt safe at the convent. The sisters were good to her. They understood her and told me she could stay with them indefinitely. Only then did I feel comfortable about leaving her. I went in search of my mother's people. That was when I met Selwyn.' He paused and looked at Anna. 'Selwyn and my mother, they—'

'It's all right, Alex. Grandfather told me how close they were, that they would have married had she—'

'Been of his class,' Alex finished for her without preamble.

'Love should matter more than class.'

'I agree, but it is not the opinion of the upper classes. I understand all about the class system in this country—it was the same in Russia in those days, before the Revolution. Had Selwyn married my mother, her position would not have been easy. To marry from dissimilar backgrounds often proves to be a recipe for disaster. It might have ended up a social mess.'

'Perhaps you're right. What happened then?'

'Suddenly my life in England offered a great deal. With Sonya settled at the convent, I did not mention her. I set her aside, not carelessly, nor thoughtlessly—never that. I loved her too much to do that—but carefully, gently. Knowing that if I was to get on with my life, to continue to provide for Sonya, that was the best, the only way—so long as I maintained silence and Sonya's secret was untold.'

Anna glanced up at him curiously, thinking it was a strange thing for him to say and sensing there was more to that final sentence than she understood just then. Recalling the disparaging remark Freddy had made about Sonya, she suspected something had happened to her here in England that was as terrible as what had happened to her in Russia, and that Freddy was in some way responsible.

'When I left your apartment a man spoke to me. He was Russian, I think, middle aged and smartly dressed. He mistook me for Sonya—Sonyasha, he called me.' Even though they sat inches apart, Anna felt Alex's body tense. His eyes had become as hard and brittle as ice.

'Victor Melinkov—Sonya's father. I can understand his mistake. Sonya is not unlike you in height and appearance. She is dark haired like you, and wears it in a similar style. Victor hasn't seen her since she was eight years old. He came to Britain in search of her, knowing this was where he would find us. He knew I would seek out my mother's people. Learning of my success was an added bonus. He thought to fleece me out of whatever he could.'

'Has he seen Sonya?'

'No. Because of her delicate mental state and not knowing how she will react to meeting her father after all these years, fearing the past will reassert itself and set her back, I've kept her whereabouts from him. But I know he's been making enquiries, watching my apartment, and it won't be long before he finds her. It was for that reason that I took her with me to America—for my own peace of mind and thinking some time away from the convent would be good for her. I left her behind once before when I went away—I shall regret doing so until the day I die.'

'I know she accompanied you,' Anna said quietly. 'I saw her.'

'How could you?'

'I was there. When I was halfway to Curzon Street I began thinking. I realised I shouldn't have left you like that, but I was angry—after seeing the photograph of Sonya, you understand. I told the taxi driver to take me to the Embankment, where I walked for quite some time, trying to sort out my thoughts. It was hopeless. In spite of all my resolve my body was my ruler. I had to see you to say goodbye, so I went to Victoria Station. That was when I saw you with Sonya.'

'And putting two and two together you made five.'

Her lips trembled into a smile. 'I never was very good at mathematics. But what I still don't understand is why all the secrecy. Why didn't you tell me you have a sister? Alex, has it anything to do with Freddy and his sister? Did something happen between Freddy and Sonya—when you left her alone?'

'Has anyone given you reason to believe it did?'

'Well, your behaviour towards Freddy in the past for one thing—and Freddy himself told me—when I happened to encounter him at Ascot. When I told Freddy I wouldn't see him again, he was furious. He—he blamed you for my change of heart, and he blamed Sonya for deceiving him. He slated her most dreadfully, Alex. Unaware that Sonya was your sister, I thought at first the hostility between you and Freddy might be because she preferred you to him, but then I thought it must be more than that.'

'Correct. You say he slated Sonya. How? What did he say?'

Her face burning with embarrassment as she remembered, Anna turned her head away. 'Oh, Alex, it was obscene…'

Reaching out, he placed his hand against the side of her face and forced her to look at him. 'Tell me.'

'He—he called her a Jewish whore.'

He nodded, pausing for a moment to digest what she had said. 'Jewish she may be, but a whore? Never. Sonya is the finest, gentlest woman I know—apart from you, Anna. She has never hurt anyone in her life.'

'How did Sonya meet Freddy?' Anna asked.

Alex got up and poured himself a brandy. Replacing the stopper in the decanter, he resumed his seat beside Anna, swirling the amber liquid round in the glass before knocking it back in one and setting the glass on the table.

'It was when she was eighteen and I had taken her to stay with Quentin and Irene in London. I remember how happy she was then, happy to spend some time away from the convent. Irene knew about Sonya and I often took her to visit her. Sonya had become fond of her so I had no qualms about her staying with them. I had some business to take care of in Geneva and was apprehensive about leaving her, but it could not be put off.

'It was while she was in London that she met Freddy Campbell—I now realise it wasn't a random meeting. In order to get back at me for finishing with Edwina…' he looked at Anna with narrowed eyes, '…did you know Edwina and I had had an affair?'

'Yes. Tamsin told me—which is more than you did after our encounter with Edwina at Maxim's.' She smiled. 'Alex, what you did in the past is over and your own business. That Edwina is a vindictive sort I could tell when I met her. What did she do?'

'Freddy is her bad, misguided, beautiful twin, and she

adores him. Our affair was short—in truth, I had no time for the woman, and I made no secret of the fact. She approached me on two occasions afterwards. I set her aside and earned her everlasting hatred for it. She orchestrated and encouraged Freddy's meeting with Sonya, knowing how furious I would be when I found out. Sonya was unable to work out how to deal with all the new things in her life.'

'Was it her first experience of life outside the convent?'

'Yes, and it was all very strange—the world of Freddy Campbell, strange but dangerous. And to Sonya, wide-eyed and innocent as she was, exciting and intriguing. Freddy flattered her and she was naïve enough to think him sincere and soon became besotted. He took advantage of her innocence.

'At the time—before Edwina and Freddy tried to blacken my name—Irene could see nothing wrong in Sonya seeing him. He was good looking, extremely charming and considerate, always saying and doing the right thing. He also belonged to the aristocracy—and that, in Irene's book, was terrible important. Any woman could count herself privileged to have attracted the attention of such a man.'

'But unfortunately he was not what he seemed.'

'Too damned right. Campbell is a world-class scoundrel, a master of manipulation, and he treated Sonya in the vilest possible way. He did absolutely nothing to earn her respect or her loyalty, yet she gave him herself both freely and without reservation. He broke through her isolation and, without her realising it, she allowed herself to be drawn. She was like putty in his hands.

'Not for one moment did Campbell doubt his power, his control over her, or his ability to manipulate that control to his advantage. At the time I was doing well and making a name for myself. Campbell was under no illusions as to my wealth, my ambition. He'd already tried to buy into my company and asked me to give him a seat on the board of Kent Enterprises before the crash on Wall Street. His addiction to drink and drugs was as legendary as his other vices, and he was totally unreliable. I didn't like him then and told him to forget it.

'However, as Sonya is my only living relative, he knew I would make a generous settlement on her when she married, and he would have to marry money in order to save himself and resurrect his family's bankrupt estate from the grave. He could not live on charm alone and being ambitious, though extremely idle, he could not live on anything less than wealth and good social connections. He was coldly rational about these matters.

'His behaviour was underhand, stealthy. Impatient to seal their relationship before I returned from Geneva to put a stop to it—because the reality of my absolute dislike for him left him with no illusions that I would in no way consider him a suitable husband for Sonya—he made her pregnant. Irene and Quentin were devastated that they had allowed such a thing to happen while Sonya was in their care. They sent me a cable, explaining what had happened and that I should come home at once. Believing Campbell loved her and that he would marry her, Sonya couldn't understand why everyone was making such a fuss. Of course, Campbell was delighted at the way things had turned out—until Sonya unwittingly told him she was a Jew.'

Alex fell silent, marshalling his memories. Anna could see the shadows of those memories pass across his face. Her dark eyes were disturbed but trustful as she waited for him to continue. She saw him release a breath too tightly held, saw his eyes close momentarily as though in prayer.

'The effect upon Campbell was appalling,' he continued softly. 'To marry a Jew is inconceivable to him. According to Orthodox beliefs, the religion is passed down through the mother's side of the family—and our mother was English and a Christian. So you see, Sonya was not actually a Jew by birth. But because her father is a Jew and for the first few years of her life she had been raised in the Jewish faith, according to society she is tainted. Campbell is obsessional in

his hatred of Jews—hence his adherence to the fascists—
which is greater than his hatred of me. When he turned his
back and walked out on Sonya, in a moment her passionate,
loyal heart was broken.

'Irene took her to Applemead to await my arrival. Not in
my worst fears had I imagined that such a terrible thing could
befall my lovely untouched sister. She was a child, inexperienced in such things. No man would dare, would have the
temerity, to play fast and loose, to interfere with the sister of
a man whose whole life had been dedicated to keeping her
safe.

'When I saw her I could not believe the change in her. She
had gone from the happy, laughing girl with a bright future
to one drained of all emotion. She was a child again, a lost
and frightened child who was confused by some unexpected,
frightening turn of events. How had she come to this? I asked
myself, as she retreated into the dreadful nightmare-filled
world in which she had struggled when I brought her out of
the fire.'

'What happened to the baby?'

'She miscarried. On the day of my arrival at Applemead
she went missing. A search was immediately put underway.
I found her. She had wandered as far as Belhaven—and tried
to drown herself in the lake. I managed to reach her in time,
but the trauma proved too much. She lost the child shortly
afterwards.'

At last Anna understood. It was like putting the final piece
in a jigsaw. 'So that was what Grandfather was referring to
when he was telling me how much he loved the lake—but
that it had some dark moments, tragic and best forgotten. It
also explains why you always made a point of avoiding it on
our walks last summer. I'm so sorry, Alex. What happened
after that?'

'When she was strong enough I took her back to the convent, but she's never recovered from the loss of her child. For
a long time she was inconsolable. I had never seen such des-

olation. As I held her trembling body close and shed tears of compassionate love, soothing her as she struggled to escape the memories that tore at her, knowing that once again I would have to carry the heavy burden of care for Sonya, I swore that if Freddy Campbell or his conniving sister ever came within my sights I would kill them.'

'But you didn't,' Anna said quietly.

'No, but there have been times when I've been close. To this day he's in my head, as ruthless and manipulative as ever. Perhaps now you can understand my anger when I saw him honing in on you, knowing the tragedy that had befallen Sonya could happen all over again—to you.'

Anna looked at him, her face grave as she considered what he had told her. 'Yes, of course I can.'

'I was afraid, Anna, afraid you might fall for him, and if it made me unreasonable and bad-tempered, then I humbly apologise. It was only because I was afraid for you.'

'I admire your courage to admit that you can feel afraid. If I had known all this, I would have avoided Freddy. How very sad it is,' she said, and added more to herself than to Alex, 'Your poor sister. When you spoke to Freddy at Olympia, just before we left, what did you say to him? Whatever it was, he looked devastated.'

'I told him that Sonya had tried to kill herself—that as a result she lost the child.'

Horrified, Anna stared at him. 'You mean he didn't know?'

'No.'

'Did he think Sonya had had the child?'

'I expect he did.'

'Then it would appear that his hatred of anyone Jewish is so great that he couldn't even bring himself to enquire after his own child,' Anna murmured softly, unable to believe anyone could be so callous, so cruel. 'That is both terrible and sad. You really should have told me all of this earlier, Alex, and about Sonya being your sister. Quite apart from the fact that everyone else appears to know, as a compassionate, intelligent human being, and your friend, if I'd been told the tragedy of Sonya's past I would have understood completely. I think I deserved your confidence.'

'Of course you did, and I should have known better than to withhold it—my reason for doing so being that the fewer people who know, the less likely her father is to find her. But I did intend telling you.'

'You said her father is Jewish?'

Alex nodded. 'Because of the way things were in Russia towards Jews—they were treated harshly by society—all his life Victor's tried to hide his Jewishness, which is something he's not proud of.'

'And you? Have you forgiven your stepfather his harsh treatment of your mother?'

'No. That's impossible. But I do see things differently. Victor has spent years in a labour camp—a hellhole, he called it, and I believe that's exactly what it was. He suffered, Anna, that I know. It's left him with a well of bitterness, but it's also given him a need to savour what future he has left, and to become reconciled with those he hurt.'

'Reconciliation and redemption can defy anything that's gone before, Alex—forgiveness, too, if you let it. You didn't turn him away when he sought you out. You gave him money to carry on.'

'And he keeps coming back for more.'

'And you give it to him. One thing I learned as I was growing up is that it's easy to condemn, but harder being compassionate. It seems to me you have shown compassion for your stepfather, even if the reason is hard for you to understand just now.'

Alex smiled softly. 'You have a beautiful head on your shoulders, Anna Preston, and a wise one, full of goodness. However, I've no intention of acting like the caring stepson all of a sudden, but filtering some money his way now and then keeps him off my back.'

'That may be so, but the time may come when he finds Sonya. Would you want him to turn up unannounced?'

'No, of course not, which is what I'm afraid of.'

'In which case, don't you think it best that you control the situation?'

'What are you saying?'

'That you talk to Sonya and tell her that her father is looking for her. How old is she?'

'Twenty-four.'

'Old enough for her to decide for herself whether or not she wants to meet him. Is she a logical person?'

'Absolutely.'

'Then she might surprise you and say she does. Give her the power to change her own life, Alex.'

'That isn't possible.'

'All she needs is the will.'

'Like you?'

'If you like.'

Chapter Fourteen

Because his emotions seemed perilously close to the surface, looking for a distraction, Alex said, 'Have you given some thought as to what you will do when you've finished at Oxford?'

Anna's enthusiasm for the new life she was planning shone passionately from her eyes. 'When I get my degree everything will be so different. It will be a turning point in my life. I'm considering going into journalism.'

'Really?' Alex knew she was passionately interested in current affairs and that she read the newspapers avidly. She was always keen to voice her opinion about the events of the day, the state of the economy and the unemployed, and so her decision to become a journalist came as no surprise. 'I suspected that you might be thinking along those lines.'

'I've been mulling it over for some time. It fascinates me. It has a freedom and a way of creating worlds and lives in such a short space. Eventually I'd love to work for the BBC. Olivia Pilkington—she's a friend of mine at Oxford—has a brother, Roger, who works on the *Herald*. He's worked there for four years now, and has become regarded as one of the paper's most valuable assets. I'm thinking of approaching them and Roger may be able to put in a word for me. At least it will be a start. What do you think?'

A silence fell. Alex was looking at her in wonder, at the fervour in her voice and the passion for creating that he had never seen in her before. He adored her and she affected him deeply, but he would suppress the desire to ask her to commit herself to him at this time, which was what he had intended. Her work must come first and would leave her no time for romantic attachments. At least she was honest about what mattered to her. She was young, on the brink of a new and exciting life, which she had worked hard to achieve. He could not come in the way of that. Already he could feel her slipping away from him.

'That if it's what you want, then that's what you must do, Anna,' he said in answer to her question. 'You've obviously given it a good deal of thought and I believe it will be as good a place as any to begin your career.'

Alex smiled in tribute to her ambition, but Anna could tell that a light had gone from his eyes. Despite his interest, she was aware that his mood had changed. There was an indefinable tension and a grimness in his features that was becoming more pronounced by the second. What had gone wrong? Why was he distancing himself from her? Despite all his encouragement throughout the time she had known him, perhaps he didn't want an independent, career-minded woman in his life. Even though she had a deep desire to become a part of his life, to include him in all she wanted to achieve, she knew that the final decision was his to make.

She was absolutely and passionately in love with him, but she had no idea how he really felt about her. By coming to Belhaven and telling her about Sonya, she had hoped he had been on the brink of a declaration of love, and now she felt foolish, surrendering to hope so quickly and eagerly. Somehow, even though her heart was splintering, she kept her smile bright and her chin high.

'Of course I shall have to find some accommodation in London—not that I intend staying there all the time. I shall get back to Belhaven as often as I can. I frequently see advertisements in the papers offering shared accommodation. At least it would keep the rent down—and—perhaps I could see you from time to time.' An indescribable expression flashed across his face. 'I'm sorry if I said something wrong,' she said lamely. 'You—you aren't being very logical. Alex. Why did you come here and tell me about Sonya if not to take up the thread of where we left off?'

'I made it plain earlier why I came. I want you, Anna— indeed, what man in his right mind wouldn't? But I have scruples enough to ignore that ignoble impulse.'

'What happened to your scruples on the night when I stayed with you? You wanted me then.'

'And you remained for that reason,' he told her bluntly. 'We wanted each other.'

'Whether it was foolish or not, I admit that I did want you. I couldn't help myself. Neither of us has anything to gain by pretending that it is over and forgotten. You told me earlier that something wonderful happened between us that night, that it changed things between us. Your letters telling me how much you missed me and that you were thinking of me all the time proved it wasn't over, if they proved nothing else. I shall never forget it, and I know you won't.'

Alex stood up and moved away from her, trying not to look like a man in the throes of some internal battle. He wanted to deny it, but he sensed that if he did she would be disgusted with his deceit. He desperately wanted her to know the truth about how he felt. He was certain that the truth couldn't hurt her nearly as much as the distance he had placed between them, but, for now, he had to let her get on with her life.

'Just for the record, about what you said earlier—you did not behave like a sexual illiterate on the night you stayed at my apartment, and what we did meant a great deal to me. And I may have teased you in the past, but I have never laughed at you. Nor did I mind when you told me how you felt. But you must try and understand that among other things you will soon be at an important turning point in your life.

You have so much to achieve. I have no intention of complicating matters for you by asking you to embark on a close
relationship at this point.'

Anna wanted to say that for him she would leave Oxford,
that she would quit her studies and walk with him to the ends
of the earth, that she would die for him if need be, but she
kept quiet. Alex was right—neither of them would be happy
with such a solution. Besides, she was not entirely sure that
he loved her as much as she loved him.

There was a knock on the door and Mrs Henshaw came in,
carrying a tray.

'Sorry to disturb you both, but I thought I'd clear away and
then I'm off to bed.' Setting the cups on the tray, she turned
and looked at them, her eyes twinkling, thinking it was about
time these two stopped shilly-shallying about and got together. His lordship would be over the moon. 'Goodnight and
sleep well.' She went towards the door. 'Tomorrow you might
be thinking about getting a tree. You'll have to be seeing Sam
Philips, the head keeper, about that. No doubt he'll have put
one aside for the house.'

Anna and Alex glanced at each other and then back at Mrs
Henshaw in bewilderment. 'A tree?' they said in unison.

Mrs Henshaw looked back at them from the open doorway.
'A Christmas tree. Don't tell me you haven't thought of it. It
is Christmas.' She went out, chuckling softly.

Anna felt as if it was the first Christmas of her life. She
was happy simply to be with Alex, despite the space he placed
between them. They dressed the enormous tree together, hung
mistletoe and did all the traditional things like roasting chest-
nuts and drinking warm punch in front of the fire on Christmas Eve. The carol singers that came from Stainton after dark
stood in the hall in front of the tree and sang well loved carols
like 'Silent Night' and 'We Three Kings', and afterwards
Anna helped Mrs Henshaw hand round mulled wine and
mince pies.

* * *

On Christmas morning, with church bells ringing out a joyful, clangourous tumbling peal, they went to the morning service. Afterwards they opened presents and ate Christmas dinner in the dining room with Selwyn, and in the evening the Ormsbys drove over from Applemead for drinks.

And then it was over.

As soon as Anna returned to Oxford she was plunged into work and weeks of cramming before she could sit her degree. She missed Alex dreadfully. There was the occasional telephone call from him, but that was all—and he always sounded so reserved, so distant. The only recreation she allowed herself was the odd visit to Belhaven to see her grandfather and, armed with a box of chocolates or crystallised fruit, a trip to the theatre or the cinema with Olivia.

Time passed quickly. At last Anna sat her exams and suddenly it was summer and she had her degree—a first in English literature. She was euphoric and immediately phoned Alex.

'Congratulations, Anna. It's fantastic news. I couldn't be more delighted, or proud. Didn't I tell you you could do it?'

Anna's eyes filled with tears of happiness. She swallowed hard. 'Yes, you did. Thank you so much for your encouragement, Alex, for having faith in me. I would never have done it without you.'

'Yes, you would. Well done. You deserve it. Are you excited—feeling like the cat that's got the cream?'

'Yes.' She laughed. 'Something like that. I'm thrilled. I can't quite believe it. It hasn't sunk in yet.'

'Have you rung Selwyn?'

'No, not yet. I wanted you to be the first to know. I'll call him when I put the phone down.'

'We'll have a mass celebration when you're back at Belhaven and down in London. How about a party at the Savoy?'

Anna smiled softly, wishing she could see him at that moment. 'Yes, that would be nice,' she said, thinking a quiet dinner for just the two of them at the Café Royal would be nicer.

'Good.' He paused, before continuing on a more serious note. 'Anna, I was wondering if you'd like to meet Sonya tomorrow. I know she would like to meet you; now your exams are over, I see no reason why you shouldn't. I've told her about Victor and I think she'd like to meet him after she's got to know you. She's apprehensive, as you can imagine, and I thought maybe you could be with me when they finally do meet.'

'Yes, I'd love to meet her at long last. I shall look forward to it.'

'Good. I'll pick you up at three.'

Set in woodland in the gentle contours of Evenlode Valley, north of Oxford, stood the Convent of the Sisters of Magdalene. The moment Anna entered its walls, she was struck by its cleanliness and order, its spirituality. There was a timelessness, a simple, orderly world of white walls and whispering quiet. Sister Geraldine greeted them warmly and ushered them into her office after dispatching one of the other sisters to fetch Sonya. The whole impression of Anna's surroundings was of air and space, the room striped light and dark from the partly closed shuttered window that overlooked the convent gardens.

'Sonya is helping in the nurseries,' Sister Geraldine informed them. 'She's such a help with the babies, and the girls just love her. She'll be along in a moment.'

'How has she been, Sister?' Alex enquired.

'Very well, I'm pleased to say. She has given much thought to meeting her father, and I think she might agree to it. At first I was worried about the effect it might have on her, but she is stronger now—both spiritually and emotionally. I think she will cope.'

Anna recognised Sister Geraldine as being the nun she had seen with Sonya at Victoria Station. The door opened and an extremely pretty young woman entered. Alex went to her and embraced her tenderly before taking her arm and drawing her forward.

'Sonya, this is Anna. Anna, this is Sonya.'

'Hello, Sonya.' Anna held out her hand and it was shaken lightly. 'I'm so happy to meet you at last. Alex has told me so much about you.'

They were about the same height. Sonya's short dark hair was clipped back with two red slides. Her eyes were green, speckled with brown, and set wide apart in a heart-shaped face. Wearing a smock over a floral print dress, she stood looking at Anna smiling shyly. There was something childlike about her.

'Would you like some tea?' Sister Geraldine enquired.

'Tea would be lovely, thank you,' Anna said.

'Perhaps you would like to show Anna around the convent first, Sonya,' Alex suggested. 'Sister Geraldine and I have things to discuss.'

Sonya turned and looked at Anna and smiled her gentle smile. 'Would you like that?'

'Yes, very much. You can tell me all about it as we go.'

Sonya happily led Anna away for a tour of inspection. Nuns going about their work smiled as they passed. 'I'm sure Alex has told you that the convent is a place of Christian charity and good fellowship, offering sanctuary to girls who find themselves in unfortunate circumstances,' she explained, rising enthusiastically to the subject to which her life had become dedicated.

'Yes, he has, and that it was the creation of Sister Geraldine.'

'That is correct—although, suffering from a lack of funds, it was only a small institution to begin with. Alex has made it what it is today—in grateful appreciation of what Sister Geraldine did for us when we came from Russia, you understand. There are a great many comings and goings, and, whatever the sins committed, no one is turned away. We are concerned for the welfare of the women and that of their babies.'

Sonya spoke in fractured English, which Anna found attractive. 'You obviously enjoy your work.'

'Yes, I love it. The girls come from all walks of life, from the most well-to-do respectable families to some of the poorest. Some of them have nothing, their families are destitute, and they have little choice but to let their babies go.'

'It must be heartbreaking.'

'The decision isn't easy for them, but it isn't as if they are letting their babies go to someone who doesn't want them.'

'It's obvious to me that you like living here, Sonya.'

'Oh, yes. It's my home—and I do so love looking after the babies.'

Hearing the quietly spoken words, Anna turned her head far enough to study Sonya's profile, thinking what a compassionate, truly nice person Alex's sister was. But there was a secret grief lurking in her gaze. She sensed it. Did Sonya still suffer from that deep inner wound inflicted by Freddy Campbell? Perhaps helping with the infants brought her the comfort she needed following the loss of her own child.

'Do you often stay with Alex in London?'

'Not really. He comes here mostly. He—he has told me my father is in London…and that he wants to see me.'

'I know. Would you like to see him?'

'I've thought about it—and I think I must.'

'Do you remember him?'

She nodded. 'Not very well. When he left us in Russia, my mother and me, I remember that I cried. I was afraid, but I don't remember why. There was so much confusion at the time.'

Before they reached Sister Geraldine's office, Anna stopped and turned to face Sonya. 'Sonya, I shall be staying with Lord and Lady Ormsby in London myself the week after next. I believe you know them, that you have stayed with them yourself.' She saw pain slash its way across Sony's face, but she went on quickly, giving it no time to establish itself. 'Why don't you let Alex bring you to town then? You could meet your father.'

'Yes, I would like that. You know, ever since we left Russia, Alex has devoted so much of his life to me, to worrying about me, but I'm better now. I'm going to become a Roman Catholic—has Alex told you?'

'Yes, he did mention it.'

'That's what he's talking to Sister Geraldine about. I've been thinking about it for a long time—years, in fact. I want to dedicate my life to what I'm doing now, and to God. I might even decide to become a nun. I'm never going to get married, you see. However the decision has been a hard one for me to make and I cannot simply dismiss my Jewishness. It distresses me to give up the religion and culture in which I was raised, but I do feel more comfortable with my mother's religion.'

Anna was arrested by the passionate intensity of her words. They were born of deep conviction—and perhaps more than a little pain. But she hid that. Sonya had a quality about her some would call strength, others fear, fear of life outside the secure walls of the convent.

'You sound very determined, Sonya.' She smiled. 'In fact, you remind me of myself when I wanted to go to university. All my life I knew that was what I wanted to do, and it was thanks to Alex and my grandfather that I got there. I have a notion you'll be a success at anything you choose to do.'

'I'm glad you think so, and congratulations on getting your degree, by the way. Alex told me when he rang to let me know you were coming. He's extremely proud of you, you know—as Lord Manson must be.'

'Yes, he's delighted and can't wait for me to get home,' Anna said, remembering how overcome with delight her grandfather had been when she'd telephoned him right after she'd been speaking to Alex yesterday.

'I can imagine. Now, let's go and have that cup of tea.'

* * *

That summer of 1935 saw the celebration of King George V's Silver Jubilee. It was an unqualified success, prompting a national demonstration of loyalty and patriotism. However, storm clouds were gathering as people felt they were heading towards war, and those who had been through the previous war were terribly depressed about unsettling events in Europe.

But all this was forgotten when Alex opened the door of his apartment to admit an impeccably dressed Victor Melinkov. Sonya was standing in the centre of the room, waiting. Victor didn't see Alex and Anna at first. He was much too interested in the young woman who was looking at him, cool, neat and contained. He bowed slightly and stood there for a lengthy moment, not moving an inch, but then he stepped forward. Taking Sonya's hands in his, he held them, gazing into her eyes with a look of complete absorption in his own.

Then he laughed, emotionally, shakily, holding her at arm's length. 'Look at you—no longer my little girl,' he said in his broken English. 'How I have missed you, Sonyasha. So many years have passed—so much time lost. We have some making up to do, you and I.'

Tears sprang to Sonya's eyes and the next moment, with all the years in between falling away, she was in his arms. 'Oh, Papa! I never thought I would see you again.'

'Sonyasha. Sonyasha,' Victor murmured, holding her close to him, patting her like a child. 'Hush now. Hush, Sonyasha.'

Sonya raised her face, wet with tears, and looked up at him. 'Why did you leave me and Mama? Why did you go away?'

'You must understand that it was the times we lived in, Sonyasha. It was a terrible time for Russia—for the people. I did not mean to hurt you. My going had nothing to do with my feelings for you or your mama. I loved you, Sonyasha, even though I never said it. It was my weakness—I am still not perfect, but I will do my best.'

She laughed and said on a note half-reproof, half teasing, 'You smell of cigarettes.'

Victor shrugged, his face taking on an expression of mock

contrition as he sat on the sofa and pulled her down beside him. 'What can I say? I am a chimney, Sonyasha, and am always saying I will give it up—and I will one day. I promise you. For you I will give it up.'

Anna, watching Sonya, saw her face had transformed, had brightened. A thread of tears ran down her cheeks soundlessly, but she was happy.

And if Alex had any doubts in his mind that Victor did not love his daughter, in that moment they were dispelled. Taking Anna's hand, he drew her into the kitchen and closed the door.

'Do you think Sonya will be all right?' she asked.

'I confess to having my doubts at first, but not any more. It's obvious that Victor is truly glad to see her.'

'I know, but don't you think we should have stayed?'

'I'm exactly where I want to be at this moment. How about you?'

There was a subtle meaning in his remark, but Anna couldn't see his expression as he busied himself making coffee. 'Me, too.'

'Good. I'm glad we have that settled.' He turned slightly and looked at her. 'You look marvellous, by the way. I love the dress. The colour matches your eyes.'

It was the first time in weeks that he had complimented her, or even looked at her as if she was an attractive woman. It brought a rush of heat to her cheeks. 'Do you? I bought it yesterday, as a treat to myself.'

'Then you should treat yourself more often.'

As Alex handed her a cup of coffee and she made herself comfortable at the kitchen table, Anna thought he looked rather marvellous himself, with power and virility stamped in every line of his powerful frame. The dark hair was as thick and well groomed as ever, the wonderful chiselled features as sharp, the tall body lithe beneath his casual cream trousers and white shirt. With her legs crossed, she sat drinking him in with her coffee, thinking how much she still loved him.

'Have you asked Sonya if she would like to go to Brooklands with us tomorrow?' Alex asked, lounging on the cooker as he took a sip of his coffee. 'I think some outside activity will do her good.'

'And what could be more thrillingly engaging than watching cars chase each other round the track at Brooklands?'

A leisurely smile lifted a corner of his mouth. 'Oh, I can think of many things much closer to home that are far more thrillingly engaging.'

Anna warmed to his words. 'I see your memory isn't fading.'

'Not a chance.'

'It appears the Ormsbys and their friends are going to Brooklands *en masse*.'

'I wouldn't expect anything less.'

'Lady Ormsby's been organising a picnic all week. Sonya knows about it, but she hasn't made up her mind whether to go or not. Perhaps Victor can persuade her. Since he's racing his Maserati, she might like to see it though, with you in your spanking new Lagonda, she'll not know who to put her money on.'

'We may not be in the same race. In any case, unless Victor finds a sponsorship or some other way of increasing his income, his racing days may well be numbered, since I refuse to finance this particular extravagance of his any longer. Where my sister is concerned, I doubt you will see her placing bets. You must have seen that she will not stand for any shenanigans.'

'I have noticed.'

'Sonya strongly disapproves of gambling of any sort. I think Victor's in for a hard time. You heard how she picked up on his tobacco habit—when she discovers he spends most of his time on the race track and in seedy West End gambling dens, his life won't be worth living.'

Anna smiled. 'Then maybe she'll be a good influence on him and hopefully, in time, you will see a reformed character.'

At that moment the door opened and Victor came in. 'I've

come to tell you both that I am taking Sonya for a drive. Perhaps when we return we can all have dinner together—a family meal, just the four of us.'

Without waiting for an answer, he went out and closed the door. Touched that Victor should consider her part of the family, Anna glanced at Alex, whose face remained impassive. 'It's good to see you getting on so well with Victor, Alex.'

He shrugged. 'We understand each other. As long as he continues to receive an allowance from me every month, I suppose he's harmless. If he makes Sonya happy that's all that counts.'

Nothing could have prepared Anna for the reality of Brooklands. Situated in Weybridge, Surrey, it was the world's first purpose-designed motor-racing track.

Alex drove Anna, Victor and Sonya to Brooklands in his Bentley. Ever since his reconciliation with his daughter, Victor was going around with a grin on his face like a Cheshire cat's. When they arrived and everyone had met up—with Lady Ormsby organising everyone and an exuberant Tamsin hanging on to the arm of Hubert Standing, and showing everyone who cared to look her sapphire-and-diamond engagement ring—Alex and Victor left them to join some of the other racing drivers.

Brooklands's magnificent oval circuit was two and three-quarter miles long with steep banking on the turns. It always attracted large crowds of spectators. Motor racing had attained such high speeds that it was imperative that protection for the public and competitors was arranged and supervised.

Seated on the crowded grassy bank overlooking the track, Anna became caught up in the noise, the excitement of it all, the smell of exhausts and the fierce rev of engines as the cars waited to start the first race. The small cars like the Morrises and the Austins, which were outclassed by the bigger cars, were in front.

'The atmosphere's tremendous. What a fabulous place this

is,' Anna remarked to Tamsin, who was seated beside her nibbling on a chocolate bar. She looked as fresh as a daisy in her white linen frock and broad-brimmed straw hat.

'Isn't it just.' Her expression suddenly froze. 'Oh dear, look, Anna. I do believe that's Freddy Campbell's Alfa—next to the blue MG.' She lowered her voice lest Sonya overheard, but she needn't have worried. Sonya had disappeared with the twins to buy ice creams.

Now that Alex had told Anna everything about Sonya's tragic past and her association with Freddy, there was no longer any need for secrecy between them. However, even though Tamsin had met Sonya and knew of her affair with Freddy, that he had hurt her and let her down badly, Lady Ormsby had considered it wise to keep the whole sordid truth from the sensitive ears of her young daughter. Tamsin knew nothing about Sonya's child or that she had tried to take her own life. It wasn't Anna's secret to tell so she left it that way.

'We should have known Freddy would be here today, it being a club day,' Tamsin went on. 'He's probably brought his Bugatti along for one of the later races—which he usually wins.'

For a moment Anna was totally incapable of speech. She stared at the Alfa Romeo, seeing Freddy behind the wheel wearing goggles. She'd had no contact with him since that day at Ascot, and she fervently hoped she could escape having to speak to him today.

'I sincerely hope he keeps well away from us, and that Sonya doesn't see him. If he goes anywhere near her, there's no telling what Alex will do.' Suddenly her eyes lit up with excitement as the cars revved louder and zoomed past the starting line when the black and white flag was waved. 'But I refuse to let anything spoil my day. We're here to enjoy ourselves, Tamsin, so hand over a piece of your chocolate— and once I've got the hang of things I intend placing a bet on the next race.'

Nibbling at the chocolate and sipping the odd glass of

champagne, she gazed in fascination as cars stopped in the pits and men in white overalls dashed out to change tyres and look under bonnets. The MG won the first race, Freddy coming a close second in his Alfa Romeo. As she watched the drivers climb out of their cars and pose for the photographs, Anna thought what a lovely day it was.

Lady Ormsby had arranged for the picnic to be eaten at teatime, which meant a light lunch in the clubhouse. It was a noisy, jolly affair. When everyone began to drift outside, Anna hung back to wait for Sonya who had disappeared to freshen up. Moving absently towards the door, she let her gaze stray to the bar area. She froze when she saw Freddy slumped on a bar stool, looking slightly worse for drink and in the process of ordering another. Desperate both to avoid him and to catch Sonya when she emerged from the ladies room and steer her in the opposite direction, she turned, only to find herself face to face with Edwina.

Edwina smiled thinly. 'It won't work, you know,' she said.

Anna stared at her blankly. 'What won't work?'

'Trying to avoid Freddy.' She cast a disapproving glance in her brother's direction. 'Although I don't suppose I can blame you. You'll have to excuse him. He's suffering from last night's hangover and well on his way to tomorrow's, having replaced the champagne he was drinking earlier with whisky.'

'Should he be racing?'

'No—but you try telling him that.' Edwina paused, raking her eyes over Anna's stunning summer blue dress. Her eyes were hostile and her heart cold, but with a practised smile, her voice forceful, cool and arrogant, she said, 'How nice you look, and how nice to see you. Are you with Alex?'

Anna wore an arrested expression, and her voice was no more than polite when she said, 'Yes, and the Ormsbys.' Edwina looked glamorous, even though she was wearing white overalls. Anna didn't stop to ask herself why she was wearing them.

'Alex is racing his Lagonda, I suppose, although how it will stand up to Freddy's Bugatti we'll just have to see.'

It was obvious to Anna that for all her smooth and charming manners, Edwina hated her, and Anna liked Edwina no better. They were two women emotionally connected to the same man—one in love with him, the other wanting him yet having suffered the public humiliation of his rejection.

'You seem to spend a good deal of time with Alex—I do read the society columns,' she was quick to point out. 'Goodness, he's a catch for any woman. What more could a girl want? Alex has it all, the looks, good connections, fashionable notoriety, and to top it all he is fabulously wealthy—although that shouldn't affect you, should it, being Lord Manson's granddaughter and heir?'

'You should know, Edwina, you wanted Alex yourself, remember,' Anna replied pointedly, keeping her temper, seemingly oblivious to the woman's carefully controlled animosity. 'And if you had looked more closely, you would have seen there is much more to Alex than that—but perhaps you never got past the size of his wallet.'

'You may rest assured,' Edwina returned with icy calm, 'that I most certainly did. Alex is a man with a man's needs—as you will know. We were good together—he was never disappointed in that department.'

The years of schooling her features into a polite mask were forgotten. The disgust Anna was feeling showed clearly on her face. 'Really? Is that why he dropped you?' Anna did not want to stand and watch insincere smiles and subtly disguised cuts. Edwina's eyes were hard and shining, ruthless as those of a cat watching a small bird. 'If you will excuse me, I must find the others.'

Anna was about to move on when Sonya appeared by her side. Edwina's eyes slid to her and narrowed upon recognition. As she raised a sleek brow, her smile positively oozed malice.

'Well, hello, Sonya,' she drawled. 'We haven't seen you in ages. Where have you been hiding?'

'I haven't been hiding anywhere, Edwina.'

Sonya's coolness astonished Anna, but then her heart plummeted when she saw Freddy, a glass halfway to his mouth, turn and look at them. His expression froze. Setting his glass on the bar, he got off the stool and swayed towards them. Anna was no longer transfixed. Fear for Sonya and what this encounter with Freddy would do to her overcame all other emotions.

Sonya was looking at him. She did not move or speak. The adoration on her face was an illumination. Her eyes shone between damp lashes, naked and defenceless. She was neither fearful nor sorry to see him again.

Freddy stared at her like someone who was seeing a ghost. Through the fog of alcohol that thickened his brain, he tried to assemble his shredded thoughts, which were all he seemed able to collect these days since Anna's defection to Alex Kent. It had cut the ground from under his feet. So too had his own father, who threatened to disown him if he failed to change his life style and to find some kind of productive employment that would benefit him and the family as a whole.

And then there was Sonya.

Ever since that day at the rally when Alex had brutally told him she had tried to drown herself and as a result had miscarried his child, he'd been dying of guilt slowly by inches, going from one heroin-induced stupor to another, and in his more lucid moments considered everything from emigration to suicide.

'Hello, Freddy,' Sonya said softly. 'How well you look.'

The sound of her voice seemed to calm Freddy. The lines of his features softened into an expression of inimitable sadness. 'So do you, Sonya—and you're wearing blue. You always did look nice in blue. Sonya—I'm sorry—I didn't know about...'

'Please don't say anything. I understand why you did it.'

'I remember my guilt and I remember my shame. I hurt you. I'm sorry.'

Anna remained motionless, unable to believe what was happening. She had expected anger, insults, anything but this. The flashes of feeling from each one of them confounded one another.

'Stop it, Freddy,' Edwina flared. 'Don't humiliate yourself like this. She is not worth it. She is nothing but a—'

Freddy turned on his sister, livid. 'Shut up, Edwina. Shut your mouth.'

'For God's sake, take hold of yourself,' Edwina rebuked angrily. 'It's the drink talking, that's what it is.'

'Is it? You think that, do you, Edwina? You may be right. Drink does loosen the tongue, and in my experience it's always the truth that comes out.' He looked at Anna for the first time. 'I was fond of you, Anna—but it was Sonya I loved. It was the money that drew me to her at first—as it was with you, I admit that—but it became more than that when I got to know her,' he said with bitter clarity.

'It was something deeper than love, something pure…' his eyes rested on Sonya's angelic face once more '…and whatever it was I'm not free of it—dear God, not yet. I loved you, but I didn't have the guts to keep you. I failed you, I know that now, and I embrace that failure.'

'Oh, Freddy. I didn't know. I had no idea you still felt like this—not after all this time.' Sonya's hand flew to her throat like a captive bird. She stood looking at him and permitted her eyes to fill up with such an excess of tenderness, of pure hopeless longing, that it shamed Freddy. He could not bear the sight of it.

Edwina's face was ghost white, her eyes as hard as ice and as cold. 'You idiot, Freddy,' she said. 'Think what you're saying.'

'Shut up, Edwina. If you say one more word, I shall knock you senseless. It is your vindictive—'

'Vindictive, is it? Everything that has befallen you is your own fault. Who was it who ranted and raved when he told me that this conniving woman had told you she was a Jew?'

'And you know how I suffered when she told me that.'

'And who was it who cried like a baby when he told me he could not marry her because of it? Don't begin feeling sorry for yourself now, Freddy. It's too late for regrets. You were the one who walked away—your fascist beliefs were far greater than what you felt for this woman and her unborn brat.'

'Damn your eyes, Edwina! Shut your mouth!' Moving closer to Sonya, Freddy looked close into her eyes. 'Don't listen to her, Sonya. I shouldn't have, but I did—to my shame and regret. But—you've changed, I can see that.'

'I was a child when you knew me, Freddy. I knew nothing of the world of men—of your world.'

'And now you do—and it's all thanks to me,' he said bitterly.

'Yes,' Sonya said. 'Now I know.'

'You always were something else, Sonya—complicated, to me, timid, but I can see you've overcome all that.' Lifting his hand, he touched her cheek with the tips of his fingers, relieved when she did not draw back. 'You were also very gentle, trustful and loving. What I did to you was unforgivable.'

'Please don't torture yourself like this, Freddy. I do forgive you.'

'Don't. I almost destroyed you—me and my fascist, antisemitic principles. God, how I despise them. I didn't deserve you, I know that now.'

'No, you didn't, Campbell,' a voice snapped from the doorway.

They all turned. Alex stood there, his eyes going from one to the other, his expression one of rage, then murder.

Chapter Fifteen

In a frozen paralysis they all watched him with the wary disbelief of innocents who are suddenly confronted with a threat they neither understand nor deserve from a marauder they had mistaken for a friend. His eyes, which he fastened on Freddy, were shards of ice.

'If you touch my sister or speak to her one more time,' he lashed out furiously, 'I'll kill you, so help me God. The truth is that you have hurt her more than you can possibly know or imagine, and I don't want you anywhere near her. You almost destroyed her. Be proud of yourself.'

Freddy's face was white, beaded with sweat. Clenching his hands and shoving them deep into his pockets in a pathetic attempt at self-control, he seemed to dissolve before their eyes. 'I am not proud,' he said, his voice level despite the murderous way Alex was looking at him. 'However it may have looked at the time, that was never what I wanted. I was wrong—seduced by men like Mosley who stuffed me with dreams of radical ideals. I was young...and too much of a fool to realise that fascism is never a justifiable instrument of policy.'

'You say that, yet you have lived since the day Sonya told you she was a Jew without thinking about what had become of her and your unborn child. That comes easy to you, doesn't it, Campbell? Anything comes easy to you except honour and decency.'

Freddy looked at Sonya, his face a mask of ravaged regret. 'I ask your pardon, Sonya. You deserved better.' He shook his head as if to clear it, and then to everyone's surprise he turned and walked away.

'Why can't you leave him alone, damn you?' Edwina flared. 'He's done nothing wrong that I can see.'

Alex turned the freezing blast of his gaze on his ex-mistress. His expression was merciless. 'You wouldn't. You, Edwina, sicken me. You are one of the dirtiest fighters I've ever met, and I've met plenty. And don't come the moralist either. You are both a hypocrite and a fool. Like your brother, you have achieved nothing and feed like a cancer on others, destroying lives. Out of malicious spite you tried to destroy Sonya and me—where Sonya was concerned you almost succeeded. If you had, I swear I would have torn you apart with my bare hands—both of you.'

Shaking with outrage, Edwina's face had become ugly with hatred. 'You despicable devil,' she hissed. 'You are a hard, black-hearted devil, Alex Kent, and I wish to God I'd never met you.'

Alex's smile was contemptuous. 'Devil? Hard?' He laughed. 'I recall you saying I'm as soft as butter in the proper hands. You had a score to settle, Edwina. Consider it settled. We are even.' He looked at Anna and Sonya. 'Let's go. I have a race to prepare for.'

Anna followed Alex out, and the last thing she saw when she turned and looked back was Freddy, who had stopped and watched them leave. His face was wretched and demented. Suddenly he was so pathetic in his futile love that Anna could no longer check her feelings. His eyes had never seemed emptier as they followed Sonya. And in their emptiness Anna glimpsed the dark side of his personality he had always tried to conceal from her. She sensed a disillusioned, embittered man. In that second she felt desperately sorry for him, and beyond the pity lay the knowledge that his blind faith to his beloved fascism was the cause of so much genuine misery.

Trembling, Edwina watched them go. How she would like to pay Alex Kent back for past humiliations. She would never forgive him. A cold gleam entered her eyes when she recalled Freddy's reaction to seeing Sonya again and the things he had said. Everything might seem wrecked, but perhaps all was not lost. She thought of the race she was entered in and smiled unpleasantly, striding towards the track where her MG awaited her, for it would seem that the solution to all her problems, hers and Freddy's, had just presented itself to her.

Away from the clubhouse Alex paused and looked down at Sonya. He was astonished and immensely proud that she had weathered the storm so well. Sister Geraldine was right. His sister was much stronger both emotionally and spiritually than she had been, and he very much suspected it had something to do with her gradual induction into the Catholic faith.

'Are you all right, Sonya? Seeing Campbell again after all this time hasn't upset you unduly?'

'No, Alex. Don't worry about me. I'm glad I've seen Freddy—really. It's helped me, if anything—helped lay the ghosts to rest.'

'Good girl.'

'I'm going back to the others to help with the picnic. I'll watch the race from the hill.' Standing on tiptoe, Sonya kissed her brother. 'That's for luck. Please drive carefully, Alex. Come and join me when you're ready, Anna.'

When Sonya had left them, Alex turned to Anna. She was watching Freddy's retreating figure. Her expression was mournful, her smooth forehead furrowed by anxious lines. In an instant all trace of gentleness had vanished from Alex's expression. His face was very tense and his tall figure dominated Anna.

'Poor Freddy,' she uttered softly. 'He—he looked so desolate, so wretched and full of regret. I almost pity him.' Looking at Alex, she saw he was observing her angrily. 'Why do you look at me like that?'

Taking hold of her arm, he pulled her behind a booth, out of sight of everyone. 'Bearing in mind his crimes, which you have heard by his own account, he doesn't deserve your pity. Forget him, Anna. He's not worth it.'

Anna knew there was no point defending Freddy, but in the light of Freddy's remorse she couldn't help being a trifle irked by Alex's harsh attitude. 'I know. Please don't be angry, Alex. I can't help feeling sorry for him, that's all. Freddy did love Sonya—perhaps he still does. I could see it in the way he looked at her. He—he looked and sounded so contrite.'

Alex's mouth tightened. 'It's a little late in the day for contrition. I try to be charitable when I can,' he said, 'but in his case it's difficult. I suppose you thought that if he said sorry I would forget everything else and forgive him.'

'No, not really. All the anger you feel because of what Freddy did to Sonya is understandable, but if Sonya can find it in her heart to think of him in a more favourable light, then maybe you should try and do the same?'

'Is that what you think?' Alex's voice was quiet and controlled. 'I suppose I should feel pity for Campbell, for he is a pitiful figure, but I don't. I could never forgive him for what he did to Sonya because I hate his guts. Not very admirable of me, I'll admit, but that's the way I feel.' When Anna opened her mouth to argue, he interrupted sharply. 'Anna, Freddy Campbell is a topic we have exhausted. Beginning today, I would be grateful if I never heard his name mentioned again.'

'No one gets a second chance from you, is that it?'

'Right,' he said implacably. 'Only those I consider deserve one.'

'How about me?' Anna dared to ask. 'Do I get a second chance?'

Unbelievably he smiled at that and raked her with a brazen stare. 'Do you want one?'

Something about the way in which he answered her question with one of his own sent her from her usual calm self to an anger that was almost uncontainable.

'Damn you, Alex Kent! You really are the most arrogant, infuriating man I know. Most of the time I don't know where I am with you. I really can't believe you can be so blasé about everything after I spent a night in your arms. I must have been an idiot, a stupid, besotted idiot. Dear Lord, it was so trite—the schoolgirl who falls in love with a handsome millionaire, or something to that effect, only in the novels she doesn't go to bed with him. I'm not some foundling you're obliged to see every time you have an attack of guilt.'

'Guilt?' Alex repeated, somewhat amazed by her spirit. Staring down into her stormy eyes and flushed face he wondered why, from the very beginning, she had always been able to get to his heart. Her face showed no sign of softening. Even so, its beauty fed his gaze and created inside him a sweet, hungering ache. 'The only guilt I ever felt where you were concerned, my love, was because I wanted you for myself from the moment I first laid eyes on you.'

The casual, empty endearment increased Anna's ire. 'Oh, shut up, Alex. I don't believe you. I'm beginning to think you only keep me hanging around out of pity and responsibility, not because you care for me. And don't call me your love. I'm not your love. You have made that perfectly clear. I never have been and I never will be.'

Alex could feel the rules he had laid down for himself where she was concerned already disappearing like morning mist. When they were apart he was able to think of something else besides his increasing sexual frustration. But when they were together, he would take one look at her and desire for her would pour through him like liquid fire and invariably lead to frustration. So fragile was his remaining hold on his self-control that he couldn't stand much more of it. He felt a consuming, unquenchable need to possess her.

A slow smile touched his lips. 'Yes, you are. And of course

I think we should discuss this matter that weighs so heavily on your mind. I have never pitied you and never considered you a responsibility. We have known each other some considerable time—and after spending a night together in the most intimate way, I think our relationship should progress to something more permanent. That is, of course, if you agree.'

Anna stared at him, afraid to believe him, afraid to trust him—unable to stop herself because she loved him. 'Alex— what are you saying? I recall you telling me that you had no intention of complicating things between us with a close relationship. Are you telling me that you've changed your mind?'

His chuckle was rich and deep. 'Now there's a persuasive argument.' Placing his hands on her upper arms, he drew her against his chest. 'Don't you want me to kiss you?'

Alex's mouth hovered barely an inch from hers. 'Yes.' Her whisper was scarcely audible.

'To see if I can still make you burn—remember?'

Remember! How could she ever forget? She had thought and dreamed of nothing else. Her ears must be deceiving her, but there was something in his eyes that made her heart beat wildly—a softness, a glowing. 'Alex, I—I don't understand…'

'Anna, you've belonged to me since I first saw you in Mr Rothwell's office. I thought you were the embodiment of every fairytale princess cruelly locked in a tower by a wicked queen and ripe for rescue. I saw a young face, serious, innocent—and very lovely. You belonged to me then and I've waited almost three years for you to grow up.'

Her lips trembled into a smile. 'I'm sorry I took so long.'

'Don't be. Whatever you do, you do it properly.'

'I've thought long and hard about what we did—about what happened between us,' Anna said, 'and I'd very much like it to happen again. In fact,' Anna murmured, her eyes fastened on his face, just six inches from her own, 'I'm beginning to

wonder if you're ever going to kiss me like you did that
night—'

Alex captured whatever she had been about to say with his
lips. They tasted each other with a hunger they both shared,
and when Anna's mouth opened beneath his and she leaned
into him, glowing waves of pleasure spread like quickfire over
his body. Their mouths clung together, Alex's courting hers
in provocative play, their sighs mingling into one breath.

When his mouth left hers, Anna's eyelids fluttered open as
a rapturous bliss washed through her. 'Oh, Alex.' She sighed.
'I can't believe this is happening.'

'Believe it, my love,' he said, 'because it is.' He raised his
head and looked down at her. Her face was flushed with desire, her dark eyes glazed with it. Suddenly his smile was
wicked and seductive. 'What do you know about desire, Miss
Preston?' he asked hoarsely.

An unexpected flush of colour mantled Anna's cheeks.
'Enough. Once shown, I have developed a taste for it, and I
suddenly feel in the mood for a little—diversion.'

'I do love you, Anna. Believe me when I tell you I have
never said that to another woman in my life—apart from
Sonya and my mother. Even when we were apart, I'd dream
of the way you felt in my arms, how it felt to make love to
you, and I'd wake up wanting you.'

'Did you really think I might have a baby?'

He raised his brows and quirked his lips in amusement. 'It
did cross my mind. Would you have minded?'

'I would have been happy about it, but I would prefer to
wait.'

'If I had weakened at Christmas, you would have stood a
good chance of starting one. Then where would you have
been—in your final year at Oxford, exams looming, and pregnant?'

She tilted her head back and looked at him, her eyes slum-
berous. 'I was greedy. I wanted it all.'

'The first you have achieved, and in the fullness of time I intend giving you the other two. I want to marry you, Anna.'

'Are you asking me?'

'I am. Ever since that night at Christmas, when I made up my mind not to stand in the way of your career, I've been fighting against my need for you.'

'Oh, Alex—and I thought you didn't care. You've been so remote since then.'

'I didn't want to distract you from your studies.'

'But I want you to be a part of my life—as I want to be a part of yours.'

'So you will marry me? And don't even think of turning me down.'

He was so sure of her. 'I wouldn't dare.'

Tipping her chin up, Alex gazed deep into her eyes and quietly said, 'I do love you, Anna—so very much.'

Hearing him say it sent warmth seeping through her system. 'I find it hard to believe.'

'Do you need convincing still?'

Her gaze fell to his lips, hovering close to her own. 'I would like that,' she said shamelessly, wanting to be kissed, 'because, until this moment, I was certain you would never say that to me.'

'Then I shall be more than happy to prove I do mean it.'

Anna eagerly met his kiss. His arms were clasped tight around her, his mouth moving with fierce tenderness over hers. She felt his hand cover her breast and she moaned, a moan that began deep within her and slowly rose to her throat. She kissed him with all the aching longing that being in his arms evoked, feeling faint with joy because he wanted her, because he loved her. Pressing against him, she fitted her melting body to the hardened contours of his. His arms tightened possessively, moulding her closer to him as he deepened his kiss.

The exquisite feeling of her in his arms, the feel of her body pressed close, her breasts against him, the taste of her kiss, the smell of her perfume, was unbearable joy to Alex. He couldn't go on—and he was afraid to stop, afraid that if he released her she would vanish. Drawing back slightly, he looked down at her flawless face and glowing dark eyes lit by the fires of love.

'I'm impatient to make you my wife. I want you to change your name to mine, so there will be no doubt who you belong to.' He trailed his finger along the curve of her jaw. 'I want you to share my bed every night of our lives together, and I want to wake up every morning wrapped in your arms. I want to fill your life with gladness, leave you every morning with the taste of my kiss on your lips. I want you to tell me you love me every day of our lives, and I will say the same to you—and show you. When the time is right I want you to give me children—sons, daughters, it doesn't matter, as long as they have your courage, your goodness.'

Happiness spread through Anna until it was so intense she ached from it. His expression was one of love, a love so intense she was humbled by it. 'And I love you, Alex, deeply. I love being near you. I love to feel your touch. I love it when you hold me, when you kiss me,' she whispered achingly, placing featherlight kisses in the warm hollow of his neck. 'I'll make you happy and give you enough children to fill the whole of London. I promise you.'

Alex grinned down at her. 'Two will be enough. I'm happy to note your mind is still on marriage and children, but for the time being will you cease trying to encourage me in your blatant disregard of your status as an unmarried woman,' he teased, her searing lips against his flesh threatening the crumbling walls of his restraint.

'Do you think marriage makes such a difference? Nothing is going to stop me wanting you.'

''Tis no simple lust that eats away at me either, Anna,' he said, lowering his mouth to hers and tenderly teasing her lips with his own, 'but an ever-raging desire to have you with me every moment. Do you have any idea how I feel every time we are alone together and I can go no further than kiss you?'

'Your torment is of your own making,' she reminded him.

'True, and I think the sooner we set a date for the wedding the better it will be for both of us. How does the week after next sound?'

'Tomorrow would be better.' She gave him an impish, sidelong look. 'Couldn't we—can't we…?' She flushed scarlet, her thoughts traversing along lines that suddenly embarrassed her.

Reading her mind perfectly, Alex laughed and hugged her to him. 'Anna, you're shameless! There will be no sex before the wedding.'

'You'll never hold out—not if we're to have a long engagement,' Anna said, slanting him a rueful smile.

'On the contrary—but I will not agree to a long engagement…two months at the most. In the meantime, I shall behave like a gentleman. I intend to treat you as you should be treated, to speak the right words a man speaks to the woman he loves, to follow the movement of gentle courtship through betrothal to marriage. I can't deny that it will be one of the longest, most painful times of my life, but imagine our wedding night, even after just a short abstinence.'

Anna looked at him, loving him. 'Yes, I can. It will be beautiful, special.'

Tipping her chin up Alex gazed deep into her eyes and quietly said, 'I do love you, Anna—so very much. Shall we tell the others we are to be married?'

'We must tell Sonya, but I would like to tell Grandfather before we break the news to everyone else. I think we should get married at Stainton Church. It will be easier for Grandfather. What do you think, Alex?'

'My darling girl, I have no objections whatsoever. We will get married on top of a mountain if that's what you want.'

'Then why don't we go and see the vicar and put things in motion when we go to Belhaven after Brooklands?'

'That sounds perfect to me.'

They were distracted by a roar of engines as the cars began to get ready for the next race. Anna linked her arm through Alex's.

'Come on, I'll walk to the track with you and then join the others on the hill. I shall worry about you, Alex, driving a car round a race track hell for leather. Can you tell me, a mere woman, what it is that attracts you to such a crazy sport? What exactly is the magic of a sports car?'

'It might interest you to know that "mere women" also race cars—and win. For me as an enthusiast the magic is the sheer joy of being in control of a machine as responsive to skill and understanding as a thoroughbred horse, and piloting a car with an engine three times more powerful than necessary—in fact,' he said, his gaze warm and intimate on her upturned face, 'it's a bit like sex.'

'Ah, now that I understand. And if it's as exciting as all that and women race at Brooklands, I might just buy myself a sprightly Alfa Romeo Monza, a red one, and bring it to Brooklands.'

'I think not, Anna. I refuse to allow my wife to go careering round a race track.'

Anna stopped and, pulling him towards her, slipped her arms round his neck, uncaring of the curious glances directed at them by people milling about. Very gently, teasingly, she said 'Why? Are you afraid I might beat you?'

Alex chuckled. 'No, but I do think you need a lot more experience in your trusty little Austin before you think of buying anything like an Alfa Romeo, so do not strain the bonds of my affection by defying me and adding one to your shopping list.'

His imperious tone didn't daunt Anna in the least, but before she could open her mouth to argue he laughed and kissed her hard on the mouth. 'I'll see you after the race.'

Anna watched him stride jauntily away with his goggles swinging from his fingers. With a spring in her step and anticipation and happiness pulsing through her veins, she returned to the hill. Sonya was sitting on the grass by herself, looking down at the track. Deep in thought, a frown creased her brow.

'I'm glad you're by yourself, Sonya. I have something to tell you.'

Immediately the frown was replaced with a smile. 'Oh?' She squinted up at her. 'What is it, Anna? I must say you're looking extremely pleased with yourself.'

Anna flopped down beside her, bursting with happiness and barely able to contain her news. 'Alex has just asked me to marry him.'

Sonya smiled with pleasure and threw her arms about Anna's neck. 'Oh, I'm so glad. I knew he would, of course, and couldn't imagine why he was taking so long about it.'

'You did?' Anna said, laughing and pulling back so that she could look at her future sister-in-law's face.

'I have never seen Alex look at any woman quite the way he looks at you, not with the same degree of warmth and gentleness. It's obvious that he adores you.'

'I hope so. I—I can't believe it.'

'You love him, too,' Sonya said.

'I know,' Anna admitted, 'and it scares me when I think just how much. What if something goes wrong? What if he tires of me? What if he finds out I'm not really the intellectual he thinks I am, but a woman who secretly hankers after staying at home, rearing children and cooking his breakfast?'

'I imagine he'd be able to sustain the shock.' Sonya laughed. 'Congratulations. When is the wedding to be?'

'Soon, I hope.'

Sonya's eyes became thoughtful as she gazed into the distance for several moments, and then she sighed and turned to Anna. 'I know how happy you must feel. I once felt as you do now.'

'Did you love Freddy very much?'

'Yes, I did, and what a love it was to me. It was new,

absolute and gloriously free—like nothing else on earth. It was so perfect, like the breath of life to me. And Freddy did love me. I remember how kind he could be, all his gestures of affection, all the times he proved how much he did care. Even when I told him I was a Jew I saw he loved me as well as hated me. I recognised in that love a genuine devotion laced with resentment and antipathy.'

'Which overrode everything else. How devastated you must have been when he left you.'

Sonya's eyes clouded with painful memories. 'I was, and you know what happened—I know Alex told you. Two people cannot live together side by side loving and hating each other. The two are genuine emotions and not compatible, and so for me there was only one retreat and that was into misery and despair. It was the convent—Sister Geraldine and her faith— and Alex that saved me.

'I did see Freddy once more after that—at a village fête. He didn't know I was there, but just seeing him brought back all the awful memories of what I tried to do to myself—and our child. I was ill for a long time afterwards, but I came through stronger.' She smiled softly. 'All that is in the past and, despite everything that's happened, I do wish Freddy well. Poor Freddy. He's a sad victim of his own emotions and,' she said, the smile she presented to Anna full of meaning, 'not forgetting Edwina.'

Anna laughed. 'I couldn't agree more. The woman is an absolute dragon. We've plenty of time before Alex's race, so let's go and help set out the picnic.'

'Are you going to tell them you're going to marry Alex?'

'No—not yet. I would like to tell Grandfather first.'

'I can understand that. He'll be over the moon, I know he will. I do hope Alex will be all right, by the way. Freddy's in the same race—though he shouldn't be driving after drinking so much.'

'I just hope the two of them remember what the race is about—that unless you're a professional racing driver, racing should be seen as a recreation, with tinkering and tuning and inventing means of making the cars go faster as part of the fun—and they don't try competing too hard against each other.'

When the picnic had been laid out on the grass—which was so huge Anna laughingly declared there was enough food to feed every spectator at Brooklands—she settled down to watch Alex's race. The cars were lined up. She could see Alex's Lagonda towards the back and on a line with Freddy's Bugatti. Victor, whose race was next, could be seen watching from the pits.

With a deafening rev of engines and at the wave of the flag, they were off on the first lap, pouring over the starting line to an ear-rending roar that went up from the crowd. They drove at a tremendous speed, each car clinging precariously to the track, swinging round curves and soaring to the top of the hill before hurtling down the other side. For a few terrifying seconds Anna thought they would become airborne. It was a Maserati that was first under the bridge on the first lap, falling behind when it was overtaken by a Mercedes.

All the drivers were experienced and it was a breathtaking show of driving. Nevertheless there were incidents in plenty. At one point two cars went careering off the track—thankfully the drivers climbed out unhurt. Alex was close up front, with Freddy on his tail.

Anna, whose nerve ends were jangling like bells, could hardly bear to watch.

It was on the third lap that Freddy suddenly fell back and drove into the pits. Anna saw him climb out. After removing his helmet, he walked away. She was puzzled by this, but didn't dwell on it. Her attention was back on the race and Alex, so she didn't see Sonya stand up and leave.

Her heart hammering beneath her ribs, Anna watched as a white MG drew alongside Alex. Going much too fast, the driver clung to the bend, suddenly swinging out so that he was just inches away from Alex, and before Alex could right his wheels the other car veered relentlessly into his and forced him off the track. There was an awful noise of screeching brakes and the scream of tyres. Alex struggled to control his car. His precious Lagonda rolled over itself, slid across the grass that formed a bank, and finally, with a crunching of metal, came to a stop on its side.

Anna saw impending death.

Unaware that she was crying or that she had got to her feet, she was bolting down the hill, screaming frantically to people to move out of her way and almost falling over one of the spectators sitting on the grass. She heard Tamsin call out to her, but she paid no attention. Fear and anguish that Alex might be hurt and worse—that she might soon be holding his lifeless form in her arms—overrode everything and sent adrenalin pumping wildly through her veins, so that by the time she reached the bottom of the hill and was running towards the accident, her imaginings had escalated to tumultuous proportions.

Through a daze of pain and confusion Alex half-opened his eyes. He was lying on the grass and someone had removed his helmet and goggles. Reaching up, he wiped the back of his gloved hands across his eyes. His vision cleared and through the stewards crowding round him he saw Anna running towards him. He tried raising his head, but the effort proved too much and he let it fall back and closed his eyes.

Anna dropped to her knees beside him, her shoulders shaking with suppressed sobs as she cradled his head on her lap and caressed his lean features. Blood trickled from a cut on his brow. 'Please, Alex! Please wake up.' Someone squatted beside her. It was Victor, concern written all over his face. Her expression was frantic. 'Make him wake up, please, Victor.'

Alex groaned, and his eyelids fluttered open. He looked up into Anna's face. Her head was surrounded by a bright halo of sunlight and for a moment he thought he was dreaming. She was looking down at him with so much tenderness in her beautiful eyes that it was shattering to behold. He smiled, the last cobwebs of his mind clearing, and he felt, somewhere deep inside him, the ebb tide of his strength flowing back again. With a sigh of bliss he said, 'I thought I must have died and gone to heaven.'

Unaware of the curious gazes fixed on them, smoothing a lock of hair from his forehead, Anna's smile was one of relief and incredibly tender. 'Thank God you didn't die. I couldn't go on living if anything happened to you. Welcome back, my darling,' she murmured.

Alex reached up and drew her head down, kissing her, his heart soaring as her lips parted and she kissed him back with all her heart. When he finally let her go, he said, 'I'm sorry if I frightened you. As much as I would like to lay with my head in your lap for ever, I think you'd better let me get up.'

'How do you feel?' Victor asked. 'Are you hurt anywhere? Any broken bones?'

Alex sat up and had to brace himself on his arm until his head had stopped reeling. 'No—apart from my head, which is surprising,' he said when he saw the sorry wreck of his Lagonda. 'My head took a knock, but apart from that I think all my parts are in working order.' An ear-splitting cheer went up from the crowd when he gingerly got to his feet. With a smile and a wave of acknowledgement, as the stewards fussed around and proceeded to have his wrecked car towed to the pits, he stretched his limbs to make sure he could still move.

A doctor appeared. 'You're lucky to get out of that alive. Come and be checked out, just to make sure—and you may need a couple of stitches in that cut. You were unconscious, so you obviously took a blow to the head—it's possible you may have concussion.'

With the cars still buzzing round the track, Alex paused and looked for the MG that had run him off the track. He'd lost control, but not before he'd exchanged a look with the other driver. Even though the driver was wearing helmet and goggles he'd recognised Edwina, and the triumphant smile she'd thrown at him told him the collision had been no accident.

His mind registered first disbelief and then hatred—a hatred so deep that all the muscles of his face tightened into a mask of rage. The bitch! The unforgiving vicious bitch! She'd tried to kill him. He stared at the MG as it sped past, violence emanating from every pore.

Anna saw the sudden hardening of Alex's face, the muscles clenched so tight a nerve in his cheek began to pulse. There was a cold glitter in his eyes as his gaze remained riveted on the white car that had collided with him. 'Is something wrong, Alex?'

'Wrong?' he repeated icily. 'Considering someone deliberately ran me out of the race, I think there is.'

'But it was an accident, surely.' When Alex didn't reply she stared at him in horror. 'Alex, please tell me it was.'

'It was no accident, I assure you.'

'But who would want to do that? Do you know the driver of that car?'

'It's Edwina.'

'Edwina? Are you saying she tried to kill you?' Anna's voice cracked incredulously, in disbelief.

'That is exactly what I'm saying.' He looked at Anna, his expression grave. 'This is between us, Anna. Keep it to yourself. Look, I shouldn't be long. Go and tell the others I'm all right—nothing to worry about.'

'I shall do nothing of the kind,' Anna retorted sharply. 'Don't you dare try getting rid of me, Alex. You gave me such a fright—and now this. I'm not leaving you. I'll get Victor to go and tell them you're all right and not to worry.'

Chapter Sixteen

Alex was a long time getting checked out by the doctor. A stitch was inserted into the cut on his brow and afterwards Anna went with him to inspect his car. The damage was quite extensive, but after much discussion with the mechanics they were of the opinion that it could be repaired. By the time they got back to their party, the racing was over. The picnic was being cleared away and carried to the cars. There was much confusion, with friends, family and servants all milling around, and a congestion of cars as people began to leave.

Victor, who had raced his Maserati and come a satisfactory fourth, joined them, looking extremely pleased with himself. 'Not bad for an old man, eh?'

'It's good that you're still so competitive, Victor,' Anna said, smiling.

'I was disappointed with the speed and performance. I didn't quite match the three that finished in front of me. Perhaps it's time to change my Maserati for a faster car. Ever since I started racing, I've dreamed of owning a six-cylinder Mercedes-Benz. Now there is a car that takes some beating.'

Anna caught Alex's eye and smiled, recalling what he had said about reviewing Victor's allowance.

'Dream on, Victor,' Alex remarked drily. 'I agree it's every inch a thoroughbred, but your Maserati is still capable of showing a clean pair of heels.'

Victor shrugged. 'Ah well, perhaps sometime we will talk about it some more.' He moved on to look for Sonya.

Slipping his arm about Anna's waist, Alex grinned down at her. 'I sometimes wonder what I've let myself in for with Victor.'

'Well, I think it's very noble of you to take care of him, considering the circumstances under which you parted.'

'The present ones aren't exactly to my liking either, but I do it for Sonya. Although, taking everything into account, he has had a difficult time of things. When he turned up in England, at first I thought it was because he was intent on punishing me for leaving him—for leaving Russia and taking Sonya with me. But later I suspected his time in the labour camp had so affected him that he conceived being reunited with his daughter as a form of atonement.'

'Does he ever speak of his time in the camp?'

'No, but I believe he was overloaded by guilt for the way he had abandoned my mother and Sonya. Perhaps he even thought he would break down unless he took a radical step to lighten his burden and come to England to find Sonya.' Alex turned Anna's face up to his and said with a sombre smile, 'I'm glad you have no objections to having him around.'

'No, I don't. I realise he can be difficult and that his outspoken, bombastic manners might not be to everyone's taste, but if one can look beyond his idiosyncrasies, he isn't all that bad. He seems honest and trustworthy, though he might drink and gamble a lot—'

'With the money I give him,' Alex was quick to point out.

Anna laughed lightly. 'You can't expect everyone to be perfect.' Her sparkling gaze was warm with love. 'I can see how effortlessly he is manoeuvring you, Alex, and the fact that you don't mind is a sure sign that you are mellowing towards him.'

Victor reappeared, a worried frown on his brow as his eyes

scanned the crowd. 'Where is Sonyasha? I want to know if she enjoyed watching me race.'

'I think she must be with Tamsin,' Lady Ormsby said, on her way to the car with a basket of leftover food. 'If she doesn't show up before you leave—and I wouldn't be long if I were you, Alex, you look quite pale, which isn't surprising following your accident—we'll take her back with us. There will be plenty of room in our car or in Michael's. Since Sonya and Anna are staying with us, it seems the most sensible solution anyway. Would you like to come with us, Anna?'

'Thank you, but no, I'll go with Alex. I want to make sure he's all right. The doctor's told him not to drive for twenty-four hours and that he has to remain still and quiet, so Victor's offered to drive Alex's Bentley back to London.' Anna was determined not to be parted from Alex just yet under any circumstances, but she did promise Lady Ormsby she would be back at Curzon Street in time to get ready for the pre-arranged dinner at the Dorchester later.

Looking pretty and vivacious, Tamsin suddenly appeared with Hubert.

'Tamsin, have you seen Sonya?' Anna asked.

'No—not for an hour or maybe more.'

Alex glanced at her sharply. 'Where, Tamsin, where did you last see her?'

'I—I think it was at the picnic, just before you had your accident. Everyone became so distracted by it that I don't really remember.'

Victor's brow took on the creases of his growing worry. His eyes continued to search the crowd for his daughter.

'Doesn't anyone know where she is?' Tamsin enquired.

'No. That's the whole point,' Alex replied irritably, his mind ranging over all sorts of horrors and recklessly crossing bridges before they were built.

'But someone must have seen her,' Victor bellowed, alerted by the panic he sensed in the younger man.

They asked several people round about if any of them had

seen Sonya. No one had. Where was she? What could have happened? Everyone became extremely anxious.

Standing beside Alex Anna felt a shiver of dread suddenly crawl up her spine. She waited until she could control the quaver of trepidation in her voice before saying, 'Alex, do you think it's possible that she might be with Freddy? He dropped out of the race for some reason.'

In all the time she'd known Alex, she had never seen him immobilised by any emotion or any event. The worse the disaster, the more energised he became to deal with it. Now, however, he stared at her as he tried to absorb what she had said, a muscle ticking in his clenched jaw, and then it hit him like a flash.

'It's highly probable.' Alex felt the first sparks of fury begin to ignite. 'Campbell! Who else?' He was infuriated with himself for not having kept a closer eye on his sister.

Victor was quiet, thoughtful, on hearing the name Freddy Campbell. Something nagged at him. He chased the recollection down the corridors of memory. A face—Freddy Campbell at Ascot making defamatory remarks about a Jew called Sonya; the same man at Brooklands; at the Phoenix Club, Freddy Campbell in the back room injecting himself with morphine. The thought of his Sonyasha in the hands of that man, with his fancy looks and fancy airs and filthy habits, caused a red hot haze to rise in front of his eyes and a dull rage to fill his being so completely that he no longer felt wholly responsible for his actions.

A thunderous frown drew Victor's brows into a single line. 'I know the bastard,' he said with a quiet, dangerous fury.

Alex's eyes flew to him. 'What about him?'

'He is here at Brooklands today.'

'I know,' Alex confirmed scathingly. 'His sister ran me off the track.'

Victor looked at him hard. 'And he is the man who hurt Sonyasha in the past? Yes?'

Alex nodded, his face grim.

'So—it was him, but you wouldn't tell me,' he said accusingly, 'so I couldn't be sure, and Sonyasha would never have brought it up. Did she speak to him today?'

'Before my race—in the clubhouse.' Alex's gaze sharpened as he stared at his stepfather. 'Tell me how you know him.'

'I've seen him before—many times, at the Phoenix Club. He is there often. He goes with his friends to smoke and inject dope—often when he's on a high after a race meeting, and when he's been racing his car.'

Victor smiled, but there was no mirth in his eyes. The cold ferocity would weaken the stoutest heart. It was clear to him now that Campbell's guilt was unmistakable. But what the hell could he do about it? He could think of nothing except the kind of unthinkable act to which some of the men in the labour camp had predicted he'd be driven to by this sort of provocation.

'After all the things he did to my Sonyasha—and now this—he deserves to live out his life in torment,' he uttered in a spirit of revenge. 'He must answer to me.'

'Victor, we're not certain Sonya is with Freddy, and, if she is, he won't hurt her,' Anna remarked in an effort to calm the situation.

'And you're sure of that, are you?'

Recalling the way Freddy had looked at Sonya, she said, 'Yes, yes, I am.' The look of silent disgust Victor gave her told her he wasn't convinced.

All at once Sonya seemed to materialise from nowhere. There were gasps of relief all round, but it was clear that she was distraught, breathing heavily, her face was ashen, her eyes wide and filled with panic. It was Alex she went to, her small hands clutching his shirt firmly. 'Alex, it's Freddy.' Her voice was frantic.

Alex took her hands in his and gripped them hard. In the midst of his own rampaging emotions and his disastrous efforts to prevent the past from intruding into present day, he was not prepared to dissemble. 'You've been with Campbell all this time?'

'Yes—we—we talked. He asked me to go away with him—to marry him.'

'And what did you say?'

'I—I told him I wouldn't—and—and he became suicidal. He's getting into his car. I tried to stop him, but he wouldn't listen. I don't know what else to do. Alex, you have to stop him. He shouldn't be driving—he's in such a state. I can't bear to think of what might happen. Please do something.'

Alex's head spun round as a red car flew past them on the grass. It was a miracle no one was run down. Freddy was at the wheel, his eyes fixed straight ahead.

Victor became a man with a mission. His face bright purple, his being filled with hate and a lust for revenge, he roared, 'I'll get him.' Springing to life, and before anyone could stop him, he had hauled the Ormsbys' chauffeur out of their black Daimler, flung himself behind the wheel and was in hot pursuit of Freddy.

'Damn the man! He's insane!' Alex fumed, chafing with impatience as he hurried towards his own car. 'What the bloody hell is he thinking of? When will he learn that vengeance is a cruel, driving master?'

Anna ran after him in alarm. 'Alex, leave it. You can't go after Victor.'

'I can and I will,' he gritted.

'Remember what the doctor said. You shouldn't be driving—not in your condition.' Realising it was pointless arguing with a man who refused to listen, she said, 'If you must go, please let me drive.'

Alex brushed his hair from his brow with an impatient hand. 'I'm quite capable of driving myself. Wait here, Anna.'

'Over my dead body,' she replied with finality, getting in the car. Throwing her a black look of exasperation, Alex flung the car into gear and rushed after Victor. Before Anna knew it, they were out of Brooklands and hurtling along narrow country roads.

'Please, Alex, slow down,' she begged.

In reply Alex pushed at the accelerator. Looking ahead, seeing Victor's car in the distance, Anna was blinking at the shimmering heat haze hovering over the countryside in the distance. She pulled the car's visor down to shield her eyes against the dazzling light. There was no sign of Freddy. It wasn't until they came to a long winding stretch of road that they saw him. Victor had closed the gap between himself and Freddy and was irately blowing his horn in an attempt to get Freddy to pull over. Surprisingly Freddy responded by stopping his car in a narrow lay-by and getting out.

By the time Alex reached them, Victor had already launched an attack. Facing a man whose visage was red with rage, his eyes blazing, Freddy stared at him in petrified horror and would have bolted past him, but Victor stepped before him, blocking his flight, his fist flying out and knocking the younger man to the ground.

Anna ran towards them, pressing a hand tightly across her mouth as her heart throbbed in sudden dread. Fear rose within her, and she could not beat it back as she watched and heard Victor's fist make contact with Freddy's jaw as he tried to get up.

'Victor, for God's sake stop,' Alex shouted, pulling Victor back as he was about to haul Freddy to his feet to pound him some more. 'Get up,' he said to Freddy.

Freddy scrambled to his feet, breathing heavily.

Victor tried pulling himself free of Alex, but he was firmly held. 'I have an account to settle with this bastard,' he roared.

'Any account to be settled will be settled without further violence.'

Freddy stared at Victor, who was no stranger to him, but he did not know him well and had no idea what lay behind what he considered to be an unprovoked attack. He looked at Alex, whose utter contempt for him was manifest in the look in his eyes—it was deadly, his face as if carved from marble, hard and ice cold. 'What the hell's going on?'

'Allow me to introduce you to Victor Melinkov, Campbell—Sonya's father. You don't need me to say more—except that it isn't wise to antagonise a man as adept at using his fists as Victor, so take my advice and go.'

Freddy backed away as the situation became clear. His bemused stare moved from Alex to Victor, whose rage had not dissipated as he strained to tear himself from Alex's grip. Without more ado he turned, his legs carrying him without hesitation towards his car. Turning on the ignition, he rammed his foot on the accelerator and, with a scream of tyres and in a cloud of dust, raced off down the road.

'Damn!' The expletive exploded from Victor's throat, and his rage mounted as he saw his quarry getting away. His determination to punish Freddy reinforced, with superhuman strength he tore himself away from Alex and was soon in hot pursuit, with Alex and Anna on his tail once more.

Freddy and Victor were close together, with Victor once more blasting his horn. Even from so far back Alex could see both men were driving erratically and that they posed a serious danger to other vehicles. Suddenly Freddy swerved to avoid an oncoming lorry, perhaps dazzled by the sun, and his car left the road, rolled down a steep embankment, hit a tree and burst into flames.

To Alex and Anna's horror, they saw Victor swerve to the left and with a tremendous lurch of springs and rubber come to a halt in thick brush halfway down the embankment.

With a screech of brakes Alex stopped the car and flung himself out. Looking down the embankment into the cloud of thick black smoke, he saw Victor's car. It had come to a halt some distance from Freddy's, still in one piece as Victor struggled to get out. Freddy, who had been thrown out of his car as it rolled down the embankment, was not so fortunate. He was lying face down in the grass. Scrambling down the steep slope, Alex went to Freddy and turned him over. His face was covered in blood. Checking the neck pulse, he realised Freddy was dead. Stepping back from the smoke cloud, he went to check on Victor.

Victor was rolling in agony on the grass, his teeth gnashing in pain. Anna was on her knees beside him.

'Victor, be still,' she whispered urgently. 'You'll only do more damage to yourself.

He was alive, but might not have escaped serious injury. His hands and face were lacerated, his leg, set at an odd angle, clearly broken. His breathing was laboured and he was holding his chest, so internal injuries could not be ruled out.

Anna looked up at Alex. He was staring down at her anxiously. His eyes met hers and she held his gaze steadily, feeling the colour drain from her face. 'Freddy? How is he?'

Alex shook his head.

Anna was overwhelmed with sadness, as tears pricked her eyes. Through their mist she looked across the grass at Freddy, whom death had released at last from the hopeless love he had carried silently in his heart for Sonya. 'Poor Freddy. He may have had his faults, but I am sorry he's dead.'

'What about Victor? How bad is he?'

'His leg's obviously broken and he's in a lot of pain. We must get him to hospital.'

They were distracted when they saw Hubert's car stop up on the road, close to the lorry Freddy had swerved to avoid. Hubert got out quickly, accompanied by Tamsin and Sonya. After they surveyed the scene, and Hubert had spoken to the lorry driver, who climbed into his lorry and drove off, they scrambled down the embankment. Alex went to his sister, whose eyes were fixed on the burning car and Freddy's inert form.

'He's dead, isn't he?' she whispered.

'I'm afraid so.'

Sonya swayed under the impact of the heavy blow and Alex's arm went around her waist to steady her. After a moment she straightened her small body away from the steadying arm and moved slowly to where Freddy lay. She sank to her knees beside him with an indefinable union of sadness and reverence upon her face. Bending over him, she gently kissed him on the brow, as one would kiss a child goodnight, then, bowing her head, she began to pray.

Standing next to Alex, Hubert said, 'Bad job. Sonya insisted on coming—couldn't stop her. The driver of the lorry has gone to phone for an ambulance. Shouldn't be long.'

Alex glanced at Victor, who was clearly in a great deal of pain. Anna was bent over him, trying her best to make him comfortable. 'Let's hope not, for Victor's sake.'

At the hospital, just before midnight, Anna was sitting alone in the waiting room. She was exhausted. It had been an awful day and she couldn't wait to leave the hospital and be alone with Alex. Alex and Sonya were with Victor, whose broken leg was in a cast and his chest, having sustained three broken ribs, heavily taped. Edwina walked past the open door. Seeing Anna, she paused uncertainly. She was about to walk on, but had second thoughts and entered the room.

Anna stood up. Edwina looked subdued, drained. There was a sick, disbelieving expression on her face and her eyes were no longer hard and bright but dull. For a split second pity stirred Anna's heart, but then she reminded herself she was in the presence of someone who had tried to kill Alex, someone who had driven her brother to his death and almost wrecked Sonya's life.

'I'm sorry about Freddy,' Anna said.

'Are you?' Edwina's lips became drawn into a feeble sneer. 'Your feelings towards my brother are well known to me.'

'I don't believe they are. If there is one thing I've learned over the years it's that what people have done or not done doesn't seem to have much effect on how you feel about them. I am truly sorry Freddy is dead.' Edwina seemed to lose confidence and shrink into herself.

'I am shocked. My parents are devastated and I'm in pieces. I don't know how I can endure it.'

'You will. You have no alternative.'

'I know.' Her defences down, Edwina's voice was as life-less as her face. 'It was an unlooked-for accident, but at least Freddy died instantly. Apparently his neck was broken.'

Anna already knew this. She also knew, from what Alex had told her after speaking to the doctor who had been in casualty when Freddy and Victor had been brought in, that the combination of drink and drugs Freddy had been taking throughout the day hadn't helped.

'Have you seen him?' Anna asked.

Edwina nodded. 'If it were only the grief I feel, I think I could bear it, but added to my stunned sense of loss is remorse and the torment of a suddenly awakened conscience.' She smiled, a strangely reflective cynical smile. 'Conscience! The irony of it. I didn't realise until now that I had one, but for the first time in my life I am regretting things I have done. I killed Freddy just as surely as if I had run him off the road.'

'Edwina, I don't think I am the one you should be talking to about this.'

'Perhaps not, but I must talk to someone or I'll go mad.' She paused to steady her voice, her eyes pleading with Anna to believe her and understand.

'You see, Freddy was not just my brother, my twin brother, he was also my soul mate, my mirror image, my other self. When Sonya told him she was a Jew, I was the one who told him to finish with her—he never could refuse me, you see. And now he is dead because of my interference. The truth is, he only ever loved Sonya. All his other women were as noth-ing compared to her. No doubt I will suffer the rest of my life for all my bullyings and bouts of temper and cutting re-marks—for alienating him from Sonya. A fitting penance for me, don't you agree? I made him unhappy during the last few years and he bore it like a gentleman—despite his drinking and the dependency he developed on drugs. I always knew how desperately miserable he was and I also knew that Sonya could have made him very happy.'

'And Alex?'

'Oh, I was driven to trapping him—but he used me coldly, humiliated me.'

'Did you really intend to kill him on the race track?' Edwina glanced at her sharply. 'Alex told me.'

'I don't know. I was angry, I admit that, and I wanted to get my own back. I was also prepared to set aside the awful fact that Sonya is a Jew and give Freddy my blessing and tell him to go ahead and marry her—and with Alex out of the way he could do just that.'

Anna could see it all. Her eyes were suddenly hard and her anger rose swift and fierce. 'You almost succeeded in your ploy to get rid of him. And Sonya, being Alex's sister would inherit his wealth. You really are quite devious, Edwina. Little wonder Alex would have nothing to do with you.'

'I do know that. But, you see, my father is facing bankruptcy, and he threatened dire consequences unless Freddy conformed to his standards and toed the line.'

'There's something you don't know, Edwina. Today Freddy asked Sonya to go away with him, to marry him, and she refused. She's decided to convert to the Catholic faith—to become a nun.'

'I didn't know that. He must have spoken to her after I saw him—for the last time.'

'That was the reason why he left like he did. So you see, even if you had succeeded in killing Alex, you would have had to look to someone else to save your family from ruin.'

'I don't blame you for sounding bitter. If positions were reversed, I'd feel the same.' Her shoulders slumped and her self-confidence seemed to ooze from her as she turned and walked to the door. She paused and looked back at Anna, her expression one of wild despair. 'Freddy was the only friend I had, and the only man who really loved me and understood me. Suddenly I feel mutilated—as dead as he is, as if I were the one lying on that cold mortuary slab. I really don't know how I will find the strength to go on without him.'

She went out, the very droop of her shoulders showing Anna that her own self-castigation was more cruel than any she could give.

Edwina seemed to be so many women in one. There was the haughtily arrogant and devious Edwina, the vindictive, vengeful Edwina, and then there was this suddenly vulnerable woman who was suffering a genuine grief for her brother. Anna did not like her. There was something terrible about her—not only terrible but merciless, self-destructive, that could eventually destroy both herself and those she loved.

Leaving Sonya to say goodnight to Victor, Alex went back to the waiting room to find Anna. She came towards him, her eyes warm with love and silent greeting. 'What did Edwina want?' he asked, having seen her leave. 'Don't tell me. She's suffering.'

'Why? Don't you think she's capable of it?' Anna asked, thinking how strained Alex looked, how grave his handsome face.

'No. Only of making other people suffer.'

'You could give her the benefit of the doubt.'

'I don't have the emotional wherewithal. Besides, don't forget she tried to kill me earlier.'

'I haven't. I confronted her with that and she didn't try to deny it. With you out of the way and feeling as they still did about each other, Freddy would have been free to marry Sonya, who would receive the bulk of your estate. She was even prepared to ignore Sonya's religion.'

Alex's expression was grim. 'I'd already worked that out.'

'Will you take her to task over it?'

'No, not now,' he said, drawing her into his arms.

'I know it was a dreadful thing she tried to do to you, but I'm glad you're not. She's taking Freddy's death hard and is

blaming herself. She did love Freddy—and they do say twins
are closer than siblings born separate.'

'Edwina's idea of love is to own and dominate, and she
has just lost her prime possession. Death affects people in
different ways. This is the first time to my knowledge that it
has hit her. She hated Freddy when he openly confessed to
still loving Sonya.'

'It was cruel of her to reject a woman who didn't present
the right credentials.'

'That's your opinion. It isn't hers. Edwina is a manipula-
tor—of people, events, anything, to achieve her own ends—
and when it comes to deviousness she wrote the book.'

'Did you know Freddy still loved Sonya, Alex?'

'Not until that day at the rally. When I told him that Sonya
had tried to kill herself and as a consequence had lost the
child, he was so upset he was shaking. I can see that now. I
must say I was concerned how Sonya would react to coming
face to face with him again. In fact, I'm surprised how well
she coped—thank God.' Anna started to pull away from him,
but he drew her back against his chest. 'No,' he said quietly,
'stay where you are. I just want to hold you. It's been a long
day. You must be exhausted.'

'So must you.'

'You did enjoy the racing?' The smile he gave her was
slow, lazy and confident.

Anna laughed in spite of herself. 'Yes, Alex, I absolutely
loved it.'

'And you will come again?'

'As to that, you will have to ask me when I've got over
today. It's been quite a day and you gave me a fright. Do you
realise you could have been killed?'

'But I wasn't.'

'And you feel all right?'

'I am now. I'm perfectly fine.' He saw the concern and the
tears shimmering in her eyes. One of them traced unheeded

down her smooth cheek. He checked it with his finger. 'Now what's wrong?'

'I don't like to think of you being hurt.'

Alex smiled reassuringly. 'I enjoy racing and there's nothing to worry about.' Jokingly he added, 'If I do come a cropper, I know I can count on you to make me better.'

'You're right, I will,' she said, and so ferociously that he laughed. 'Have I told you how much I love you?'

'Not today.'

Anna glanced at the clock on the wall and smiled. 'Considering it's one minute past midnight, I haven't had the chance.' Slipping her arms around his waist, she pressed her lips to the V where his shirt opened at his throat. 'But I do love you, so very much, and I can't wait to be your wife.'

'And have you thought any more about what you propose to do with your time when you are—unless you've decided to devote all your time to your husband, of course, which I would not object to in the slightest?'

'I fully intend to devote as much of my time to you as I possibly can—as much as my work as a journalist will allow.'

Alex saw a knowing twinkle light her eye and he looked at her suspiciously. 'Has something happened that you haven't told me?'

'Yes, but I haven't had a chance to say anything. Roger Pilkington phoned to tell me that the *Herald* might be interested in taking me on. I have to present myself and my credentials at the paper's office in Fleet Street next week. Oh, Alex, I'm so excited.'

Alex hugged her, genuinely pleased. 'That's wonderful news, Anna. Congratulations—although I might change my mind if you are given too many assignments abroad.'

'Congratulate me if I get the job.'

'You will. Do you remember what I told you before you left Gilchrist, when you were sitting your exams? I told you then that I wouldn't argue with the inevitable. Whatever you do, I'm enormously proud of you. Always remember that.'

'Thank you for your support, Alex. I couldn't have done it without you. By the way, have you given some thought as to where we will live when we're married? For Grandfather's sake I would like to spend as much time at Belhaven as I can.'

'I understand that and I don't care where we live. As long as we are together, that's all that matters. The house is vast, so there will be plenty of room. Besides which, Belhaven is your inheritance. As far as my work is concerned, I can easily drive into London or take the train—or work from Belhaven, for that matter. It isn't a problem. The apartment's large and perfectly situated for our work, so I suggest we live there when we are in London. What do you say?'

'That it's a perfect solution.'

His expression suddenly became sombre. 'You know, Anna, when I look at you and remember my lonely past, there are times when I cannot believe I have found you. You have reinvented my life and filled it with meaning, laughter and love. Thank you.'

Anna looked into his eyes and smiled, a smile of such blinding sweetness, of understanding and love that made Alex's heart ache. 'You are welcome,' she whispered.

Alex gazed down at the beautiful creature in his arms, his eyes moving over her tired face, first concerned, then tender, then containing something Anna had become familiar with, something she recognised as wonderful and welcome—desire. It was absolutely shattering to her self-control. The truth was that he wanted her and she wanted him. They both knew it.

'Do you realise that we haven't eaten since lunch?' he said quietly. 'I missed the picnic.'

'Are you hungry?'

He nodded slowly, and Anna's heart fluttered at the husky intimacy she heard in his voice when he said, 'Starving.'

'Do you mean that in a sexual context?' she asked, her gaze fastened to his firm lips hovering so close to her own.

'Shame on you,' he uttered with mock reproof. 'You should be completely innocent of such thoughts. You're outrageous.'

'Utterly,' she agreed.

'Since you mention it, what are you offering?'

'Food, of course.'

'Where? A restaurant?'

'No, it's too late. I have a better idea. When we've taken Sonya to Curzon Street, we could eat at your apartment. It's much cosier than a restaurant, don't you agree?'

'Absolutely. And afterwards? Do you have you anything in mind?'

His voice was seductive, ever so persuasive, and his eyes gleamed. Anna could smell his skin, feel the heat of his body. A smile played on his lips, curving gently, and an errant lock of hair had fallen across his brow. He was a magnificent male, utterly irresistible, and just looking at him filled her with a delicious sense of expectancy she couldn't deny. Drawing a shaky breath, she was ready to call an end to their being apart.

'Alex, I know what we said—what we agreed, but—but can I stay with you tonight? I want us to be together, as we will be when we're married. This sexless arrangement is driving me crazy already.'

Alex looked at her in disbelief, then as he saw she meant it he smiled in dawning delight. 'It's just as hard for me—but we made a deal.'

'You did. I didn't.' She reached up and kissed him with enough ardour to make him groan. All the love that had accumulated through the years of her childhood and the months she had spent apart from this man who was soon to be her husband was in that kiss. With an effort that was almost painful, she drew back and said, 'Now what do you say?'

Dragging her back into his arms, losing the battle, Alex informed her, 'The deal's off.' His mouth opened hungrily on hers. He felt the soft lips parting willingly for his searching tongue, the delicate arms slide around his neck. With unselfish ardour she offered herself to him, and he knew when they

were alone he would take it hungrily. She was everything he
had ever dreamed of, and more. His hands shifted restlessly
over her waist and the sides of her breasts, holding her tightly
to his aroused body while he kissed her until they were both
on fire and wanting more.

Footsteps in the corridor brought them back to their senses
and reluctantly they drew apart.

Pulling her back for one fervent kiss, his eyes sultry, his
lips warm and moist, Alex murmured, 'Tomorrow we'll go to
Belhaven to see the vicar. The sooner I make an honest
woman of you the better I shall feel.'

Anna laughed delightedly, laying her hand against his
smoothly shaven face. 'I couldn't agree more.'

Never had Anna believed she could feel such intense happiness. They spoke to her grandfather as soon as they arrived
at Belhaven. With an adoring Alex looking on and her eyes
shining with the joy of her first love, after gently hugging her
grandfather, she knelt beside his wheelchair and took his hand
in hers.

'I appreciate that this is all so sudden, but Alex and I,
well…' she beamed across at Alex where he was leaning
against the mantelpiece in a rakish manner, hands thrust into
his trouser pockets, black hair sleek, silver-grey eyes on her,
so disgustingly single-minded, he had no idea of the effect he
was having on her susceptible female heart '…you can see
how things stand between us, can't you?'

Alex relinquished his stance by the fireplace. Scarcely able
to conceal the rush of joyous delight and satisfaction, Selwyn
grasped his hand and wrung it fervently. His wish that these
two should marry had advanced further than he had hoped.
Alex had assured him repeatedly that he would never marry,
and yet here he was offering for Anna like any other man in
love with a beautiful girl.

The face Selwyn lifted to the man who had entered his life
at a time when it had been nothing but an empty shell, the

man he had come to look upon as a son, was joyous, his eyes misted with tears. 'That's splendid news, just splendid. For you to marry is my dearest wish. I was wondering how much longer it would take you to get round to it. Are you happy, Anna?'

'I'm *very* happy,' she said softly.

'Then I couldn't be happier for you both. Alex is a fine man, and an exceptional one. I give you my blessing gladly.'

Later, Anna was moved to tears when she opened a little box and saw the most beautiful solitaire engagement ring gazing out at her. Alex took it out and placed it on her finger, before taking her in his arms and sealing their engagement with a kiss—a kiss that held all the memories of the past and the promise of the future.

At a small party at Belhaven the following day, Alex proudly announced that Anna had consented to be his wife. An effusion of delight and congratulations ensued, and no one seemed in the least surprised, the Ormsbys having suspected for some time that the happy couple nurtured feelings for each other.

Anna's wedding day dawned bright and clear. It was to be a wedding such as the people of Stainton had not seen in many a year, and the whole district would be celebrating.

Anna sat up in bed, the first thing she saw being her wedding dress and veil—a simple, beautiful creation in white silk and lace, hanging on the wardrobe. She hugged herself as she thought of Alex and relived the night they had spent together at his apartment six weeks ago, and several since then, when they had rediscovered each other and he had taught her the meaning of true passion.

He would keep her awake most of the night, making love to her either with exquisite tenderness, which she found tormentingly sweet, or he'd be urgently demanding. After each time she would drowse in his arms, and he would hold her as if he would never let her go.

Anna loved him more deeply and more tenderly than she had ever dreamed possible, and in return she felt loved, cherished and wanted as never before in her life.

Sighing contentedly, she got out of bed for what she knew would be the happiest day of her life. They were to spend the night at Belhaven and tomorrow set out on their honeymoon to Italy after spending three days in Paris. When they returned to London, she was to start work as a trainee journalist on the *Herald*, having been offered the position just three days after her interview.

Because she had become so much a part of Stainton, with every citizen prepared to welcome the guests, the entire village had been decked out in bunting and the small Saxon church lavishly filled with bouquets of flowers. In it generations of Mansons had worshipped and were interred. The guests, just family and close friends, would be limited at the afternoon wedding ceremony and the small intimate reception held at Belhaven, but more friends and acquaintances had been invited to the evening reception.

Anna had managed to talk her grandfather into attending the wedding. Incapacitated as he was, he was unable to give her away, so Lord Ormsby had stepped in to do the honour. Alex was staying at Applemead and would travel to the church with Lady Ormsby, Michael and the twins. Victor, who was on crutches and had been allowed out of hospital for the event, was also staying at Applemead.

Sonya and Tamsin—the bridesmaids—Anna and Lord Ormsby were drawn in two open carriages to the church. Scores of smiling estate workers and villagers, all dressed in their Sunday best, lined the route and jostled round the church, each one straining to get a look at the bride.

Inside the church, as the organ swelled, Alex stood with his best man and close friend, industrialist Jeffrey Stevenson, and watched Anna walk down the aisle. It was the most poignant moment of his life. A drifting swirl of white lace and carrying a bouquet of fragrant white lilies, she moved towards him. When she stood beside him, his expression was so intense, so profoundly proud, that Anna's heart ached. 'I love you,' he whispered.

'I know,' she murmured simply, her face aglow.

She lifted her eyes to his, and in their fathomless depths Alex saw sweet acceptance and all the love in the world. He also saw a promise of a perfect future together, of his unborn children and of quiet joy.

* * * * *

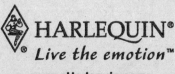

Harlequin Historicals®
Historical Romantic Adventure!

From rugged lawmen and valiant knights to defiant heiresses and spirited frontierswomen, Harlequin Historicals will capture your imagination with their dramatic scope, passion and adventure.

Harlequin Historicals . . . they're too good to miss!

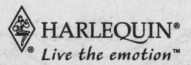

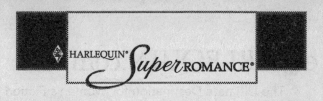
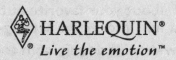

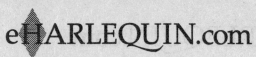